Praise for Stephanie Kuehnert's
brilliant debut novel
I WANNA BE YOUR JOEY RAMONE

"Stephanie Kuehnert has written a sucker-punch of a novel, raw and surprising and visceral, and like the best novelists who write about music, she'll convince you that a soul can indeed be saved by rock and roll."

—John McNally, author of *America's Report Card*

"Kuehnert's love of music is apparent on every page in this powerful and moving story. Her fresh voice makes this novel stand out in the genre, and she writes as authentically about coming of age as she does punk rock. She's titled the book after a great song by Sleater-Kinney, and both that band, and the iconic Joey Ramone, would be proud of this effort."

—Charles R. Cross, *New York Times* bestselling author
of *Heavier Than Heaven: A Biography of Kurt Cobain*

"Some books play at trying to be 'edgy'; some books try to hit the right notes; but Kuehnert's prose doesn't notice labels. It just is—which is the purest kinda edge. Teeth. Punk. Combat boots. Attitude. Feminism. Family. Girls with guitars. Relationships that jack you up. Sharp things of the not-good kind. Friendships. Love. . . . It's _____ loved it."

_____ bestselling author
of *Ink Exchange*

"A wonderfully written and evocative story of a mother and daughter parted by circumstance and joined by music. I heartily recommend it."

—Irvine Welsh, author of *Trainspotting*

"*I Wanna Be Your Joey Ramone* is intense, raw and real; a powerful and heartbreaking weave of Emily Black's public dream of making music and the intensely private one of finding her elusive, missing mother. Emily, a gutsy, passionate and vulnerable girl, knows exactly what she wants and strides straight into the gritty darkness after it, risking all and pulling no punches, but leaving us with the perfect ending to a fierce and wild ride."

—Laura Wiess, author of *Such a Pretty Girl*

"Stephanie Kuehnert writes with dramatic flare and all the right beats, as she spins a story with punk rock lyrics, big dreams, and one girl not afraid to reach out to her lost mother through music, while enduring intense journeys in between. A debut like an unforgettable song, you'll want to read I Wanna Be Your Joey Ramone again and again."

—Kelly Parra, author of *Graffiti Girl*

Learn more about debut author Stephanie Kuehnert and see her mix CD song picks for

I WANNA BE YOUR JOEY RAMONE

at www.stephaniekuehnert.com.

This title is also available as an eBook

I Wanna Be Your Joey Ramone

Stephanie Kuehnert

POCKET BOOKS   MTV BOOKS
New York London Toronto Sydney

Pocket Books
A Division of Simon & Schuster, Inc.
1230 Avenue of the Americas
New York, NY 10020

First MTV Books/Pocket Books trade paperback edition July 2008

POCKET and colophon are registered trademarks of Simon & Schuster, Inc.

For information about special discounts for bulk purchases, please contact Simon & Schuster Special Sales at 1-800-456-6798 or business@simonandschuster.com.

Manufactured in the United States of America

10 9 8 7 6 5 4 3 2 1

Library of Congress Cataloging-in-Publication Data

Kuehnert, Stephanie
  I wanna be your Joey Ramone / Stephanie Kuehnert.
     p. cm.
   1. Punk rock musicians—Fiction. 2. Women rock musicians—Fiction.
3. Mothers and daughters—Fiction. I. Title.
   PS3611.U3513   2008
   813'.6—dc22
                                                      2007048888

ISBN-13: 978-1-4165-6269-6
ISBN-10:   1-4165-6269-9

For Mom

I like the comfort in knowing that women are the only future in rock 'n' roll.

—Kurt Cobain

ACKNOWLEDGMENTS

I would like to thank Caren Johnson, agent extraordinaire, for believing in this book from the first chapter and working so hard to make sure it saw the light of day.

Jennifer Heddle is the woman who ultimately made that happen. She truly understood my characters and their world and provided priceless suggestions for revising. In short, she's the dream editor. Thanks also to Jane Elias and everyone else at MTV Books who ensured that this book turned out perfectly.

I couldn't have done any of this without my writing partners in crime, particularly Katie Corboy. She's read every draft and her advice triggered many breakthroughs, not to mention her friendship means the world to me. Jenny Seay and Vanessa Barneveld read the last draft very quickly as I revised and provided invaluable feedback and cheerleading. All three of these ladies challenge me to write as well as they do.

Randy Albers, chair of the Columbia College Chicago Fiction Writing Department, is hands down the best writing teacher in the world. He mentored me from the formative undergraduate years through my master's thesis, working with me during summers, and when he was supposed to be on sabbatical, to get this book out the door.

Thanks to John Schultz and Betty Shiflett for creating the Story Workshop Method and, as a result, the amazing Columbia College Chicago Fiction Writing Department community. I'm grateful to everyone I met there, particularly the faculty who helped me and this novel grow, including Craig Gore, Ann Hemenway, Gary Johnson, Antonia Logue, Patty McNair, Joe Meno, Alexis Pride, Chris Rice, and Sam Weller; the staff, Linda Naslund and Deborah Roberts, who always looked out for me and taught me copyediting; Sheryl Johnston, who has been so supportive; and most of all my peers, the people who encouraged me, read my work, motivated me with theirs, and built a real "literary scene" in Chicago, especially Amber Abrahamson, Bobby Biedrzycki, Julia Borcherts, Ira Brooker, Nicki Brouillette, Nicole Chakalis, Brian Costello, Joe Deir, Rob Duffer, Max Glaessner, Aaron Golding, Monique Lewis, Tony Luce, Anna Medakovich (okay, you're film, but whatever), Richard Santiago, Felicia Schneiderhan, Mike Sims, Jantae Spencer, Jessie Tierney (special thanks for the author photos), and Joe Tower. And to Frank Crist, devoted friend and brilliant writer, who passed away while I was revising this book, I tapped your manic energy to finish, so it's for you, man.

Then, the other authors who've been my mentors, guidance counselors, and in a couple of cases, drinking buddies: Dorothy Allison, Hillary Carlip, Charley Cross, John Mc-

Nally, Kelly Parra, Don Snyder, Irvine Welsh, and everyone on the Teen Lit Yahoo loop.

Of course, those outside my writing world have been equally essential. My best friend, Katie Lagges: everything I write about long-lasting, true friendship is based on her. My family, particularly my little brother Dan, who doesn't know how much *I* look up to *him*. Jenny Hassler, a super-b individual who volunteered her amazing web design talents. Eryn Mulloy, who sends me surprises by mail and the sweetest encouraging notes. Tai Little and Lindsay Stanford, who have bolstered my sanity through the years; Kathy Lesinski, my newest sanity-keeper; Chris Lempa, who makes sure I stay true to my punk rock ethos; and Kelly Lewis for being admirably feisty. Jme, Dan, Scott, and everyone at the Beacon, 'cause a writer is only as strong as the folks at her favorite dive bar.

The foundation of this book and my desire to write in general is music. This story was born of my fantasies about a rock world where girls rule, and I can only hope it pays fitting tribute to the women who've inspired me. Sure, Nirvana gave voice to millions of freaks like me and the Sex Pistols introduced me to punk rock, but the first time I heard Courtney Love scream that she was "pretty on the inside," it saved my angry, thirteen-year-old girl soul. Then, ten years later, when rock 'n' roll was suffering at the hands of macho dudes and whiny Pearl Jam knockoffs, I heard Brody Dalle of the Distillers, and she restored my faith. There's also Sleater-Kinney (one of whose songs this book is named for), Mia Zapata (gone too soon), Babes in Toyland, Patti Smith, PJ Harvey, Kim Deal, Kim Gordon, and Pink, among many others—but my biggest rock star heroes are my friends, Heather Lynn of the Capricorns and Tamra Spivey of Lucid Nation.

Saving the best for last: Scott Lewis, love of my life, your unending encouragement and sense of humor keeps me going. And to my mom, Nancy Napp, who I admire more than any rock star, who has supported me more than anyone, and who is responsible for everything I am, this book is for you.

1.

I'm your worn-in leather jacket
I'm the volume in your fucked-up teenage band
A pack of smokes and a six-pack
I'm the dreams you had walkin' down the railroad tracks
You and me

I'm your first taste of romance
I'm your first broken heart on a Saturday night
Guys like us ain't got no chance
But I'm the thing that keeps you and me alive
But not forever

So take me down the road
Take me to the show
It's something to believe in
That no one else knows
But don't take me for granted

—Social Distortion
"Don't Take Me for Granted"
Sex, Love and Rock 'n' Roll

Rock Gods

Altars. Saviors. Rock 'n' roll. I braved my fear of spiders, dust plumes as thick as L.A. smog, and the stench of dog piss that the last owner of the house had let permeate the basement to tirelessly search my father's record collection for my next holy grail. Sitting on that cold, dirty, painted cement floor in my blue jeans, with the Wisconsin winter creeping through the tired walls and windows of our house, I dug through crates of albums, feeling their perfect square edges poke between my fingers. The slap of plastic dust cover against plastic dust cover was so satisfying, but the best moment came when I found the record I wanted, slipped it out of its paper jacket and onto the record player. The needle skipped and skittered for a few seconds until it found its groove, the first chord scratching its way through the speakers, a catchy chorus reverberating in my ears. Earthquakes. Rock gods.

Music was in my blood. My mother left me with my father when I was four months old so she could follow the beginnings of punk rock around the country. Detroit. New York. L.A. We never heard from her again. Neither of us was resentful. She had her reasons. At least that's what I told myself.

Two months after she disappeared, my dad moved us from our tiny apartment in Chicago to Carlisle, Wisconsin, the small farming town fifteen miles beyond the Illinois border where he and my mother had grown up. When we first returned to the land of lush fields, acres of corn, and barns that sat fat and yawning at the ends of dirt roads, people talked. It was just that kind of place, a small, tight-knit community; any deviation from the norm was grounds for discussion.

Before areas were incorporated, when land was simply land, Carlisle was born of a general store that farmers flocked to from miles away. Back then, the men talked about their work while picking up seed and parts for aging equipment. Their wives came for cloth and the foods they could not raise themselves. They exchanged advice about family matters and gossiped about the other women who had asked them for advice.

As the years passed, the government bought up land to build roads, and corporations turned family farms into giant factory farms. People moved closer together, and from the general store sprung a main street scattered with businesses. Two miles away a food-processing plant opened. The sprawling community shrunk into a town made up of the farms that remained nearby and the former farming families who took jobs at the plant or opened storefronts. Side streets attached themselves to Main Street in a neat grid near the center of town, but farther out, roads meandered around fields. From above, the layout of Carlisle looked

like straight hair—parted in the middle by Main Street—
suddenly gone curly at the ends.

But everyone still knew one another. Everyone still gathered in front of the store or at the tavern to talk. No modern-
ization would ever change that.

I don't want you thinking I'm from some completely backwoods town, though. I grew up with all the modern com-
forts: indoor plumbing, cable TV. What set Carlisle apart
from urban areas was the way everyone clung to history. Not
like this-war-started-on-this-date history, more like where-
was-your-grandfather-during-the-blizzard-of-1921 history.
From snippets of conversation, I knew who I was, who my
family was, and how we fit into town lore. The most popular
topic from the time I came to Carlisle until the day I left
was the high school football team. The second most common
topic was the people who didn't seem to care about normal
things like football, the people who just weren't quite right.

Like Paula Collins, whose parents had both perished in a
barn fire when she was sixteen. She inherited all the money
they'd squirreled away and the land they lived on, and she
never left, never married, never rebuilt that barn. Or Norma
Lisbon, who was well on her way to being the town drunk
even before her son, Eric, killed himself. After Eric died,
her husband stopped speaking, became a total mute, and
Norma was drunk, disorderly, and doing something gossip-
worthy nearly every day.

Or like my family . . .

My parents, Michael Black and Louisa Carson, had created quite a scene in 1974, when they sped out of town on
my father's motorcycle. As a teenager, I walked into many

discussions about it at the local gas station and grocery store, but my favorite version, the only one I took as gospel, was the one my mother's best friend, Molly Parker, told me.

It was an unusually warm day in April when Michael and Louisa fled, Louisa's eighteenth birthday, and she made sure all of Carlisle knew that she was an adult and finally free to leave the tiny town that had smothered her with old-fashioned morals. My father concentrated on the drive, thinking the only way to save the girl he loved from all the anger that ate away at her heart was to help her escape. His black leather jacket and wild, coffee-colored curls made him look so dark he almost blended in with the road, which was appropriate because before Michael Black was seen in the company of Louisa Carson, no one in Carlisle had ever noticed him. As she had since she arrived in the town at the age of ten, the pretty but untamed doctor's daughter, Louisa, was the one causing the ruckus. Burning down Main Street on the back of his Harley, she held on to Michael with one arm, her bleached-blond hair tangling like corn silk in the wind as she turned dangerously in her seat to shout obscenities and shake her fist at Carlisle. Outside of Carlisle Groceries and Meats, a crowd of middle-aged women doing their weekly shopping and work-worn men picking up packs of smokes on their way to the job gathered to gawk at the spectacle. Louisa tugged off her black high heels and whipped one through the window of the grocery store, the other against the Old Style sign that flickered above the doorway of JT's Tavern. With that final act of aggression, she wrapped both arms around my father's chest and never looked back.

So, when my father returned almost three years later in

a blue Chevy Impala with me, Emily Diana Black, asleep in the backseat, everyone had questions. They contemplated why he'd returned alone, wearing a wedding ring and carrying a milk-skinned baby with a shock of hair as dark as her last name, and blazing, green eyes that left no doubt she was Louisa's. They theorized about why Louisa had left him and wondered if I would end up as wild as she had been.

Molly overheard one of the many conversations in Carlisle Groceries and Meats soon after our return. As Molly put little jars of baby food into her basket, Mrs. Jones, wife of the store owner, openly discussed the situation with her customer, Sarah Fawcett. "Well, Michael had some of those hippie tendencies. That's probably how he ended up with that woman," she stated frankly, pushing the paper bag with Sarah's things across the counter to her.

"Oh, I remember," Sarah agreed. "Long hair, and that bike, of course."

"Yes." Old Mrs. Jones tightly clamped her thin, pasty lips together to give a dramatic moment of pause before she shared her vast knowledge. As one of the most well-known people in Carlisle, she considered herself the authority on every topic. "Michael was from a good family. Not a *rich* family like hers," she added snidely, "but the Blacks have lived around here forever. I don't know what he saw in that girl, but I'm sure she was a terrible wife, which'll drive even the gentlest man to his wit's end eventually."

Sarah nodded enthusiastically: at the time she was a young wife, seven months pregnant, and wished to prove she had the moral fiber that others from her generation, such as Louisa, lacked.

Molly emerged from the aisle and headed angrily toward the counter. Mrs. Jones continued, "I'm sure three years drained the rebellion from him . . ." When Molly slammed her basket down, Mrs. Jones paused and stared at her from wrinkly eye sockets, then finished her sentence. "Now he's back to raise his daughter right."

That was the consensus of the town. When my dad took work at the plant, people seemed to remember that he was the quiet son of a respected farmer, so they disregarded any of his remaining eccentricities, such as never removing his wedding ring, and the talk simmered down to a whisper until I reached my high school years.

My dad and I lived in a house that was big but cheap, weathered but solid, old but transformed by the rock 'n' roll energy that he and I breathed. My dad raised me on music. Our living room was a temple, plastered with posters of Bowie and the Rolling Stones. A framed, signed Beatles record hung over the stereo, which was our altar in the center of the room. A photograph of my mother sat on the left speaker, and an ever-changing stack of records on the right. My dad's taste ran the gamut, from classical to blues to punk to folk. Even into his forties, he amazed me by discovering the best underground bands before I did. Three records never left that stack on the speaker: one each by Johnny Cash, Leadbelly, and the Clash. The basement held crates and crates of other records, and as I grew older, that became the place I ran to immediately after dinner.

I knelt on that cold cement floor, dust clouds poofing up around me as I flipped faster and faster through the albums. "There has to be something good in here. Don't tell me it's all folk crap," I complained, craving noisy guitars the way other nine-year-olds hungered for candy.

"That's rock, too, Emily," my father chided from behind me, looking slightly disappointed that I wasn't finding nearly as much satisfaction in his old record collection as he did. His dark eyes drank in every album cover, mouth twitching with a memory, a line that wanted to be hummed, or words in the record's defense that would have been wasted on me.

"No, it's not noisy enough," I replied. I wanted something that you could feel in your throat when you played it loud, something that churned through your stomach and shook you to the tips of your toes. Something that scraped out your insides and made you want to dance without them. Just as I searched for the steepest hill to ride my bike down, I hunted for music that would provide the greatest thrill.

My dad's wavy hair fell across his brow as he laughed softly. Everything about my father was soft except for his hardworking hands. Just twenty-one when I was born, he still looked young, more like an older brother than a dad. However, since he stood over six feet tall, so much bigger than I was, I always viewed him as my protector. As tough as I acted, on many occasions I buried my tear-drenched face in one of his flannel shirts to be soothed by the sound of his voice or the thump of his big heart. Most important, he was also my playmate. He went along with my nightly exploration of the records, sharing in both the delight and the seriousness of my mission.

"It's gotta be noisy, huh?" He smiled impishly. His brown eyes sparkled like they were lit by stage lights. "Your mother would be proud of you," he said. The glimmer in his eyes changed just slightly; a sense of longing always emerged when she came up in conversation.

"Are any of Louisa's records around here?" I asked. I rarely referred to my mother by anything other than her first name. She was even more distant than the rock gods in *Rolling Stone*. I had nothing of hers but photographs. I possessed the energy and voices of my icons through their music, but I remembered neither about Louisa.

"Somewhere. I don't know if you're old enough yet," my father teased, scooting away from the crate to stretch out on the floor.

"Louisa left some records with you!" I exclaimed, my hair slicing through the air between us as I twisted around to look at him. I'd been asking that question since I was five years old, but he never answered. I knew I had to have those records. They would be my mother. They would let me know her voice, her thoughts, the stories she would have told me before bed. They would help me re-create the moment I knew I would never remember: the night she decided she could no longer ignore punk rock's summons and kissed me good-bye. "I'm old enough! I can't believe you've just let 'em rot down here, Dad! Damn!"

"Emily, don't swear," he scolded affectionately, leaning back with his hands behind him.

"I'm sorry. I just want them so bad . . ." I took a breath, imagining how I would finally create my own altar, how I would stack Louisa's records right next to the little stereo that sat across from my bed. "I just *know* they're so cool!" I exhaled, curling my dusty fingers in my long, tangled hair and then leaping onto my father. He sat up quickly to catch me.

"You are certainly Louisa's daughter." Dad grinned. "Nine years old and you want to make the windows rattle and the floorboards creak with blasting speakers." He slid me off his lap, stood up, and led me past his tool bench, the furnace, and boxes full of Christmas decorations to a little closet that I'd never looked in, certain it only contained bugs and mice. It was surprisingly clean, and up on the top shelf perched a red milk crate with about twenty records in it. My holy grail.

Play it harder. Play it faster. Louder. Harder. Faster. So loud-hardfast that I forget your name. After all, did I even know it in the first place? Those were the first lyrics I composed myself. I wrote them the summer I turned fourteen. As a little girl I felt the music in my gut and in the tips of my fingers, making me want to sing at the top of my lungs and learn to play guitar as well as my father. When puberty hit, I started to feel music between my thighs. My legs stretched long and slim, and my hip bones jutted out. I dressed in vintage blue jeans so worn they clung to me without being tight in that trashy way the girls with big, ratted bangs at my high school preferred. My hair, still as dark as my name, hung straight and thick, dusting the middle of my back when I pushed it behind me. The only makeup I wore then was black eyeliner and red lipstick.

Every weekend I walked around town with Molly's daughter, Regan. Since I was a baby, I'd spent my days in Molly's home while my father worked. Molly treated me like the sister of her two girls, Regan, who was only four months older than me, and Marissa, who was four years older. My dad told me that Louisa would have loved it that I was best friends with her best friend's kid. Regan even looked like Molly, a tiny but feisty girl who stood a few inches shorter than me, the red highlights in her chocolate hair glistening in the sun as we prowled the streets of Carlisle.

Main Street had changed since Louisa made her dramatic exit sixteen years earlier. Two blocks beyond Carlisle Groceries and Meats a strip mall had sprung up where Main Street became County Highway PW, the speed limit jumping from twenty-five miles per hour to forty-five right in front of the entrance to the brand-new Wal-Mart. Regan and I spent our Saturday afternoons in that vast, brightly lit emporium of crap, shoplifting everything from sodas to candles to black bras.

On those treks down Main Street the summer before freshman year, I heard whispers of my mother's name. People talked because of how much I'd grown to look like her on the outside, but I knew that I was most like Louisa on the inside. I understood why she'd hated Carlisle. Like all small Midwestern towns, it evolved slowly. It lagged at least a decade behind when it came to any cultural advancement. As the rest of the country moved into the nineties, Carlisle hung on to 1979. The women still had badly feathered hair. The men who whistled at Regan and me from their battered pickup trucks still had Styx and REO Speedwagon blaring through the speakers. Louisa, who'd entered her teenage years in 1969, lived in a town still stuck in the fifties. Like her, I saw two ways to escape Carlisle: sex and rock 'n' roll.

For the first time, I thought I heard my mother's voice inside of me. *Play it harder. Play it faster. Louder. Harder. Faster. So loudhardfast that I forget your name.*

The first guy I slept with was a musician. Sam thought he was destined to be the biggest rock god the world had ever known. I thought so, too, but hell, I was only fourteen. Back then, we spent our days at Wal-Mart and our nights at River's Edge, an abandoned warehouse three miles from the outskirts of town and just as far from the nearest farmhouse. Kids came from all over two or three counties to listen to the raucous, angry music that bands pounded out at the Edge, the closest thing rural southern Wisconsin and northern Illinois had to underground rock, and the only place where Regan and I could find cute punk boys.

The afternoon before I met Sam, as Regan and I slid black lace panties on in the fitting room at Wal-Mart, she shouted over the partition, "Tonight's the night, Emily. We're going to find you some sexy punk to fuck out at River's Edge." We'd made a pact at the beginning of the summer that we wouldn't enter high school as virgins. Since Regan had hooked up with a guy at River's Edge the previous weekend, it was my turn to seal the deal.

I zipped up my jeans and shouted back to her, "I don't care what he looks like as long as he's in a band." I was, of course, being somewhat sarcastic. He had to be in a *good* band.

"That's my girl." Regan laughed as we stepped out of our stalls at the same time. The clerk standing outside the fitting room, a plump woman with an overprocessed perm, gaped at us, horrified.

"You're Molly Dahle's daughter," she hissed at Regan, flecks of spit curdling her coral lipstick. "You better watch it or you're gonna end up just like your mama," she continued, wearing the look of a satisfied hog, "knocked up at sixteen."

Regan glared at the woman, her hazel eyes turning the color of embers. She dropped the clothing that we'd been pretending to try on and corrected, "Parker. It's been Molly *Parker* for eighteen years now. Let me guess, you were prom queen? Class of '74? And you laughed your ass off when my mother dropped out to have my sister. But here you are now, fat and old, and my mother is still as thin and pretty as she was back then. Not to mention she's happily married, whereas you . . . I bet you haven't gotten laid since prom night, you dried-up—"

"Shut up!" the woman bellowed, cheeks flaring and watery blue eyes bulging. Wal-Mart shoppers from intimate apparel to housewares gawked.

Regan gazed innocently at her audience. When she wasn't glaring or cursing, Regan's size made people think she wasn't a day over twelve. She backed away from the clerk, acting shocked. "I'm sorry, ma'am," she said sweetly, but loud enough for the silent store to hear. "I thought the customer was always right."

Regan and I sashayed through the racks of clothing toward the aisle. I glanced back and saw the store manager storming toward the clerk. I had no doubt she would try to tell him whose children we were, but the beauty of the new Wal-Mart was that it was run by folks from outside of Carlisle and even attracted many of its customers from surrounding towns. At Carlisle Groceries and Meats, Regan and I had been watched since the age of five for signs that we were like our awful mamas. At twelve, when we got caught smoking cigarettes behind the store, it was attributed to the evil we'd sucked down in our mothers' milk. But the managers of Wal-Mart viewed us as their corporate offices instructed. We were customers and the employees were not to let petty, small-town gossip interfere with proper customer service. As the manager lectured the clerk about this, Regan and I exited without suspicion, new underwear beneath our jeans and purses stuffed with stolen makeup and lighters.

Still snickering, Regan and I trekked through town, passing houses with big wraparound porches, painted bright shades of white, yellow, blue, and red. Downtown Carlisle was the nicer part of town. Farther south, the sun-faded and boxy houses looked as if a major snowstorm would reduce them to a pile of waterlogged boards. Our families lived in the area in between. At the intersection of Main and Laurel, we parted ways. "Marissa and I will meet you at the Edge at eight tonight," Regan reminded me.

Of course, they were late.

My dad dropped me off on his way to play music with the guys from his high school band. It wasn't a serious project, but Dad joked that it kept him in touch with his roots and helped him escape my noise.

I waited for Regan and Marissa on the outskirts of what was used as a parking lot at River's Edge. Cars lined up next to the warehouse, their tires treading worn gravel, broken glass, and thick ruts of dirt. Where I sat, grass struggled to grow in gnarly tufts, nourished by spilt beer and cigarette butts. Just a few feet away from me, it was lush, green, and tall, which made the area surrounding the warehouse look like the patchy head of a balding man.

No one knew where the name River's Edge came from. There was no sign that a river had run anywhere nearby in the last century, the nearest being the Pecatonica, five miles away. Maybe it was the name of the company that once owned the building. Even my dad, who met my mother there eighteen years earlier, had no idea. But I enjoyed the rural tradition of legend, and River's Edge was steeped in it.

In the late seventies, when someone—maybe the cops, maybe the electric company—noticed that the warehouse was being used, they shut it down for a couple months. Then someone—or maybe a few people—bought the property. No one knew who'd done it because nothing at the Edge changed when it secretly reopened. Making it into a legitimate club would have meant security, controlling underage drinking, and taking a cut from the money the bands made. The mysterious owner just left an old paint can with a sign that said "Donations" on the wooden table by the door where bands put their flyers and sold their silk-screened T-shirts and low-quality demo tapes. We all kicked in cash whenever we could so the electric bill could be paid and the roof kept leak-free.

River's Edge ran like a co-op. Volunteers did sound and lighting. Bands scheduled themselves on a calendar backstage. There were three slots a night and rookie acts who didn't know anyone else to sign up with chose a random date and opened by default. Bands from farther away called their friends to be added to the calendar. It created an intricate underground rock network so appreciated by everyone that fighting was rare, despite the edgy, volatile nature of the music.

During my dad's time, the sound at River's Edge transitioned from folk to garage punk, and it managed to survive the plastic metal of the eighties. Punk rock still thrived when I started seeing shows there, music that shared some similarities with what was brewing in the Pacific Northwest at the time, but we played it faster, like our lives depended on it. I have no idea why my father allowed me to hang out there. He probably assumed I went to appreciate music the way he'd raised me to, not realizing that rock possessed me the way it had my mother. If he'd had any idea that I was getting drunk and checking out boys, he would have tightened the reins. But my dad was very trusting and I was very good at concealing things from him.

I took a swig of cheap, watery beer and squinted through the fiery red light of the setting sun, searching for Marissa's black Pontiac. Pollen tickled my nose and late-August humidity thickened the hazy air. I finished most of my drink before Marissa and Regan showed up. Regan stumbled out of the passenger's door with a half-empty bottle of wine in her hand. Marissa stepped out gracefully, a lit cigarette dangling from her bloodred lips. Regan and Marissa both wore the same shade of lipstick, but other than that they looked nothing alike. Marissa resembled their father, tall with sandy hair and aquamarine eyes, while everything about Regan was dark; she inherited the Native American features of Molly's father. Marissa stood fluid and curvy, possessing the elegant confidence that Regan and I hoped we'd find in our own bodies in the next four years. At the same time, Marissa was still bad-ass enough to be our idol. The black halter dress she wore revealed the phoenix tattooed on her left shoulder and her creamy arms, toned from years of playing bass guitar.

We were a mismatched trio. Although I acted like the third sister, I obviously wasn't. Paler than both of them, my skin exuded the spooky glow of a full moon. They were both lean and muscular, and I was bony. Truly, we were not a trio at all. Regan and I were the inseparable pair, and Marissa the kind older sister who provided rides, tried to impart wisdom, and sighed when we ran recklessly ahead, ignoring her.

"Good evening, Emily." Marissa reached through the window into the backseat of the car for a beer. "Help yourself to the good alcohol," she added, noticing the Old Milwaukee I held.

I set down my can and stood up as Regan loudly slurred, "Tonight we're getting Emily laid!" She chucked a box of condoms at me, which were most likely the rightful property of Wal-Mart.

I rolled my eyes and threw the box back at her.

"That's all she's been talking about since we got in the car. Having some regrets about sleeping with that drummer last weekend, Regan? Need someone to share in your misery?" Marissa teased, her cheeks rising with her smile.

Regan stuck her tongue out at her sister and bent down to retrieve the condoms. "No, I just want her to get it over with. The first time's no good anyway. It's like opening a wound."

Marissa chuckled, rounding the car to meet us. "How would you know, Regan? You've never had a second time. Maybe it's always like that."

Regan raised her bottle of wine, uncoiled one of the fingers wrapped around the neck, and jabbed it in her sister's face. "How do you know, Marissa?" she mimicked. "Maybe I screwed that drummer twice."

Marissa shook her head wisely, her long hair shimmering. "If you had any more sexual experience, you would know that no teenage drummer could do it twice in an hour. Besides," she added with a giggle, "I know you overheard me saying that 'opening a wound' thing a couple years ago."

Regan blushed indignantly. "Shut up!"

"Oh, Regan," Marissa sighed, "you'll learn. You're both too smart to end up little groupies." She patted us on the tops of our heads in a motherly fashion and started toward the large, gray building. I watched her black high heels clicking steadily through the dirt and imagined that they were just like the pair Louisa had furiously thrown as she exited Carlisle. I wanted more than anything to combine the cool dignity of Marissa with the uninhibited rage of my mother. And I was convinced that Regan was right, that I would just have to get rid of my virginity to do it.

The opening chords of a fast punk song reverberated inside the warehouse. Feedback sizzled like lightning flashing across the darkening sky, beckoning us. I grabbed a fresh beer from the car and linked my arm with Regan's as we strode toward the entrance. She took a big gulp of wine and pondered her sister's words. "We're not groupies, are we, Em?" she asked, sounding somber.

"Nah, we're just bored."

Regan's enthusiasm was quickly renewed. "So, you'll let me pick out a guy for you tonight?"

"What the hell," I agreed, swallowing half the beer to catch up with her drunkenness. "You'll probably pick a better one than I would."

"Great!" Regan squealed. She ripped into the condom box and handed me a strip of them. "You'll need these, then. Better safe than sorry!" I pocketed them as she pulled me through the wide doors of the warehouse. "When I find him, I'll give you a sign."

Signs were the only way we could communicate inside. No one really monitored the noise level at River's Edge since there were no neighbors to complain. The warehouse had great natural acoustics. Across one end stretched a stage, built back before my father's time. It was ridiculously large, allowing bands that shouldn't have been performing outside of their own basements to feel like they were playing at an arena. The stage was located near a side door, so equipment could be unloaded easily. The small backstage area had a dingy, olive-green couch and a few raggedy chairs. Throughout the warehouse, ladders on the wall led to a catwalk that snaked all the way around the inside, eighteen feet above the floor. Sometimes kids climbed up there and watched the band, legs dangling through the metal rails. They dared each other to dive into the thrashing crowd below, but no one ever did.

Audiences ranged from twenty to two hundred kids. Regan and I always scanned for faces we recognized from school. A crew of three older boys, all of whom wore the same leather jackets and spent lunch smoking in the parking lot, showed up semiregularly, but it looked like everyone else was at the game—football, basketball, baseball, whatever season it was. The kids at River's Edge arrived in groups of three to five. Like us, they attended rural high schools filled with guys who donned Packers jerseys every Monday and chicks who wore their boyfriends' varsity jackets with miniskirts or too-tight, acid-washed jeans. At school, multicolored hair, shredded and patched clothing, and studded, spiked accessories stood out like a neon billboard in the middle of a cornfield would, but at River's Edge those things blended right in.

By my senior year, when some of the local bands had begun to make names for themselves, more people started showing up—some of them from as far away as Milwaukee and Chicago—to see the legendary place where those country kids had gotten their start. They were probably disappointed to find it was much like any other club on the inside—dirty and dark, the concrete floor covered with that slimy mixture of ashes and beer—and we were the same group of kids found at any rock show. After all, it was the nineties. Just because we lived in the sticks didn't mean we were completely cut off from subculture. We just took more shit from our neighbors and classmates for looking strange.

The crowd thinned at the back of the warehouse by the main doors, but the area up to fifteen feet away from the stage was packed with sweaty, bouncing bodies. Regan barreled in, shoving burly guys twice her size out of her path. She liked to be right up front, getting slammed into the stage with the rhythm of the song. For some sick reason, I enjoyed being trampled and bruised, too. It was another phase that Marissa said we'd get over soon enough. Unless she really loved the band, Marissa stood at the back, splashing her drink on anyone who stepped on her toes. Since she played in July Lies, one of the best bands in the area, Marissa was queen of the scene. Regan and I could have shared her glory, but we liked to get hot, sticky, beat up, and dirty with the masses.

That night, however, Regan dove into the crowd on a mission; I knew she noticed him when I had. Sam's band was playing when we walked in.

I'd never seen or heard them before. They had a dumb name, Dead Smurfs or Mikey's Mom or something like that, but Sam was definitely practicing to be a rock god. His guitar hung low so that everyone could see his bare, tattooed chest. He had unwashed, blond hair that picked up the color of the lights. He thrashed a chord so hard that a string snapped, lacerating his finger, and he let it bleed. His voice was guttural and sexy. The music was fast and loud, just the way I liked it.

I pushed through the pit, grabbing at Regan, who always danced with her elbows swinging to knock away all the bigger bodies threatening to crush her. She threw her arm around me in a sweaty embrace and then shoved me in front of her so that I was standing directly in front of Sam. Entranced by him, I couldn't even tell if he was genuinely a good musician or if he just knew how to manipulate acoustics and energy. All I saw was that he oozed sex and danger. Regan agreed. After two songs, she pelted him with condoms, which she must have drunkenly decided would be a good sign.

I whipped around, mouthing "Bitch!" at her. She laughed hysterically and pointed over my shoulder. I turned back to see Sam smiling down at me, his baby-blue eyes thirsting for fame.

It wouldn't be the last time I was deceived by a rock god, but it was the only time that my disappointment was unforeseen. Of course, I hadn't expected or even wanted romance, but I had craved at least the pleasure of pain. I thought Sam would touch me with the raw power he used to play guitar. I thought he would kiss me and leave bruises on my skin as black-and-blue and dangerous as his voice. And I thought he would be able to satisfy the burn between my legs that surged every time I heard a distorted guitar. I slept with him because we worshipped at the same altars, because he oozed frenzied, furied rock energy, because I knew I could absorb it, make it mine. He thought I loved him for his inevitable future rock-god glory, but I had no interest in watching from backstage or vibing to the records he made, gleaming with gratitude that I was his muse. I thought that if we fused together, the world would screech like an amp so charged it caught fire. But it wasn't anywhere near that good.

I waited for him behind the stage and he made a beeline for me. After he introduced himself, Sam kissed me hard, shoving me against a steel beam. He tasted like stale beer. He bit my lower lip before thrusting his tongue into my mouth and exploring it violently. I dug my fingernails into his bare back and raked them down, feeling his skin splinter like weak wood. The scratch would become my trademark, the signature I left on every guy I hooked up with. He moaned into our kiss and I felt his pleasure vibrating down my throat and into my stomach. Sam pulled his hot mouth away from mine just enough to whisper, "Let's go outside."

Behind Marissa's car, we tumbled to the ground, pulling our T-shirts over our heads and tugging off each other's jeans. Night had fallen while Sam's band played, but the moon lit the sky. Our nakedness was protected from the eyes of others by darkness, though we could still see each other clearly. Sam rolled on top of me, hands groping greedily, stripping off my underwear and then his own as he sloppily sucked on my neck.

"Whoa!" I firmly planted my palm against the Celtic cross tattooed on his chest. "Condom?"

"Uhhh . . ."

"Right pocket of my jeans," I demanded.

"Oh. Good," he mumbled, scrambling backward and rooting through the pile of balled-up clothing at our feet.

Yeah, thank god for Regan. No matter how hot and heavy the action, I wasn't about to risk babies or STDs.

When he finally got the thing on, he climbed back on top of me. Then he was inside me. I closed my eyes waiting, at first, for the powerful, hungry feeling I'd felt in his initial kiss. After a few minutes, I opened one eye, still expecting, at the very least, the bleeding ache that Regan had mentioned. Nothing. It didn't feel like dancing while getting bruised by shoulders and elbows and knees. It didn't even feel like drunkenly screaming along to my favorite song. There was nothing raw or even energetic about it. The only thing remotely musical that I could compare it to was tapping my foot. The band inside butchered an Iggy Pop song. As the tone-deaf singer wailed, *"Can you feeeeel it?"* I wondered the same thing. And the answer was, "Not really."

I opened both eyes to see Sam thrusting into me in a way that was so not rhythmic that I doubted whether he'd ever heard music, let alone played it. His eyes squeezed closed, brow furrowed in intense concentration. I thought briefly that maybe I was in so much pain I was numb, but then I felt bits of gravel and broken glass digging into my butt. His sweaty hair fell into his face; the moonlight that trickled through it made it look translucent, as fragile as a spider's web. That's when I saw past the grimace on his face, the tattoos that he'd probably conned someone into giving him, and realized how much he resembled a little boy. He was probably two years older than me, but his inevitable lack of experience still didn't justify my disappointment.

I groped behind me for the beer that I'd left nearby, praying for a swallow of lukewarm backwash to alleviate my annoyance. Sam's breathing got faster and more labored, like he was working really hard. He pressed his cheek against mine, his chest rubbing against my black bra, which he hadn't even bothered to try to remove. I felt his leg muscles twitch and then he collapsed against me, leaving me with the impression of a dying fish.

When he finally rolled off of me, I quickly pulled on my jeans. Sam sighed. "I'm going to write a song about you," he murmured.

I stifled my laughter with the beer can I'd found. Before he could make any more embarrassing statements, I got dressed and walked away. My idea of rock gods had been ruined. They were nothing more than little boys wearing stolen scowls. I knew that the next time I saw Sam play, I would realize his songs sucked. He would be nothing without his rock-god hair flying, his arms flailing, his chest dripping sweat, and his intense eyes zeroing in on every girl in the audience who believed him to be raw power. I would notice that he couldn't even play four chords. And most important, I'd know that the sex wouldn't even last through three songs.

"Maybe he was just really bad," Regan said, peering sympathetically at me as I lay stretched out in the backseat, reveling in my disillusionment. The wind blew in from both her and Marissa's open windows, and I hoped that the smell of dirty barns was cleansing me of the scent of Sam's sweat.

"Well, regardless of that, I learned one thing. No guy fucks like they sound when they're onstage or blaring at top volume on your stereo. And I'm sure this knowledge will change my life," I quipped cynically.

Regan winced. "I swear I'll pick a better one next time."

"So will I," I said with a laugh.

"You girls need to do what I did," Marissa chimed in. She turned down the original version of "Gimme Danger" that I insisted she put on so my memory of the song wouldn't be tainted, and met my eyes in the rearview mirror. "Start your own damn band!"

Regan and I fell silent, but as the car sped toward the same part of Carlisle Louisa had blazed out of, I knew we both were thinking that Marissa was right.

SKIN

April 1981

Introduced as Scarlet, she followed the haunting rhythm out onto the stage with her hips swaying and torso winding. All the girls before her had danced frenetically to fast pop songs, garbed in sequins and glitter. They tossed their gowns in the gutter, rubbed their tits, and splayed their legs with wild abandon in an attempt to suck up the sloppy, post–Mardi Gras energy like powder through a rolled dollar bill. The old men in the back of the club watched the dancers with empty eyes, hungrily swallowing bottles of cheap beer. They wiped their perspiring hands on faded slacks and—only once or twice a night—retrieved a grimy bill from their pockets and threw it at a stripper's feet.

They were not the ones the dancers worked to impress. Girls gyrated and writhed to plastic ballads for the men who sat right up front: the conventioneers who slid their wedding rings off before going out on the town and the college boys still too intoxicated to realize that Mardi Gras was over. They screamed catcalls, grabbed their crotches, and overturned the torn vinyl chairs, but their rowdy behavior was excused because they tipped well.

After all, the club was at the edge of the French Quarter, a dim hole-in-the-wall on Esplanade that tourists only found when they turned off Bourbon Street and stumbled aimlessly in what they thought was the direction of their hotel. Bleary-eyed, they ignored the sticky floor, the chipped tables, the hum of the neon sign above the bar, and the gaudy gold curtain that functioned as the only decoration on the small stage aside from two black poles.

Scarlet stepped through the curtain to do her last dance at two A.M. Her voluminous, crimson hair cascaded down her back and over her shoulders, covering her breasts. She wore a shimmering, pearly skirt slit up to her hips on both sides, revealing legs the vulnerable pink of the inside of a shell. She sauntered to the front of the stage, green and purple lights illuminating her ghostly skin. Her rib, hip, and wrist bones jutted out, looking as though they could scratch through her delicate surface like coral. As the hollow voice that skimmed above the plodding, icy beat of the music sang about a woman giving away the secrets of her past, Scarlet tossed back her hair, pulled off the skirt, and opened her seaweed-green eyes all in one fluid motion. She looked out at the grimy heads of the regulars, averting her gaze before she caught a glimpse of herself in the smudged mirrors behind them. Then, she peered down at the red-faced, younger boys. One of them, thick-necked, bloodshot eyes wide, hollered, "She's a goddamn mermaid!" and stuffed her gold bikini bottoms with a ten-dollar bill.

She shut her eyes again, dancing as she would naturally at a nightclub, a concert, or in the room she remembered with flimsy white curtains, a battered radio, and a bassinet beside the double bed. She twisted her body to a song too obscure for anyone to recognize, and thought about things that no one in the crowd would know. About the way her legs had gotten long when she was fifteen and every man and boy stopped to stare at them as she kicked up dust on her trek to school. About a thin-lipped teacher who wore a bra tight as a straitjacket to flatten her chest and constantly told her, "Those legs will get you into trouble." About a lover left behind in the room with the white curtains whose gentle face she didn't dare picture while dancing, who told her, "Those legs will save you." And lastly, as the melancholy song about losing control crept into her ears, Scarlet thought about its singer, who had hanged himself less than a year ago. She let his voice possess her as her fingers fluttered to her throat, first pulling the strings of her top tight, and then untying them, letting the fabric fall away. She felt hands tangling around her legs, clawing at her hips, her stomach, and her thighs to stuff more money in her skimpy underwear. *It's only skin,* she thought, *they could rip away layers and layers of it and never get inside of me. They'll never penetrate my thoughts. They'll never even learn my name.*

Scarlet disappeared behind the gold curtain and went downstairs to the dressing room she shared with eight other girls. She sat on a metal folding chair in front of the mirror that spanned an entire wall and tossed her head back, carefully removing her red wig. She pulled her long, flaxen hair out of the two snaky coils beneath the hairnet, scratching at her tawny roots to relieve her sweaty scalp. After slipping into a pair of well-worn jeans and a T-shirt, she carefully wiped her makeup off with a damp tissue, attempting to erase all traces of Scarlet. But it was not until she got on the streetcar at Canal and St. Charles that she retrieved the felt bag she kept stashed at the bottom of her purse. Inside was a gold wedding band, and when she slid it on, she became the woman she would never let her audience know: Louisa Black.

Normally, the ring was just another part of Louisa's ritual, the final action she took to become herself again and sever any mental connection she had with the person she pretended to be at work, stepping away like an actress after playing a difficult role. Louisa had come to regard the ring as the simple symbol she reduced it to when people asked her about it. "Yes, I have a husband," she always told them, speaking with an affectionate tone yet offering no explanation as to who or where her husband was.

But that night, when Louisa put her wedding ring on, she clearly pictured Michael. She didn't see him as she had first seen him, with his long fingers dancing over the strings of a guitar. She didn't have a flash of the shy smile he wore when they were married in front of a judge in Chicago. Instead, Louisa was momentarily blinded by her image of Michael right before she'd decided to leave him: lying in their bed in his pale blue pajamas, his back propped up against the wooden headboard with their baby girl sleeping soundly on his lap, her rosy cheek pressed against his chest.

As Louisa bent down to kiss their daughter before setting her in the bassinet beside their bed, she noticed how soft Emily was, thought about how she fit so perfectly against her body when she nursed. Emily's skin felt like velvet or satin; it was like Louisa's second skin. A skin that Louisa would have to shed.

Since Emily's birth, Louisa had been having the same dream of sitting in the kitchen nursing Emily, but with the milk going red. Bloodred. Louisa noticed it at the corner of Emily's tiny lips, spreading quickly toward her cheeks, and, before long, her baby face resembled raw meat. Emily tried to pull her mouth away, began to shriek, but it was like her suckling had turned on a fire hose. She started choking, but Louisa froze, keeping her at her breast until Michael rushed in. "You're killing her!" he shouted, but he couldn't do anything, because as Emily turned blue, so did he. They both died right in front of Louisa while her breasts continued to leak blood.

The dream was always the same and she had it every night. She awoke racked with guilt, unable to fall back asleep. She spent her days feeling less and less capable of caring for Emily. She didn't have the words to explain it to Michael. Besides, nothing he could say could comfort her. Normal mothers didn't see things like that night after night. Louisa felt that the dream's message was clear: she did not deserve this child. She promised herself that if she had the nightmare one more time, she would leave.

Louisa paused, didn't want to set Emily down. She imagined holding Emily in her arms for years, her daughter growing rapidly like she had inside of Louisa's womb. Her arms, legs, all of her would lengthen and strengthen. She would learn to speak, her voice musical but commanding. And Louisa would keep her snugly in her grip, pressed against her chest, until Emily was too big to hold. Too big to be hurt by Louisa's secrets and memories. Or by the nightmare. If only she could stay awake until Emily was grown. "Pray," she whispered to the sleeping infant as she reluctantly put her to bed. "Pray my dreams are sweet as you from now on, so I don't have to go away."

Louisa squeezed her eyes shut as she slipped beneath the covers beside Michael. His arms found their way around her immediately, his lips brushing her neck, but the dream was beginning. She could feel the blood heavy in her breasts.

As she pushed the memory back, Louisa stepped off the streetcar in front of the dilapidated building she'd been living in for months. The yellowing sign, barely visible in the ghoulish shadows of the streetlights, proclaimed it the St. Charles Hotel, but it was really a bar, open twenty-four hours a day, with three floors of rooms above it that were rented for twenty dollars a night or seventy-five dollars a week. Louisa's room was on the third floor. Her view consisted of the on-ramp to I-10 and one of the many blocks of St. Charles Street that tourists avoided as they passed through the run-down section between the French Quarter and the Garden District. Louisa was lulled to sleep each night by the muffled music that never ceased in the bar below. She kept a knife on the scarred nightstand beside her because she shared a bathroom with her constantly revolving next-door neighbor. This was how she'd lived since she left, and she knew it was exactly what she deserved.

The summer after my freshman year—when faded yellow ribbons still hung all over Carlisle even though Operation Desert Storm had ended in the spring—I followed Marissa's advice in my own twisted way. I started a band, but didn't let it stop me from pursuing guys at River's Edge. Regan cajoled her parents into buying her a drum set, and I got an electric guitar for my fifteenth birthday. I'd had an acoustic since I was five and learned to play it before I could write my name, but the night that my dad gave me the electric was special. It reminded me that once upon a time things had been simple. I'd been Daddy's little girl, and all that mattered to me was making him smile, which he did most when I sang or mastered a new song on guitar.

As soon as I'd rolled into double digits, people started comparing me to Louisa. I heard it so much that by the time I hit twelve I didn't think of myself as Emily or Regan's best friend or Michael's only child. I thought of myself as Louisa's girl, and I strove to live up to her outrageous reputation.

People said that at thirteen, Louisa chopped off all her hair in history class just because she was bored, and the ragged pixie cut that she wouldn't let her mother fix only made the boys pine for her more. She was the girl older guys always went for. I heard that she never dated anyone in her own grade, but apparently she hated the men who called to her from pickup trucks as much as I did. One spring morning her sophomore year, she and Molly showed up without any books because on their way to the bus stop, they'd hurled one at every driver who commented on their legs. Louisa's expressions of loyalty also had a veneer of danger. On prom night, she danced with Molly on the roof of the high school gym since Molly wasn't allowed inside, being pregnant and all. Even Luke Parker and Eric Lisbon, who was Louisa's boyfriend at the time, hadn't dared to go up there. Of course, Louisa was the kind of girl who always got away before the cops came. The day she bid farewell to Carlisle by shattering glass with high-heeled shoes flung from the back of a Harley, they showed up after she was long gone and gaped slack-jawed at the damage she left in her wake.

I was so obsessed with the image of a woman I had never known that my dad often faded into the background. Louisa was fantasy. He was routine. He drove me to school every morning and tucked me in every night. I'd observed the lines that curled around the sides of my dad's mouth when he laughed, watched the molasses waves that dipped down to meet his chin when he shook his head, known the pattern of the black stubble that peppered his jaw, and felt his fingers ruffle my hair for so long that he became a part of my shadow. It was Louisa's face I yearned to see when I got up in the morning and her features that I searched for in mine when I looked in the mirror. But, of course, I would never admit how much I cared. That would make me seem like a little lost, motherless lamb, and I couldn't stand the idea of anyone thinking of me that way. So I acted like her instead. Everyone seemed to expect it of me and playing her role made me feel like I knew her.

But I was most myself with my father. Every night he and

I retreated to the living room after dinner. He stretched his long, tired limbs out on the couch and alternated between sips of coffee and drags from a cigarette. I "played DJ," as he called it, putting on a song, excitedly talking over it about the musicians' techniques, and then putting on a new one before my first selection had even ended. He smiled throughout the whole procedure, truly affected by my great discoveries, and never hesitating to point out when he thought I was full of crap. We communicated almost entirely through this game of song and response. Every couple of weeks, our conversations would turn into all-night discussions that ranged from the influence of jazz on punk to the burgeoning riot grrrl movement to why Bill Clinton's saxophone playing made him an interesting presidential candidate.

On the night of my fifteenth birthday, however, we weren't speaking. I put on one record and left it alone. I planted myself in the rocking chair across from my father's couch. He sat with his head bent over his mug as if he needed to watch each granule of sugar dissolve. He had not acknowledged my birthday that morning or after I returned from Regan's. Thinking that he'd truly forgotten about it, I gave him the silent treatment throughout dinner, and he simply hadn't spoken. As angry punk rock blared, I glared at him, fuming.

His lips slowly snaked upward and finally, he couldn't take it. He tried to force his mouth into a frown, causing his face to light up with the exaggerated expression of a jack-o'-lantern. "What's wrong, Emily?" he asked with that absurd smirk.

My face flushed as I became aware of his ruse, but I

acted as if I hadn't figured it out. "I realize, *Michael*, that you aren't a woman. You didn't carry me around inside you for nine months and go through agonizing labor . . ."

"Don't call me by my first name. My name to you is Dad."

I narrowed my eyes, and he narrowed his back at me. My lip curled up at the left, and his curled at the right. My chin dropped to laugh, and his followed the same arc. I shook my head, realizing for the first time that, except for my green eyes, I was the spitting image of my father. "Well, don't pretend to forget my birthday!" I shouted, half amused and half exasperated.

"Did you actually think I forgot?" he teased, sliding a small box out of the breast pocket where he usually kept his cigarettes.

"No!" I denied, snatching the package from him. I unwrapped it quickly, completely mystified by what it could be. It looked like a jewelry box. When I was ten, he'd given me what I thought was Louisa's only piece of jewelry—an antique silver locket. I wore it every day, even polished it when it started to tarnish. But I didn't take such special care of it because it had been Louisa's. Inside the shiny oval was a picture of my dad at eighteen. I treasured the necklace because it reminded me of him more than it did her. Now, I was almost afraid to open my gift, thinking it was something else of Louisa's, that he, too, had begun to associate me with her. But I removed the lid to find a red guitar pick and a note in my father's scratchy handwriting that read, "Look in the basement."

I raced downstairs to find the floor plastered with paper

arrows pointing toward the closet that had once held Louisa's records. Dad stood behind me while I opened the door. After carefully setting the hard, black case on the floor, I unlatched it and raised the top slowly. A guitar. The blue body sparkled brighter than any lake I'd ever seen. The white pick guard glistened like a pearl. My eyes followed the frets up to the headstock. "Holy shit, it's a Fender Mustang," I spoke in quiet awe.

"My 1969 Fender Mustang," my father added. "That I'm giving to you."

I whirled around. Since his head was right behind my shoulder, our faces were just inches apart. "How do you keep this stuff hidden from me?"

There was a faraway look in his eyes. "I was playing that the night your mother first saw me at River's Edge." He met my gaze seriously. "Don't end up like her, Emily. Don't search for the music in other people. Play it yourself."

I immediately glanced down, afraid that in my eyes he could see every boy I'd met at River's Edge.

He let any traces of sorrow drain from his voice. "C'mon, baby, plug that sucker in and play me a song." He ruffled my hair, forcing me to look up at his gleeful face. I realized that he was innocently unaware of the things I'd done, which was unfortunate because that was part of the reason I continued to do them.

The next morning, Regan and I cleared a space in her basement to rehearse. I brought over my guitar and my stereo. We learned to play from it, strumming, singing, and thrashing along to everything from my dad's Beatles records to the Patti Smith album Louisa left behind to the seven-inches I got monthly from the Sub Pop singles club. Regan broke sticks and I snapped strings, my hands a mess of bloody blisters. We spent our afternoons making music, but we still spent our nights at River's Edge or with the boys we met there.

In my head I had made a transition. I was no longer Emily Black, toy of the rock gods; I was Emily Black, future rock goddess picking out her own groupies. If the boys could have their playthings, why couldn't I have mine? I was demanding equal rights. However, since no one but my dad, Regan, and her family had ever seen me play music, by all outward appearances I was just a slut. I asked for nothing more of the guys I slept with than the use of a condom. I spent no more than two weeks with them and had a couple of occasions that were identical to my night with Sam, in which I exchanged only a few sentences with my chosen partner. I was not fully aware of how it looked to others. Heads never turned when I left the Edge and the heads that did turn when I stumbled out of a field or the alley behind JT's Tavern with my lipstick smeared on my chin belonged to people older than my father. They buzzed about Louisa, which I thought they would have anyway, so I just concerned myself with the way it made me feel.

Of course, I knew what love was. I saw the passion Molly and Luke still shared after nineteen years of marriage and the devotion my father still had for Louisa almost fifteen years after she left us. But I knew that the only thing I loved that much was music, so I had no desire to search for a person to fill that role. Sex to me was like drinking or dancing at a crowded show. I wanted to reach new levels of excitement. I wanted to feel something, even if it was sickness or bruises. I wanted to be entertained. My quest was to find a guy who could do that job well. But it was no-where near as important as learning to play my own music. I shopped for records in a much more dedicated fashion than I shopped for boys.

I shopped for boys like I shopped for shoes. I tried on guys with soft voices and with screams that mangled my ears. I tried out one of the black-haired, the red-haired, and the brown-haired variety before I settled on blonds as my type, but I never distinguished between natural and bleached hair. I had two guys that touched me tenderly and one that covered every inch of me with bite marks and scratched me as hard as I scratched him. Neither type aroused me any differently; I actually preferred the other three boys who performed at a level in between. I never allowed any of them to be as lazy as Sam was, but despite their attention, I never felt more excited by any of them than I had by him. Lying beneath, beside, or on top of them, I didn't perceive what I was doing to be wrong, and I certainly didn't consider myself inferior to them. *After all,* I thought, *I'm giving them nothing more than skin and they will never forget me.*

April 1981

Louisa made friends in every city she touched down in, but she never had trouble saying good-bye. In fact, she hardly ever said it. Her exits usually weren't planned;

the urge to flee would come over her in the middle of the night, just as it did in New Orleans. But although her stay in New Orleans was one of her shortest anywhere, it was also the only place where she'd become regrettably close to someone.

Colette had introduced herself the very first night Louisa came to town. Louisa arrived in New Orleans after midnight, checked into the St. Charles Hotel, the first place she saw upon exiting I-10, and took the streetcar into the French Quarter to find a nice place to drink. Despite the fact that she'd driven from New York City with just a three-hour nap at a truck stop in Tennessee, Louisa knew she wouldn't be able to sleep. She wandered down Bourbon Street, but the bright lights and loud celebratory atmosphere conflicted with her mood, so she turned off on Ursulines. Between Royal and Chartres, she found the perfect place. Large stone steps led down into the bar. Inside the old building that had likely once been a mansion, the walls were made of gray stone and the floors and bar of deep brown oak. At the back of the bar, French doors were propped open and a brick walkway led to a patio that seemed to be getting the only breeze in New Orleans, but Louisa decided not to go outside, instead ordering a rum and Coke and carrying it to a table in a dark corner.

She noticed Colette immediately. It was hard not to; she had the body of Farrah Fawcett, but her clothes were pure punk rock. Everyone—especially the men—paused to stare at her. Tall and slender with short, jet-black hair sprayed to stick up in fierce chunks and spikes, Colette wore a black miniskirt, torn tights, and a vivid red shirt that advertised an obscure movie from the sixties with a photo of the unknown starlet's face, eyes wide like a frightened animal and lips slightly parted.

Colette sat at a table next to the jukebox with four friends who were as skinny, pale, and crazy-haired as she, but totally nondescript by comparison. Louisa hung around for an hour just enjoying the atmosphere and Colette's laugh, which reminded her of Molly's—constant, loud, from the gut, and completely unrestrained. Colette put a Runaways song on and sang along in her whiskey-and-cigarette-tinged voice as Louisa finished her second drink and headed for the door. Before she could exit, she found a red-fingernailed hand wrapped around her arm.

"Where are you from and why are you leaving?" Colette demanded, her bright blue eyes glittering.

Colette's interest was piqued as soon as Louisa said that she'd just arrived from New York. "No shit! I'm gonna move there in a month or two. Whenever I save up the money. I want to be a singer. In a band. Did you see a lot of bands there? Did you hang out at CBGBs? Did you meet Blondie?" Colette spoke in a quick, clipped manner that covered up what Louisa soon found out was a North Carolina accent.

Colette's life story bubbled from her lips as Louisa took a seat beside her. "I ran away from my hometown more than a year ago, when I turned seventeen. I hated that small-town bullshit. But it sounds like you've lived in a lot of big cities, so I guess you wouldn't know what that's like." Colette paused to gulp her Jack and Coke, leaving another red lipstick print on her glass.

"No, not at all," Louisa murmured.

As the cocaine Colette had snorted earlier wore off, she calmed down, and she reminded Louisa of Molly even more: an intelligent, sarcastic girl with big dreams. That's probably why Louisa made the mistake of opening up to her.

Colette got Louisa the job at the strip club where Colette had worked since arriving from North Carolina. They often went drinking together after work. Louisa usually spent her nights off alone, Colette out with other friends, but one night Colette showed up at her hotel.

"This is the ugliest room I've ever seen," Colette announced as she plopped down on the bed next to Louisa and examined exactly how badly the brown blankets clashed with her purple tights.

"How'd you get my room number?" Louisa asked, slamming shut the notebook she'd been writing in and pacing toward the window.

"Asked the bartender. You really should get an apartment in the Quarter," Colette continued, peering down at the pockmarked, threadbare carpet.

"I thought I was going to New York with you in a few weeks."

Colette, distracted by the notebook, ignored Louisa's statement and asked instead, "You writing juicy secrets in there?"

Louisa stared hard at the on-ramp to I-10. "I don't have any secrets."

"Sure, you do. Like your husband." Louisa's right hand clamped instinctively around her left, covering her wedding ring. Since she had her back to Colette, she didn't see the younger woman pick up the letter on the nightstand and the photograph that was tucked neatly beneath it. "And whoever this little girl is."

Louisa flew across the room in a whirlwind and ripped the picture out of Colette's purple-painted fingertips. She cupped the wallet-size photo in her hand and glanced down at the four-year-old girl with long, ebony hair held back by green barrettes that matched her forest-colored velvet dress and her flashing jade eyes. Louisa took a few steps to her left and placed the photo on the rickety dresser.

"Who is she?" Colette asked quietly, her eyes as wide as the starlet's had been on the T-shirt she wore the first night Louisa met her.

"Emily. My daughter," Louisa whispered in a voice that seemed disconnected from her body. She avoided Colette's gaze by inspecting a scratch in the wood a few inches away from the photograph.

"Did he . . . did your husband take her away from you?" Colette ventured, her voice wavering. Louisa knew Colette's father had kept her mother out of her life since she'd cheated on him when Colette was six.

"No, Michael would never do that!" Louisa exclaimed. She felt as if the wind had been knocked out of her, saying their names aloud.

"No, of course not," Colette muttered, more to herself than to Louisa. "He wouldn't send you pictures if he had."

"He doesn't send the pictures. He doesn't know where I am."

"Who sends them, then?"

Louisa ignored Colette's question and continued her own train of thought in a daze. "I left them. I left Michael and Emily." Her throat throbbed as she spoke their names again.

"Why?" Colette's voice rang out like a child's, sounding almost like it could have come from the girl in the picture.

Louisa turned slowly to face her and looked her in the eye. "Because I had to. Because I wasn't good enough for them." She set her jaw firmly, signaling that she had nothing else to say on the matter.

The night after she spilled her guts to Colette, Louisa threw open the door to her room, retrieved the money that she kept hidden in a cigarette pack in her suitcase, and spread it out on her sagging bed. She combined it with the two hundred dollars she'd made that night, counting out a total of fourteen hundred dollars. She mulled over where to head next.

Initially, Louisa had had great plans for each new city. In Detroit, she wanted to meet Iggy Pop. In New York, she wanted to drink with the Ramones. She went to Los Angeles to open a club with a woman she met in New York. All of these ventures failed. After a couple years of traveling, her stays in the major cities got shorter and shorter. She kept ending up in places that she never intended to visit, like Toledo and Oklahoma City. And deep down, Louisa knew that it was because more than anything she just wanted to go home.

Denying that thought, as she had for almost five years, Louisa swept the money off the bed and into her purse with one hand. She didn't have to glance around to figure out what to pack next. There was no closet. Louisa kept all of the costumes that she wore to work in a black duffel bag. She dumped the cosmetics lining the sink into that. She'd only half unpacked her regular clothes into the dresser, so emptying the three drawers back into the suitcase was easy. After fifteen minutes, Louisa left room 310 as she'd found it when she checked in: the bedsheets rumpled, a cigarette smoldering in the ashtray, and long blond hairs stuck to the basin of the sink. She just added the one touch she left in every place she stayed. Kneeling on the dirty yellow carpet, she pulled the middle drawer out of the dresser, and using a bottle of red nail polish she'd kept aside while packing, she inked her initials and the date in the back corner of the drawer.

While tossing her bags in the dented trunk of her Impala, Louisa glanced at her long-expired Illinois plates and wondered if she would ever stay someplace long enough to replace them.

She decided to go west, see more of California. An acquaintance of Colette's had just come from there. He'd talked up bands like Social Distortion and the Circle Jerks and said that the hardcore scene had reached a boiling point when the not-so-beloved former governor, Ronald Reagan, had taken office as president earlier that year. After Louisa had driven for a mile, the windows rolled down to let the humid green air that snaked off the Mississippi River kiss her farewell, Louisa looked in the rearview mirror and said, "Bye, Colette." Startled by the sound of her own voice, she completed her apology silently. *I really would have taken you with me, but last night you let me tell you about them, and I can't be around someone who knows.*

On Labor Day weekend, the official end of my summer and beginning of my sophomore year, I picked the last River's Edge guy using the same methods I always had. He was to be conquest number eight, and of course, I didn't foresee him as being the last at the time. I watched all three bands that played River's Edge each night carefully, knowing that sometimes the first was better than the last, and sometimes none of them were good enough at all.

Number Eight's band was the second to grace the stage. The chorus of their first song was so catchy that I left my beer with Marissa so I could use both hands to push my way up front. I danced with my eyes closed to pick out the instrument that carried the song. I'd learned from my first experience that the singer was not necessarily the most talented individual in the band even though he was assumed to be the leader. I wasn't a groupie, so I had no interest in screwing for status. The guitar riff definitely dominated the first song. I noticed during the second that the guitarist had an impeccable instinct about when to use the distortion pedal, which was often overused by newly formed bands in the early nineties. I opened my eyes and scanned the stage. I had standards. I only chose guys whose looks were equaled by their musical abilities.

"He's cute!" Regan proclaimed, bouncing up beside me and indicating the guitarist. His bleached hair fell into his face as he leaned into a powerful riff, hiding everything but his strong jawline and the curve of a wan lower lip. While the singer jumped around the stage in nothing but baggy camouflage shorts to show off his toned abs and pierced nipples, the guitarist was fully clothed. The long sleeves of his shirt were tattered, presumably because of the ferocity with which he played his instrument. The only skin visible was on his hands and through the small hole in the left knee of his jeans. An unassuming rock god. A rare breed. One that I had yet to find.

"Number eight!" I shouted, turning to Regan and sarcastically licking my lips. "He's mine!"

She shook her fist at me with a smile. "Dammit! You always call them first," she complained. Then she lifted her thumb from the fist, giving me a sign of approval. "Good luck," she yelled solemnly before bouncing away. Those were our rules. She who calls him first gets him. I'd lost a few with great potential to her that summer, but on all occasions was informed that I hadn't missed much.

Number Eight was from Rockford. That's all I heard over the din of the Edge. As we walked outside to his van, I contemplated asking him to clarify the name of his band, even his own name, but I could procure that information if he proved himself worthy. He wasn't. That didn't surprise me, but what happened afterward did.

He pulled on his boxers. I was already dressed and had my hand on the door handle when he said, "So, who do you want next?"

I whipped around, my arms banging against the passenger seat and the sliding door. "What?" I asked incredulously.

His hair obscured a self-assured smirk. "Well, we've heard about you, of course."

I blinked. Regan and I had not recorded a tape. We weren't even thinking of playing the Edge yet. I quickly realized that he couldn't have heard about my band because no one except the adoring fans in my daydreams had. What he meant hit me faster than six consecutive shots of whiskey and made me feel sicker than any alcohol could. "What have you *heard* about me?"

"Well, we heard that you set the standard at this place. You pick the best band." He ran his hand from his right nipple down to his stomach as if seductively stroking his own ego. "And you *do* the best band."

My vision swam. "What?" I raged. "Who the hell do you think you are—Slash? Do you think I screwed a series of roadies and the drummer to get to you and now I want Axl?" I gestured angrily out the front windshield toward River's Edge. "This is not some cock-rock joint! I am not some groupie! I have a band too, you know. You should be honored . . ."

I stopped because he was laughing at me. Not just giggling at my foolish indignation, but red-in-the-face, slapping-his-bare-thigh, hysterically laughing at me. I shrunk back, defensively crossing my arms over my chest as ugly reality set in. I hadn't been considering the consequences of my actions. What I was doing wasn't just a little bit slutty. I'd put my future reputation as a musician in jeopardy. In my mind, I was already a rock star. I'd convinced myself of it. And I'd deluded myself into thinking I was making some sort of equal rights statement by using guys the way rock gods used chicks. But to the rest of the world, I looked like a groupie. Who was I kidding?

Number Eight abandoned his modest rock-god act, pouting his lips to mock me. "Awwww, you're in a band, huh? Do you play an instrument? Do you sing as good as you suck dick? Do you— Ahhhh! Jesus Christ!" he wailed after my fist slammed into his face. Blood gushed from his formerly pretty nose. Hitting him felt like I had wanted sex to feel.

"I have yet to meet a guy who knows more about music than me. In fact, I have yet to meet one who knows how to fuck!" I sneered, reaching behind me to open the van door, satisfied by the tears mixing with the dark blood that dripped into his once superior mouth. I could feel my eyes growing as black as my hair when the words for the final blow came to me. "Maybe one day I'll let you open for my band," I spat, slamming the door on the skinny boy who suddenly seemed so much smaller than me.

But I never felt as tough as I acted. I stalked away from Number Eight's van and looked helplessly at River's Edge, knowing I couldn't go back in there without having a tantrum. I wanted to climb up onstage and scream that I wasn't a groupie, but I knew that that would only make things worse. When I mounted that stage for the first time, staring out at the audience instead of up from it, it would be with dignity. So I did the only thing I could think of. I trudged three miles back to Regan's house, trying not to cry.

By the time I arrived, Marissa's car was already parked in the driveway and both her and Regan's bedroom lights were off. When they hadn't found me at the end of the night, they'd simply left, assuming that I'd gone off with some guy—because that's what I did and everyone knew it. I couldn't hold it in any longer. I slunk behind the house, sat on top of the picnic table, and bawled. I paused momentarily to take the joint that Regan and I had rolled earlier out of my cigarette pack. Between sobs, I inhaled lungfuls of smoke that did nothing but burn my throat and make my head pound. I tossed the joint away. Nothing tasted good anymore. Nothing felt good anymore. I was bad from skin to bone, and everything I did or thought about was as horrible as me. Tears ran all the way down my neck, soaking my shirt.

When I felt her arms on my shoulders and remembered that touch could be affectionate instead of just empty, I thought my sadness had made my secret wish come true. "Louisa?" I asked hopefully, but I found myself staring into Molly's worried brown eyes.

"What's wrong, baby?" she asked, like I was one of her real daughters. She was tuned in to me in the same way she was to them. She sensed my tears in her dreams, knew exactly where I was, and came running, dressed in a wrinkled T-shirt, her russet hair in the messy braid she slept in. But it wasn't enough.

I threw myself against her and cried pathetically, "I want my mom."

Molly's delicate hands rubbed my back in circles the way my father did when I was sick. "It's about damn time," she sighed.

I let myself sob hard, chest heaving until I was exhausted. When I finally stopped, Molly held me at arm's length, staring into my eyes, her face wrought with guilt. I knew then that she knew what had happened to my mother. I had probably known subconsciously since the first day of third grade when our teacher had forced Regan and me to sit on opposite sides of the room. "I've heard about you two girls," she clucked, and it was a couple years too soon for her to have heard something bad. "I know that you're inseparable." And we were. Sisters in every sense except blood. Just as Molly and Louisa had been. And that kind of bond runs deeper than marriage ties, maybe even deeper than maternal instinct. If I refused to talk to anyone in the world, I would still talk to Regan. I knew that for Louisa and Molly it was the same way.

Molly had the permanent expression of a mischievous sixteen-year-old, like she hadn't aged a day since she'd had Marissa, but in the dim moonlight, remorse bruised circles under her dark eyes and traced lines around them. "I don't know where she is anymore, Emily." Tears rode the wrinkles like riverbeds. "She hasn't written me in four years. The last address was in Boston and it's no good anymore. I should have told you about it earlier, but . . ."

"I never asked," I concluded woodenly. I'd asked Molly to tell me stories about what Louisa was like when they were growing up. I asked my dad what their time in Chicago together was like. I never asked either of them anything about Louisa leaving. I blindly accepted the vague story my father told me about Louisa needing to follow the music, because I liked that legend.

Molly bit her lip, her hand grasping mine. "I shouldn't have waited for you to ask. Baby . . ."

She continued, but I wasn't really listening. She talked

about my mother showing up in the middle of a cold November night—the night she left us. Molly's words sketched an image of Louisa as tear-streaked and red-eyed and confused as me. And I didn't want to hear it. My mother was a woman of myth. Her shoulders had never been shaken by sobs. Her commanding, verdant eyes had never shed a tear. She was not randomly wandering because she was in pain. She followed her ears. She consumed the rumble of the drums, ferocious guitar riffs, throbbing bass lines, throaty voices, angelic voices, claw-your-eyes-out yowls. She hunted music. Lived it. Knew it better than anyone.

"The idea of never being able to talk to her again . . . So when she said she'd write me if I didn't tell . . ." Molly gulped in air and pulled her hand away from mine to desperately rake it through her hair.

"She made you promise, didn't she? If Regan made me promise, I would have kept the promise," I murmured, needing to comfort Molly and, even more, needing to make her stop acting broken, stop talking like Louisa had been broken.

"Yeah." Molly went silent for a moment. Then her eyes snapped up to meet mine. She looked startled, like she'd suddenly awakened from a hypnotic trance. "You need to know why your mother left."

I panicked. I did not need to know why my mother left. Not then. I couldn't handle it. That night, my image of myself—rock goddess, totally in control, making little wannabe boys play her game—had been shattered. I was not ready to have my vision of my mother demolished as well. "Louisa was a free spirit. She left to follow the music. I was born when punk rock was dawning in America and she wanted to be there." I told Molly what my father had said almost word for word.

Yeah, I didn't just like that legend, I needed it. I drew my strength from it. That's why I'd never questioned it. My mother wasn't there to hug me and comfort me and bandage my wounds when I fell down, but at least I knew she was beautiful, fierce, and driven by rock 'n' roll, and that gave me something to aspire to.

Pity spread across Molly's face. "Emily . . ."

"No!"

Louisa did not leave my father and me in tears or too numb to cry. She had smiled at us and kissed us good-bye and said that it was time for her to go meet Iggy and Joey and Patti, and my dad had held the door open for her because everyone knows that goddesses come and go as they please. I had to believe that. That legend protected me from my deepest, darkest secret fear: that I was the reason my mother left. I'd ruined her fun, drained her life of joy, and she had to run away to get that back. She had to run away because she didn't love me.

"No!" I snapped viciously at Molly, leaping off the table. "I don't need to know. Not tonight. Not after everything . . ."

Images of my long-legged, smiling mother vanished, replaced by Number Eight's smirk. Molly rose and guided me back to the picnic bench. "What happened tonight, Emily?"

"I did something stupid. In fact, I've done a lot of stupid things lately." I hesitated. She looked like a bigger version of Regan, but even in my distressed state, I wasn't going to mistake the two.

Molly broke the ice with laughter like she always did. "You think I don't know what kind of stupid things you've been doing? Your dad and Luke are blind to what their little girls become when they hit fourteen. But I was you once. Not to mention I went through this a few years ago with Marissa. Please, tell me what hurt you so bad that it made you ask for your mother for the first time in your life."

I couldn't tell her the whole story, so I summarized. "This guy called me a slut. But I guess I kind of deserved it."

"Oh, Emily, that's crap. You've got to think about your actions, but no guy ever, *ever*," she emphasized, "has the right to degrade you. There isn't one man in this world who's any better than you. Obviously that guy wanted you to think that what he does is fine, but when *you* do it, it's wrong. And a lot of them will try to make you think that about a whole bunch of different things. You can't ever take it to heart."

"Well, I punched him," I informed her, deadpan, studying my knuckles, still inflamed and throbbing from the blow.

Molly cackled so loud that dogs across the street barked. "That's my girl," she managed between chuckles.

I remained angry with myself, thinking of all the greedy boy-hands that had grabbed at every inch of me that summer. "I should call my band Tainted Skin."

Molly shook her head. "Did you crack him good?"

"There was blood." My lips twitched into a smile. "And then I told him that someday he could open for my band."

Molly put her hand over her mouth to suppress hysterics. "I'm sorry. Please don't tell your dad that I laughed. He'll think I encouraged you to be violent."

I raised my eyebrows. "I really don't intend to tell him any of this."

"You shouldn't do things that you can't tell your daddy about. If you can't tell him, you can be damn sure it's gonna end badly. That's what I told Marissa. Straightened her right up," Molly said, maintaining a serious tone and her grin at the same time. "You're cheering up now, aren't you? Laughing is good for a girl. I think you should call your band She Laughs. And make music that people can dance to."

She gazed into the distance, fingering my disheveled hair. "You should've seen the way your mother danced. That's the way I remember her. Dancing at River's Edge. Nothin' that happened and nothin' nobody says about her will ever take that image away from me." Molly's eyes flickered trance-like again, but she smiled wistfully. "She found the secret rhythm in the song. People would be jumping around, pushing each other, and your mom'd be standing a little farther back, just swaying. No one went near her, not even accidentally. Tainted skin, my ass—you got untouchable skin just like your mama. People would watch her, sometimes pay more attention to her than the band. The song would end, she'd stop, applaud like crazy, and look at me and crack up. I'm sure she's still out there dancing, but I bet she don't laugh like that, not without you and your daddy."

"And you," I whispered, the ache in my chest and the echo of Number Eight's words disappearing. My entire view of River's Edge had changed. Despite the grimy floors, the stale air, and the onslaught of feedback that filled it, it was a temple. My mother hadn't gone there in search of boys like I'd always thought, like I'd mimicked. She'd danced on long legs, lifting her bleached hair off of her sweaty neck, closing her sage eyes, and drinking in the music. Her laughter still lived there, waiting to be awakened by a really good song, maybe a song that I would write.

"What you just told me, that's what I really needed to hear about Louisa tonight," I told Molly softly.

She squeezed my shoulders, drawing me into her embrace again. "Call your band She Laughs, Em. Keep laughing and dancing and don't take no shit."

The Worst Thing You Could Do

Regan was the last person in the world I thought would fall in love. Well, almost. The last person besides me.

The morning after the groupie incident with Number Eight, I went down to Regan's soundproofed basement to rehearse before she even woke up. I played "Louder, Harder, Faster," the first song I'd ever written, over and over again on acoustic guitar. It was a song about sex with rock gods that I'd come up with a few months before I'd even lost my virginity. I snarled the chorus: *"Play it harder. Play it faster. Louder. Harder. Faster. So loudhardfast that I forget your name. After all, did I even know it in the first place,"* and played so viciously that eventually a string snapped, lashing into my pinkie. I swore and sucked on my injured finger.

"Careful there," Regan said with a smirk, wandering into the room in her pajamas. She plopped down on the couch beside me. "Haven't heard you play that one in a while."

"And I'm not playing it again," I mumbled around my finger.

Regan took the guitar from my lap and started to remove the broken string. "Why? It isn't *that* bad."

"It is after last night."

She arched an eyebrow and I sighed, rubbing my finger on my dirty jeans as I launched into the story. I concluded with my three-mile walk of shame and my conversation with her mother.

"Well, at least we got a cool band name out of it," Regan consoled.

I picked at the flap of skin on my pinkie. "Yeah, great, but no one's going to respect us because they think we're groupies."

"You're right. No more sleeping with musicians."

"After last night, no more sleeping around for me, period," I said. "Our music is all that matters to me."

Regan nodded solemnly. "Me, too. No more guys. They're boring anyway. From now on we just focus on the band. Okay?" She extended her pinkie and I smiled and wrapped my injured one around it. "Now let's write some new songs," she said, grinning.

So, a pact was made. But that was before Regan laid her eyes on Tom Fawcett.

Tom was a lanky loner a year younger than us. He'd transformed from an ostracized band geek—whose president-of-the-PTA, church-fund-raising-queen fascist of a mother made him wear ill-fitting, button-down shirts and dress pants—into a scruffy punk-rocker kid in one summer. He stalked into the lunchroom on the first day of school with the baby fat shaved off his razor-sharp cheekbones, bleached hair erratically sticking up around black headphones, a Social Distortion T-shirt, and ripped jeans. The look in his long-lashed, heavy-lidded brown eyes told everyone who'd pushed him around in the past to back off. And he might've been hungover on his first day of high school, which was pretty cool.

When she saw him, Regan's jaw dropped. It was like when Christian Slater shows up in the cafeteria for the first time in *Heathers*—except, fortunately, Tom didn't shoot anyone. "How come I never noticed . . ." Regan stammered with that wide-eyed look Winona Ryder had when she noticed her ill-fated love interest for the first time.

"That's Tom Fawcett, dude." I shrugged, appreciating his beauty, sure, but not finding it earth-shattering.

"I know, but . . . Emily, he's like . . . cool. How come we've never seen him at River's Edge?"

"Yeah, right," I scoffed. "Like Sarah Fawcett would let her precious only child hang out with delinquents like us."

Regan shook her head, awestruck. "I can't believe *he's* related to her. I can't believe *he's* from Carlisle."

And I knew then that she *wanted him* wanted him. Like wanted him to be her boyfriend. This was ground neither of us had treaded before. I would have understood if she wanted to break our pact to sleep with him. But to fall for him? To want him for more than a night or two? And to obsessively watch him from afar, incapable of talking to him, like some typical lovesick teenager? The change in my best friend was disturbing to say the least.

* * *

The madness went on for two months, but when Regan decided to be Rizzo from *Grease* for Halloween, I hoped she'd start acting like a badass Stockard Channing again and less like a sappy Olivia Newton-John.

"Aren't you guys a little old to be dressing up and going around asking for candy?" Marissa teased as she walked into the bathroom that she and Regan shared while Regan and I were putting the finishing touches on our costumes.

The bathroom adjoined their two bedrooms, and it hadn't been painted since they were little girls. It had this rubber-ducky border around it. By the time Marissa was twelve, she was embarrassed by the ducks and started defacing them. Regan joined in even though she was only eight at the time. The ducks had X's over their eyes, rainbow-colored feathers, and comic-strip thought balloons above their heads filled with back-and-forth banter between Regan and Marissa. Like, next to the toilet, a Regan duck threatened, "If you don't pay me for my bracelet that you flushed last night, Mom and Dad will get a list of every bad thing you've done since I was born." Marissa's duck poetically retorted, "Sisters that betray die in gruesome ways."

I stepped out of Marissa's path so she could grab her makeup bag from the side of the sink. "We plan to be big rock stars one day, remember? Our whole lives will be about dressing up and getting candy. Isn't that what you're going to do now?"

July Lies was about to leave on their first big tour, opening for a Minneapolis band that had just scored a major-label deal. Marissa would be playing bass in midsize, all-ages clubs across the country because the singer of that band had caught a July Lies show at River's Edge. I was bursting with pride for Marissa, not to mention feeling supercharged because she'd proven that big things could happen, even to bands from Carlisle. Regan, on the other hand, refused to be happy for her.

Before Marissa could answer me, Regan grumbled, "And she's not taking us." She slumped onto the toilet, crossing her arms over her chest.

Marissa turned away from the sink, her fawn-colored waves flying through the air like a shampoo commercial. She stared down at her little sister and sighed with a mixture of sympathy and annoyance. "Regan, you're in school."

Regan narrowed her hazel eyes. The dreamy look that had been polluting her face evaporated. The only time Regan wasn't thinking about Tom was when she was being pissed off at Marissa for leaving. "I still don't understand why you couldn't have waited until summer to tour. Then we could have come with you."

"What, as little roadies?" Marissa laughed, which was very much the wrong thing to do.

Regan leapt to her feet, stomping her black high-heeled sandals angrily. "As roadies? As an opening band! Don't you remember your *other* band? She Laughs? The one you quit last weekend when you decided to tour with July Lies?"

Marissa shook her head, still smiling. "You mean my little sister's band that I agreed to play bass for until they found a bassist? You haven't even played River's Edge and you want to go on tour? Please, Regan, let's not get into this again. I need to finish packing. Besides, I don't think Rizzo would throw a temper tantrum. Emily, how could you have let her win?"

As soon as Marissa glanced over at me, she started cackling. I'd put my bright yellow beehive wig on. "Damn," Marissa giggled as she surveyed my lemon-colored, fifties-style prom dress and matching heels. "Frenchy, right? When she goes to the big dance? No wonder you gave in. Wow, you look . . ."

"Like a pineapple," I quipped, quoting the line from the movie. As pasty as I was, I knew I looked horrendous in yellow. But when Regan and I watched *Grease* at two in the morning a couple weeks earlier and decided to be Pink Ladies for Halloween, we'd gotten into a terrible argument over who should be Rizzo. Like a screaming-at-each-other, me-storming-out-of-her-house-and-walking-home-in-the-middle-of-the-night-and-then-not-speaking-for-practically-a-week kind of fight—and Regan and I never fought. Ultimately, I decided that since I related to Rizzo in real life, Frenchy would make a better costume. And I had to let Regan have something. She was taking the Marissa-going-on-tour thing really hard. She thought Marissa had a familial obligation to bum around Carlisle until we were old enough to escape with her, even though it was the fall of 1991, aptly dubbed by Sonic Youth as the year that punk broke, and Marissa needed to take advantage of the spotlight waiting to shine on the next great unknown band.

Marissa sidestepped a mound of laundry to stand in the doorway and admire us. "You both look awesome! Really authentic." She proudly clapped her hands.

I paused in my application of pink lip gloss to study Regan. She did have Rizzo down from the shoes to the capris to the partially unbuttoned, cleavage-revealing red blouse. She'd even customized a pink jacket with "Pink Ladies" on the back in perfect black cursive letters. Regan pressed her lips together as she finished applying scarlet lipstick. She met her sister's eyes in the mirror. "Well, you can't find much in Carlisle except for out-of-date clothing." She smiled at Marissa, showing that she'd given up the argument. And she was probably thinking about Tom Fawcett again.

"I've got something for you!" Marissa exclaimed suddenly. She rummaged in the linen closet and threw black pillowcases at us.

Regan rolled her eyes. "We aren't *actually* going to trick-or-treat. We just like dressing up for Halloween."

I nodded in agreement, careful to keep my heavy wig from sliding off.

"Sure you are! And this is your first stop!" Marissa led us into her bedroom. She opened the bottom drawer of her dresser, her turquoise eyes dancing.

Regan and I knew what was in that drawer. We took from it as often as we could without being noticed. Marissa had kept an overstocked, makeshift minibar since she was fourteen. God knows how she did it, seeing as they kept those bottles behind the counter. As she was at everything else, Marissa was probably just a more artful thief than Regan and I, though we had no trouble pilfering her stolen goods. We'd been holding our noses and draining little bottles of vodka and tequila since we were twelve, back when we were able to get drunk off of just one.

Marissa scooped up handfuls of tiny Jose, Jack, Bacardi,

Fleischmann's, and Absolut bottles, then dumped them into our pillowcases. "Trick or treat!" She grinned, happy to corrupt us one last time before she left.

We stuck around until five thirty to see Marissa off when her band came to pick her up. Then we went wandering in search of something fun to do. We seemed to forget every year that a holiday didn't suddenly make Carlisle an interesting place to live. There was a pumpkin-carving contest at the annual Harvest Festival on Main Street. The adults there were a terrifying reminder of what we'd become if we didn't escape Carlisle: folks who lived for Halloween, Fourth of July, St. Patrick's Day, and Christmas because they loved to dress entirely in the color scheme of the holiday and wear appropriately themed socks. Little kids masqueraded as the cartoon characters of the moment—Belle from *Beauty and the Beast* and Bart Simpson—and bobbed for apples. Teenage girls in sexy kitty costumes plotted to sneak off and make out with meathead teenage boys who tossed pumpkins around like footballs.

It was pathetic and Regan and I wanted none of it, so we headed for the older, less populated part of town. A pickup truck swerved down the street next to us.

"Hey, sluttzzzz!" three guys slurred. Drunken football players whipped an egg in our general direction but missed.

"Fuck you!" Regan and I shouted after them in unison. I wished we had something to throw, but I wasn't wasting one of the little liquor bottles.

We broke those out as we cut through a couple fields and

a thatch of trees. "Tom's place is, like, two houses down the road that way," Regan announced, pointing with a bottle of Absolut in her hand and a dopey smile on her face.

Ignoring her Tom comment, knowing I'd be hearing more as she got drunker, I focused instead on her drinking habits. "Why are you drinking all the Absoluts? First you drank all the Joses, and now you're going to drink all the Absoluts, aren't you?" On the other hand, I downed my bottles in the same order I used to eat my Halloween candy—one of each from least favorite to favorite, then starting over at the beginning again. I would have enough for about four rounds.

We'd arrived at our old grammar school playground and Regan plunked down on one of the swings, looking confused. "Yeah. I don't want to mix them up. If I drank the gin, then vodka, then rum, then tequila, then whiskey like you are, I would puke. Why the hell are you doing that?"

I started to swing, the fabric of my yellow dress dragging on the ground until I caught some air. "They're all going to end up mixed together anyway."

Regan jettisoned her heels, burying her bare feet in the dirty sand. "Why do you start with the Fleischmann's? You hate gin."

"To get it over with, end on an up note." I gazed dizzily at the rest of the playground as I swung. A few yards away from the swing set, there were three plastic animals—a duck, a horse, and a frog—that rocked back and forth on giant springs. I kicked off one lemon-yellow high heel midswing, aiming for the frog, but I missed.

"That's the stupidest method, Emily. You should drink the ones you like first. Once you get drunk, you won't care."

"Yeah," I said, releasing my other shoe and watching it land on target against the duck's ass, causing it to rock forward and spring back. "But when I puke, I usually taste the last thing I drank, and it doesn't seem as bad if it tastes like something I like."

"That's why we have the peppermint schnapps, though. So you can puke minty fresh." Regan patted her pillowcase, where she carried the bottle we'd stolen from Carlisle Groceries and Meats a couple weeks ago.

"Put that stuff down and swing up here. Let's have a contest, see who can jump farther."

Always up for a competition, Regan pumped her black-clad legs to catch up with me. When she finally did, we counted, "One, two, three!" and released. I landed closer to the plastic animals than she did, but only because the slick taffeta material of my dress caused me to slide across the sand on my knees, shredding the bottom of the dress along with the skin on my bare legs.

"Dammit!" I whined, examining the damage. The combination of sand and the tulle layer of the dress had left a bloody rug burn on my knees and shins.

Regan came over with our pillowcases, sniggering. "Here." She thrust mine at me. "Alcohol makes everything better."

So we sat in the sand and drank. The long shadows from the swing set and the trees behind us faded into true darkness. It wasn't long before the conversation turned, as I expected, to Tom Fawcett.

"Have you noticed the way he, like, slllings his backpack?" Her tongue drunkenly stuck on "slings." She awkwardly rocked forward off her hands to do a feeble imitation. "He sort of slouches and sighs into it. This little barely noticeable sigh of, like, being that weirdly beautiful boy in a sea of jock/hicks. Like—"

"I definitely should not have let you be Rizzo," I snapped. "This is the most un-Rizzo behavior I've ever seen. You're like Sandy drooling over Danny freakin' Zuko. Yuck!" I threw an empty minibottle of Absolut at her. "Why don't you just hand over the pillowcase and the Pink Ladies jacket, because you're too goddamn pure to be pink."

"Shut up!" Regan's fake eyelashes weighed her eyelids down, but now she just looked wasted, not sultry, which was the original intent. She raised her finger slowly, and it hung there, pointing at me accusatorily until she came up with words in her defense. "He's, like, my Kenickie, okay? You can go right ahead and be Marty and screw a bunch of guys, but I have my Kenickie, okay?"

"I'm Frenchy!" I snorted. "And if he's your Kenickie, don't you need to sleep with him, think you're knocked up, and avoid him until graduation before you can be all gross over him?"

"He's my Kenickie," she slurred again, reaching for the peppermint schnapps. She was down to her gin bottles and avoiding them like the plague, probably because, as I predicted, they'd make her puke if she drank them. "'Cept he's hotter. Like Kurt Cobain. And he plays guitar and we should get him to join our band and make us really famous."

I snatched and almost hurled the schnapps bottle at her, but I didn't want to waste the alcohol, so I tossed my cigarette butt at her instead. "Ow, bitch!" she muttered, brushing it off her pants, where I was satisfied to see it left a burn mark.

"*I'm* the guitarist, and you and I will make the band famous, not some stupid guy." I pounded my palms against the sand. "You're selling me out for dick!"

"Oh, Emily." She clambered toward me, eyes getting misty so her eyeliner ran slightly. "I love you." She flung herself on me in an awkward drunken hug, managing to take the schnapps bottle out of my hand in the process. "I would never sell you out for dick." She slid down beside me, taking a contemplative drink. "I know it's freaky how much I like him. It creeps me out, too. But I do and I know he plays all sorts of instruments. Remember he was in band in grammar school?"

"Regan!" I laughed. "Everyone had to be in band in grammar school."

"Okay, yeah, but I overheard him talking to the music teacher, and he, like, plays everything, bass, guitar, drums, piano, even violin. He's like a prodigy. We should let him in our band."

I liked that phrasing a lot better. "Let him? I guess we could *let* him, if he's, like, really good."

"Awesome!" Regan jumped to her feet. "Let's go tell him."

"Tell him now? Like, show up at his front door wasted? You think his evil mom is gonna let us in? She'll call the cops."

A sly smile crept across Regan's face, making her look much more like Rizzo and the Regan I was used to. "You know his mom is at Harvest Fest, selling candy apples for the church choir or whatever. And besides, his room is way at the back of the house, right above the back porch, so all we have to do is climb this tree and get on top of the porch roof . . ."

My mouth distorted in horror. "Have you been stalking him?"

She shrugged and lit a cigarette. "Let's call it preplanning." I grimaced, but she yanked on my hand. "C'mon, Em. It would be a very Pink Lady thing to do. And it's for the band."

I sighed and allowed her to pull me up. "I guess if it's for the band. I don't know if it's a good idea for us to be in a band with someone you want to hook up with, though."

But Regan waved off my concern. We collected our pillowcases and shoes and started toward the road, leaving a litter of empty airline liquor bottles, cigarette butts, and tattered yellow prom-dress scraps on the playground behind us.

When we reached Tom's house, we went around to the back. Like most yards in Carlisle, it wasn't fenced in. Regan had apparently spent some time in that yard because her description of it was dead-on. A tree provided easy access to the roof of the enclosed back porch below Tom's bedroom window. Sober, it would have been a simple feat. Drunk, it was slightly more complicated and definitely noisier than anticipated.

We stuffed our shoes into our pillowcases, where they clanked against the few remaining liquor bottles, and then we twisted the tops of the pillowcases around our wrists. There was a low branch on the tree that seemed to be thick enough to support us. We couldn't see much beyond that; the dim light above the back door barely sliced through the darkness.

Regan mounted the branch first. She gripped with both hands, jumped, kicked her legs up, wrapped them around it, hung upside down briefly, and then swung herself up to a sitting position. It was gracefully executed. Then she scrambled onto the next branch to give me space. I just stared up at her shadowy outline.

"C'mon, Emily," she hissed.

I pointed at the torn remains of my yellow skirt. "I'm not wearing pants."

"Oh, no one's looking. When did you get so modest?"

I shrugged. The skirt was just an excuse, really. It was the upside-down thing I feared, certain all the alcohol in me would rush to my head and then back out of my mouth.

"Emily, come on!" Regan repeated, forgetting completely about whispering.

"Shh!" I swung up onto the branch the same way she did. When I got on top of it, I lay there for a moment, squeezing my eyes closed to stop the ground from spinning.

"I see London, I see France . . ." Regan taunted.

"Shut up!"

"Shh!"

I stood awkwardly and climbed successfully all the way to the second-to-last branch, but practically fell grabbing for that last one. My shin scraped against jagged bark, reopening and deepening the wounds I'd sustained earlier. "Dammit!" I cursed, feeling blood trickle down my leg.

Regan was already shimmying across the branch that

spanned out over the porch roof. "Shut up, Emily!" she reprimanded, not monitoring the volume of her own voice.

I peered through the darkness to the shadowy ground a story below. "If I die, you better marry this guy," I grumbled.

She didn't hear me over the crackling of the twigs she crushed as she slid off the tree onto the roof. Neither of us landed very quietly. The drunken thunder of Regan's feet on the roof was as loud as I always imagined that fat-ass Santa really would be.

When I got onto the last branch, I wrapped my arms and legs around it and slithered along backward, moving like a caterpillar with my pillowcase dangling down like an oversize cocoon. Positioned above the porch, I released the branch and landed right on my butt.

I rose, rubbing my sore tailbone and staring down at the blood glistening on my legs. "Regan, this better be worth it." I rummaged through my pillowcase for one of the little Jack Daniel's bottles.

Regan explored the roof in the faint light coming from Tom's window. Apparently, he hung out there often. A couple beer bottles were stashed in the gutter, and next to the window, Regan discovered an ashtray, or at least what Tom used as an ashtray. It looked like a malformed ceramic bowl, probably one that he'd made for his mom in art class in third grade, judging by the craftsmanship and the pink glaze. As I limped over to her, Regan reached into it and removed a small pipe coated in resin. "Ooooh, naughty boy!" she chirped with delight.

"Just the way you like 'em." I laughed, my annoyance disappearing as alcohol numbed my aching limbs.

She set the ashtray and pipe down and headed for the window that led into Tom's room. Due to his lack of response to the clatter on the roof, I assumed Tom wasn't inside, but figured we could wait and surprise him. Regan pushed the partially open window the rest of the way up, placed her palms on the sill, and put her legs through, like an excited kid propelling herself down a waterslide.

It turned out that Tom was indeed inside, innocently sprawled out on his bed, reading a magazine with headphones on. And he responded the way any fourteen-year-old guy would if he saw long, definitely female legs coming through his window. "Holy shhh—" I heard him begin to declare, but Regan was quick.

I scrambled through the window headfirst to see what was going on, landing not so slickly again, this time on my elbows. My pillowcase shot across the hardwood floor in front of me. I looked up to see Regan straddling Tom on his bed, her hand clamped over his mouth. She'd wrapped herself around his lanky body like a spider preparing her flailing prey. Grinning maniacally, Regan yanked the headphones off of Tom's ears with her free hand. "Shh!" she growled insistently, and removed her other hand from his mouth.

"What the hell are you doing here?" Tom moved with such force that he sent Regan tumbling toward the edge of the twin bed. He shot backward, drawing his long legs to his chest, wedging himself into the corner of the wall his bed sat against, and jerking the headphones out of his stereo in the process. The room suddenly filled with blaring distorted guitar and the voice of a punk chick midscream.

I scuttled across the floor and hit the stop button. "What

the hell are you trying to do? Get us caught?" I whispered scornfully.

"Yeah, what the hell?" Regan added, sitting up and scooting to the foot of his bed, visibly pissed that he'd knocked her off of him.

His bewildered brown eyes wide, Tom slowly looked back and forth from me to Regan. Regan smoothed her blouse and removed her dark brown, curly wig, which had been knocked to one side in the tussle. She tugged at her short, red-streaked hair so it was appropriately disheveled, glowering at Tom the whole time. I calmly pulled a little bottle of Bacardi out of my pillowcase and stared right back at Tom when his gaze fell on me. Then I stood and perused his room. It was pretty clean for a guy. The fault, I assumed, of his Nazi mother. The hardwood floor was neatly swept, though now my blood stained it. A couple of band posters hung on the wall and three crates of records and tapes sat next to the stereo. I busied myself flipping through them until Tom broke out of his shocked silence.

"Uhhh." He rubbed at his temples and then slid his hands back into his tangled, bleached hair. "Am I awake?" he asked softly, probably not meaning to say it aloud. Regan smirked again and reached across the bed, pinching his leg through his flannel pajama pants. "Oww! What the hell?" He grabbed her hand.

She wrenched it away from him, still smiling. "You're awake."

Their eyes locked. "What are you doing in my room?" Tom repeated.

Without taking her eyes off of his, Regan bent down

and retrieved her pillowcase. She brought out the bottle of schnapps and shook it. "We're here to get you drunk and molest you," she informed him, straight-faced.

Tom went white. "My dad's, like, down the hall," he said, and gulped.

I snickered, shaking my head, and Tom ripped his eyes away from Regan's, his face going from pale to bright pink in a matter of seconds. I strode across the room to where a few guitar cases and a practice amp were, the only stuff, it seemed, that Tom touched in his own room. I pointed at a bass that was out of its case. "You play that?"

"Yeah. Why?" he managed to ask.

"Are you good?" I demanded, assessing him critically.

"What does this have to do with—"

"The orgy?" Regan giggled, taking a swig out of the schnapps bottle and offering it to him.

"Oh my god." Tom put his scorching face in his hands. "Why are you in my room?"

"Oh, you know you're going to call all your little friends as soon as we leave," Regan taunted.

Tom snatched the schnapps bottle. "I don't have any friends."

"Neither do we, so this is perfect."

"What's perfect?" Tom coughed, obviously overwhelmed by the peppermint in the massive swig he'd taken. He handed the bottle back to Regan, grimacing in distaste.

"You joining our band. Here"—she offered him my pillowcase—"pick your poison."

He selected a mini tequila bottle. "You want me to join She Laughs?"

"How'd you hear about our band?" I asked at the same time that Regan inquired, equally as incredulously, "Tequila's your favorite, too?"

He slipped back into stunned, shy-boy mode again, eyes darting back and forth between the two of us. Regan, by the pacified little smile on her face, found it to be cute, but I was irritated. I repeated my question. "How did you hear about our band?"

"Oh, uhh, I guess I overheard you. It's all you guys ever talk about." He blushed again and decided to drain the little Cuervo bottle to compensate.

Regan was pleased by this development. "*You* listen in to *our* conversations?"

Tom took this to be criticism. He threw his hands up in the air, twitching wildly. "You guys stalked me and climbed in my bedroom window!"

"Shhhh!" I hushed him. "And I didn't stalk you. Regan did."

She glared at me over her shoulder. "Emily!"

"What?" I shrugged, unlatching one of Tom's guitar cases.

Tom's face changed from exasperation to awe when Regan looked back at him. It was endearing, really. The poor kid had been tormented to such degrees by our charming hick peers that the concept of any girl being attracted to him blew his mind. I'd seen plenty of guys who *acted* as though they didn't know they were hot, but Tom clearly had no clue. I waited for him to stutter about the whole situation some more or for Regan to make one of her usual witty remarks, but they just awkwardly stared at each other.

I took the guitar out of the case and strummed a few

chords, but neither of them seemed to hear. "If you guys want to have sex now, let me know and I'll leave."

Tom leapt off the bed like I'd branded his ass with my words. He stood next to the open window as if he was preparing to evacuate his own room. "This is not normal. I mean, I can't imagine that this is how people usually get asked to join a band."

"Well, are you going to join or what?" Regan asked.

"You climbed in my window in your Halloween costumes!" Tom exclaimed.

"Trick or treat. Join our band. What do you want us to say?" I put the guitar down. "At least you know you'll have fun."

"Uhhh, yeah, I mean . . ."

"Tom, who are you talking to?" A woman's voice came from the hallway, footsteps closing in.

Regan and I scrambled to our feet and rushed over to the window. I dove right through without any hesitation and headed straight for the tree. I should have stuck around to see the look on Mrs. Fawcett's face when she walked in and found Regan up on her tiptoes like a dancer, her alcohol-soaked tongue jammed down Tom's throat.

"Regan Parker!" Mrs. Fawcett bellowed, her voice shattering the silence of that pristine Carlisle night. The reputation she'd so carefully built for her family slid out of her hands and crash-landed in the sea of airline liquor bottles, wigs, and high-heeled shoes spilling out of the black pillowcase at her son's feet.

Regan pulled her mouth away from Tom's, running the edges of her top teeth lightly over his bottom lip to make him shiver. "See you at band practice tomorrow," she said as he opened his eyes dreamily.

"Yeah," he whispered, watching her disappear out the window.

As Regan and I shimmied down the tree, we heard Tom's mother scream, "Regan Parker in my house! How could you?"

And then the backyard reverberated with Tom's laughter.

Songs My Mother Never Taught Me

When I was a baby, my father sang me to sleep with old blues songs. I took my first steps to the Beatles and learned to dance to the Clash. But the first time I realized I could claim the energy that blasted from the stereo as mine, possess it, *be* it was when Regan and I blackmailed Marissa into taking us to our first show at River's Edge.

That summer Marissa was sixteen and constantly in trouble. Regan and I were twelve and bratty as could be. Most of our schemes involved tormenting Marissa. We "borrowed" her clothes and ruined them. We played with her cosmetics and left them unusable. And our favorite activity? Listening in on her phone calls.

One afternoon we overheard her promise to meet a boy at eight. She was supposed to be grounded for smoking pot in her room. (Regan and I had ratted her out for "burning some weird-smelling incense.") Just before Marissa's appointed meeting time, Regan and I stationed ourselves in the shadows next to the toolshed. We watched as Marissa eased open her bedroom window and made the leap to the shed's roof with her guitar case strapped to her back. When she got to the bottom of the tree next to the shed, we pounced.

"Where do you think you're going?" Regan asked smugly as we blocked her way, arms crossed over our practically nonexistent chests.

Marissa groaned, "Not tonight, Regan," and tried to push past us.

Regan grabbed Marissa's wrist. "Hot date? Mom didn't unground you, though, did she? Emily, why don't you go ask her? Marissa and I will stay here."

"Yeah, right. Like you can hold on to me." Marissa easily jerked away, her armload of silver bangles jingling.

"No, but I can scream—"

Regan should have known better than to give Marissa warning. Marissa slapped her hand over Regan's mouth before she could utter a sound and pinned Regan against her the way gunmen hold their hostages when using them as shields from the police.

Regan's angry hazel eyes darted from me to the house, urging me to yell for Molly. But Marissa's blue eyes seared into me from over Regan's head. "Emily, please don't. Scott Anderson asked me to play bass for his band, July Lies. My first show with them is tonight at River's Edge. They're really good. Scott's dad was in your dad's band, you know. This is my big chance."

I studied Marissa in the faint golden glow cast from

her bedroom window. She wore artfully ripped jeans and a Smiths T-shirt she'd rescued from the thrift store and carefully constructed into a tank top that fit her perfectly. She'd curled her tawny hair into big waves that framed her precisely made-up face. Regan squirmed in her grip, shaking her head no, but my gaze wandered to the bass strapped to Marissa's back. She'd been practicing for four years. And she'd brought my dad into it. He'd told me so many stories about what it had been like to play at River's Edge, Louisa smiling up at him from the front of the stage.

"Okay," I said softly, "we'll let you go."

Regan thrashed around and tried to yell "Emily!" through Marissa's palm.

I met her eyes, quieting her when I added, "But . . . the next time Molly leaves you in charge of us, you're taking us with you to River's Edge."

Marissa agreed immediately and Regan begrudgingly approved the deal.

Two weeks later, I walked into that warehouse for the first time and stared around in awe like I'd entered the Sistine Chapel. It was as smoky and dingy and loud as I'd always imagined. The perfect rock 'n' roll setting filled with so many scruffy, tattooed, colorful rock 'n' roll people. The opening act was an all-girl band. They kicked off their set with a blistering cover of "Chemical Warfare" by the Dead Kennedys. Regan and I dove into the pit with no fear even though we were the smallest kids in the place. It quickly became clear that the girls onstage weren't the best musicians. They played some mean covers, but their original songs consisted of indecipherable yelling over feedback-laden, poorly arranged power chords. But it didn't matter. I stared up at the girl who fronted the band, rocking out in knee-high black leather boots and a badass leopard-print skirt, and I knew that *that* was what I wanted to do.

I'd been fantasizing about what my first gig with my own band would be like ever since. After losing my virginity to a pathetic excuse of an aspiring rock god and then being called a groupie by an even bigger one, my fantasies became increasingly elaborate. I daydreamed that even though it was our very first concert, we headlined and at least a hundred kids were there. I imagined that most of the people up front would be girls like me and Regan who slammed in the pit as hard as boys and chose only the best bands to mosh to. Mixed in with those girls—hopefully being brutally shoved around by them—would be the pseudo rock-god boys that I'd slept with. They would gaze up at me with a mixture of regret and envy in their glistening eyes, begging my acknowledgment between songs, but I would stare right over their heads like I had no idea who they were.

As un-punk as it was to do so, I even planned out what I was going to wear: a short, sea-green, velvet dress that I'd found at a thrift store in Madison. I thought it complemented my father's Lake Placid–blue '69 Mustang and that it just looked hot. I wanted to be a million times sexier and more mysterious than the false deities whose arrogance I'd fallen for at River's Edge.

Our first show took place in April of my sophomore year. It could have been sooner, but we'd seen bands play River's

Edge after rehearsing together once or twice. We had no interest in getting booed like they had, so we decided to wait until Tom had been in the band for six months.

July Lies actually invited us to play with them. Of course, that meant we weren't set to headline like I fantasized, but we got second billing. Not to mention July Lies drew a huge crowd since they'd recently signed to an indie label in Minneapolis. Label reps would be there. If we played well enough, maybe they'd want to sign us, too. Marissa's success had definitely proven to me that my wildest dreams could come true.

The day of the show I paid little attention in class. This wasn't new; I studied rock 'n' roll performance more avidly than any subject in school. I'd been to over a hundred concerts and I hadn't even reached my sixteenth birthday. Observing established bands, I kept notes on how to arrange a set list (at least four fast songs before slowing down for a ballad), how to interact with the audience (for the mysterious rock star, speak only occasionally to thank the adoring crowd and introduce new songs), and general pointers (you don't need theatrics if you're a good musician, but make sure your live sound varies from your album sound).

I'd reviewed those notes and practiced guitar until midnight the night before my first gig, so instead of making up answers on the history quiz I had to take that day, I drew different versions of our band logo below each question. And I guess I was also humming one of our songs, because Jackie Jenkins kicked the back of my chair midtest.

"Will you *shut* up?" She emphasized "shut" with a crack of her gum.

This caught Mrs. Trot's fine-tuned ears. She stalked over to my desk in the back of the room.

"Girls, what's the problem?" she hissed, trying not to disturb the rest of the class.

Jackie, however, was an attention whore. She loudly complained, "Emily's singing to herself again."

I rolled my eyes. "I think Jackie's having auditory hallucinations."

"I don't know what that means, but I'm not the druggie."

I took particular offense to this comment because, though I drank whenever and whatever I could get my hands on, I'd stopped smoking pot and forced Regan and Tom to give it up as well. I'd been reading a lot of rock bios that made the stuff they said in health class seem true. Pot and sniffing glue led to coke and heroin, which led to too many dead rock stars. "I am not a druggie," I said. "But I think those diet pills you and your little cheerleader friends take at lunch instead of eating might qualify."

Jackie automatically tuned out any criticism. She flounced her sun-kissed curls and retorted, "Well, if you're not a druggie then you must be retarded. Only retards, like, sing to themselves."

"Oooh, I bet it hurt your brain to come up with that one!"

"Enough!" Mrs. Trot snapped, but then she noticed my test. "She Laughs? Is this some kind of joke, Ms. Black? Because I'm not laughing and you shouldn't be either, since you're well on your way to failing this class."

I protectively slid my paper toward me and snarled, "It's not a joke. She Laughs is my band's name. And we're playing a show tonight, which is way more important to me than this quiz."

"Oh my god," Jackie cackled. "You *are* a joke. A band? A show? Where, in your basement with your two loser friends? Oh wait, they're probably in the band, right?"

The rest of the class chortled along with her. I'd never hated Carlisle more. "Shut up, bitch! Ten years from now—"

"Emily Black! Principal's office now!" Mrs. Trot roared.

"No, I don't think so." I snatched my backpack and logo-covered test. "I'm outta here."

I ran down the hall to Regan's math class and knocked on the window of the closed door. Regan sat in the last row, and as soon as she saw me, she stood up and grabbed her things, ignoring her teacher's objections. We swung by Tom's science class and signaled him in the same fashion. He followed without hesitation.

"Why did we even come here today?" I grumbled as we headed for the exit. The principal's office was right next to it, and as we pushed our way through the big glass doors, a secretary came running out of the office.

"Parker, Black, Fawcett!" she barked. "Where do you think you're going?"

"Rehearsal!" Tom smirked, grabbing both Regan and me by the hand and breaking into a sprint.

I'd never expected Tom to mesh with me and Regan so well. I thought he'd be around for a month or two until Regan got bored. But she hadn't, and even if she had, I wouldn't have let her kick him out of the band. Surprisingly, he turned out to be the key ingredient to She Laughs' sound.

Before he joined, we were a stereotypical, angry-girl punk

band. I relied on fast power chords, and Regan concerned herself with volume over accuracy when it came to drumming; I didn't sing, I screamed like the victim in a slasher movie. We had melodic influences, but we ignored them. Aside from July Lies, who had an indie, Sonic Youth vibe to them, punk ruled River's Edge, and the harder you played the more respect you won. Besides, Regan and I were pretty pissed off.

The first few times he played with us, Tom dutifully learned our songs. But when I brought a new one in, he pushed his scraggly bleached hair behind his ear, straightened to his full six-foot height, and asked, "Can I make a few suggestions?"

I wrinkled my nose distrustfully because this was not how things worked. I came up with a riff, then Regan and I jammed on it. But Regan was still all doe-eyed over him, so she said "Of course" before I could object.

Tom knew me well enough by then to cut to the chase. "The bands that are getting real attention like July Lies aren't your average punk band. You've gotta use everything you know about music to create a unique sound. You guys have Black Flag in your record collections, but you have the Bangles, too. Pop songs aren't all bad. You want to write something that sticks in people's heads. Catchy, like the Ramones or Nirvana. Also, if you don't dial the amps up to eleven, you might be able to hear Emily's vocals." He stared poignantly at me with slightly bloodshot brown eyes. "You write great lyrics and Regan says you belt it out like Billie Holiday in the shower. You shouldn't scream all the time or you'll ruin your real voice."

That made me blush furiously and I wanted to say something sarcastic, but instead I conceded. "Okay, what would you do with that song?"

Tom's lips curled into a small smile. "Your dad loves the blues, right? Did he teach you slide guitar?" When I nodded, he instructed, "Open with it, and give the audience something they're not expecting. Now, your lyrics are great, but in the verses, your voice should go down an octave and draw out the last notes of each line. In the chorus, pick up the pace like you're used to." He snapped his fingers to demonstrate. "Your phrasing should be clipped, staccato. And how do you two feel about harmonies?"

A new dynamic was born: I composed, Tom arranged, and Regan provided the beat. We wrote songs with texture. Punk rock's razor edge tinged with the blues and underscored by the simple rock 'n' roll melody you'd find on the oldies radio station. Sometimes I crooned like Billie, sometimes I raged like Courtney Love.

My father taught me how to play guitar, but Tom taught me to be a songwriter. So I developed a soft spot for him.

But I shouldn't have folded on the drug rule, not at the last rehearsal before our first show.

After we ditched school for Regan's basement, Tom grew increasingly agitated. Quitting pot wasn't a big deal for me and Regan, since we were drinkers, but Tom usually relied on smoking a bowl to help him relax. As the afternoon wore on, Tom continually stopped in the middle of songs, put his bass down, and paced the room. Finally, I unplugged my guitar, retrieved the bottle of tequila Regan kept stashed behind her kit, and shoved it in his face. "Here, drink this and calm down."

He smacked it away. "Why the hell is this okay and pot isn't? It makes no sense. Wait," he spat, "it does. Booze calms *you* down. *You* need it to go onstage tonight, but who cares what *I* need."

We stood there, hands on hips, glowering at each other. Regan tapped out a steady beat on the cymbals, refusing to get involved, which she had done since I initiated the no-drugs rule. "Fine," I spewed through gritted teeth. "I just want to get through this rehearsal. Then you can go score some drugs, okay?"

He showed up at River's Edge stoned, and then smoked some more with the July Lies drummer and other randoms hanging around backstage. "That's some strong-ass weed," I heard a kid with a blue Mohawk remark. Tom nodded with his eyes at half-mast and a dumb grin on his face.

I glared at Regan. "If he screws this up, he's out of the band."

She shook her head, hair freshly dyed burgundy for the occasion. "He's not going to screw it up. You need to relax. Maybe you should get in on the next bowl."

"Oh yeah, that's a *great* idea!"

I ignored her and Marissa's pleas to chill out and watched Tom decline into a near comatose state. When Regan told him it was time to set up our equipment, he just blinked at her.

"He can't even talk!" I exclaimed furiously.

Regan rationalized, "He doesn't have to talk to play bass."

"He has to walk to get onstage. He has to make sure his bass is in tune." I ticked off these responsibilities on my fingers, my voice growing more panicked with each one.

"Well, if you hadn't been such a control freak for the past few months, he wouldn't have gotten so high. We're a high school band for Christ's sake, not a chart-topping—"

"Regan!" I yelled, frustrated by her lack of loyalty to the band, and to me. "I don't want to top charts, I just want a band that's good enough to get us the hell out of here. I thought that's what you wanted, too."

She sighed heavily. "Just go set our shit up and I'll get him onstage."

At an abandoned warehouse, you are your own roadie. The drums were already onstage behind the first band's kit, but I had to check my guitar and microphone and, since he was incapable of doing it, Tom's bass. I did it quickly, probably too quickly, but at River's Edge there was none of that wait-half-an-hour-for-the-band-to-come-on crap. The last thing I needed was an impatient crowd. As I finished, Regan pushed Tom onstage and he somehow managed to strap on his guitar.

His playing was off to say the least, and that in turn threw Regan off. Regan was never, ever off. She was the most natural drummer I'd ever seen. Tom had her really worried. He stood stock-still, his head hanging down from his neck like a fat tomato about to fall from the vine. Sweat mixed with the hair that flopped in his face. His fingers moved sluggishly, always a note or two behind, and hit the right chord only half the time. I made things worse by playing faster, thinking he'd speed up, but he just slowed down more. And the one thing that could have slightly made up for our wretched musicianship—my vocals—was drowned out. I hadn't checked the microphone as well as I should have. Out of frustration I screeched the words at the top of my lungs. My voice cut out completely by the end of the fifth song, so I ripped the cord out of my guitar and stalked offstage, leaving Tom still playing and Regan staring after me.

Marissa found me drinking a warm beer on the hood of her car. Exactly the spot she'd found me in almost two years earlier when I'd been feeling sorry for myself because I'd lost my virginity to such an unworthy guy. And she said exactly what she said back then: "The first is always the worst."

When I didn't respond, she pointed at the guitar lying in the gravel by the front tire. "You can really play that thing. You can tell that your dad's had you messing around with it since preschool. You're not just a punk guitarist sloppily pounding out chords, Emily, you've got really refined technique. Even Lucy from my label said she's never heard a kid play like that."

I ignored Marissa's compliment. "She called me a *kid*?"

"Emily, you are a kid. Why is that a bad thing? Why have you and Regan wanted to be twenty-five since you were ten? This is the best time of your life. You have no responsibilities—"

"That's easy for you to say! You have a record contract. You moved to Minneapolis. I want to grow up fast to get out of here!" I screamed, but I sounded childish, my voice scratching and dipping because it was all used up.

"You'll get out, Emily." Marissa brushed a strand of my long, black hair off my sticky forehead and I batted her hand away. "Listen," she said firmly, "you can leave on your eighteenth birthday like your mom did. You can tour and move wherever you want, but you'll find out what I have. July Lies is not a Minneapolis band. No matter how much you hate it, this is where you're from. You're a Carlisle band, or if you really can't stomach that, you're a River's Edge band."

"They'll laugh us offstage if we try to play here again," I scoffed.

"No, even with your timing off and your mic problems, you were still one of the best bands these kids have seen." Marissa smiled at me with genuine admiration. "After you guys work the kinks out, you're gonna be huge."

Though I brushed off her compliments, I did take them to heart. Without those words, I might have broken up the band that night and given up on music forever, and it was not the time to give up on rock 'n' roll.

Everybody remembers how Nirvana exploded in the early nineties, but it was particularly significant to Regan and me. Marissa had taken the two of us to see them at a hole-in-the-wall club in Madison for my thirteenth birthday in 1989. We moshed up a storm just an arm's length away from the band that would become the biggest of our generation. It would be a lie and a cliché to say we knew they'd get huge. Scruffy kids with loud guitars from middle-of-nowhere towns like Aberdeen, Washington, and Carlisle, Wisconsin, didn't get huge. Guys with poodle hair from L.A. got huge. But as we drove home through the black Wisconsin night, the windows rolled down despite the stench of dead skunk rotting on the hot asphalt, all we wanted was what Nirvana had at the time.

"Someday I'm gonna see the country in an old van with July Lies," Marissa declared over the blaring radio.

"Yeah," I sighed, fantasizing about the band I hadn't even formed yet.

By the time She Laughs played its first show, Nirvana mania was in full effect. The next time we saw them live, they performed in an arena. I was so amazed by the size and intensity of the crowd that I didn't even jockey for my usual spot up front. I just stood in the middle of it all, marveling that a small-town band had done this.

Punk never became the mainstream in Carlisle, though. People wore flannel, but it was no fashion statement. The jocks that ruled our high school called Kurt Cobain a fag because he wore a dress in a music video. Nirvana wouldn't be cool until they were on the classic-rock station. Carlisle was that stagnant. But at River's Edge, the air felt electric and full of promise. The heyday of the garage band had arrived. We all had a shot at being the next Nirvana.

She Laughs' audience grew every time we played. After our disastrous first performance, Tom swore off pot for good, so the only problems we faced onstage were the occasional broken string or drumstick, and those were generally signs of a good show.

Junior year, Regan's parents and my dad bought us an eight-track recorder as a joint Christmas present. We recorded our first demo tape in Regan's basement. It was hard to choose ten songs for it because by then we had thirty. For cover art, we cut out one of the logos I'd drawn on my history test: She Laughs in swirling letters around a pair of sultry, smirking lips. We even left printed above it: "List the key events leading up to World War I." We silk-screened T-shirts with the same logo and sold them alongside the cassettes. We made enough money to pay for gas to go on a short tour of Madison, Milwaukee, and Minneapolis the summer before senior year. We set the gigs up ourselves and were elated by the turnout, at least fifty cheering kids per city.

Finding fans outside the boundaries of River's Edge was an important step for us, but my biggest thrill came when I spotted a girl on Main Street in Carlisle wearing a She Laughs T-shirt. My dad actually noticed her first as we emerged from Carlisle Groceries and Meats. "A fan!" he exclaimed proudly, gesturing across the street. She looked about fourteen and emulated Regan with her messy, cherry-red bob.

She saw me and screamed, "Emily Black, you rock!" My dad joyfully clapped me on the back and the girl's sister sneered at me. It was Jackie Jenkins. She'd gotten booted off the cheerleading squad after showing up blitzed at homecoming. Life wasn't going nearly as well for her as it was for me.

Things only got sweeter when Marissa came home for Christmas with a signed contract in hand from DGC Records, Nirvana's label.

"*You're* the next Nirvana!" Regan shouted as they embraced.

Marissa pulled me into their hug, vowing, "You guys are next!"

The three of us screeched so loud and long that the neighbors called the cops. Luke told my dad, "Now everyone's going to think I'm an axe murderer," but the two of them lit up cigars like Marissa'd announced she was pregnant, because in our families a record deal was better than a baby.

New Year's Eve 1993, we opened for July Lies again at River's Edge. We had almost two years' worth of shows under our belt. The audience had swollen to nearly eight hundred people and they weren't just there to see July Lies. Tom was sober, as were Regan and I because our parents had come out. Our dads stood off to the side, but Molly and Marissa danced in the middle of the melee at the front of the stage.

Maybe I imagined it because I saw Molly out there, but a few yards from the stage, I caught a glimpse of long, blond hair. I couldn't see her face. She was too far away and she had her arms up, waving in the air to the steady riff of my guitar. But my stomach clenched and I thought, *Louisa*.

My gaze locked on her as I wailed the last chorus: *"You're sixteen years lost and I'm sixteen years found. You couldn't teach me how to live, but I figured out how. I figured out how!"*

I clenched my eyes shut for a few seconds while I held the last note and Regan pounded out the final three drumbeats that closed the song, but when I opened them I'd lost sight of the blond. I spent the next song only half focused on the music, combing the crowd for her. Then I abruptly ended the set two songs early with a garbled "Thank you, good night," set my guitar down onstage, and ran off, leaving Regan and Tom as bewildered as they must have been that very first show.

I dashed through the backstage exit into the parking lot. I ignored the goose bumps that instantly shot across my sweaty skin. I wove in and out between rows of cars, stamping down snow with my combat boots, and stopped in the middle of the lot, craning my neck every which way in search of her.

"Emily . . ." My dad appeared behind me and threw his leather coat over my bare shoulders. I was in a black spaghetti-strap dress and fishnets in zero-degree cold.

"Did you see her?" I asked, still staring around desperately.

"Who?"

"Louisa. She was, like, ten rows back, dead center. Then, she disappeared."

"Emily . . ." His chocolate eyes were shot through with concern.

My face crumpled. "I'm not crazy, Dad, I swear."

He pulled the coat tighter around my body. "You're not crazy for thinking songs like that would lead her back here. That's the kind of music she loved. We can go inside and look if you want," he suggested, but I saw the skepticism behind the gentle smile.

"No. The stage lights, they mess with my vision sometimes. And I don't even know why I thought of her." I shrugged off the coat, rejecting comfort like I always did when I felt like a fool. "I didn't write those songs for her. My music's not about her at all."

I'm sure he saw straight through that lie, but he went along with it. "Okay, then," he said. "Let's go get a good spot for July Lies."

THREAT

Rock 'n' roll trumped love in my world. Sophomore year I'd decided guys were a distraction I couldn't afford if I wanted to make it as a musician. I still felt the same way by high school graduation. (Yes, I graduated high school. Tempted as I was to drop out and get my GED like Tom had, my dad would have killed me.) I remained down on relationships despite being in a band with a couple.

Fortunately, Regan and Tom didn't gross me out with constant PDAs. In fact, Regan held out on sleeping with Tom for over a year because she, of all people, had some sappy notion about being in "true love" this time. Of course, when she made the mistake of confessing that to me, I teased them both relentlessly.

Out of nowhere, I'd ask, "So, have you slept together yet? You know, Tom, Regan responds pretty well to 'put out or get out.'"

Karma bit me in the ass one sunny June afternoon a couple weeks after graduation. I showed up early for rehearsal and walked in on them in Regan's basement. I screamed and turned my back, stammering, "I'm going outside for a cigarette."

Tom joined me a few minutes later, a giant grin on his flushed face. He sheepishly apologized. "Sorry about that. She was practicing when I came over. She's the most beautiful thing on earth when she's drumming. That's how musicians fall in love, watching each other play." He'd gotten disgustingly gooey-eyed as he spoke, but then he smirked and tousled my hair like a big brother instead of little Tom Fawcett who I had *let* in the band so my best friend could hook up with him. "You'll see, it'll happen to you one day."

"Gag me, Tom." I swatted his hand away. "And I don't have any plans to fall in love. I don't even plan to have sex again until we're rich and famous. Then, maybe the occasional cabana boy or Calvin Klein model."

A month later, Johnny Thompson waltzed into my life. Our bizarre courtship began with a She Laughs show at River's Edge two weeks after my eighteenth birthday.

The performance Johnny witnessed was nothing special. We played as hard as we always did. When I got onstage, the passion for music that my father had instilled in me since birth rose up from my gut like a tornado. The first notes we hit summoned pure energy from the crowd like great gales of wind. And it just kept building and building. By the end, I was nothing but throat and fingers, voice and guitar, a wave of sound. And then I wanted to be in the audience. The jostling, bruising, hot sweat of colliding bodies was part of the experience for me, the culmination of everything I loved about rock 'n' roll. Well, that's the beautiful, visionary version of it; the bottom line is that I was impulsive.

I didn't stage-dive at every show; in fact, I hadn't for quite a few before that one in July, but that night the vibe was just right. I slung my guitar aside and leapt into the audience of sweaty-faced kids and twentysomethings. They were a rainbow of hair colors, a collage of grins, bare arms covered with tattoos or bracelets, and T-shirts that blared names of assorted bands, including mine. Hands lifted and tossed me, fingers wrapped around my legs and arms, and then released as the current took me elsewhere. I found out later that Johnny had been one of the many whose fingers had pressed against my biceps, ankle, even brushed my thigh, but I certainly wasn't aware of him at the time.

When I ended up near the left side of the stage, I felt Tom's hand close around my wrist to haul me back up. My leaps always freaked the hell out of him. I tilted my head, trying to look up at him, but the stage lights blinded me. I grinned maniacally and yanked my arm out of his grasp, letting the crowd pass me toward the center. Then I kicked my legs out, forcing them to set me down, and shoved my way to the front like I had as an audience member.

Regan met me there and helped me onstage. Her fuchsia hair was sweat-plastered against her head, her high cheekbones driven even higher by her huge smirk. Unlike Tom, Regan didn't panic; she understood and fed off my adrenaline rush. However, after she fished me out of the crowd, her smile faltered, and she gestured wildly at her neck.

I sat back on my heels to catch my breath and ran my

hand across my neck, asking, though it wasn't even audible to me over the ringing feedback from my guitar and the crowd's screams, "Am I bleeding?"

Regan shook her head adamantly, slapping a spot slightly lower, just above her chest. I didn't get it until she mouthed, "Necklace."

I looked down, genuinely alarmed, and saw that the oval locket and red guitar pick that I always wore on a metal ball chain around my neck were gone. I got up quickly, nearly twisting my ankle in the process. The heel on my left shoe was broken and my right shoe missing. I staggered over to the mic while Tom unplugged my guitar to reduce the noise level. I blinked at the audience—all open mouths and raised hands—trying not to let the situation faze me. I pulled off my left heel and displayed it. "Okay, guys, you can keep the shoe. I really liked it because it came with the dress, it's vintage, it's got this cool beadwork, but whatever, keep it. But I want my necklace back. That necklace means a lot to me. Please toss it up here."

I stared out at the crowd, unable to make out individuals beyond the first few rows of people. I knew that they'd reacted as to be expected; in fact, at any other place I probably would have gotten my clothes ripped off or worse. Losing the necklace was entirely my own fault, but I still wanted it back.

I decided to test the pull I had over them. "I asked nicely, but now I'm telling you, if I don't get the goddamn necklace back, we will never play here again."

Five seconds later, it landed just a foot in front of me, locket and pick still miraculously attached to the chain. As I bent over to retrieve it, my right shoe landed in front of Tom. He brought it over, shaking his head in awe.

I returned to the microphone, necklace clenched tightly in hand, and gave the audience a little curtsy. "Thank you! We'll see you in a couple weeks," I told them, and headed offstage. It took all the grace I possessed to pull off that exit.

I sat on the couch backstage in silent amazement, just turning the necklace over and over in my hands until Tom ducked in to say that he was leaving. He had this weird reverse stage-fright thing where he got incredibly nervous after the show and had to get out of there. He always loaded up the equipment and volunteered to drive it back to Regan's. He'd even done it before he could legally drive.

His departure snapped me out of my stupor and got me thinking about music again. "You don't want to stick around?" I asked, opening my guitar case. "Work on some new songs?"

I always asked, but he always shook his head, allowing a slight smile to flirt with his otherwise anxious expression. "Emily, I never stay. You start the songs. We'll work on 'em tomorrow when we rehearse."

Regan and I had created a tradition of staying after every show, waiting around for our friends and fans to finish their beers and conversations and trickle out of River's Edge. When it emptied, we remained backstage or reemerged onto the stage, sitting at the very edge of it. And we wrote. Well, mostly I wrote. Regan usually chain-smoked and listened. Occasionally, when I came close to perfecting a song or stumbled upon a tune that she liked so much she couldn't resist, she pulled out her drumsticks and beat out a rhythm on whatever surface was in front of her. I never had to write down the chord progressions, I just played until my fingers had them memorized. Lyrics I recorded in a notebook that I carried with me at all times.

This process could go on all night and often did. Typically around the time she ran out of cigarettes, Regan would murmur, "I'm gonna go."

Sometimes I went with her, but mostly I stayed, not leaving until the sun rose the next morning, shining through the crack beneath the side door. Every once in a while, I'd wake up late the next afternoon to Tom's or Regan's gentle prodding, having fallen asleep in a little ball at one end of the couch, my guitar, notebook, and an overflowing ashtray on the floor beside me.

I always brought clothes to change into after the show and was just lifting the ends of my hair out of the neck of my T-shirt when Johnny sauntered backstage. Regan warned, "Em, there's a guy . . ."

But before she could finish, Johnny tapped me on the shoulder. "Hey, Emily Black. Is that your real name?" he demanded without even introducing himself.

I whirled around, my face a mask of irritation. He towered over me a good six inches. His spiked hair—bleached but streaked with a brilliant red—had wilted from the heat of being in the crowd. It hung in hair-sprayed chunks like daggers pointing down at his glittering, gray eyes. I would be lying if I said I didn't notice those eyes or the way his sweaty T-shirt clung to his thin but well-defined torso, and his jeans hung low on his bony hips. I noticed, but that didn't mean I was going to do anything about it. I hadn't done more than notice for years.

"I thought everybody had cleared out of here." I looked over his shoulder at Regan, who glared at the back of his head from her usual chair.

"Me, too," she answered icily, irritated as I was by the intrusion.

Johnny didn't pick up on our cold reception. "I was outside talking to your bassist. I'm Johnny and I'm from Chicago. I thought I could set up some shows down there for you."

"Tom? I thought he left." My eyes stayed fixed on Regan's.

Johnny shook his head, the sparkle of his metallic irises pulling my gaze to his face. "Is it your real name?" he insisted.

"Yeah, it's my goddamn name." I snagged the lit cigarette that dangled from Johnny's hand and inhaled from it, claiming it as my own.

Johnny's lips curled upward as he laughed. "Whoa, didn't mean to piss you off. I just thought it sounded cool, the kind of name that's asking to be famous."

Regan and I exchanged a glance. Both of us had him pegged as a sleazy promoter trying to pass himself off as a scenester. There'd been a few of those showing up lately, all of them unsuccessfully trying to work their way into their pitch by hitting on me. Regan and I tormented them ruthlessly until they ran off with their tails between their legs. We didn't like people who thought they could take advantage of us just because we were girls.

"If I get famous, it won't be because of my name. No one ever needs to know my name, just the band's." I tapped the cigarette precisely so that ash landed on Johnny's black canvas sneaker. He didn't flinch, which admittedly impressed me a little bit.

I'd given him the perfect opening to state exactly what he could do to get She Laughs' name known, but he didn't take the bait. Instead, he snatched the cigarette back. "I know. That's how I feel about my band, too."

"That's a new one," Regan jeered, the cracked vinyl on her seat squeaking as she pulled her bare feet up on to it. "None of the other promoters pretended to have their own band."

Johnny pivoted to face Regan and mirrored her cold stare. "I'm not a promoter. This is my band. We're playing a show in Chicago next weekend. That's what I was talking to Tom about." He withdrew a flyer from the pocket of his torn jeans and offered it to Regan. She refused, so he handed it to me.

I inspected it, repressing laughter. "My Gorgeous Letdown?"

"My first girlfriend broke up with me in a letter. That's how she addressed it."

"So you named your band after it?" I asked incredulously as Regan snickered.

"Well, where the hell did you get She Laughs?" Johnny took an angry drag from his smoke.

"Regan's mom came up with it. After I punched a guy who laughed at me when I said I was in a band." I seized his cigarette again. Johnny snatched my wrist before I could inhale from it. I tilted it back in an attempt to burn his hand.

He quickly recoiled. "You should call your band the Arrogant Bastards," I said with a smirk.

"Why? Because I came back here and tried to talk to you? You played a good show. That's all I wanted to say. Just because you're the queen of some backwoods scene . . . Whatever." His scowl exaggerated the sharpness of his cheekbones.

I grabbed his elbow before he could storm off. "Excuse me? If this is such a nothing scene, then why the hell are you here?"

Johnny wrenched out of my grip. "Because I heard you were good. And you are. So I thought you'd be a fun band to play with. Your bassist seemed into doing a show with us, but he said—"

"We're not opening for your stupid band just because you're from Chicago. We're not a bunch of hicks starved for the big-city lights." I expertly flicked the cigarette just to the left of Johnny into the can next to Regan's chair.

"Christ, how'd you get so cynical?" Johnny flung his hands up in exasperation.

I narrowed my eyes. "Because up until three years ago I was involved with a lot of guys like you."

"Guys like me? What does that mean? I'm sorry. I mistook you for a girl band with talent, not another one of those psycho anti-male bands—"

"We're not a fucking 'girl band'! We're just a band. And we can book our own gigs, thank you very much! We would never open for your horrendously named band," I fumed. The "girl" thing always got me riled. As if having ovaries had any impact on musicianship.

Johnny was equally pissed. He screwed up his face like a petulant child and retorted, "I wasn't going to ask you to open for my band. We would open for you!"

At that I collapsed onto the couch in a fit of giggles. It was almost as good as one of the guys I'd hooked up with in the past coming back and begging to open for She Laughs.

"What?" Johnny raged, his fair skin flushing almost violet.

"I'm sorry." I took a deep breath to calm myself and wiped tears of hysteria from my eyes. "I think we got off on the wrong foot."

Johnny blinked uncertainly. "Okay . . ."

I turned to Regan, who had her arms wrapped around her knees, chin balanced on top of them, watching the exchange with mild amusement. "How about it, Regan? Should we let Johnny and the Gorgeous Letdowns open for us in Chicago?"

"We should hear a tape first," she said.

I cocked an eyebrow and swung my gaze in Johnny's direction. He coolly tapped another cigarette out of his pack, clearly trying to decide if we were messing with him. He lit the smoke and snapped his Zippo shut. He stared directly at me and exhaled. "Fine, I've got a tape in my car. Come listen to it."

Regan stretched her arms overhead, yawning. "Not tonight, I'm tired." Her feet thumped to the floor one after the other. "You can leave a copy with us."

But Johnny's silver eyes remained locked on mine, daring me.

No. I didn't do this anymore. I didn't flirt with guys like him. I didn't go anywhere with them.

Then again, this was different. He'd hunted *me* down instead of the other way around. And, admittedly, I liked the little rush of power that gave me. I found myself saying, "I'll listen to it now."

The three of us headed for the parking lot and as Regan hugged me good-bye, she whispered, "If you really want to play with his band, don't sleep with him."

My chuckle broke the blissful, late-summer-night silence. "I know that."

Regan shook her head. She recognized what I didn't want to admit: the reckless instincts and impulses I'd repressed for almost three years had taken over.

I slid onto the cluttered cloth seat on the passenger's side of Johnny's car. My feet crunched Coke cans, empty cigarette packs, and fast-food bags. "Sorry about the mess," Johnny said with a shrug. "Been living out of my car for a few days. Was up in Madison meeting with a label about putting out our EP. Everyone was talking up She Laughs, so I decided to come down here and check you out."

It was probably one of the most girly things I'd ever done, and I don't know why it happened—sudden, inexplicable nervousness?—but I giggled when he said "check you out."

Bemused, Johnny's voice softened. "What's so funny, Emily?"

I didn't like being caught in a moment of vulnerability. "Just you, the situation. It reminds me of so many other guys," I remarked flippantly.

He frowned. "I don't want to remind you of anyone."

"Well, why don't you play me your tape? If you're as good as you say you are, you'll blow thoughts of anyone else out of my mind, right?"

"Hey, I never claimed to be that good. We're definitely not better than you." He leaned toward me, twisting his body between our two seats to rummage in the back for his tape. His T-shirt rode up, revealing a sliver of pale abdomen. He obviously worked out. All the other rock gods had had nicely toned arms, as musicians usually do, but none of them had had abs like that. I bit my lip and forced myself to look away. A tape sitting behind the gearshift caught my eye. I'd never met anyone besides my father with that tape.

"You like Loreena Campbell?" I exclaimed. She was a blues songstress from Chicago who my parents had gone to see religiously.

Johnny sat up, his demo loosely in hand, stunned as I was. "I love her! You've heard of her? How? I didn't think her music made it out of Chicago."

"My dad. He listens to her, a lot of older blues, just about everything really."

Johnny nodded emphatically, pointing at me with that look you get when you finally identify something you couldn't put a finger on. "That's why I like your voice so much. You're like the punk-rock Loreena Campbell." I couldn't help beaming at that. "I saw her very last show at a bar in 1981," he continued.

"Yeah, right," I snorted. "How old are you?"

He laughed, pushing tendrils of red-streaked hair out of his face. "Twenty-two. It was my first concert and I almost didn't get in. I was nine years old, standing with my mom, singing Loreena's songs to the bouncer, trying to win him over when Loreena herself walked by. She made them let me in 'cause she liked the way I sang."

"You're shitting me."

Johnny's eyes grew wide as the full moon glowing through the window behind him. "I'm serious. It was the best day of my life. I decided right there that I was going to start a band."

I shook my head, amazed. "I never thought I'd meet a punk guy who was into Loreena Campbell."

Then I realized I'd never had a conversation like this with any guy besides Tom and my dad. It put Johnny on a new level and I was uneasy about that. I decided to move the conversation into an arena where he would surely disappoint. "Why don't you put on your tape?" I suggested.

As I anticipated, it was mediocre, like all those opening bands whose generic sound drones on and on while you pray *Please, god, let this be the last song before the main act* because you're so bored. This should have triggered an immediate opening and slamming of the car door, perhaps with some laughter to drive in the last nail, but no, I couldn't stop thinking about how he liked Loreena Campbell and Loreena Campbell had liked him. His voice *was* really good, and the guitar work definitely had potential. He just needed to lose the overly fuzzed out, angsty thing.

As I thought about this, I noticed him leaning toward me, shirt riding up again, and when he kissed me, I kissed him back.

The way he kissed me made me forget all the reasons behind my self-imposed vow of celibacy. Nothing besides singing had ever made my mouth feel so good. I barely remembered to come up for air every once in a while. If he learned to play music as well as he kissed, he'd be the world's biggest rock god. He tangled his fingers in my hair, tracing his nails down my scalp, making me shiver. The way he touched me made me forget every guy I'd ever been with, so during the second mediocre song on his tape, I took off my top. He smiled, and lifted his shirt over his head. While he did this, I quickly popped out his tape and put in Loreena Campbell. I don't know if this pissed him off because when I turned back, all I saw was abs. He maneuvered through the gap between the front seats into the back, and I followed, straddling his lap.

Under the blazing heat of the morning sun, the smells of stale cigarette smoke, stale fries, and not-so-stale sex collided, jarring me into consciousness. Waking up half naked in the backseat of Johnny's car scared the crap out of me. The last time I'd slept with someone, it ended with me feeling completely helpless. I couldn't believe I'd exposed myself to that possibility again.

I struggled to sit up, but Johnny's embrace kept me pinned to the seat. I was pleased to note the awkward angle of his head: right cheek mashed against the window, neck cranked back like I'd instinctively shoved his head off of my shoulder in my sleep. But at the same time, I fought the urge to kiss his smooth, white throat. And I knew if I glanced down toward his bare chest, I'd be toast.

No. No more mistakes. Back to celibacy.

I poked him awake. "I gotta go." I wondered why I hadn't said that the night before. I'd never actually stayed with a guy I'd slept with for more than ten minutes after completing the act. Sometimes, I'd agree to meet them later, but I'd never fallen asleep beside them.

"You said that last night." Johnny yawned. He tightened his grip on me, trying to set his head on my shoulder.

"I did?" I squirmed to loosen his grasp.

"You did. I convinced you that you were too tired to drive."

"Oh."

"Was I so bad that you blocked it out?" he teased.

"I'm always confused in the morning until I get coffee." This was true, but I avoided his question. He wasn't bad. He was good. I hadn't known "good" existed until him. But he didn't need to know that. He still struck me as slightly more than self-confident.

"Let's go get some coffee, then," he suggested, kissing my cheek. He was aiming for my lips, but I moved out of his path, reaching into the front for my T-shirt.

"No. I should get over to Regan's. Practice." I tugged my shirt over my head, fingering the chain around my neck as I pulled it on top of the T-shirt.

Johnny lifted the locket from where it fell against my chest. "So, what's so special about the necklace?" He ran his forefinger over the silver oval, pressing the tiny button that opened it. "Who's inside?" He lowered his eyes to study the faded black-and-white photo of the stubbly face I had memorized. "Boyfriend?" he asked, without any inflection to indicate if he cared how I answered.

The lie was posed on my tongue, but strangely I felt the need to tell him the truth. "It's my father." I brushed his fingers away and snapped the locket shut. "It was my mother's. One of the only things of hers I have, besides her old records."

"She was a musician, too?"

"No. Well, I don't know, maybe she is. She loved music. We don't know where she is now, though." I trained my eyes on the vacant parking lot as I spoke. Why was I compelled to tell him these things? I didn't talk to the guys I slept with, not like this anyway.

"No wonder you wanted it back."

"Yeah." I stared him down. "I shouldn't do impulsive shit like that. I could lose things that I care about." *Impulsive shit like sleeping with you and losing my focus on my career.*

"Nah, you're too tough. No one could take anything from you."

He seemed to grasp my meaning, which freaked me out. I leaned into the front seat for the rest of my things.

Trying to lighten the mood, he gibed, "So you're Daddy's little girl."

My head snapped around, all the muscles in my back tensing. "Shut up!"

His smirk disappeared. "Jesus, Emily, calm down. It was a joke."

He kept me on edge because, deep down, I actually liked him. I didn't just find him attractive, our personalities clicked and clashed in all the right ways. "Sorry. And, yeah, I guess I am."

"That's fine." That cocky lip curled up again, but he used

the intensity of his gaze to make it appear almost sensitive. "I guess you could say I'm a mama's boy. My dad bailed on us when I was five, so I'm really loyal to her. When someone walks out on the family, you either fall apart or get tight. I'm sure you know what I mean."

I glared at him. "No, I don't know what you mean. My mom wasn't like your dad. She didn't just *bail*," I mimicked snottily, and reached for the door, but he took hold of my arm.

"Well, she left, right?" he contended.

"Yeah." I jerked away. "But not 'cause she cheated or whatever typical bullshit your dad probably pulled on your mom."

His eyes blazed, but he inhaled slowly to cool them, speaking to me gently again. "Hey, leaving is leaving, the effect is the same. But we're stronger for it."

I didn't want to get into I-survived-the-single-parent-home therapeutic crap. "Listen, I don't want to talk about this with you. We're not friends. I don't even know your last name."

"Thompson. John Christopher Thompson. Pretty boring, huh? See why I was so jealous of you for having a rock 'n' roll name like Emily Black?" He tried to charm a smile from me.

I shrugged. "You already go by Johnny. Just come up with an adjective that describes you and make it your last name." A devious look crept across my face. "Too bad Johnny Rotten's already taken."

"Oh, is that what you think of me?" He pretended to pout. Then he pointed to his hair. "Can't I be Johnny Red? We'd make such a cute punk couple . . ."

"Couple?" I choked, scooting closer to the door. "Yeah, right. I don't date. I'm focused on my music. Nothing else. You just distracted me last night."

"Johnny Attraction?" He gestured at his bare chest.

I refused to look anywhere but his face. "Don't flatter yourself, Johnny Bastard."

He shook his head, keeping his silver eyes on mine. "I don't like that one."

"Johnny Threat."

"Where'd you get that?" he smirked.

I flashed an impenetrable smile. "I'm not telling. Besides, you have to act like it's your real name for it to work."

I wasn't about to let him know that the name came to mind because he was a threat to my long-standing resistance to romance. That his couple comment had actually made me feel warm and mushy inside, just for a moment.

He held his hands up, surrendering. "Okay, fair enough. But you'll at least let me buy you a cup of coffee for coming up with such a great name, right?"

As he groped around on the floor for his shirt, my fingers found the door handle. "No. I have to go practice."

"Hey, I thought you said I could come with you. So we could all talk about the show in Chicago? Maybe a few shows?"

"Yeah," I said, slipping out of the car and his reach. "Right. Sure, just follow me." And with that innocuous phrase, I let him into my life.

2.

Rock and roll is what I'm born to be.

—Patti Smith
"Ask the Angels"
Radio Ethiopia

SLEEPWALK DANCING

November 1986

Sirens screeched down the street outside of Louisa's Minneapolis apartment. She paused at the window, watching two police cars followed by a fire truck, their red lights slicing through the evening shadows. The glow briefly illuminated a yellow cab. It sat in front of Louisa's building, blinkers on as it unloaded passengers. Louisa resumed packing. On her walk home from a show at the 7th Street Entry the night before, her cheeks getting chapped by the wind, she'd decided it was time to leave. She couldn't take another Midwestern winter.

She scooped up four glasses from the coffee table and brought them into the kitchen. Two were relatively clean. Louisa rinsed these and set them aside. The other two were sticky with the remnants of whiskey sours, her current drink of choice. One of them had cigarette butts floating in sludgy brown liquid; the other had a flyer stuck to the bottom. She tossed both glasses directly into the garbage. She'd accumulated too much stuff over the past two years in Minnesota anyway.

Louisa hadn't figured out where she was going next until she glanced at the drink-ringed flyer she'd peeled off the glass. It was from a show she'd seen in September, a noisy rock band from Boston she'd loved. Boston winters were bad, but not as bad as Minneapolis, she decided, and if the scene was hot, who cared about the weather. She folded up the flyer to shove it in the pocket of her jeans, but dropped it when the doorbell buzzed loud as a fire alarm.

Louisa opened the door to Colette, who had a three-year-old girl with honey-colored hair clinging sleepily to her leg. "I'm sorry to do this to you again, Lou," Colette said with a trembling lip, "but Nadia and I have nowhere else to go." Before tears could overflow from Colette's big blue eyes, Louisa ushered them in and used her teakettle for the last time to make Colette a mug of steaming black tea.

Louisa was not nearly as shocked by Colette's appearance on her doorstep as she had been in 1983, the first time it happened. Back then, Louisa lived in San Pedro, California. She hadn't seen or heard from Colette since she'd left her in New Orleans two years before. But apparently Colette had come to regard Louisa as an older-sister figure during that brief time in the Big Easy. When Colette got into trouble, Louisa was the first person she thought to track down through her transient friends. At the time, Louisa was about to leave San Pedro for D.C., where a new form of hardcore punk was emerging, but she couldn't bring herself to close the door on Colette, lost and lonely at twenty-one, with a brand-new baby whose father's identity was as hotly contested as the origin of the heavens. Louisa let her in, thankful that Michael didn't have Colette's kind of connections. Then again, he understood why she needed to be alone.

Louisa set Colette on her feet in California and then continued to wander, summoned by music, a new band with a different sound that could be "It," anything that could prove the healing power of rock 'n' roll had not failed her. But inevitably, Colette and baby Nadia would appear at her door and ride along for a while.

"I got mixed up with the wrong guy again," Colette sighed, gratefully swallowing the tea and sandwich Louisa made for her. Nadia had eaten half her sandwich and promptly curled up against her mother for a nap. "He was dealing drugs out of my apartment. I came home last week and found the door kicked in. I knew the Santa Cruz police would be looking for me. Not to mention social services." She gave Nadia a squeeze. "I had to get as far away as possible."

"Boston far enough?" Louisa gestured across the room to the open suitcase on her bed. "I wanted to go tonight."

"Boston sounds great."

A couple hours later, they left Louisa's apartment, Louisa carrying the last bag and Colette with Nadia on her hip. Colette shut the front door and paused to grab Louisa's mail. "Want this?" She offered the envelopes to Louisa. Louisa fanned them out as she took them in her free hand. She let the bills flutter to the ground, but shoved the envelope with the familiar girlish handwriting and a Wisconsin postmark in her pocket. Molly still wrote to her even though it had been ten long years since Louisa had abandoned her husband, child, and best friend. Ten years almost to the day, Louisa realized.

Fueled by sleeplessness, Louisa drove while Nadia slept in the backseat, strapped in and sitting completely upright with her head tilted toward her left shoulder. Her unruly curls, which she wouldn't let Colette cut, brushed the scuffed leather seat. Colette slept as well, her pale cheek pressed against the cold window on the passenger's side like it was a pillow. Three hours into the drive, as they neared Baraboo, Wisconsin, Louisa's intuition guided her off of I-90/94 onto US-12. *Just a shortcut,* she told herself as she crossed the Wisconsin River.

Louisa no longer headed east toward Boston, but slightly west toward a place she'd spent years avoiding. South of Mineral Point, Louisa followed the backcountry roads to the abandoned warehouse, River's Edge, where the best music she'd ever heard had been played by friends, acquaintances, and most beautifully by the man who later became her husband. She parked in the gravel lot, but did not get out. She saw tire ruts in the frozen mud and rusted beer cans in the weeds. *The kids still come here,* she thought, cracking the window as she lit a cigarette, and when she glanced down at the ground just below, she saw a thin wire glinting in the moonlight. A broken guitar string. *And the kids still play.* But when her mind turned over the next thought, *Maybe Emily will come here someday,* her throat seized up and she put the car into drive again.

She continued her ghostly tour, driving southeast on County Highway PW, whose curves she knew as well as the curves of her own hips. She slid silently into the sleeping town. Where the highway became Main Street, she slowed below the required twenty-five miles an hour to gaze into the darkened windows of JT's Tavern and Carlisle Groceries and Meats, both of which looked the same as they had over twelve years ago when she'd fled with Michael on her eighteenth birthday.

Reaching the southernmost outskirts of Carlisle, Louisa turned onto an out-of-place, winding street that rose and fell with tiny hills like shallow breaths. The houses were ill-spaced, sitting like faded wooden blocks tossed to the ground haphazardly by a cranky child. Fields stretched out behind them, already harvested clean in preparation for winter. Louisa stopped in front of a house painted a violent shade of red that looked like dried blood in the darkness. She sat waiting for the ghosts to emerge: herself and Eric Lisbon. Perhaps she would even see the moment when Eric dragged her inside and all the music she'd loved and collected from River's Edge drained from her open mouth instead of a scream. She'd have to spend years searching for it again.

Colette stirred beside her. "Where are we, Lou?" she asked, blinking sleepily. Taking in her surroundings with a squint, she added, "Why are we in some little podunk town?" She honed in on the house down the driveway from them. "That place gives me the creeps."

Louisa whispered, "Me too."

Colette stretched, touching the roof of the car. The sleeves of her leather jacket dipped to reveal a group of silver bangles that clinked together, breaking the silence like a crash of cymbals. "I can drive, y'know. I got some stuff that would wake me up."

"No, I needed to stop here to remember why I can't go home." Louisa clutched the steering wheel. If only she could drive the car at a hundred miles per hour right through Eric's house and demolish her memories, but they were indestructible. She sank against her seat, defeated.

Colette gaped at her. "What are you talking about?"

Louisa trained her eyes on the shadowy fields beyond the red house. She forced her voice to sound strong. "This is *my* podunk town, Colette. This is Carlisle. And the stuff that happened in that house? That's what I've been running from."

"Yeah? You know if you want to talk . . ." Colette shifted uncomfortably in her seat and trailed off like she expected to be shot down. She'd asked Louisa about her past on a few occasions, but Louisa always clammed up like she had in New Orleans.

This time Louisa would've told the story even if she hadn't been asked. She couldn't help it. Everything was rushing back.

"Eric." The name scratched its way out of Louisa's throat like a rusty nail dragged across a chalkboard. "Eric Lisbon was my high school boyfriend and he lived in that house." Louisa gestured down the driveway at the bloodred building.

"I met him the summer after my freshman year. My best friend, Molly, her boyfriend, Luke, and I saw his band play at this old warehouse, River's Edge. Eric was the guitarist. He impressed me so much that I sent my friends home and waited for him in the parking lot afterward. I sat on the hood of his van, smoking a cigarette, trying to seem cool. And it worked."

Louisa glanced over at Colette, who didn't seem to know if she should smile. She nodded, straight-faced, urging Louisa to continue.

"He put his amp down, ran his fingers through his inky

black hair, and hopped up beside me. He said, 'Louisa Carson, to what do I owe the honor?'

"I was so flattered. He was two years older than me. He never acknowledged me at school before. Or maybe he had, I just never noticed him until I saw him onstage. I said, 'You know who I am?'

"He stared right at me with these dazzling hazel eyes and said, 'Of course I do. I remember when you first moved to Carlisle, started stirring up trouble with Molly, and making things more interesting. Not to mention brightening up the place with your beautiful smile.'

"I didn't want to blush, so I complimented him back, told him he'd put on the best show I'd ever seen. He teased me and asked how many shows I'd been to, like I was so young it had to be my first. So I took a drag off my cigarette to look older and said, 'Plenty.'

"Then he pinched my cigarette between two fingers, took it from my mouth like a lollipop, and tossed it to the ground, saying, 'You're too pretty to smoke. It'll give you wrinkles.' I didn't know whether to chew him out or kiss him. I gave him this playful little butterfly kiss and he laughed, grabbed me by the arm before I could slide away, and laid a full one on me." Louisa paused and reached for her pack of smokes. She pushed the car lighter in and offered Colette a cigarette.

Colette accepted and asked, "Your first kiss?"

"Yeah, unfortunately." Louisa remained silent until she was able to light up. She knew she needed to smoke to keep talking. Finally the lighter popped and Louisa went on. "Eric and I were inseparable for the rest of the summer, until I went to England.

"My cousin Amelia was nineteen and she'd just moved to London to go to school. My dad agreed to let me visit her because he thought if I saw the rewards of studying abroad, I'd focus on my schoolwork more. But Amelia had found the beginnings of punk rock to be a hell of a lot more interesting than her studies. Instead of taking me on a tour of the campus, she bleached my hair and took me to Kings Road. She bought me a stack of records and a whole new wardrobe with her tuition money. The only school-related thing that Amelia introduced me to was David, a classmate of hers with a brilliant aquamarine Mohawk and even brighter blue eyes." Louisa sighed.

"That British accent made me forget about my boyfriend back home. But when I returned to Wisconsin three weeks later, I went right back to Eric because I never thought I'd see David again and I was in love with Eric, right?"

"Yeah?" Colette's eyes lingered doubtfully on the house looming in front of them.

"You can tell it's gonna end badly, can't you?" Louisa asked, but Colette didn't answer, so she continued. "Eric had a temper. He didn't like the bleached hair. He called all of my new clothes 'slutty.' We fought for most of my sophomore year and then I met Michael around my sixteenth birthday." She cracked a smile for the first time since she'd started talking.

Colette turned to her, recognizing the name. "Your husband. You left Eric for him?"

Louisa studied the cherry of her cigarette, her tone softening. "Not exactly. Michael and I were friends. He used to give me guitar lessons before the bands went on at River's

Edge. But yeah, I had a crush on him. I just couldn't figure out how to break up with Eric. He scared me. So what did I do?" Bitterness crept into her voice again. "I let him catch me with Michael. It was innocent, of course. Michael's not the type to steal someone's girlfriend. But Eric seeing me with Michael's guitar around my neck was as good as him catching us in bed. Eric was that jealous."

"You did it on purpose?"

"Kind of. I met Michael at River's Edge on a night that Eric's band was playing, so I knew Eric would arrive early."

"What'd he do?" Colette couldn't keep her anxious eyes off Louisa, but Louisa still focused on the end of her cigarette, reminded of how Eric's gaze burned into her that night.

"Nothing at first. He ignored me, played his gig. Molly was five months pregnant at the time. She didn't feel well, asked if I would be okay getting a ride home with Eric. I thought I would. He'd called me every name in the book before, but he'd never hit me or anything. I figured he'd yell, maybe we'd finally end it, and he'd drive me home. So after the show was over, I waited by his van. The whole parking lot cleared out by the time he got there. He'd been inside getting wasted and even angrier at me." Louisa's breath hitched and she took a long drag to cover the sound. "When he found me he beat the shit out of me. Then he left me in the parking lot. Like roadkill."

"Jesus Christ . . ."

Louisa held up her hand to silence Colette without looking at her. She lit a fresh cigarette from the one she'd almost finished. "Michael found me there. I guess he liked to stay late at River's Edge and practice guitar. When he walked out to his motorcycle, he heard me crying. He wanted to go to the police, but I begged him to take me home. He dropped me off and I went in the front and out the back. Straight over to Eric's because I was completely humiliated that Michael had seen me like that. I didn't want him or anyone else thinking I was this helpless, battered girlfriend. And I planned to end it that night if it killed me. Which I wish it had."

Exhaling heavily, Louisa rolled her window down halfway. She needed the slap of cold air to keep her from crying. Her eyes landed on the sagging front porch. It had been sturdier back then, but the chipping coat of white paint matched her memory. "It was stupid to go over there. I knew his parents were out of town. I knew he was drunk and he'd just beat me up. But you never think someone is capable of crossing that line . . ."

She saw herself: bruised, hem of her dress torn, but defiant, banging on the door. Eric answered, coming from the bathroom, still zipping his fly. The evil, crooked grin. "Here to make up, baby? I guess I should be unzipping . . ." Wrenching her inside with one big hand around both of her skinny wrists.

Louisa ripped her focus from the blackness outside the window, desperately seeking Colette's familiar face. She needed to see that someone else was beside her, that she wasn't trapped alone in the car with her nightmares. "He dragged me down to his basement, to this little bathroom the size of a closet . . ."

Louisa could smell that cramped room. Piss, mildew, the whiskey on Eric's breath. He brutally shoved her to the floor, her knees bashing against the concrete. She tried to scramble to her feet, but he pushed her down again. Her head banged into the underside of the rusty sink and she rolled onto her back, clenching the top of her head in pain.

Eric laughed and jumped on her before she could curl into a ball to protect herself. He sat on her legs and pinned her arms over her head with one hand, reaching up her skirt and tearing at her underwear with the other. After tugging his pants down, he slapped his calloused hand over her mouth and commanded, "Stop screaming! No one's going to hear you." Louisa hadn't even realized she was making a sound.

She struggled against him, but it didn't matter. He slammed her around the grimy bathroom like a rag doll, jamming himself into her for what felt like an eternity. When he finally finished, he drunkenly passed out on top of her. Louisa thought she'd suffocate beneath his weight, but she managed to slide out from under him.

Eric's father's gun collection was displayed in the corner of the basement across from the bathroom. Louisa limped over to it, picked up a handgun and pressed it to her temple. *Count to three, then fire. It will all be over,* she told herself. But she counted all the way to one hundred and couldn't do it. Noticing a phone on the wall, Louisa lowered the gun. She cradled the receiver between her cheek and her shoulder, and dialed with her free hand.

"I need you," Louisa whispered hoarsely when Molly answered. "I'm at Eric's."

"What happened?" Molly asked, panicked.

Before Louisa could respond, Eric stumbled out of the bathroom, pulling up his jeans. "Louuuzah," he slurred. "Where'd you go? I wasn't through with you." He immediately spotted the phone, jerked it away from Louisa, and put it to his ear, demanding, "Who is this?"

Louisa could hear Molly shrieking, "What did you do to her?"

Eric let her shout for a moment, a slow smile spreading across his face. Then, glaring into Louisa's eyes, he taunted, "I fucked her. So hard that she won't ever think about fooling around with Michael Black again."

Molly screamed indiscernible threats until Eric cut her off with a snarl. "I'll do what I want to her. She's mine."

Then his hand dropped to the waistband of his jeans. Louisa felt the cold weight of the gun in her palm. She couldn't let him hurt her again.

Eric had been so focused on the phone that he hadn't even seen the gun, not until it was pointed in his face. Before he could reach for it, before he could even say her name, Louisa fired.

She didn't remember hearing the shot; she didn't remember watching him collapse. She just remembered—very vividly—how he looked dead. His forehead caved in like a rotten melon, hazel eye missing from the right side where the bullet entered, the skin around the wound pulpy like papier-mâché that would never dry. Shattered pieces of skull, red gore, and tufts of his greasy black hair were all that remained of the back of his head.

Louisa had gaped at him until Molly arrived and found her sitting on the cold basement floor, half-naked, covered in blood, some Eric's, some her own. The gun lay between Louisa and Eric's body.

"He did this to himself, Louisa," Molly rationalized,

kneeling in front of her. "He killed himself when he raped you." Molly wiped the gun clean and pressed it into Eric's hand. She carried Louisa out to the car.

While Molly gathered the scattered remnants of Louisa's torn clothing and erased every trace of her from that basement, Louisa stared through the windshield, unable to pull her eyes away from the ugly, bloodred house.

Listening to Louisa's tale, neither could Colette.

"Eric's death was written off as a suicide," Louisa finished. "No one ever suspected it. Guys his age in our area, sometimes they got drunk, looked out at those dead fields, and saw no future. But he didn't kill himself. I did. I shot him point-blank."

"And it's haunted you ever since," Colette completed.

"Yes." Louisa nodded. A fat tear rolled down her cheek and her voice shook. "I could've had a future. I tried to have one with Michael. But when I had that baby . . . I couldn't be around her. I'd done something too awful."

"Honey," Colette said, shaking her head, "I done way worse things than you."

Louisa's eyes probed Colette's. "You killed someone?"

"No, but neither did you, really. You acted out of—"

Louisa put up a hand to dismiss what Colette was about to say. "Don't give me that self-defense crap. Michael had me convinced of that for a little while, but . . ." She paused and then stated firmly, "I ended a life, Colette."

"What kind of a life?" Colette sneered. "I am not saying that you should just brush off shooting somebody—hell, I can't even brush off the time I accidentally ran over a rabbit—but I'm saying that, because of the circumstances, it's not the worst thing you've done and it's no worse than shit I've done either."

"What's the worst thing I've done, then?" Louisa anxiously scrubbed the wetness from her face.

"Leaving your little girl."

"No." She shook her head so violently that strands of her hair whipped against the window. "That's the best thing I've done. She's got a better life without me. I did a horrible thing, Colette. I wasn't worthy of Michael and I didn't deserve to raise that little girl." To put a stop to that discussion, Louisa addressed Colette's other comment, thinking that if Colette had committed a comparable act, it might ease her own conscience slightly. "What's the worst thing *you've* done, then?"

Colette turned in her seat to gaze at Nadia. "Dragging this little one toward all my dreams that just wind up being nightmares." Then she looked up at Louisa again. "Go home, Lou," she urged, tears collecting at the corners of her heavily kohl-lined eyes.

Louisa faced forward, grasping the steering wheel so hard that her knuckles went white. "I can't. I'm not ever going to be able to. When I left, I thought I was going to find myself out on the road somewhere, in a song at a show in some other city. I thought the music would heal me because that was the only time I felt okay. Listening to the radio, or watching someone play, especially Michael."

Colette placed her fingers on Louisa's shoulder. "I know what you mean. A good song can make you forget everything. You feel like it was written just for you, that the singer knew your pain. But Michael actually did. His were the songs you needed."

"I know." Regret filled Louisa's voice. "But I figured it out too late."

"Maybe not."

"No." Louisa slammed her body back against the seat to knock Colette's hand away. "Don't you understand? Michael's a good man. He's got a decent job. He's raising our daughter to be a strong, beautiful, *good* person." She swallowed a whimper and turned pain into self-loathing.

"And never mind the evil thing I did. Let's set that aside for a minute. What about how I've spent the past ten years? Drinking? Doing drugs? Stripping? I didn't let rock 'n' roll save me. I became the ultimate rock cliché! I let go of Emily back in 1979 when I became a stripper. I only followed the music the way I intended for three years. I went to Detroit for a year. Then I went to New York, where I met a girl who said she wanted to start a club in L.A. And I thought about that old warehouse, River's Edge. The place where I discovered music, where I met Michael, and I thought, 'That's it. If I can create a place like that, I'll create enough good energy to get rid of all the bad inside of me. Then I'll be able to go home.' Nope." Louisa laughed cynically.

"That girl bailed on me as soon as we got to California. It took me two months to find a job and when I did it was at the slowest bar in Hollywood. When I finally had enough money to make rent on time for the first time, I came home to find my apartment had been robbed. I didn't have a bank account. I kept my money under my mattress and of course it was gone. So I cried to my coworker and she ripped an ad out of the paper for me. Amateur night at a strip club. 'You're pretty enough,' she said. 'You'll make it all back in one night,'" Louisa mimicked, raking her fingers through her hair in disgust.

"And I did it. I fought tears onstage, thinking how ashamed my daughter would be if she knew that this was the kind of woman her mother was: a murderer who abandoned her child and went on to earn money by taking her clothes off."

"You were just trying to get by," Colette soothed. "She'd understand that, or she will someday. And Michael, he really loved you, so he would understand, too."

Louisa tossed her cigarette out the window and viciously shoved the car lighter in again. "Yeah, Michael's really loyal. He knew the truth about Eric and he stuck by me. He begged me not to leave. And how'd I repay that? By cheating on him. I remember the date I did it, Colette! October fifth, 1980. I'd been back in New York for a year. I'd saved all that L.A. stripper money to get back there and was determined to make an honest living. So I bartended in the East Village and one night this guy comes in. I set a drink down in front of him and he goes, 'Amelia?' and I go cold because I think he said, 'Emily.'"

"Your cousin Amelia . . ." Colette handed Louisa the cigarette pack she fumbled for.

"Yeah. My favorite cousin. I named my daughter for her because she died in a car wreck in London a few months before Emily was born. So I'm staring at the guy and he's staring at me like he's seen a ghost. Then I recognize the blue eyes, even though his hair doesn't match anymore."

"David. The guy from London."

"Yeah, David." The cigarette lighter popped and Louisa

resisted the urge to press it to her lips instead of the cigarette between them. "David and I did shots till closing and then instead of going home, I ended up at his hotel room. He pretended I was Amelia. Apparently, he'd been in love with her, but never got to tell her until she was bleeding to death in his arms on the side of the road. And I pretended. . . . Well, I was drunk and had been alone for nearly four years and it just happened."

Louisa remembered the way her clothes slid to the floor like petals wilting off a flower. How she couldn't decide if it was easier to close her eyes or open them. Open, she could see quite clearly that David wasn't Michael; closed, Michael was all she could see. She settled on closed when she looked up and saw that she'd left her wedding ring on. It glittered in the light cast from a billboard glowing through the window. But even with her eyes shut, she could still feel the ring, the metal cold and numb as her body.

"He fell asleep as soon as it was over. Of course, guilt was eating me up so I couldn't do the same. I considered myself married." Louisa's fingertips glanced over the gold ring on her left hand. "I still do. So, I slunk out of that hotel, went home, packed my things, and was out of New York before sunrise. I headed for New Orleans, where, as you know, I went back to stripping, started doing coke, and sleeping with random strange men on the really lonely nights."

Colette hung her spiky black head. "Because of me." She reached for Louisa's hand, then decided against it. "Maybe if you got rid of me . . ."

"No," Louisa snapped. "Not because of you. I would have done it no matter what. Don't you get it? I had nothing left. I betrayed my daughter, my husband. I left them to try to get rid of all my ugliness, but instead I've *become* it."

Colette was crying, one hand still hovering near Louisa's, the other rubbing her own eyes, smudging dark makeup across her face. "Let's go to Boston and get clean. Then maybe I can be the mother Nadia deserves and you can feel good enough to go home. Boston," she begged, likening Louisa's failures to her own. "Fresh start."

"Boston," Louisa repeated, but she added, "Last chance. Supposed to be a good college town. Maybe I can get my act together. But if I can't—" She was cut off by Nadia's shrill wail.

"Oh, baaay-beee." Colette's voice became a singsong cleared of the tears. She climbed between the seats, settling beside her child. "What's wrong? Bad dream?"

Louisa glanced back at them guiltily. "Shouldn't have told you that story with her around. Probably gave her nightmares."

"No. She was sound asleep. She just has bad dreams sometimes. It's normal." Colette lifted Nadia out of her car seat. Nadia didn't even open her eyes. Her cry simmered down as she turned her head toward her mother's body, pressing tightly against her breast. "Just drive and I'll sing to her a little bit. She'll be out again in no time."

Louisa started the car, but before she headed for the highway, there was one more place she needed to see.

When she'd left Michael and Emily, she hadn't gone directly to Detroit. She'd come to Carlisle first, stopping at River's Edge, then at the Lisbon house, just as she had this time. And lastly, she'd gone to see Molly. She'd crept inside through the unlocked back door and padded upstairs.

Her footsteps woke baby Regan and Louisa hurried to comfort her on instinct. As soon as she picked her up, Regan quieted, but Molly came running into the room anyway. Seeing Louisa there must have alarmed her. Louisa was supposed to be in Chicago with her own child. Louisa set Regan back in her crib and tried to leave without explanation, but Molly stopped her before she reached the back door.

"What the hell are you doing, Lou?" she demanded.

"I just can't do it anymore," Louisa said.

Molly knew she was referring to Eric Lisbon. She tried to reason with Louisa, of course, but guilt is the hardest emotion to convince someone to rationalize.

The dawning sun had streaked the sky the purplish color of a bruise and the roosters down the road had started to crow before Molly gave up. Both her and Louisa's eyelids had puffed to twice their normal size, their eyes a bloodshot mess from crying. Molly squeaked, "If you just write me, I won't tell anyone where you are. I just have to know you're still out there. That there's hope . . ."

"Okay," Louisa agreed, but she refused to hug Molly good-bye because she knew if she did, she'd never let go.

The letters from Molly always came addressed to Louisa Carson-Black, the name Louisa continued to use because she, too, held out the hope that one day she could be that person again. Every time she moved, Louisa sent Molly her new address. She wrote little more than that and the names of the bands she'd been seeing. No I miss you's. No questions about Michael and Emily. Molly sent her updates on them anyway. As far as Louisa knew, Molly had kept her promise and hadn't told Michael where Louisa was. But

Molly made sure Louisa knew where he was. She included his address every time even though it never changed. By this point Louisa had it memorized.

While Colette cooed to Nadia in the backseat, Louisa cut through the middle of Carlisle. She slowed as she reached Laurel Street and stared up at the tall, gray house that sat perched on top of a hill at the end of a gravel drive. Her eyes filled with fresh tears as she studied the motorcycle parked in front of the garage. It wasn't the same one, of course. Michael insisted on trading that in for a car as soon as he found out Louisa was pregnant, the car that had finally died on Louisa the previous winter in Minneapolis. Louisa almost emitted an audible sob when she saw the large wooden construction next to the house. A ladder led up one side and, across a short bridge, a slide went down the other; two swings hung beneath. Something Michael had built for Emily, she was certain.

Louisa accelerated suddenly, wheeling the car around in a U-turn.

"Lost?" Colette questioned.

"For a second."

For ten years, her brain echoed.

Back on the highway, pointed in the direction of Boston, Louisa fingered the most recent letter from Molly, the one Colette had rescued from her mailbox before they left. She'd give it one more shot, send Molly one more change of address. If she couldn't find the strength she needed to get over the things she'd done—all of them—in Boston, she'd give herself over completely to this sleepwalk dance that took her from place to place. No more writing Molly. No more using Michael's last name. No more false hope.

BRIDGE

I had this dream. About my mother. A really simple dream, but I'd been having it for as long as I could remember. I see her on the other side of a long, foggy bridge. She looks just like this picture my dad took of her a couple months before she left, bright eyes, blond hair blowing in the wind—except she's in the shadows, so the color of her eyes and hair are muted, and her skin's washed out. I run to her, but the distance keeps growing between us and time's passing, years speeding by. When I finally reach her, she's an old woman who looks like she's lived a harsh life. Her face is covered in wrinkles, her flesh is sagging off her bones, and her hair has mostly fallen out, so all that's left are these pathetic, stringy tufts.

I thought about that dream while I stood in Johnny's tiny studio apartment, gazing down eight stories at the Kennedy Expressway, reveling in the sheer number of people in Chicago. I could stand there for fifteen minutes and see more people in their cars racing in and out of downtown than lived in all of Carlisle. And I wondered if my mother had driven away from my father and me on that very expressway.

I jumped when Johnny came up behind me and placed his hand, cold from the beer he was carrying, on my shoulder. "You realize you sold out that show." He referred to our first gig with his band, which we'd finally agreed to do after he hounded us for a month.

"Seriously?" I spun around, snapping back into reality. Still dripping with sweat from the intensity of the show and the hot summer night, I pressed the icy bottle against my forehead before opening it. "I saw it was packed in there, but sold out?"

Regan accepted a beer from Johnny and asked, "How'd that happen? I mean, a few kids from Chicago used to come up and see us, but we never really had much of a reputation down here. Your band must have been the draw." It was a flattering comment, seeing as the audience had obviously been most enthusiastic about our set. The great show we played must have lightened Regan's mood, because she had never been so kind to Johnny before. She still acted incredibly wary of him for some reason. But if he kept plying her with booze, he might win her over. She downed half the beer in one gulp and had been eyeing a bottle of tequila on his kitchen counter since we'd come in.

"Well, actually, I didn't give this to you guys yesterday because I didn't want to freak you out, but I wrote a review of your last show at River's Edge, so tonight was pretty well advertised." Johnny grabbed a newspaper from the countertop that separated his living/sleeping space from his kitchen.

I lunged across the room and snatched it from him.

"What page?" I demanded, plopping down between Tom and Regan on the futon that doubled as Johnny's bed so they could read along with me.

"Fifteen. Normally they have a picture, but I didn't have one, so . . ." His voice faded out as I started to read. It was the first article I'd ever seen on my band.

> Like most people outside of southern Wisconsin, I'd never heard of She Laughs, a three-piece punk band from a tiny town just north of the Illinois state line. I first caught wind of the buzz around them in Madison, Wisconsin, where my band was meeting with some people from Fist Fight Records. [Ed. Note: Look out for the first EP by My Gorgeous Letdown, on Fist Fight, in the early months of 1995.] She Laughs was *the* topic among several kids on State Street. When I asked one girl about them, she declared them to be "the best band in the Midwest," a sentiment I immediately dismissed as gross hyperbole. But they were playing a show that night, so I decided to take a detour on my way back to Chicago and check them out at River's Edge, a warehouse just outside of their hometown, Carlisle.
>
> Both River's Edge and the area around Carlisle were dubbed a "burgeoning musical mecca" by several of the big rock rags in the spring of 1993 when July Lies came barreling out of that region with their major label debut. Unfortunately, July Lies never got the mainstream status they deserved, and none of their rural Wisconsin contemporaries registered on the ra-

dar. But the members of She Laughs were still in high school then. Now singer/guitarist Emily Black, drummer Regan Parker (her older sister is Marissa of July Lies), and bassist Tom Fawcett may be poised to do what July Lies couldn't.

The warehouse was packed with nearly four hundred people, all of their eyes on Emily Black as soon as she walked onstage. Her long, raven hair emphasized her snow-white skin, but she was no porcelain doll. The bloodred lipstick and tattered vintage dress she wore made her as rock 'n' roll as the shiny blue guitar she played.

The band's energy really exploded when Regan clicked her sticks together three times to start the second song, a new one called "Two Miles Down." The guitar and bass built like a wave, Emily's voice the crest. *"The phone rings two miles away. It's not over. It's not over,"* she began, soft and angelic. As the music drove faster into the chorus, her voice scratched into a scream. When the song came to its furious end, her darkly lined eyes squeezed shut as she wailed the last *"It's not over."* As she struck the final chord, her eyelids snapped up, revealing eyes as green as all-consuming envy—the envy every musician will feel in their gut when they hear this song and realize that She Laughs truly is the best band in the Midwest. The teenage girl on that bench on State Street was not exaggerating; in fact, she might not be giving them enough credit.

She Laughs has the ability to become one of the

best bands *period*. They play solid, catchy, honest rock 'n' roll. While the influence of punk is most obvious in their raw, loudhardfast songs, the melodies that lie beneath reveal that they were raised on the Beatles, and a lot of Emily's guitar work and throaty singing style pay homage to her love of the blues, her voice particularly reminiscent of Chicago blues songstress Loreena Campbell.

She Laughs roared through a thirteen-song set, Regan and Tom laying a hard-hitting backdrop for Emily's guitar and vocals, her lyrics a perfectly woven web of growled threats and whispered pleas. The crowd sung along with "Temper Tantrum," "Skin," and "Hollow Mirror," some of the oldest She Laughs songs, all of which appear on a well-circulated demo. Spectacular new songs like "Vacancy" and "Two Miles Down" had the audience joining in by the last chorus.

Catch She Laughs' first Chicago show Thursday, August 25, at Fireside Bowl.

"I'm not that . . . I mean, I don't really . . ." I didn't know what to say. He'd painted me as an established rock star, an image you would see on a poster or a T-shirt. I felt a surge of pride, but at the same time I didn't know if I deserved that kind of attention.

Regan was more succinct. "Nice love letter, Johnny." She smirked, swilling the last of her beer.

He blushed. "What the hell are you talking about?" he asked defensively.

Regan laughed. "It's a great review, don't get me wrong.

And I'm thrilled about the publicity, but it's all about Emily. The obsession is kind of obvious."

It was my turn to blush. In an attempt to cover up for it, I shoved Regan playfully as I rose and stalked back to the window. "I'm the singer, dude. People are going to focus on me. Unfortunately," I added with a slight snarl.

"I really didn't mean to do that. Maybe it's just 'cause I'm a singer, too." Johnny shook off his embarrassment and changed the subject. "Listen, article aside, you guys could really build a reputation down here. There are so many more places to play than up in Carlisle. Would you consider moving down here?"

"Consider it?" Tom exclaimed, coming out of his usual postshow jitters and speaking for the first time that night. "We've been planning to leave Carlisle since we were born!" He joined me at the window. Together, we silently plotted how to make the city beneath us clamor at our feet.

Other than daylong excursions to Minneapolis and Chicago, I'd only been outside of Wisconsin twice. People from Carlisle didn't travel much. I think it was a combination of not having the money to do so and not wanting to deal with what might lie outside their little community. My father, who'd bucked tradition in so many other ways, clung to the unspoken no-travel policy. It was as if that three-year jaunt to Chicago with Louisa had been enough for him. The only two trips we took—in the spring and the fall of 1986, practically ten years after Louisa had left us—were to her parents' house in St. Louis.

I was a few months shy of ten on our first journey. Though it had been planned for weeks, I was still irritated when my father woke me up at five in the morning and forced me into a flowery dress, white tights, and Mary Janes I didn't even know I owned. "Where did all this stuff come from?" I yawned grumpily as he laid out what looked to me like doll clothes. I pulled the covers over my head.

He yanked them off. His wakeful cocoa eyes glistened. His face was closely shaven, curls still damp from the shower, and he smelled clean, like Ivory soap. "Molly picked it out when I told her we were going to see your grandparents. We both thought you should look presentable. Put these tights on."

"Tights are itchy!" I objected, mentally cursing Molly. I'd known my father couldn't have come up with such a costume alone. It suited him just fine that I dressed like a tomboy. I wrested my blankets back.

"Emily, don't make me dress you. Put the clothes on and let's go. It's going to be a long drive."

When I emerged into the kitchen, rubbing angrily at my sleep-crusted eyes, Dad was seated at the table, armed and ready for further torture. Standing me in front of him, he brushed my hair thoroughly, spraying detangler, which buried the coffee smell that filled the room beneath its baby-shampoo scent.

"That hurts!" I howled as he attacked my snarls.

"I'm sorry, honey. I just want you to look nice when you meet your grandparents." He slid his left hand down my long hair. I felt the cold metal of his wedding band against the nape of my neck as he pressed firmly at the roots of my hair.

"Why the hell do they want to see me now, anyway?"

"Emily, do not swear!" He raised his voice, sounding unusually formidable.

I whirled around, causing the comb to tear through the last tangle, and stared at him. Not only was he forcing me to look different, *he* looked different. His face, with the bow-shaped lips and dramatically arched cheekbones that we shared, was the same, but he wore a serious expression. He'd attempted to tame his wild, espresso-colored waves. He sported slacks instead of jeans, a button-down shirt instead of a flannel, and had even polished the dress shoes I'd only seen him wear to my school conferences. I narrowed my eyes suspiciously at him and repeated my question. "Why do they want to see us now?"

He tried to force his mouth into his usual easy grin and joked, "Maybe they want to meet their hundred-dollar-a-year investment," but it came out stiffly.

"They don't have to send me fifty bucks for every Christmas and birthday," I scowled. "They can't pay me to look this way, or you either." I tried to muss his slicked-back hair.

He caught my hand gently, holding it between his palms. His soft brown eyes met mine. "Emily, I want you to have a family. And since mine's never forgiven me for running off with your mother—"

"I have a family. It's you!" I snapped. I had a hard enough time defending that to my peers and teachers. He was supposed to be on my side.

"I know, baby." He ran one hand halfway down my hair, then cupped my chin. "Of course, you and I are family, but I want you to have more than just me."

"I don't want or need anybody but you!"

He smiled sadly. "Your mother's parents love you—"

"Then why haven't they ever come to visit? Why don't they call?" I yanked my hand away from his and folded my arms across my ugly, floral chest, the material much more slippery than the comfortable T-shirts I was used to.

My father sighed. "It's complicated, Emily. When your mother left, they—"

"What? They blamed her?"

He rubbed his forehead the way he always did when he got frustrated. "No. Emily, will you listen for a second?" he asked in a low, rumbling, serious voice, the only tone of authority I ever responded to. I nodded quietly. "Your grandparents, they felt guilty. They were the ones who came to Chicago and helped me pull myself together. They tried to convince me to move down to St. Louis, which was where they'd gone after your mother and I left Carlisle."

Even though this was something I hadn't heard before, I wouldn't let curiosity stop me from pouting. I squeezed my folded arms tighter. "Why didn't we move there?" It sounded a hell of a lot better than Carlisle to me.

"Because I knew if I was going to raise a child by myself, there was no way I could do it in a city. I'm not from the city, Emily. I went with your mother to Chicago because that's where she wanted to go, but it's not in me. This is where I'm from, this is what I know, and I didn't know nothing about raising a little girl, so I figured I better do it in a familiar place." The expression on his face was indecipherable, like he couldn't decide if he was going to smile or weep.

"Were Grandma and Grandpa Carson mad at you?"

"No, but Louisa's leaving probably hurt them more than anybody besides you."

"It didn't hurt me," I reminded him stubbornly.

Dad ran his hands over my hair, smoothing it once more. He gently uncrossed my stiff arms as he spoke. "Okay, then it hurt them most. Just like it would hurt me more than anything if you went away and I never heard from you again. But older people deal with their hurt differently than younger people. Their generation was taught not to let it show so much. I think they've avoided Carlisle and you and me because we would remind them of Louisa and make them sad. But like I told you when your grandpa called, your grandma's sick, and she's been asking to see you."

He stood up, grabbing his travel mug and keys with one hand and taking my hand with the other.

Six hours later, as we arrived in front of my grandparents' house, I understood why he'd made me dress up. Our house was big, but their house was huge. The lawn manicured and the outside perfectly painted, their house seemed a work of art, not friendly and worn-in like ours. The backyard was a sprawling garden that, I found out later, my grandmother still attempted to care for despite her weakened state from aggressive treatment for breast cancer. For the first time I could remember, I felt intimidated. I hung cautiously behind my father, stepping very carefully in shoes that pinched, unlike my ratty old sneakers.

My grandfather answered the door. He stood a few inches shorter than my lanky dad, but he was the kind of man whose presence took over the room. He'd fought in World War II, and even though he'd gone into medicine afterward and became, as people in Carlisle deemed him, "the friendliest doctor around," his body posture and face still bore that military trademark.

He shook Dad's hand, saying gruffly, "Michael," and then gazed down at me, uncertainty flashing in his blue eyes. "Emily," he said, and an awkward moment passed before he decided to bend down and hug me. I expected his embrace to be like his handshake, stiff and swift, but he lost some of his well-drilled composure, falling across me like a heavy, wet blanket. I patted his back lightly. I always shied away from anyone's touch, unless it was my father or a member of Regan's family.

My grandfather immediately regained his poise, calling, "Elizabeth, your granddaughter is here. Do you want me to send her in?"

Though we were there to see her, I only have a few clear memories of my grandmother, and the first was my initial sight of her. I wasn't sure what to expect. Everything seemed so formal, me being "sent in" like I was visiting royalty. And would her face be all sunken, like kids with leukemia on TV? Would she be bald? He was giving her adequate time to put her wig on by announcing us, right?

I became abnormally shy again, gripping my dad's hand and half hiding behind him as my grandfather led us down a narrow hallway with perfectly polished wood floors. Once we got to the living room, I inhaled the air carefully, certain it would have that sick, sterile hospital smell, but it was just stale. The curtains were drawn, making it so dark I couldn't tell the color of the walls. A large TV sat to our right as we entered. A soap opera was on, and I watched the big green bars on the screen get thinner as my grandmother reduced the volume.

I didn't want to glance to my left, where I knew she lay on the couch. I had a feeling that she would resemble my mental image of my mother, except shriveled and wasting away, a vision I knew would cause nightmares. Instead, I stared straight ahead at the fireplace. Ceramic figurines and framed photographs lined the mantel. I was dying to examine the pictures, certain that there'd be some of Louisa among them. Dad only had photos from the time he was with her. I wanted to see her as a child, desperate to know how alike we really looked. When I finally got to peruse them later, I was disappointed to find only pictures of me and of my grandparents through the years—their daughter conspicuously missing from all of them.

"Emily," I heard my grandmother say before I looked at her. Her tone convinced me to wager a glimpse in her direction. It wasn't the raspy voice of an invalid, more of a hopeful, almost youthful sigh. She sat propped up against numerous pillows on the couch, covered in a rose-colored blanket.

"Grandma," I responded, feeling my father nudge me gently toward her.

She laughed musically. "I still feel too young to be called that. Come here and give me a hug. I haven't seen you since you were a baby."

I trudged tentatively over to her. She didn't look like an old lady, really, and especially not a sick old lady. The light wrinkles, laugh lines around her mouth and eyes, were all that gave away her age; her sun-starved skin and slow movements all that shed light upon her illness. Her hair—which must have been a wig, but I could hardly tell—was as dark as mine, but streaked with a dignified gray and worn in a short bob. Her smile, which widened as I approached, was exactly as I had pictured Louisa's to be, and her glittering jade eyes mirrored both mine and my mother's.

I sat down carefully beside her, and she embraced me tightly. As we pulled apart, tears streaked her cheeks. "She looks so much like her mother, doesn't she, Robert?"

My dad smiled at this, but my grandfather's face faltered, and he looked away.

My grandfather acted incredibly stiff and formal around me that day. It seemed especially pronounced compared to the way my grandmother doted on me, asking me questions about everything. Not until that evening, when she finally felt well enough to show Dad and me her garden, did my grandfather finally crack a smile.

My grandparents' backyard was vast. At the bottom of their deck, lush green grass bled into aisle upon aisle of electrically bright flowers. A stone path wove between the sections of different plants. I followed my grandmother, who was wrapped in a large winter coat despite the mild spring temperature, toward her roses. There was grace in her step, though she walked rather slowly.

Unable to mimic her elegance, I tripped over one of the stepping-stones, landing on my knees. Dad held out his hand to help me up, but I batted it away, cheeks burning, and sprung to my feet. A streak of dirt ran up each of my shins, standing out horrifically against the whiteness of my tights. The bottom of my dress was grass-stained. Embarrassed and expecting my father to be mad at me for ruining my clothes, I lashed out before anyone could say anything. "I told you I hated these dumb shoes! They made me slip! I told you I hated this whole damn outfit!"

Dad looked as if he was about to laugh until I swore, to which he responded with a hissed "Emily!"

But my grandparents chuckled, my grandfather especially. "I was starting to wonder if she really was Louisa's daughter, prim as you had her looking, Michael. You brought her some clothes she likes, I hope." All traces of military firmness vanished, his face more resembling the kindly small-town doctor he once was.

I nodded frantically. Grandpa ruffled my hair the same way my father always did and said, "Go inside and change, kid. You'll have more fun out here with your grandma if you can get dirty."

After that, the trip was a blast, and I came back overjoyed, telling Regan and Marissa that I had a real family with grandparents just like theirs. But it all ended in the fall of 1986 when we took our second trip to St. Louis, this time for my grandmother's memorial service.

We brought her ashes to a tree in the Missouri Botanical Garden that my grandfather had had dedicated to her. It was in a beautiful spot that she would have loved, right outside the Japanese Garden. We had a private service, just me, my dad, and my grandpa on a foggy October morning. The leaves had begun to change, including the ones on my grandma's tree, which were bright gold and orange. That's what I noticed the most, the slices of color coming through the gray.

The pastor of my grandparents' church said a prayer when we first arrived, but after he left we stood in front of the tree for what felt like hours. Watching my grandfather cry was one of the worst experiences of my life. He still had to act so tough; he couldn't sob like he obviously needed to. Tears leaked out of his eyes, and he scrubbed at them with his handkerchief and loudly blew his nose.

Uncomfortable, I studied the bridge into the Japanese Garden. The fog prevented me from seeing to the other side, and I became convinced that my mother would stroll over it at any moment, like she did in my dream. She had to know her mother was gone and feel drawn to say good-bye.

My grandfather glared at the tree. "She was supposed to outlive me, you know. That's why you marry a woman ten years younger than you," he said, his offbeat sense of humor trickling through his sorrow. Then he murmured, "Elizabeth, Louisa . . . an old man's got nothing left." I noticed he stared at the bridge, too, as if he was begging both of them to walk over it.

Dad took a few steps toward him. "You've got us, Robert. You're welcome to stay . . ."

"Bah!" He cut his hand through the air, dramatically dismissing the idea. "What did you say when we offered that after you lost your wife?"

"Louisa's not dead!" I interrupted heatedly.

My grandfather's eyes got glassy, and he started to say something that was probably along the lines of "She's dead to me," but instead he stopped, gazing at me sympathetically. He knelt down in front of me, hugging me while he asked my father, "What got you through that, Michael? What got you through losing Louisa?"

Enveloped in my grandpa's arms, I couldn't see anything but the bulky, tan material of his coat and the white trunk of my grandmother's tree. I wanted to see my father's face because he sounded near tears when he said, "My little girl."

"My little girl," my grandfather repeated. "That's all that can get me through this, too. I need to find my little girl."

"She doesn't want to be found!" I insisted, recoiling from him.

My last memory of my grandfather was his solid, square jaw, and the determined expression on his face when he said, "That's too goddamn bad."

After that, he roamed the country, searching for Louisa, never stopping in Carlisle to visit. He sent updates describing the beauty of Boston Harbor, the Golden Gate Bridge, and the Cascades in Oregon, but returned to St. Louis my senior year, alone. I told myself that I would book a show down there as an excuse to see him. And living in Chicago, I'd be even closer.

We spent three days in Chicago following our first gig. Tom and Regan started apartment hunting that very night. They circled a bunch of two-bedrooms in the back of the newspaper that contained Johnny's review of us, but when they showed them to me, I said, "Did you see the rent? You've been dating three years, why can't you share a bedroom? You know we're going to have to rent rehearsal space, too. I don't know how—"

"Emily!" Regan interrupted. "The three of us would split the rent."

I furrowed my brow, momentarily confused, and when I got it, I wrinkled my nose. "Oh! I can't live with you guys. That would be way too weird."

Regan's hazel eyes lost their gleam and her voice fell flat. "But I always thought we'd live together when we left Carlisle."

Of course I'd always pictured it that way, too, but ever since that time I walked in on them . . . I knew they needed their space. Besides, I had a bunch of doubts about moving to Chicago. Part of me hoped that if I told Regan we couldn't live together, she'd say we couldn't move. But instead she debated with me about it for a while and then started circling one-bedrooms for her and Tom and studios for me.

They went to see a dozen places over the next two days and were ready to fork over their life savings to sublet from a guy in Logan Square who wanted to get out of his place on Labor Day weekend, but I kept holding out.

Much to Regan's delight, Saturday night Johnny took us to a dive bar he knew of where ID wasn't an issue. We claimed a booth by the window and I nursed my beer and stared through the smudged pane, watching cars circle the block, drivers seeking an elusive parking spot. Across the table from me, Regan's excitement level rose with every shot of tequila she took. After the third, she and Johnny double-teamed me. "Are we going to do this or not, Emily? Where are you going to live?" she demanded.

I shrugged.

Beside me, Johnny's floppy red spikes swayed as he preached at me like a minister on Sunday morning. "How many venues does Chicago have? How many labels is it home to? Carlisle has one and zero, respectively. They get that." He jerked his chin at Tom and Regan. "Why don't you? You know you aren't going to be content waiting tables in a farm town and playing gigs on the weekend. You want to be a rock star."

"No, Mr. Ambition." I glared into Johnny's pompous gray eyes. "*You* want to be a rock star. I want to be a musician."

"Oh, are you calling me a sellout again?" He playfully stuck out his lower lip and crossed his tattooed forearms over his chest.

We'd debated this often. Truthfully, we both wanted to be rock stars. The difference was that Johnny took a business-oriented approach to stardom, hustling to get meetings with the right people, whereas I chose to let the music bring them to me. On his second visit to Carlisle to see us, I told Johnny straight up that She Laughs could do that because we had a unique sound. Johnny had talent, but his band wasn't bringing anything new to the table. The world didn't need another guy who alternated between screaming at and whining to the chick who wronged him, even if the record execs kept shelling out money for those bands. Johnny had looked for a second like he wanted to punch me, but then he kissed me instead.

That was our way of flirting: he brought the M-80s, I brought the gasoline, and we both carried matches in our back pocket. We got a bigger charge out of bickering than holding hands.

But at the moment, I wasn't flirting. I was making a major life decision, and he didn't get it.

"Listen," I snarled, swallowing the rest of my warm beer. "Just because you've been up to Carlisle to see me a few times and we've spent the last couple nights crammed like sardines in that box you call an apartment doesn't mean you know me. Regan does, but apparently she's gotten so caught up in the excitement that she's forgotten." Regan's expression sobered and she started twisting her magenta hair nervously around her finger. "Her parents have each other. Tom's been trying to escape his mother since he left the womb . . ."

Tom's brown eyes darted to the scuffed wooden table; he hated being involved in arguments.

Johnny's palm fell across mine. "But all you and your dad have is each other."

Every muscle in my body stiffened except for my right hand, which bucked like an untamed horse to dislodge Johnny's. That had been exactly my point, but *he* wasn't allowed to say it. Pseudo rock-god boys didn't get access to my emotions even if they did have decent musical chops and could teach me a thing or two about the biz.

"No, that's not what I meant," I lied. "You guys just got me so worked up . . . Listen, the real issue is money. Even with everything I've saved from my crappy waitress job, I can't afford to live alone in Chicago. Case closed."

"Em!" Regan slammed her beer bottle on the table.

"So live with me," Johnny said calmly.

My head swiveled slowly, a look of abject horror plastered across my face as I met his nonchalant smirk. "I don't even like you!" I protested. That wasn't really true, but for some reason it came out ahead of my other reasons, like "I've only known you for a month," and "Your apartment is smaller than my bedroom."

Johnny didn't flinch; he'd gotten used to matching me gibe for gibe. "How come you keep making out with me, then?"

I tossed my hands in the air, flailing them in Regan's direction. "Tell him I have a bad habit of sleeping with boys in punk bands."

Clearly as thrown by Johnny's suggestion as I was, Regan's eyes jumped back and forth from me to him. She finally said, "You used to have a bad habit. I don't know what the hell this is. But I do know it's time to get out of Carlisle."

When I arrived home late Sunday night, I found my dad parked at the kitchen table, ready to greet me the moment I walked through the back door. Normally, he waited up for me while lounging on the couch, where he could comfortably read a book and listen to a record. It was like he knew something was up.

His eyes drilled into me as I propped my guitar case against the wall. "Gig go well?" he asked.

I pulled out the chair across from him. "Yeah, it did. In fact, it sold out." I didn't scoot the chair all the way into the table. I needed to distance myself from him in every way in order to give the speech I'd been rehearsing the entire three-hour drive home. I'd come up with some metaphor about the Chicago music scene being my version of college and . . . Crap. As soon as I glanced up and caught a glimpse of Dad's encouraging grin, I forgot the whole speech.

"Tell me about it."

I knew he meant the show, but instead I blurted out, "Regan and Tom got an apartment in Chicago. They want to move next weekend."

His smile crashed into a frown. His gleaming brown eyes got muddy and the lines around them became more defined as he blinked back tears. "I always knew you'd leave and probably end up there. But so soon?"

"Opportunities . . . ," I murmured. I battled with the need to comfort him. If I hugged him, I'd start crying and take it all back. When a tear of his own slipped free and his hand flew up to hide it, I couldn't fight it anymore. I jumped up from my seat and pulled him into my arms. I wept, too, harder than he did, so that soon he was smoothing my long hair, consoling me.

"I'll visit all the time," I blubbered. "And when I get a place, you'll visit me, too. I'll find one soon. I don't want to stay with Johnny long."

"Johnny?" My dad's arms straightened, pushing me back in order to stare me down. "That scruffy guy who slept on our couch the last couple of weekends?"

I sniffed and rubbed my damp eyes. "Yeah. The guy who got us the show. We stayed with him this weekend and—"

"No." He let go of my forearm so he could jab a finger in my face. "You are not moving to a strange city with a strange guy."

That's when the yelling commenced. The last time my father raised his voice at me was when I'd lit a cigarette in front of him for the first time at fifteen. This argument ended the same way. The purplish red tone in his cheeks faded as he suddenly realized: "If I say no, you're just gonna lie to me, aren't you?"

So when I left the following weekend, Dad and I were on good terms, but I couldn't look back at him when I drove off. I knew he stood at the top of the driveway in a gray T-shirt and jeans, his wild waves of hair teased by the humidity. He would be unsure of what to do with his hands, like he always was when nervous. The heat would cause moisture to form along his hairline and shirt collar. Watching me not looking back would bring it to his eyes. He wouldn't lift his anxious hands to wipe the tears away, though; he'd let the heat and the quickly climbing sun dry them. After ten minutes or so, he'd light a cigarette and go inside, yielding to the idea that just as he and my mother had when they were my age, I'd left with no intention of returning.

I showed up at Johnny's with two suitcases and four crates full of music. My guitars and amps had gone in Tom's van and would be delivered to the practice space we'd share with Johnny's band. After Johnny helped me lug in my stuff, I announced, "This is only temporary and it sure as hell doesn't make me your girlfriend."

"Whatever," he said, but he couldn't fight the smile that danced across his lips.

After two months, I was still living with Johnny and I'd finally stopped correcting people who called him my boyfriend, but I fought my fuck-and-run instincts every time I woke up and found him beside me. I hated feeling attached. I thought about the wounded expression my father tried to hide when the subject of Louisa came up, or how frail my grandfather looked the day of my grandmother's memorial service. I didn't like seeing the two men I admired most so weakened, and I was determined—no matter how fun the person or how good the sex—not to care for someone so much that that could happen to me. My relationship with Johnny was based entirely on music and making out. I kept him at arm's length emotionally. If he asked me how I felt about something and wasn't referring to a song or a movie or food, I gave him a hard look and changed the subject.

And if Johnny had been there on the cold November morning when my dad called to tell me my grandfather was dead, I probably would have found an excuse to storm out of the apartment and never come back.

Johnny'd left for his record-store job half an hour before the phone rang. My father didn't like that I was going to be alone after receiving such bad news. He only agreed to hang up if I promised to call Regan, which I did, numbly asking her to bring over two packs of cigarettes and "something strong," without any explanation. It was eleven in the morning, but she went along with my request, no questions asked.

I still lay in the fetal position next to the phone when Regan arrived. She knelt beside me, wispy strands of her newly dyed lavender hair falling into her worried eyes. She cupped a hand around my shoulder, and I sat up to give her a hug.

She'd inherited her mother's silent power of comfort, her fingers falling over my back like a gentle rain. She smelled like sleep, like I'd just wakened her, which I probably had. It reminded me of the times I'd woken in the middle of the night at her house after having the dream about my mother and gone down to the kitchen for a glass of water. Molly always appeared with a warm embrace that coaxed me into talking.

I'd been having that dream but with a different twist since we'd moved to Chicago. "I have this dream" were the first words I managed to say to Regan. Tears I hadn't felt myself crying worked their way into my mouth as I began to tell her about seeing my mother at the far end of a bridge. "I walk toward her and get so close that I can see her arms outstretched. So I start running, but when I get a few feet away from her, I can tell she doesn't even see me. She's staring in the distance, and then she whispers, 'Daddy.' Over my shoulder, I see my grandfather. They hug, and I scream both of their names, begging them to include me, but they never do."

Regan continued to stroke my back and tried to make sense of my outburst. "Your grandfather went searching for Louisa, right? Do you think he knows where she is?"

"Regan, my grandpa's dead. My dad just called me and I called you and he's dead. He died all alone and I'll never see him again." I choked out the words, sobbing.

Regan's chin trembled as if she was going to cry, too. She held me tighter, repeating, "I'm so sorry, Em."

Then Regan introduced a method of comfort that her mother never had. "Tequila?" she offered, extracting the bottle of glittering gold liquid from a paper bag.

I daubed my eyes and allowed a smile. "That's exactly what I need."

Soon we had a nice spread going: saltshaker, lime slices

laid out on a plate, ashtray, cigarettes, matches. All we could possibly need. I sat on the floor, Regan across from me, leaning against Johnny's bed. I was supposed to consider it my bed, too. He'd told me, "Everything here is yours now." Not that there was much, but the only things I considered mine were the CDs, records, clothes, books, and guitars I'd brought with me. The apartment itself was part mine since I paid rent on it, but that was it. I'd chosen to live with Johnny because it was convenient and I liked the view, but I wasn't about to get into sharing possession of stuff. I couldn't go from avoiding any possible romantic relationship to acting like we were married.

After we'd done several shots, Regan ventured, "Maybe your grandfather didn't die alone. Maybe Louisa was with him. Maybe that's what the dream meant."

"No, she wasn't." I snapped acidly. "Like I told him years ago, she didn't want to be found."

Regan bit her lip. "Emily, why have you always been so convinced of that?"

My face hardened with indignation. "*Convinced?* I'm not convinced, I *know.*"

"Hey, I didn't mean to make you angry." She put her hand on mine. "I just mean how do you know?"

I ripped my arm away from her. "Because . . ." Fortunately, I didn't have to go any further. The door opened, and Johnny sauntered in.

He tossed his hoodie on a chair and gestured at the half-empty tequila bottle. "This is what you do on your days off, huh? How did you get to be 'the best band in the Midwest' without even rehearsing?"

He was joking, but I wasn't in the mood for it. "Since when did you become our keeper?" I snarled, getting up and stalking past him toward the bathroom.

"What the hell, Emily?" He reached for me, looking genuinely confused, but I dodged his grasp.

In the bathroom I scrubbed my face, trying to pull myself together. I could hear Regan's murmured voice explaining the situation to him, but her question rang in my ears. I knew exactly why it made me so defensive. The idea that my mother was running away from everyone and everything was the thin shield that protected me from the thought that she was running away from me.

"Em," Johnny called softly through the bathroom door. "I'm really sorry about your grandfather."

I opened the door to face him. "I'll be fine," I said curtly, shrugging off his attempt to hug me and moving toward the closet to shove some clothes in a bag. "I'm going to the practice space now. I won't be back till late, and I'm leaving early tomorrow for St. Louis."

Some people decide to profess their love for you at the most inappropriate time. Johnny was exactly that type. At the last rest stop before St. Louis, I dug into my bag for my Loreena Campbell tape. Knowing I would listen to it at some point, Johnny had tucked the article he wrote about She Laughs and a note inside of it.

Emily— Regan was right. This was my love letter to you. I hope this doesn't scare you but rather provides the

*comfort you wouldn't let me give by coming with you: I
love you. And when you come home, I hope you won't be
so distant. Believe me, caring about someone terrifies me
just as much as it terrifies you. Yet another reason we're
perfect together. So please let me in. I promise not to
hurt you. Love, Johnny.*

I shredded the note, sprinkling it out the window as I
drove over the Mississippi, thinking he had me all wrong. I
wasn't terrified. I was irritated by his attempts to understand
me when there was nothing to understand. I slept with him,
we lived together, that was all I had to give. Why couldn't he
just leave it at that?

The next afternoon, my father and I scattered my grandfather's ashes at the base of my grandmother's tree. The day
was as damp and gray as it had been for her memorial service.

Some time passed before my father broke the silence.
"Ready to go, Em?"

"Yeah," I mumbled. As we started walking, I glanced over,
noticing he'd saved some of the ashes in a small silver box.
"What's that for?"

"Louisa."

"Louisa? How are you going to give them to her?" I snorted
as we reached the edge of the bridge that led into the Japanese Garden, koi rioting beneath it.

"Dunno." He shrugged and slid the box into the pocket
of his leather jacket, then pulled out two quarters. He nodded toward the fish-food machine. I held out my hands beneath the spout as he put his money in. "Figured maybe
she'd want it someday."

"You're never going to see her again," I said viciously, in order to disguise my hopefulness when I added, "unless Grandpa found her and told you where she is."

"He didn't. He told me that you were right, she didn't want to be found," my father stated simply, fighting hard to keep sorrow out of his voice and his dark eyes.

"Oh." I felt betrayed by my dream. For a second I'd thought maybe Regan was right and it meant something even though I'd been telling myself for years that believing Louisa would come back was as naive as believing in Santa Claus. Worse, because when you found out that Santa Claus didn't exist, you felt foolish, but being reminded that you'd never known your mother and never would? That made your heart ache, even if you'd tried to build concrete walls around it like I had.

"I know he was telling the truth, too. He said if he tracked her down, he wouldn't let her go without seeing her kid."

"Why?" I ambled toward the center of the bridge, hands full of brown pellets. "I wasn't the one who needed to see her so badly. He was."

My dad used the other quarter, food emptying into his big palm. "I think he needed to bring her back to us. So we could all be a family."

There was that word again. To everyone else, it was like a puzzle, and they needed Louisa as the connecting piece between generations. Not me, though. I'd grown up fine without her. Whole. At least that's what I told myself.

I stared down at the fish that clamored for the food I held. When my dad joined me in the center of the bridge, I told him, "Well, he didn't find her, and you won't either, so there's no point in saving those ashes."

After a moment of silence, he whispered, "Your mother loved both of us."

I glared at him. I was already aching from the loss of my grandfather; why was he trying to make it worse by making me long for *her*? I felt my defenses go up and my words came out harsher than I intended. "So what? You think that means she'll come back? Whatever gets you through the night."

Stoically, he shook a few pellets of food down to the waiting fish. "There's always the chance she'll come back."

"No, she won't. Love leaves." I opened my hands, releasing all the food in a rain down upon the koi.

Dad took my hands and pressed the rest of his fish food into them. I saw the tears glistening in his eyes and felt incredibly guilty. "I want you to know she loves you and I want you to love her."

"I can't."

"Why, Emily?" he pleaded.

I cast my hands up, showering fish food all over the wooden bridge. "You know why!" I roared, tears burning down my face. "Because you're here and she's not. And I hate myself for wanting her, because she clearly didn't want me!"

He threw his arms around me, kept me pinned even though I squirmed and pounded my fists against his chest. "Your mom wanted you as much as I did. She loved you so much that she thought she wasn't a good enough mother for you. That's part of the reason she left."

"What?" Adrenaline surged, giving me the strength to break out of his embrace. My boots crunched fish food pellets into dust as I backed away. "That's the good-mother thing to do? Leave? Didn't she realize that would screw me up worse?"

"You're not screwed up, Emily!"

"Yes, I am, Dad! I wouldn't even let Johnny console me about Grandpa. He wrote me this love note and I threw it in the Mississippi River. And you know why?" I continued to stagger backward over the wooden bridge as Dad lurched forward, reaching for me. "Not because I don't like him. He's smart. He's gorgeous. He loves music the way I do. He challenges me. He's exactly my type. But I think that one day he'll get up in the middle of the night and leave me like Louisa left you. And I won't let anyone hurt me like she hurt you."

"Like she hurt *us*."

His fingers fell around my wrist, but I recoiled sharply, screeching, "No!"

Then I stumbled over an uneven board and he jumped to catch me. His arms enveloped me and I beat my fists against his leather coat again, but weakly this time. Suddenly, I was crying too hard to fight him.

Dad just let me sob, my entire body quaking, but he didn't let me collapse. When I quieted, he said, "Emily, no one will ever break your heart like she did, I can promise you that much."

For the first time in my life, I didn't deny the words, didn't tell him that she had hurt him and her parents but not me. I took a longing glance at the foggy far end of the bridge and buried my face against his chest in an attempt to stop searching for her.

He smoothed my hair. "I can't tell you that love isn't scary, though. You can't control what other people are gonna do. Like I couldn't control it when my eighteen-year-old daughter told me she was moving to Chicago and planned to live with some guy she'd only known for a month."

I craned my neck to look up at him. "Dad, I'm sorry."

He shook his head, smiling. "No, like I told you, I always knew you'd leave Carlisle as soon as you could. And, yeah, I was concerned about Johnny, but it makes me feel better to know that he loves you. It should make you feel good, too."

I nodded and hugged him tighter. Listening to his heartbeat like I always had for comfort as a child, I felt my own heart crack open a little bit. Maybe I could let Johnny in, tell him about my missing mother, admit she was the driving force behind my music and who I'd grown to be. After all, my father was right. There was no way Johnny could hurt me worse than Louisa had.

SOURED

After a few months in Chicago, I didn't recognize my life. And it wasn't just because when I went outside, I found myself surrounded by towering skyscrapers instead of unending cornfields.

There was the boyfriend that I never knew I wanted. I grew closer to him every day. He dropped the *L* bomb again upon my return from St. Louis and I actually said it back. I kept saying it until I meant it. And when his lease went up for renewal in December, I summoned all my courage to sign my name alongside his on the new one. Admittedly, I had to do it with my eyes closed, my signature coming out even more illegible than usual.

Then there was the success with She Laughs, which was happening the way I'd always dreamt it would. At first it seemed like we'd simply traded our regular shows at an abandoned warehouse for shows at a bowling alley that doubled as a punk club. But when I gazed out at this new audience (from a much smaller and lower stage than I was used to), I remembered that this was a crowd who had a bunch of other options. There were plenty of other shows, parties, and clubs they could go to, but they chose to see us, and they kept coming back and bringing their friends. When you generated a buzz like that in Chicago, you attracted real attention pretty quickly.

I'll never forget the night Johnny busted into the women's bathroom at the Fireside. We'd just gotten offstage and Regan and I were trying to restore sweat-streaked makeup before the headlining band went on. Johnny shoved through the line of girls waiting for the one functioning stall and nearly crashed into the graffitied wall when he slipped on the slush that people had been tracking everywhere.

"You have to get out here now!" he demanded, grabbing us both by the wrist.

No one was particularly fazed by seeing a guy in the girls' bathroom, but a chick with blue liberty spikes snapped, "Chill, dude, we all want a good spot up front."

Johnny was not headed toward the stage, but he did take her advice and collected himself before marching us straight into the back bar, a separate room near the entrance where Regan and I were not technically allowed. He ignored our shouted questions, shushing us as we approached the bouncer, who let us pass when he said, "They're with me." When we reached a very flustered-looking Tom and a lanky guy with stars tattooed on his fingers and an unruly, ginger goatee, Johnny pushed us in front of him. "Emily and Regan, meet—"

"Frank from Capone Records," I whispered in awe.

Capone was the biggest punk label in Chicago. Frank

warmly shook my hand and said, "I was just telling Tom that I'd love to put out your first seven-inch."

It came out just in time for my dad's fortieth birthday in March. He marveled over that three-dollar record, studying the sleeve, weighing it in his palms.

"It's not gold, Dad," I told him, rolling my eyes, even though I'd done the same thing in private.

He grinned as he lowered it onto the turntable. "One day it might be. Especially since it's on the radio now."

"After midnight and only because we're going to do that show—"

"Shh." He dropped the needle onto the record and fell into a cross-legged position in front of the stereo, sitting in a trance—hands in his lap, eyes closed, head bobbing—the way I used to do when I was playing DJ. When the song ended, he immediately flipped it over to side B.

He did that about five times, repeating "God, you're so good" whenever there was silence.

Finally, my embarrassment boiled over and I put my hand firmly on his. "Please stop."

He smiled at me over his shoulder and relented, carefully returning the record to its sleeve. "No wonder the guy from Q101 wanted to book you as soon as he heard this." Then he reassured me for the thousandth time, "It's okay you're missing my birthday dinner for it. You've given me the best present I've ever gotten right here."

I shook my head guiltily. Johnny'd had drinks with someone who put together local music showcases for the big alt-rock radio station and gave him a test-pressing of the seven-inch. He called Johnny two days later. The headliner had dropped out of their March show and the station wanted She Laughs. Problem was it was scheduled for the night of my father's birthday and Molly already had this big dinner planned. I'd offered my dad and Regan's parents tickets to the show instead and Molly had been all for it, but my dad came up with a million excuses. Hotels in Chicago were too expensive. He couldn't ask for that time off work. Forty meant he was too old for that kind of thing.

"Chicago's filled with memories of Louisa for him," Molly sighed when she called to back up my father's decision that I play my concert while he kept to his original plans in Carlisle. "He really wants to visit you and see you play, but it's going to take a while."

I had to leave Carlisle by noon on Dad's birthday to get back to Chicago in time for sound check. And even though my dad seemed to be content with my decision, that night in the green room, just ten minutes before we were to go on, Regan plunked down beside me on the couch to express her displeasure for the millionth time.

"I still think we should've turned this down and you should've had dinner with your dad. You shouldn't listen to every single thing Johnny says. If they thought we were that good, they would have booked us for another show. I don't know why Johnny gets so involved with everything and I really don't get why you always defer to him. You used to trust your gut."

I glanced across the room where Johnny showed off our seven-inch to a music critic he'd invited. "Johnny helps because he wants to see us succeed," I told her, just as I'd repeatedly told myself. "I don't 'defer' to him, and I do my share of arguing with him. But I listen to his advice because he knows the business end of things better than us and he knows Chicago. I don't know about you, but I still feel really lost here sometimes. I mean, in Carlisle, I could have gotten to your house blindfolded, but here I keep taking the train in the wrong direction," I joked in an attempt to lighten the mood.

Regan arched an eyebrow. "So that's why you never come over."

"Regan . . ." I reached for her hand, but she moved it to tighten her blond-streaked pigtails. I let my fingers fall to the shabby couch and tugged some stuffing through a small hole in the fabric. "I see you at rehearsal every day," I argued defensively. "Though I am getting sick of you showing up late and stinking of tequila."

Regan ignored that remark, her hazel eyes fixed angrily on Johnny. "If Johnny's so good at playing the music biz, what the hell's going on with his band?"

"Regan, you know the bassist quit because he didn't like the new direction they were going in. A direction I suggested, by the way, that Johnny went with because he listens to me, too. He's auditioning people, but he has a record deal already, as you're well aware."

"Right." She fluttered her long eyelashes. "But for some reason, he's convinced you to hold out on signing with Capone Records, so we don't have one."

"Only because he thinks we can land a bigger deal," I insisted.

"And never mind my opinion that we should start out by working with an indie. Let's not learn from my sister, who's fighting to get out of her contract with DGC so that July

Lies can go back to No Wave Records, a company that actually promoted and understood them. Let's just sign to a major label as the token punk band and get totally shafted—"

"Guys!" Apparently, Tom had noticed our bickering.

When we both whipped our heads around and spat "What?" he cowered slightly.

"We have to go on in ten minutes," he meekly reminded us.

Regan pushed herself off the couch. "Fine, guess I better go pee."

"AKA do a shot."

Regan flipped me the bird. I shook it off. I had to. We needed to go onstage. And we did such a good job that all was forgotten afterward. The energy of the music had us hugging again like it did after every show.

So I chalked the incident up to Regan feeling the same way I had when she'd first fallen for Tom: a little bit of jealousy and a strong aversion to change. And since there was so much change going on for both of us, who could blame her. Sure, she continued to show up late and a little toasted to rehearsal and it pissed me off, but as long as she kept playing well, I couldn't really complain.

But Johnny and his band were usually leaving the practice space when Tom and I were arriving, and by May, he'd waited around with us for Regan often enough to form his own opinion. That's when I learned the hard way about mixing business and pleasure. It ruined perfectly good sex.

"Emily . . . Jesus . . . ," Johnny sighed as he rolled off of me. He kissed my cheek and put his head down next to mine. I could feel both of our bodies emanating warmth, my skin still pulsating in every place he'd touched.

"I love you," I told him. I'd been using those words for six months, and they finally felt natural.

My eyelids slipped down and I gazed at him through the blur of my lashes. Johnny and I made each other melt. Like me, Johnny looked hard as nails when he was onstage with his band or anywhere in the outside world. He turned the sneer into an art form. Combined with his slate-gray eyes that went dark as a threatening sky when he was angry, his sneer actually looked menacing, not ludicrous like it did on the majority of the punk boys who affected it. However, when we were in bed together, all of that was gone. Johnny's sharp cheekbones were offset by soft, almost girlish lips that fluttered into a little smile. His eyes glowed a silvery light. Everything about him became tender. And it made me go soft like that, too.

But that morning, Johnny's voice broke into my romantic thoughts: "Emily, there's something you really need to think about."

"Hmmm?" I responded, still spacey.

"I don't know the nice way to put this, so I'll just say it. You need to find a new drummer for your band."

My body tensed and my head snapped to the side to face him. His lips clenched in a straight line and his gaze emptied of any mushy affection. He'd gone into full-on business mode.

"What the hell are you talking about?" I demanded. "Regan and I *are* the band. There is no band without Regan."

"I know you feel that way and I didn't want to say anything, but I don't think Regan's committed to the band anymore. All she wants to do is get drunk." He kept his voice level, acting sympathetic while he did this little head-nodding thing in an attempt to subliminally convince me he was right.

I couldn't believe he'd brought this up not even five min-utes after sex. My brain spun. "We're a punk band, Johnny! Getting drunk is synonymous with that." And what I didn't tell him was that I couldn't lecture anyone about using sub-stances to cope with the fruits of success. When I'd whined about the crazy hours I had to keep between work and the band, one of the girls I waitressed with introduced me to her late-night study aid: her roommate's ADD medication. I only used it occasionally because I had no interest in falling victim to the rock 'n' roll junkie cliché. But really, it seemed like slightly stronger NoDoz, perfect for the days after late gigs when coffee wasn't going to get me through a morning shift, an afternoon rehearsal, and time with Johnny.

He propped himself up on his elbow, looking down on me. "Emily, I've told you since the day I met you that you are so much more than just a punk band."

Yeah, he did keep telling me that. Sometimes as a genu-ine compliment and sometimes as ammunition during our occasional drunken spats over She Laughs' direction. He'd lay out all these plans and then fly off the handle when I joked about him being domineering. But those fights were supposed to take place at night before the angry makeup sex, not first thing in the morning during postcoital calm.

I sat up furiously, the sheet slipping from my shoulders, exposing them to the chilly spring breeze that blew through the window next to our bed. "Are you my manager or my boyfriend? You can't be both, and I don't even want a goddamn manager."

I wrenched the sheet off the bed, wrapping it around myself before I stormed across our tiny one-room apartment to the bathroom.

"Emily, come here," Johnny pleaded. "I'm just trying to look out for you because I love you."

I glowered back at him. "If you loved me, you would know that Regan is like my sister and no one could ever make me abandon or betray her. Especially not a guy." My last words dripped with venom. I slammed and locked the bathroom door.

Seething, I paced back and forth in the small space between the door and the shower. The oversize T-shirt that I wore as a nightgown was draped over the towel rack, so I dropped the sheet and put that on. I needed to relax. My fingers started to itch, and my arm muscles tingled. The only thing that would soothe me was playing guitar. Fortunately, since the bathroom doubled as my sanctuary, the only place I could go for privacy in our apartment (and being an only child, I thrived on privacy in ways I wasn't aware of until I moved in with Johnny and had none), I kept an old, acoustic guitar in the corner of the room, next to the toilet. I sat down on the side of the bathtub with it. After a few minutes, I'd totally forgotten about Johnny, finally perfecting a riff I'd been struggling with.

"*In the winter, no one knows. In the winter, she don't go,*" I sang, my voice a scratchy murmur. Then it arced into an edgy wail: "*In his failure, I am sold. In his room, she grows old."* I played the song through twice and sighed with accomplishment.

"That's a great riff," Johnny commented through the door.

My aggravation returned the moment I was reminded of his existence. I got up and banged on the door. "Go away!" He didn't respond. After a moment of silence, I added spitefully, "It may be a good riff, but it won't be a song without Regan. She's one of the best damn drummers out there."

I waited for Johnny to argue, but he surprised me. "You're right," he said softly. "And I'm really sorry about what I said. It was out of line."

I unlocked the door, opened it just a crack, and peered out suspiciously. Johnny sat directly across from the bathroom, his back against the short wall that separated our kitchen from the rest of the apartment. He took a drag from his cigarette and looked up at me, his eyes as placid as they had been in bed before he dropped his bombshell. "I am really sorry, Emily. I know Regan is like your sister."

I nodded and stepped out of the bathroom.

He held the cigarette pack out to me, a peace offering. I accepted, easing onto the floor beside him. I decided I would just overlook everything that happened between the sex and the cigarette. I put my head on his shoulder, ignoring my increasingly nagging doubts about his intentions when it came to my career. But I shouldn't have ignored my growing concern about Regan.

Two weeks later, she failed to show up to rehearsal. Tom and I waited for an hour at the practice space. Normally, we would have let it go, but we had a show to play that night with Johnny's band and we needed our drummer.

"You stay here and wait in case she's on her way. I'll go by your place and check if she's still there," I instructed Tom, but he obviously had the same gut feeling I did.

"I'm coming with you. She's not on her way. This has been getting worse and worse. Something's wrong this time." Tom's brown eyes flickered with concern, making him look eerily like my father.

"I really wish you wouldn't have said that."

Even though I felt it, too, hearing his words worsened my worry. Despite the heat of the windowless room, I shivered. Tom put his arm around my shoulders, steadying me as he led me to his van. But as soon as I was in the passenger's seat, I was myself again. I reached over and pounded on the horn when slow cars pulled out in front of us.

He pushed my arm away. "Emily, please calm down! We'll be there as fast as we can. She's probably just passed out."

After Tom unlocked the security door to his building, I flew up the stairs, taking two at a time. I banged frantically at the apartment door with both fists. "Regan, wake up! Let me in!"

Tom was seconds behind me, so I moved aside to let him unlock the door. We both expected to find Regan passed out on the couch, bottle of tequila in hand, snoring away to *Seinfeld* reruns. The front door opened right into the living room. *Seinfeld* blared from the TV and a bottle sat on the coffee table, but it was obviously yesterday's, converted that afternoon into an ashtray. The couch was empty.

Tom hurried to the bedroom while I went to the bathroom door. I rattled the knob and found it locked. "Tom, she's in here!" I called before hammering on the door. "Regan, let me in!" I was silent for a moment, but after hearing nothing except Tom's heavy footfalls in the other room and canned laughter from the TV, I delivered a swift kick to the door with my steel-toed boots. Because of my height, I only succeeded in splintering the bottom. Tom got it open with one more determined kick, revealing Regan passed out next to the toilet, curled up like she'd tried to sleep there. A fifth of tequila lay tipped over on the floor beneath the sink, a thin, golden layer of liquor barely visible along the side of the bottle. We would have expected this scene—if it hadn't been for the blood.

Regan wore the clothes she usually slept in: Tom's faded Pixies T-shirt and plaid boxer shorts. The boxers were soaked with blood, her thighs sticky and red. I dropped to my knees and crawled over to her.

"Jesus Christ! What happened to her?" Tom screamed.

I pressed my hand against her neck, which was thankfully still warm, and worked my fingers up toward her chin, feeling for her pulse. I didn't breathe until I found it. I couldn't tell if it was fainter than it was supposed to be, and in my muddled panic, I couldn't figure out how to maneuver my hands so that I could feel her pulse and my own. I wanted to listen to her breathing, but Tom was still yelling. "Is she dead? Did she try to kill herself? Christ!"

His face went from ashen to scarlet as he screamed, and back to gray again as he tried to throw himself on Regan. Even though he had eight inches and over fifty pounds on me, I managed to catch him.

"Tom, cool it!" I held him above me like we were frozen in a wrestling match. "She's not dead. She's just . . ." I glanced from the blood to him, knowing I had to make sense of it before he totally flipped and made things worse. Alcohol. Blood coming from between her legs. Tom. It clicked. "I think she may have had a miscarriage or something. She drank too much and . . ." I paused because Tom had gone ghostly white.

"She never said anything about being . . ."

"Tom, there's no time for this, okay? She's losing blood. She's probably got alcohol poisoning. She's unconscious. We need to call 911. Can you call 911?" I tried to keep my words slow and even. He didn't say anything, his eyes filling with tears. "Okay," I said, sliding out from beneath him, allowing him to lie down on the floor beside Regan. "I'm going to call. Don't move her. Just hold her hand." I lifted his heavy palm and placed it on Regan's arm before dashing into the living room in search of the phone.

I found it on the couch, and as I rapidly fired off the address to the operator, I noticed prescriptions on the table next to the saltshaker and mangled slices of lime. Antibiotics and painkillers, both prescribed for Regan. I rushed back into the bathroom.

Tom's face was pressed against the back of Regan's neck, buried in her blond-streaked black hair. "I love you so much. Why didn't you tell me what was wrong?"

I felt like an intruder as I knelt over them. "Tom, the ambulance is on the way," I whispered. His head rolled back, strands of his chin-length hair stuck to his damp cheeks.

"She's been so far away lately." His voice shook. "What if she doesn't wake up?"

I extended my arms and he sat up to hug me. "She's going to wake up," I said, trying to sound sure of it. I numbed myself to keep him calm while worry churned in my stomach. I wanted to know what the prescriptions were for, if it had something to do with what happened to Regan, if she had some weird illness I wasn't aware of. But instead of asking Tom these questions, I stroked his back and reminded him, "I've known Regan all my life. She's the toughest girl in the world. She's going to be fine."

While sitting in the waiting room at St. Joseph's Hospital, I realized I'd been playing grown-up. The job, the apartment, the boyfriend, the band, and all the wheeling and dealing that went along with it. It had been like the punk-rock version of the board game Life. Spin the wheel, move along toward that goal of happily ever after, the million-dollar record contract, or whatever the hell I was supposed to be working for.

Then suddenly it wasn't a game anymore. Regan had almost died and she'd only turned nineteen a few months ago. I wasn't even nineteen yet, but there I was, in charge. I had to handle everything because when we got to the emergency room, Tom couldn't even speak. I had to sit him down in a chair and shove a *People* magazine into his hands, hoping he'd read about the never-ending O. J. Simpson trial to take his mind off of it. I had to call Regan's parents and get screamed at by Molly that we were out of control. I had to tell the admitting nurse everything that I knew. And when I handed over the prescriptions, I had to take in the information that Regan hadn't had a miscarriage, she'd had an abortion and medicated her pain in a way that could have killed her by thinning her blood. And I kept this information to myself because I would not be the one to break Tom's and Molly's hearts. Mine was broken enough, because before that, Regan had always told me everything.

When she woke up, Tom let me go in first, mumbling something about seeing his grandfather hooked up to machines before he died, and needing to know how she looked before he could face her. I told him I understood, left him with the unopened magazine on his lap, and followed the gray-haired nurse down a long, white hallway, which twisted and turned into other long hallways. I tried not to notice the sterile, antiseptic scent or the smells of blood, urine, vomit, and general sickness that lurked underneath. I didn't want to imagine Regan in the context of all this. Finally, the nurse stopped outside a room and told me Regan was in the far bed, by the window.

I tried not to look at the other patient as I passed her bed, but I couldn't help it. Fortunately, the sight of the girl was comforting. She wasn't hooked up to any beeping, buzzing equipment; she simply slept, perfectly normal except for the hospital gown visible above the sheets. I took a deep breath, hoping Regan would appear the same way.

As soon as I passed the curtain that separated the two beds, my eyes fell on Regan. She didn't look quite as good as her roommate, but not as bad as I feared. An IV dripped into her left arm. The hospital made her seem smaller than she was, her body enveloped in the whiteness of the bed. Her face was pale, and deep circles surrounded her eyes, which she struggled to hold open.

"Hey," she croaked.

I couldn't figure out how to speak to her at first. I wanted to yell at her for scaring me and Tom, but at the same time I wanted to crawl into the bed and just hold her. Instead, I reverted to the sarcasm that I always used in order to keep from bawling. "Regan, we're not famous enough yet for you to pull this rock-star-drinking-yourself-to-death crap," I joked as I sat down at her bedside.

She smiled weakly and squeezed her eyes shut. "I would laugh, but I think my brain would explode, my head hurts so bad." She glanced away from me, back toward the curtain. "Is Tom here, too?"

"Yeah, he is. We both . . . we both found you."

"I'm really sorry." Regan cried soundlessly, tears rolling out of her bloodshot eyes and down her swollen cheeks. She lifted her right hand to rub them away, but they kept coming. Her nose started to drip, too. I reached behind me for the tissue box on her bedside table and handed her one.

"Can you . . . ? What the hell happened, Regan?"

She swabbed her face with the tissue, patting her eyes dry before she spoke and summoning a stony expression. "I had an abortion."

"I know. They told me that. But I mean, why didn't you tell me? So I could have been there?" My face puckered, lips trembling at the thought of her leaving me out.

The strength she'd drawn on when she told me about the abortion failed. Tears streamed down raw, red skin, and her voice cracked. "Because I haven't really been able to talk to you since we moved here."

I felt like I'd been sucker-punched, and I'm sure I looked it. I was speechless; my mouth opened and closed several times, fishlike. I wanted to deny that our friendship had fallen by the wayside, but I couldn't anymore.

Regan reached for me and I let my hand fall like a stone onto the bed, next to hers. She wrapped her fingers around mine and squeezed them so hard, I would have cried out if my vocal cords functioned. "I'm not saying it's your fault. I shut down. I got freaked out, and I didn't share it with you, or Tom, or anyone but Jose Cuervo." She attempted a halfhearted smile. "I mean, it's stupid. We got our wish, right? We got out of Carlisle, and the band's really taking off. But it scared me to death. This city's so goddamn huge, sometimes I feel like I'm just one of the hicks we made fun of at home. And I don't feel like I deserve the success that's been happening so fast. I'm not good enough. I don't measure up to you."

"You're just as good as me," I finally managed, squeezing her hand back. I felt like an asshole. I'd told Johnny how great she was, but when had I last told her?

Regan rolled her eyes. "Your boyfriend doesn't think so. You're the one that's good. You *are* the band." Anger seemed to be building within her, but then the tears were back again. "So I'm scared to move to the next level with the band, but I'm also scared to lose the band, and, more important, to lose you. I feel terrible, like I'm trying to cheat you out of your happiness. Rock 'n' roll is your dream. And you put up with me when I fell for Tom; I should do the same for you. But Johnny's different. He's . . ."

She was being so diplomatic. And I didn't deserve it.

"He's Mr. Ambition," I whispered, adding bitterly, "and just call me Mrs. Ambition because I must be pretty swept up in it if you thought I would ever, *ever* play music without you."

Daubing her eyes with a Kleenex wetter than her face, Regan implored, "Emily, don't be so hard on yourself."

"No, Regan, be harder on me! Tell me I'm a bitch because I am. I saw you turning into a drunk, and did I bother to cancel rehearsal once and say 'Let's get some coffee and talk about what's going on with you'? No, I didn't. All I thought about was the next gig, or going home and getting laid. I'm such a shitty friend." I sobbed so hard, I was surprised Regan deciphered my last sentence, but somehow she did. She tugged on my hand, drawing me into the bed beside her.

"You're not. You're no worse than me. After all these years, I didn't know how to tell you I was scared. We've never been the best at addressing our feelings. We're both more . . ." She paused, biting her lip to find the right words. "Action-oriented."

She was right. Since childhood, the two of us had been a blur of activity. We weren't the kind of girls who cried at sappy movies together. We discussed our love lives like jocks in a locker room, never stating how we actually felt about boys. Sure, one of us broke down sometimes, got upset, got hurt, got pissed, and the other one was supportive, but not in a "let's talk" way. We'd just go to a show or write a song or get wasted together. As much as we shared, me telling Regan that her drinking had started to scare me or her telling me that our band's success intimidated her was not something either of us could comfortably do. We let feelings become static in the background, slowly building like the feedback from an old amp that's ruining the clean tone you want for the song. And the amp finally shorted out.

I wrapped my arms carefully around Regan, mumbling into her tangled hair, "I'm so sorry."

She slowly turned onto her side to face me, pressing her forehead against mine. "I'm so sorry, too." We kept going back and forth apologizing until her face went stony again, except for her lower lip, which quivered violently when she said, "I did the right thing, right, Em? I couldn't have been a mother. Not now. No matter how much I love Tom. Someday . . ."

Petting her hair, smoothing it against her tearstained cheek, I soothed, "You did the right thing."

"The way I was drinking . . . I wasn't healthy. And if I reacted that way because of my fears about being a good drummer, imagine how far I would have run when I started worrying about being a good mom."

My hand stopped midpet; I visibly bristled at the combination of those words: "run" and "mom."

"Talk to me about it, Emily," Regan urged, trying to summon me back to our safe place, but I'd snapped out of it.

I sat up abruptly and glowered at her. "About what?"

"About your mom. About feeling abandoned."

She'd turned into a shrink in that hospital bed. I got up, gingerly so as not to hurt her, but as quickly as I could. "I don't feel abandoned."

Her arms remained outstretched, but I stayed out of her reach. "Emily, let's be honest with each other. We're not little kids anymore. We can stop playing tough. I mean, hell, look at me. Don't you think it's time to stop playing tough?"

I stared at the IV dripping into her vein, her sallow skin, and weakened frame. "It's not about being tough, and Louisa has nothing to do with this. I know I've done some rotten things since we moved here. Becoming obsessed with the band, with Johnny, letting him change me 'cause it's nice to have the rock god worshipping me for once. We can talk about those things, and I'll apologize for the rest of the night, but . . ."

Regan's raised voice was ragged, her throat thick with phlegm. "Emily, please sit down and listen to me. I feel so bad for not telling you this. I need to tell you."

She was my best friend, and she was in the hospital, so I did what she wanted and returned to my chair, but even though she was crying again, I didn't take her hand. I felt betrayed by her mention of Louisa at an already emotional time.

"I'm shocked I didn't get knocked up sooner. Like my mom," she sniffled. "I'm a slut. Was a slut before Tom. But do you know why I slept around?"

"Because you were bored?" That had been my personal logic.

"Partly. But partly because it seemed expected. My mom got pregnant young, so obviously she was a slut. And everyone said my sister slept around, but she probably wouldn't have even gone through that phase if it weren't for Jeremy Pearson spreading rumors about her because she refused to sleep with him."

"Yeah . . . ," I said slowly, trying to figure out where she was going with this. We'd discussed these things before. Regan was a keen eavesdropper; we learned everything we knew about boys and sex from conversations Marissa thought were secret. But I figured I had an opportunity to keep Regan from talking about Louisa, so I took it. "I hate Carlisle. Everyone's so high-and-mighty about what a perfect little town it is, talking shit about our families, when homegrown, local boys like Jeremy Pearson—"

Regan cut me off with a murmur. Staring down at the white sheet that covered her, she added, "And Eric Lisbon."

I blinked hard. "Eric . . . Louisa's . . . Why do you keep bringing this back to Louisa?"

Regan's orange-ringed irises wouldn't focus on me. She stared at the thick curtains, behind which night had fallen quickly. She paused and I hoped her voice would give out, because I knew she was about to tell me something about Louisa that I didn't want to hear. "Because Eric's name came up once."

She pushed herself up on her elbows and forced her eyes to meet mine. "Remember how my mom and Marissa used to have those fights all the time because Marissa was doing what you and I started doing at River's Edge a couple years later? She was fifteen, I was eleven, and I used to hang out in our bathroom so I could hear my mom reaming her in her bedroom. Most of the time I had no idea what they were talking about. The time Eric came up was no exception, but even when I understood it, I didn't know how to tell you." Regan pressed her fingers to her temples and grimaced. "You see, my mom finally got through to Marissa when she mentioned your mom. She told Marissa not to get in over her head like Louisa had with Eric Lisbon. I don't have all the facts—my mom was crying so hard I could barely understand her—but I think the reason Louisa left is because Eric Lisbon raped her when she was younger and she never got over it." Regan's eyelashes dipped down, her face tense with guilt.

I don't know what made me say it or even if I believed it, but I blurted out, "That isn't true. You must have misheard. I mean, Louisa, she was tough, like us. If that happened to her, she would have survived it. Like you're going to get through what happened today. My dad would have gotten her through it, like Tom's gonna get you through this. And I am, too. Your mom and my dad, they would have taken care of her, like me and Tom'll take care of you."

Regan looked doubtful, and clearly had more to say, but then Tom appeared, having finally gathered his strength to face her. He crawled into bed beside her, enveloping her completely in his arms. His hair, half blond and half brown, fell into his face. He'd been letting the bleach grow out. It really changed the way he looked. He wasn't just this kid who Regan had a crush on anymore. She needed him and he'd been there for her in ways that I hadn't.

"I should give you your privacy," I muttered. "Go tell Johnny what happened and that we're taking some time off."

Regan looked up at me gratefully, but Tom's eyes filled with concern. "Em, why don't you wait for me? I'll talk to him with you."

"Pffft." I brushed him off. "I can handle Johnny."

Skepticism took center stage on Tom's face. "He's probably going to be pretty pissed we missed tonight's show and didn't even call."

"He'll understand," I insisted. "And," I added with mild annoyance, "I can take care of myself." The balance hadn't shifted that much. Tom might have become better at taking care of Regan than I was—something I would have to work on—but there was nothing I couldn't deal with. *Just like Louisa,* I reassured myself, mentally dismissing what Regan told me as I hugged her and Tom good-bye.

However, when I finally left the hospital at close to midnight, I found myself sneaking into my own apartment in a way I'd never even snuck into my father's house, because I knew that Johnny was definitely going to be mad, and I wasn't actually sure if I could handle it.

Relieved to find the apartment dark, I crept in hastily, shutting the door to prevent the hall light from leaking in and waking Johnny if he was sleeping. I closed myself into total darkness. Four steps in, Johnny growled "Emily!" from somewhere in the black abyss in front of me.

Startled, I jumped, but quickly regaining composure, I scanned the room for the source of the voice. In the left corner, approximately where our bed was, I spotted the red glow of his cigarette. I waited for him to turn on the light, but he didn't. "Regan's in the hospital, Johnny," I informed him without any hint of apology in my voice.

"So that's your excuse for not showing up, not even calling me to let me know that you weren't intending to play the biggest show of your career. The one I set up for you, for us. I whored myself to get major-label A&R people to come . . ."

I wished he could see me rolling my eyes at that one. He needed to stop acting like he didn't want to be a well-connected rock star. And I had to stop allowing his ambition to take over my life.

"I never asked you to do that," I said. "In fact, you never asked *me* if that was what I wanted. But it's really beside the point, okay? I watched my best friend almost bleed to death tonight. I just want to sleep—"

"Ha!" Johnny scoffed. "What did Regan do this time? Get drunk and try to kill herself? I told you that she was dragging you down with all her crap. She's a lush! What did you expect?"

Seething, I kicked the bathroom door, pretending the cracking wood was Johnny's skull. "Regan's a lush? Jesus Christ, look who's talking!" I ranted. "I'm sure you've got your bottle of whiskey right next to you. At least drinking doesn't make Regan an *asshole*. Oh, wait . . . I forgot! The asshole-drunk thing is part of your whole punk-rock act, isn't it, *John*?" I paused briefly. If I'd quit then, I probably could have left quietly, but I'd never been good at quitting while I was ahead.

I stalked toward the glow of his cigarette, punting everything in my path for emphasis. "You are so fake. You bring me down here so we can be this perfect little punk-rock couple, another part of your image. Every day you remind me how good I am, how I'm gonna be such a big rock star, and you just want to help me. Bullshit! You're just using me to get ahead. You created this buzz for my band and set up shows, which you so graciously let me headline because you think that if some big label tries to sign me, I'll say, 'Oh, you have to sign my boyfriend's band, too,' because I *owe* you for rescuing me from Carlisle and helping me make a name in the big city. I could have done it myself, *John Thompson*," I jeered, emphasizing his given name because I knew how much it pissed him off. Since I'd dubbed him Johnny Threat, he'd all but legally changed his name to that moniker. I felt him sneering at me through the darkness, which enraged me further, so I continued, "Your band sucks and you know it. Especially compared to mine—"

I stopped when I heard his whiskey bottle shatter against the wall behind me, sending tiny shards of glass into the back of my arm and splattering me with what liquor was left in the bottle. "You asshole! You want to fight me, go ahead, but fight me fair," I screeched, turning around and groping for the light switch.

When I finally hit it, the blast of brightness from overhead momentarily blinded me. "Oh, I wouldn't fight a girl," Johnny mocked from behind me. The tone of his voice was low and even. He was not sloppy, goofy, make-you-laugh drunk. He was dark and bitter. "Besides, I know a way to hurt you worse."

"What are you talking about?" I whirled around to face him. He didn't have to answer. He sat on our bed, still fully clothed in torn blue jeans and a sweaty black T-shirt that clung to his thin frame and muscled arms. He'd backed all the way into the corner, leaning against the wall with my guitar in his lap. The one my father had given me. "Where did you get that?" I demanded.

"From the rehearsal space. After you didn't show up at the venue when you said you would, I went looking for you guys. I noticed that you forgot this." He drummed his fingers on the perfect blue body.

I met his bloodshot eyes, such a stormy gray they were almost onyx. Red blotches covered his face, reflecting the mixture of wrath and alcohol. I stomped toward him. "Give that back!"

"Why? You obviously don't care about your music as much as I thought you did. So you must not care about this." He hissed the last sentence like a snake, flecks of spit dripping from the corner of his sneer.

I decided to try the calm approach because he was drunk, pissed, and he had my guitar—a very bad combination. "Johnny, you can think whatever you want about me. I understand why you're angry, just give me my guitar."

"Why? You don't deserve it. You've had everything handed to you, everything I've wanted, and you need to learn how to appreesshhiate it," he slurred.

"Johnny, I do appreciate it, but Regan was—"

"Oh, shut up, Emily!" He withdrew the pocketknife he always carried and slashed along the neck of my guitar, slicing all the strings.

The little twang they made as they snapped sounded like a child crying out. I was done talking. I leapt at Johnny, swinging for his jaw. My fist connected with the cigarette that dangled from the corner of his mouth, burning my knuckles slightly but his upper lip far worse.

He screamed, flinging his hands up to his face. "You bitch! I'll kill you!"

I snatched the guitar from his lap and ran with it into the bathroom, where I promptly locked the door. Being sober, my reflexes were good, but if I'd been thinking clearly, I would have run out the front door. Instead, I sat down on the toilet and examined the neck of the guitar to see if he'd scratched the wood when he cut the strings. Then I noticed the swollen blister across my middle and ring fingers, and as soon as I caught sight of that, my hand started to throb. Survival instincts kicking in, I prepared to dash for the front door. But Johnny was now on the other side.

"Let me in!" he thundered.

I backed away from the door as he pounded on it.

"Emily, don't think I can't break this door down!" He heaved his body against it and it shuddered. My first instinct was to protect the guitar, knowing that I was far less breakable than it was. I threw a towel down in the bathtub and laid the guitar on top of it.

Johnny changed his approach, kicking the door. I heard the wood splinter. I closed the shower curtain, hoping that if he didn't see the guitar, he would forget about it. I pivoted to face the sink, scanning it for anything I could use as a weapon.

The door broke open. Johnny lost his balance and fell forward into me, a blur of limbs flushed an angry crimson.

"Get off me!" I shoved him backward, sending him stumbling into the wall, tripping over the laces of his sneakers and the toilet. Johnny was several inches taller than I was, but he probably only weighed about thirty pounds more, and as drunk as he was, I doubted his ability to get the upper hand after he fell. I shouldn't have.

I ran immediately for the front door, but as soon as I unbolted it, he pinned me against it with his body, his chest pressed against my back, his legs straddling mine. He shouted, "Don't leave me, Emily," words contorting midsentence so the last part of it sounded like a sob. His drunkenness had taken him from furious at me to afraid of losing me. I was beyond confused. I had no idea what the fight was about anymore, but I still needed to escape. I elbowed him in the ribs and he groaned, but he didn't double over as I hoped he would.

"Get the fuck off of me!" I shrieked, and luckily that scream was punctuated by a police siren roaring down the street. My eyes widened with the hope that one of our yuppie neighbors had actually decided to call the police. I let out a bloodcurdling yelp. "Get off—"

Johnny clamped his left hand over my mouth, suddenly as aware of our surroundings as I was. "Shut up!" he rasped. "Someone's going to call the cops." He tried to wrench me away from the door, bending my neck backward with all the pressure he had on my mouth. I bit into the flesh of his palm.

He recoiled enough for me to shout, "I want someone to call—" Then his hand went back over my mouth, and I felt a prick in my right side. I almost bit him again, but I realized that somehow, drunk as he was, he'd managed to keep ahold of his goddamn knife. It was in his right fist, the blade pointing inward, aimed just above my hip. I was trapped.

His tone shifted, became creepily soothing. "Don't make me cut you, Emily. I don't want to. This has gotten really out of control, baby. We don't need to get arrested. Let's just talk. I love you, Emily."

Love? This was not how people who were in love behaved. I wanted to tell Johnny that, but I'd frozen at the realization that I, Emily Black, had somehow ended up in a relationship with a guy who had a knife pressed in very close proximity to one of my major organs—liver, kidneys, whatever was located on the right side of my body.

Even as I tried to think of a way to get out of the situation, all I could do was wonder how I'd missed the warning signs that Johnny was capable of something like this. He'd been a bastard at times, but I really never saw it coming. The same way, I realized, I had never *ever* imagined anyone could hurt Louisa.

I mean, *my* mother, raped? In every other tale about her, she was so strong. And I prided myself on taking after her in that way. Like her, I was tough. Unbreakable. Indestructible. And yet I had no idea how to get away from Johnny.

Then, suddenly, Johnny dropped the knife. I was so freaked that I didn't recognize why he did it, or why he backed away from me, but then I heard the voice that he obviously had. "Police! Open up!" it boomed.

I lifted my trembling hand and opened the door to find two of Chicago's finest standing on the other side. I never thought a day would come that I would be so happy to see a cop.

While Johnny fled for the bathroom, trying unsuccessfully to close the busted door on a male officer who was built like a marine, I met the steely eyes of the policewoman who stood in front of me. The way her black hair was combed back into a bun beneath her cap, pulling her skin taut, gave her a severe appearance, but the longer she looked at me, the more she softened. I don't remember saying anything, but the officers seemed to know right away that I was the victim. After I told her everything, she asked, "Do you want to come down to the station and press charges?"

"No. I just don't ever want to see him again."

Annoyed with my response, she huffed, "If you don't press charges against him, all we can get him on is disturbing the peace. He could come back here and try to kill you all over again."

I glanced over my shoulder into the bathroom, where Johnny sat on the toilet with his arms wrapped around his knees like a shamed child while Marine Cop berated him. "He wasn't really trying to kill me . . ." But remembering the knife in my side, something that I never thought him capable of doing, I relented. "I don't know, maybe I need a restraining order or something. But can we do this quickly? I just need to go home. To my dad's. In Wisconsin."

THE BLACK NOTEBOOKS

After leaving the police station around two in the morning, I shoved crates of CDs, records, and tapes into the trunk of my car. Fortunately, I kept that stuff pristinely organized, so even in my rush I didn't leave anything behind. Clothes were another story. I grabbed a basket of dirty laundry and everything I saw hanging in the closet and tossed it all in the backseat. I ran around the apartment throwing random items into a backpack, but I left behind a bunch of stuff, including my favorite July Lies T-shirt. I remembered the most important things, though.

I set my wounded guitar in its hard plastic case and piled it on top of the clothes. And then there was the photo of Louisa that I'd kept framed on the stereo speaker in my room at home. After I'd moved out, I tucked it away between the pages of a book and only looked at it when Johnny wasn't around. At least I hadn't shared that little piece of my soul with him, I thought. I slipped the picture out and dumped the book—a stupid collection of fairy tales my dad used to read to me as a kid that I'd known Johnny would never flip through.

The photo lay on the seat beside me as I sped out of Chicago. It was a black-and-white my father had taken. Louisa had his guitar in her lap, gently resting against her pregnant belly. A smile lifted her lips, but her eyes seemed haunted. It reminded me of the iconic photographs they always put on the cover of *Rolling Stone* when a rock star dies. The kind of pictures that trigger admiration, sorrow, and so many questions in the viewer's mind.

I glanced at it as I crossed over into Wisconsin. Questions were the only thing bringing me back to Carlisle. I did not want to slink home after less than a year. Maybe Dad had thought it was the place to go when things got rough, but I did not want to follow in his footsteps.

As I turned onto Highway PW, my stomach sunk and I felt sicker with each sign I passed that warned of a change in speed limit. There was a pattern to them on the county highways. When you were surrounded by wide-open fields, you could go fifty-five. As the farms got closer together and you reached the outskirts of a town, it dropped to forty-five. Then it plummeted to twenty-five, becoming the strip that locals knew as Main Street.

When I reached Carlisle's Main Street at six in the morning, I caught sight of Mrs. Jones hobbling up to the front of her store. She turned and watched my car as it passed. I knew she recognized me despite the cloak of early morning shadows. She'd tell her first customer, "Emily Black is back. Didn't even last in the big city as long as her daddy. Came crawling back alone just like he did, too."

And with my luck, the customer would be some evil person I went to high school with, like Jackie Jenkins. She'd smirk and say, "So much for her stupid band."

That image, along with the memories of finding Regan in a pool of blood and the sensation of Johnny's knife against my side, pushed me into the darkest place I'd ever been. When I arrived at my father's house, instead of going for the coffee that had started to auto-brew, I grabbed a bottle of red wine from the top of the fridge and yanked the cork out. I slumped at the round kitchen table to wallow in my lowest low.

The bottle of wine had been three-quarters full and I'd nearly put it away by the time my dad got up at six thirty. The summer sun streamed in through the windows that lined three of the four kitchen walls, lit up the creamy countertops, and stretched lazily across the golden oak floor. I sat in the darkest corner of the room, holding my head in my hands, hair draped like a veil over my face and down my shoulders. I only parted that black curtain to tip the bottle into my mouth. I drank sloppily, letting droplets of wine settle into the cracks in my lips, blending with my faded lipstick.

My father sleepily slurred, "Lou—" before catching himself and exclaiming, "Emily!" I'm sure he'd never wanted to see me looking the way I did, but he'd probably always expected to find her like that.

I raised my head to look at him. I'd been so lost in thought, I hadn't heard the creak of the stairs and the floor in the hallway as he approached. "Dad," I said weakly, blinking at him with bloodshot eyes.

He ran around the table, parental instincts kicking in and shocking him awake. Kneeling beside my chair and clasping my hand, he asked, "I've been worrying since Luke called and told me about Regan. Why didn't you call me? I left you all those messages. Or did you come straight from the hospital?"

"You left messages?" The pain in my voice turned to ire. "Then he heard the messages. He knew exactly what was going on!"

"What are you talking about?"

I jerked my hand out of my father's, and my fingers flew around the neck of the wine bottle. I took an angry swig, wine streaking my chin. "That asshole Johnny," I raged, slamming the bottle down.

My dad snatched it away from me, setting it out of my reach. "What about Johnny?"

"You see this?" I flipped back my hair to reveal scratches on my neck. "And this?" I pointed to bruises on both arms. "When I came home from the hospital he freaked out and tried to kill me and the police came. He was pissed because we'd missed the gig he'd set up. But he knew why we'd missed it all along because I'm sure he got your messages—"

I stopped when I heard the wine bottle crash. Dad had flung out his arm and violently swiped it off the table as he stood. The bottle didn't shatter, but the wine that was left inside broke like a red wave across the floor. His eyes were black. "Is he in jail? You better tell me he's locked up right now because otherwise I will kill him," he gnashed through gritted teeth.

I swallowed hard; I'd never seen him so angry. With his jaw clamped in rage, his fists clenched, biceps bulging, and posture stiff, he looked like a completely different man. "They told me that in . . . *domestic disputes,*" I spat the words, "they have to take someone in and they said it was obvious that he was the one who . . . I got an emergency restraining order, but they told me to think about pressing assault charges, to come to the station this morning and do it or they couldn't hold him after that."

"What are you doing here, then? Why didn't you call me so I could come down there? Jesus Christ, let me get my keys so we can drive back to Chicago." He pivoted, heading for the back door, but stopped midstep when I let out a high-pitched shriek.

"No, Daddy, I just want it to be over!" I dropped my head into my hands again.

His anger disappeared as quickly as it had come, and he rushed back over to me. I wrapped my arms loosely around his neck and buried my face in his shoulder, breathing in the comforting smell of him. "I shouldn't have let you go. I never should have let you go," he murmured into my hair.

I wanted more than anything to sob like I was small again. But even as I felt my father's tears dampen my hair, I couldn't cry. I pressed my hand against his cheek, trying to absorb the wetness and the repeated mantra of "I shouldn't have let you go." I said, "You couldn't have stopped me, but I shouldn't have left."

He guided my hand away from his cheek and cradled it in both of his hands, studying me. "I shouldn't have let her leave."

My thin eyebrows wrinkled in confusion. "Dad, you couldn't have stopped me," I repeated.

He stood up, letting my hand slide out of his. "No, I mean your mother. I shouldn't have let her leave us." He paced toward the coffeepot to pour himself a cup, only to spill a quarter of it as he sat back down. "There's so much more you could have had, stuff you needed, if she'd been around."

He had never said anything like this, and it alarmed me. "Dad"—I reached across the table toward him—"all I've ever needed is you."

He curled his fingers into a fist and shook his head violently. "No, you should've had her, and you should have had all of me, not this cripple that I've been because she left me." He beat his fist against his heart.

"Dad, you weren't like that!"

"Emily!" he snapped, but his voice immediately softened with regret. "I couldn't even visit you because that city reminds me too much of her. She's been gone for nearly nineteen years and god knows how many nights I spent thinking about her instead of giving you what you need."

"It's okay." I squeezed his hand to reassure him. Then I refocused on what I'd come to him for. "You can give me what I need now."

He squeezed my hand back. "Anything."

But as I spoke, his expression changed from concerned to questioning to full of doubt. "I need the truth. When I drove into town this morning, the first thing I saw was Mrs. Jones and I imagined the way she's going to talk about me. And don't say she's not going to. People talk about us, Dad. About us and about Louisa. Remember how I would come home crying about it? You always said, 'Just don't listen, Emily. Those people don't know anything about your mother.' And then you'd tell me some cute little story about you and her. About how Luke and Molly and Marissa came down for your wedding and Marissa cried because she wanted Louisa to hold her during the ceremony, so you guys got married with Marissa on Louisa's hip. Or how all Louisa listened to while she was pregnant with me was Patti Smith, so no wonder I came out wanting to be a rock star. And those stories were fine when I was a kid. I just wanted to find out as much as I could about my mother. But still, every time I went anywhere, people put their heads together and whispered. I'd hear her name, yours, mine, Molly's, Eric Lisbon's—"

Dad cut me off with a growl. "What about Eric Lisbon?"

I glared at him. "I don't know, Dad. Why don't you tell me? 'Cause I'm not supposed to believe them, right? I'm not supposed to believe that her poor, lovesick boyfriend Eric killed himself because you stole her from him. I'm sure there's another explanation, right? And what about the thing that Regan just told me? She said she overheard Molly saying that Eric Lisbon raped Louisa. Is that true?" Tears finally streamed down my face and I started to shake. "Was Louisa weak just like me?"

"You are not weak. You're tough, you're smart, you're a brilliant musician—"

"Answer the goddamn question, Dad! Did Eric Lisbon rape Louisa? Is that why she left?"

My father sighed and for the first time in my life, he couldn't meet my eyes. He stared into his coffee. "She . . . Your mother left because she . . ." He stopped and rubbed his temples like he was fighting bad memories. "You know why your mother left. She was a free spirit. She wanted to tour with bands, follow punk rock."

"That's a fairy tale," I scoffed. "A bedtime story you used to tell me. After what happened yesterday, I can't believe in it anymore. I watched my best friend practically die because I was too wrapped up in my stupid music to notice she had a problem."

"Emily, don't call your music stupid . . ."

"Tell me the truth!" I banged the table for emphasis. "What did she do? Or what did someone do to her that she just couldn't live with?"

I waited a long time for him to respond, but he just shook his head slowly back and forth. Finally I rose, heading for the back door.

"Where are you going?" He shot out of his chair.

"If you won't tell me the truth, I'll go find it."

He trailed after me down the back steps to the driveway. "What does that mean? Emily, please come back here!"

Before I opened the driver's door, I went to the door behind it and yanked my guitar out of the backseat. "You can have your guitar back, Dad. I'm not playing music anymore." I slid the case across the gravel toward him.

"Emily!" he cried. "Don't do this. Don't leave me like she did."

I turned and glared at him, holding the car door open, ready to hop in. "I'm not. 'Cause she left to follow the music, right? I'm running away from it. My obsession with it almost killed my best friend, and Johnny's obsession with it almost killed me."

He shouted my name again, but I slammed the door and cranked the engine. Music roared from the speakers. Patti Smith's voice crooned at me to "ask the angels," but I cut her off. I rammed my finger into the eject button and tossed the tape through the window as I peeled off down the driveway and out of Carlisle for good.

July 1992

Louisa was always acutely aware of Emily's birthdays. On the morning of Emily's sixteenth, she awoke thinking, *Sixteen.* She rubbed away mascara and clumps of sleep to peel her eyes open. It was nearly one in the afternoon. She and Colette had been hitting the Whisky or the Jabberjaw or some bar in West Hollywood every night for over a week. It was Tuesday or Wednesday, Louisa wasn't really sure, but she knew the date, July 7. She felt Emily's name kicking around in her stomach, the same way her feet had pattered inside of her womb all those years ago. She felt the number sixteen pulsating beneath her skin.

Louisa stumbled to the bathroom, passing Colette, who napped on the couch, music videos on the TV barely audible. The water in the shower seemed to thump out the same pattern, speaking to Louisa. *Sixteen, my baby's sixteen.*

She had no idea what Emily's life was like anymore because she no longer received updates from Molly. Louisa had completely given up on returning to her old life after her "fresh start" in Boston had failed miserably. She'd searched for a legitimate job for three months until resigning herself to stripping again out of desperation. Then came the pills.

She needed them to numb herself to what she was doing, but getting strung out made her active line of work impossible. The last night in Boston, Louisa passed out in the dressing room and woke up in the parking lot to the manager clocking her, calling her a dumb junkie whore who put his club's license in jeopardy. Louisa didn't talk back, just collapsed to the ground, not even balling up to protect herself from his blows like she had when Eric had beaten her back at River's Edge.

Colette came running out, throwing her stilettos at the manager, clawing his face, and shouting that it was the worst place they'd ever worked. The next thing Louisa knew, she was in the car, Nadia and their few possessions packed in the back. As Boston grew smaller behind them, Louisa studied her black eye in the mirror, knowing it meant she would never go home. She took off her wedding ring and cut contact with Molly completely. It was too cruel to let Molly go on believing that one day she could be convinced to come home, and it hurt too much to get news about the daughter she knew she would never see again.

Over four years had passed since Louisa had fled Boston and decided she'd never feel good enough to return to her family, but it never stopped haunting her. She'd moved on but hadn't forgotten. She still expected her wedding ring to catch on her hair as she washed it. And drugs, alcohol, even the meanest hangover couldn't mask her longing for Emily, especially on days like this one.

After Louisa dressed, she meandered back into the living room. Nadia sat on the floor in front of the couch, doodling in a notebook on the coffee table. Louisa regarded the little girl with the moon-shaped face. Her hazel eyes were always wide and wondering, but her sun-streaked hair often fell over them, a shield between her and the world. Her presence was the exact opposite of Colette's wild, loud nature. Nadia soothed Colette. After hard nights—fights with boyfriends in crowded clubs or when she drank to the point that it stirred memories of her lonely North Carolina teenage years with an overprotective father—Colette crawled into her daughter's bed. Nadia would sigh, roll over, and embrace her mother, pressing her little body against Colette's and wrapping her fingers in Colette's stiffly hair-sprayed hair, comforting her without even waking. Sitting there in front of the couch, Nadia resembled a gatekeeper, protecting her mother.

For a moment, Louisa doubted her decision to give her daughter up. Maybe Emily could have consoled her like that, healed her. But then Louisa looked more closely at Nadia. She seemed like a miniature adult. Emily hadn't been like that at nine, Louisa knew from the letters and pictures Molly'd sent back then. At nine, Emily was as pale as Nadia was tan, and her mint-green eyes were replicas of Louisa's, mischievous, beckoning silly trouble. Well, Louisa's had been like that once; now they were as serious as Nadia's, introspective and distant.

Life should have turned out better for Nadia, and it almost had.

Oakland came after Boston. Things hadn't improved there, but after a year of fighting with drug dealers in the living room while Louisa snuggled next to Nadia on the bed, trying to keep her from crying, Colette decided that the part of California she really loved was L.A. Louisa chose to continue north to Portland, and she and Colette parted ways.

Colette's luck changed in Southern California. She met an actor named Brad and they got married in the fall of 1989. Brad even paid for Louisa to fly down and be Colette's maid of honor. Colette vowed to Louisa, "Now I won't have to come running to you anymore. And my little girl"— she squeezed Nadia, who'd been allowed to wear fairy wings with her mini bridesmaid's dress—"will never want for anything again!"

Then, in the summer of 1990, just after Nadia's seventh birthday, Colette banged on the door of Louisa's apartment in Portland. "I cashed in big, baby. Big!" she exclaimed as she thundered into the living room in her chunky black shoes, fluffing her magenta-tipped hair, which matched her magenta-striped stockings. Nadia trailed behind like the train of a garish wedding dress, her honey-colored head bowed as she chewed on her nails.

It was the first time Colette had ever shown up without tears threatening to spill from her seafoam eyes, clutching Nadia like a life preserver. Instead Colette glowed, her skin a healthy tan, teeth movie-star white, makeup shimmering. Louisa smiled as Colette plopped down on the overstuffed gray sofa. "Did you win the lottery or something?"

"Better. Alimony." Colette beamed. Nadia perched on the couch next to her mother, drawing a small, plastic animal from the pocket of her overalls. She cupped the little lion in her hands and peeked at it with a furtive smile as if the twenty-five-cent vending-machine toy were a long-lost jewel.

"You and Brad are getting divorced?" Louisa gaped.

"He was"—Colette's hands, still glittering with the various platinum bands Brad had bought her, clamped over Nadia's ears—"screwing his agent. Ha! He was such a terrible actor, I guess I should've wondered how he was getting those roles."

"Wow, I'm sorry to hear—"

"Don't be! He's got to pay for a house, clothes, accessories . . ." Colette gave an exaggerated wink, clasped Louisa's hand, and transferred a small vial into it. "And babysitters. I want you to come back to L.A. and live with us, let me repay you for all the times you've bailed us out."

"You don't have to do that. After Oakland, I'm done with California, and I'm trying to be done with this." Louisa passed the vial back to Colette.

"Well, you don't *have* to do that. I need to quit anyway, for Nadia." She flicked her fingers around the vial like a magician making a quarter disappear up his sleeve. "But California, c'mon, Louisa! Portland is, like"—Colette's thickly mascaraed lashes fluttered—"you might as well move back to Wisconsin."

Louisa's jaw clenched at the reference. Then she said, "I left my daughter because I knew she'd be better off without me. Why do you want me around yours?"

"'Cause Nadia loves you and she likes having more than just me around." Colette turned to the pudgy-cheeked girl. "Right?"

Nadia wrinkled her brow. "I miss Brad."

"But you would like it if Louisa came to live with us, right? That would be fun. All girls."

"Yeah." Nadia nodded, her golden face lit up by a full smile.

"Can ya really say no to that?" Colette pressed.

Louisa's green eyes remained full of lingering doubt. "I don't know. The scene here is good and I was thinking of going farther north. Olympia. Seattle. Something amazing is happening there."

"How dreary." Colette screwed up her face and turned to her daughter with an even goofier expression that made Nadia giggle. "Tell Louisa the scene is always great in sunny Los Angeles."

Nadia mimicked Colette's words exactly and then added what probably made much more sense to her: "You can sleep on the floor in my room."

"I'll come," Louisa finally agreed with a sigh, "but just for a little while. You know how I feel about staying in one place for too long. Bad things happen."

But before she knew it, two years passed, the longest Louisa had gone without packing up and leaving. She'd moved to L.A. to make the divorce easier on Nadia and Colette. Unfortunately, Colette's way of coping involved heavy partying, and Louisa found herself sucked right back into it. She watched the scene in the Pacific Northwest erupt as she'd predicted, but the vial of coke in her handbag made her forget her desire to be there instead of California. She and Colette also forgot about Nadia's needs more often than they should have.

Louisa pushed her thoughts and memories aside, returning her attention to Nadia, who still sat in front of a sleeping Colette. "Hey, Nadia," she managed to say. "You bored?"

Nadia glanced up from her drawing and nodded. Her best friend, Brenda, had been gone for almost a week, visiting her grandparents, and Nadia had nothing to do but ride her bike alone in the parking lot.

"Let's wake your mom and go somewhere," Louisa suggested, sparking a grin from Nadia. "Come on, let's tickle her feet!"

They each attacked a bare sole until Colette's pearly painted toenails were flying through the air and she was up, giggling.

"We're bored, Mom," Nadia declared.

Pulling Nadia onto her lap, Colette scraped long fingernails through her own unruly hair and lit a cigarette. "Shopping?" she suggested, blinking her sapphire eyes.

Colette took them to her favorite Melrose boutiques, where Nadia played dress-up and dutifully commented on all the outfits Colette tried on. Louisa let her mind wander again. Her heartbeat sounded out the syllables of her daughter's name, and now images of Emily were coming into her head, too. She had a box of photos and letters from Molly in the back of her closet. She rarely looked at them anymore, but she felt driven to go home, sift through them, and trace her daughter's journey right up to the cusp of becoming a teenager; Emily's sixth-grade school photo was the last one Louisa had received.

"Lou?" Colette called from the cash register, where she flicked through her wallet for a credit card that wasn't maxed.

"What?" Louisa asked as she slowly headed toward Colette and Nadia.

"Aren't you going to get something to wear out tonight?"

"Oh, I don't think I'm gonna go."

"Not gonna go? It's going to be such a time! Becca's in town. You know you're going." Colette wagged her head and turned to her daughter. "I think Louisa is, like, on a sugar crash or something. What do you say we go get dinner at Pink's? I think she needs a hot dog and a big strawberry milk shake."

Nadia's face brightened. "I think *I* need a hot dog and a milk shake!"

"You do, do you?" Colette scrawled her signature across the receipt, grabbed her bags in one hand, her daughter's hand in the other, and paraded out the door, Louisa straggling behind.

When they finally got back to their apartment, Louisa shut herself in her room, poured out the box of letters, and read over them until it got so dark she was forced to turn on a light. As she did so, Colette rapped on the door. "You better get in the shower. Nadia's in bed, the babysitter'll be here in half an hour, and then we can cruise."

Louisa opened the door a crack, pushed her hair behind her ear, and said, "No, really, I'm not feeling so hot. You should just head out. Cancel the sitter. I'll be here."

It took a little bit of convincing, but finally Colette was backing out of the parking lot and Louisa was alone except for Nadia's soft breathing down the hall. Louisa returned to her closet and brought out another box containing letters. These letters, however, were all in Louisa's handwriting, all addressed to Emily, and all still bound in black spiral notebooks.

Every birthday, at Christmas, and on some late nights when she couldn't sleep, Louisa wrote her daughter a letter. The letters always started the same, with a reference to the occasion, something like, "Merry Christmas, Emily! Have you been good this year?" or, if there was no occasion to reference, simply, "Hi, baby." The second line was always the same, too: "I miss you." And from there, Louisa went on to ask Emily things about herself, what she liked, how school was, what music she listened to. When she ran out of questions to ask her daughter, she considered telling her about her life, but she always stopped short, certain there was only one thing that her daughter wanted to know—why Louisa had left her when she was just an infant—and that was one question Louisa wasn't ready to answer. So she would sign the letter, "I love you with all my heart, Mom," and close the notebook. She spent the next couple days thinking about whether to send it to Molly and have Molly pass it on to Emily, but of course she never did. She just accumulated tattered notebooks filled with unsent letters.

Louisa searched for a pen on her nightstand. The state of it—crisscrossed with razor-blade scratches filled in with a white film of cocaine, scattered pills that she knew by size and color, and empty glasses that smelled of sticky-sweet drinks—told the story of her life in L.A. Louisa's cheeks burned in shame, but it made her all the more determined to write the letter. Sixteen was an important age, a turning point, Louisa knew. After all, it was the year her own life had changed, the year the thing had happened that would eventually keep her from her daughter.

Happy Birthday, baby. I miss you, Louisa started, as usual, but the third line was one she had never written before. *I wish I could be there,* and that was where the letter shifted. *Maybe you wish I could, too, but you shouldn't. I'm not coming back, Emily, and I guess it's probably time that I tell you why. I don't want you to think that I left because I didn't want you. I wanted you more than anything I've ever wanted, and so did your father, and I'm glad I was able to give him the best part of me—you. Just as I wasn't able to be the mother I dreamed of being, I also wasn't able to be the wife he deserved. You'll find that sometimes there is a huge valley between what we want to be and what we're capable of. Or maybe you won't, maybe the only ones who have those limitations are people who've done terrible things. People like me.*

The worst night of my life was the night I left you and your father, then drove up to Carlisle to say good-bye to Molly, my oldest and truest friend. But it had been coming for years, a result of the second-worst night of my life.

That was when Louisa knew she was about to confess the whole gruesome story. She knew as soon as she put his name down on paper for the first time, she wasn't going to be able to stop.

I suppose—if the folks in Carlisle still love to chatter as much as they used to—that you've heard about Eric Lisbon, the boy I dated when I was your age, right before I met your father. I'm sure they still talk about his suicide and maybe they still blame me for it. I listened to people gossip about that for almost two years before your dad and I ran off together. They talked about how much Eric loved me and how I'd obviously broken his heart when I cheated on him with Michael. That's fanciful Carlisle storytelling for you. Eric didn't really love me, not the way people are supposed to love anyway, but, despite that, I was never involved with your father while I was with Eric. However, I was responsible for Eric's death and I'm actually surprised that no one ever figured out how. You'd think that in a town that loves to theorize about everything, someone would have wondered if Eric really pulled that trigger himself.

He didn't. I did. And that's why I'm not with you today.

Louisa lifted her pen from the page. She felt she needed something—a line, a pill, a drink—if she was going to relive the rest, but she stopped herself, thinking, *This has to be totally coherent. If you are finally going to tell this, you have to do it right.* Instead, she lit a cigarette, inhaling and exhaling slowly until it burned down to the filter. Then she was ready to finish.

Louisa described it to her daughter the same way she'd told Colette the night they'd driven through Carlisle— explained how Eric had beaten her, raped her, and how she'd shot him when he came after her again. But telling the story to Emily didn't absolve Louisa of her guilt. She wrote bitterly, *Molly says the rape was Eric's suicide. She says if he hadn't wanted a gun to his head, he would have kept his dick in his pants. She says if I hadn't killed him, she would have, or Luke would have, or your father would have. All three of them tried to reassure me in their various ways, your father doing the best job by taking me away from Carlisle, giving me a chance at a new life.*

It was supposed to be a beautiful life. You were supposed to grow up in the city my parents had taken me from when I was ten, thinking they were protecting me by raising me someplace quieter and safer. But then, when I was about five months pregnant with you, as far along as Molly was with Marissa when I killed Eric, everything came rushing back. I dreamt about the rape and the murder almost every night, and I was convinced that you could see those dreams. Maybe you could, maybe buried deep in your subconscious are both of those horrible scenes. I felt worse and worse each passing day, but I hid it from your father, from Molly, from everyone.

I thought once you were born, once you came out healthy, perfect in every way, it would all dissipate. But it didn't. I still had nightmares. I heard Eric's voice in my head, repeating what he said before he dragged me down to his basement and raped me: "You think things are over between us, Louisa? It'll never be over."

He was right. It wasn't. Even though you were no longer inside of me, I felt like I passed all of my guilt on to you in my breast milk. And I knew it would never end. It would be in my kisses, my hugs, the food I cooked, my whispers. It was surrounding me and I didn't want it to rub off on you or your father. You shouldn't pay for what I've done. And besides, how could I teach you when I had made so many mistakes? How could I tell you about right and wrong when I had done the ultimate wrong? So I left.

I know this story doesn't match up with the one your father told you. You're probably pretty angry about being lied to, and if that's the case, be angry with me, not your dad. I made him swear to me that he'd keep my secret. He begged me to stay and he asked, "What am I supposed to tell Emily?"

I told him to make you hate me so much that you didn't want anything to do with me. To tell you that I'd run off with another man. But he said he couldn't do that, he loved me too *much. I told him that if he loved me, he'd swear to keep my secret, so you'd never have to be haunted by it. I told him to tell you I left to follow rock 'n' roll. To let you think I was a free spirit so you'd have a free spirit.*

And at first, I did follow the music. I thought maybe I just needed some time by myself to grapple with things. Then I'd be able to be the girl your father fell in love with before the murder, the girl who sat beside him on a makeshift stage in an old warehouse learning to play guitar. That version of me would have been a good mother. But I can't be that person again, there is too much bad in me. I hope you can understand, and I hope you won't ever try to find me. All I can do is damage you.

Louisa stopped writing and eased her cramped body out of bed to check on Nadia. The little girl was lying on her side, facing the door, as if she was waiting for her mother to come in, needing her. She breathed lightly but did not wake when the dim light from the hall hit her face. Louisa wished she could take Colette's place that night and lie down beside Nadia, have the girl comfort her. More than anything, she wished she could transport herself to Wisconsin and lie down beside her own daughter. Emily wouldn't be a little girl anymore, though; she would probably be almost Louisa's size, almost her shape. But her expression would be as peaceful as Nadia's when she slept, as innocent.

Louisa closed the door and walked back to her room with that sense of innocence in mind. She skimmed her letter. Was she really going to bring this nightmare on her daughter? The nightmare she'd feared she was passing on throughout her whole pregnancy? Was she going to let Emily know—at this vulnerable age, when she was probably confused enough about her own identity—that her mother was a murderer? No, she couldn't.

She added three more lines to the letter. *Like with all the other letters, I won't be sending this one. I never wanted you to know, and I'm not going to tell you now. After all, you've been better off all these years not knowing.* Then she closed the notebook and put it away in the back of her closet, realizing that she'd never write in it again.

"I need to know the truth, Molly, about my mother and why she left."

I spoke into the grimy receiver of a Milwaukee pay phone. I'd waited three days to make the call, figuring that was how long it would take for Regan to be well enough for Molly to bring her back to Carlisle. I'd actually hoped Regan would answer because she wouldn't have been as hysterical as her mother. Molly started screaming as soon as I said hello. Apparently everyone was worried about me, my father had barely slept since the morning I'd left, and Regan would be able to get healthy a lot faster if I was by her side. When she finished ranting, I told her I'd consider coming home if she gave me the information my dad had refused me.

Molly sighed. "Emily, you've been through a lot. Regan scared us all to death and your dad told me about what happened with Johnny—"

"I don't want to talk about that. Tell me about Louisa."

Molly ignored my stern words. "If you just came home, so we could help you deal with that stuff, then we could talk about everything else."

I slammed the palm of my hand into the side of the metal enclosure surrounding the phone. My extra coins clattered on the surface where they sat. "Everything else? Louisa is not everything else. She's the reason behind everything I do. I've never been able to admit that until now, but you had to see it. I spent my entire life trying to understand her through the music she supposedly left to follow. I started my own band so that maybe . . ." I stopped myself, still not willing to admit that I'd been hoping my songs would bring her home. That sounded so naive. *Then again,* I thought angrily, *Dad and Molly encouraged that childish fantasy, didn't they?*

I scraped a quarter up and down the telephone cord like I used to scrape my pick against my guitar strings at the end of an intense song. I missed my guitar. Reminding myself why I didn't have it, I said, "I screwed up my band. I learned that music doesn't heal, it doesn't save. It ruins lives. If my mother really thought it was going to fix something for her . . . well, no wonder she never came home."

"Emily," Molly pleaded, "your life isn't ruined. Your band isn't ruined. Regan and Tom are in Chicago waiting for you to come back, so you can work through all of this together."

The quarter slipped through my fingers and hit the cement. "What? Why didn't she come home with you? I couldn't go back to Chicago even if I wanted to."

"Don't let a bad relationship ruin—"

"Don't let it ruin my life like it did Louisa's?"

"No, that's not what I meant—"

"Regan told me what she overheard you say about my mother. Did Eric Lisbon rape Louisa? And what does it have to do with her leaving me?"

Molly paused for so long that I wondered if she'd hung up on me, but then I heard her inhale and exhale cigarette smoke. Finally she said, "Regan never should have told you that."

"Why, because it isn't true?" God, how I wanted to believe it wasn't.

"Because as close as Regan and I are to you, Louisa's story and her reason for leaving are between you, your father, and Louisa."

Blind rage filled me. I slammed the receiver against the side of the phone three times and it took every ounce of will-power not to hang up. Pressing the phone to my ear again, I growled, "Listen, I know my father told you to say that. He probably thinks it will bring me home to talk to him. But I'm not coming back to listen to his fairy tales anymore. After what happened with Johnny, I can't hear his crap about how much he and my mom loved each other. Obviously something was wrong or she wouldn't have left. And I'm going to find out what that was. If you won't tell me and Dad won't tell me, I'm going straight to the source. The last time you heard from Louisa, she was in Boston, correct?"

"Emily, that was eight years ago."

"Was that the last time you heard from her?" I insisted.

When Molly emitted a painful "Yes," I hung up on her. I had my starting point.

I returned to where I'd been staying to collect my things. Milwaukee wouldn't have been my first choice because it was still in Wisconsin, but I'd left my dad's house sleep-starved and low on gas. It was about as far away as I could get. Besides, I had acquaintances there who let me crash with them without asking too many questions. And they had connections. When I mentioned that I was going to be driving a long way and wished I had some pills like the ones that my waitress friend in Chicago provided me after particularly rough nights, a green-haired girl named Dawn told me she could do better.

I gave her forty bucks and she brought me two plastic baggies of pills. "The white ones will get you up and the blue ones will bring you down when you're ready." Then she revealed a tinfoil packet. "And this will make you feel invincible."

"What's that?"

Dawn beckoned me over to the coffee table and spilled white powder out onto its mirrored surface. She expertly chopped two lines and handed me a rolled dollar bill.

I hesitated. Cocaine, the biggest rock-star cliché. Then I remembered that it didn't matter. I wasn't going to be a rock star. Music wouldn't mean a thing to me again until I found my mother, the person who'd made me believe in it in the first place. And I was going to have to drive through Chicago on my way to Boston. I needed to feel invincible.

Louisa's picture became my compass. I taped it to the dashboard as I drove across the country. When I got to Boston, I taped it to the wall above my bed, the place where I'd always hung rock posters in the past.

Of course, I couldn't cut music out of my life completely. Even though I doubted the myth about Louisa following punk rock, it was still all I had to go on. I went to concert after concert, trying to integrate into the scene with the hope that an older bouncer or club regular might remember her. It hurt like hell to watch other people onstage doing the thing I used to love so much. I had to numb myself to it. I used alcohol for that purpose when I could, but found it harder to scam drinks underage in Boston than it had been in the Midwest. Instead, I took speed to keep me upbeat enough to talk to everyone, figure out if they might know Louisa. Soon, drugs filled the void that music had left. Chopping coke finely with a razor blade made my fingers feel like they were gripping a pick and hitting the strings hard and fast. Codeine and Valium put me in a sleep so deep I didn't dream about my guitar or shows I'd played or songs begging to be written.

I used my old lyrics notebook to record clues about my mother. I spent nine months in Boston and only met a few people who thought maybe they'd seen her around. If it wasn't for my drug use, I may have never gotten a real lead.

A dealer came to my house one night and brought along his girlfriend, a chick with bluish black hair who looked about ten years older than she was. She paced around while her boyfriend and I negotiated. Then she stopped in front of my bed, squinting at Louisa's picture with heavily lined brown eyes. She tapped it, announcing, "Hey, I knew her. Jimmy, come over here, see if you remember her name."

"Chill, Mary." Jimmy tried to continue his conversation with me, but I was already approaching Mary, urging him to follow.

"Do you guys remember her? What was her name?" I asked, wanting them to recall on their own, not just go along with what I said.

Jimmy glanced at the photo and shrugged. "I meet too many people. Who is she to you anyway?"

Disappointment made my words hollow. "My mother."

Mary's squint moved from the picture to my face. She stared into my eyes so deeply that I got a chill. Then she snapped her fingers. "You've got her eyes. Louisa. I'd never forget those eyes."

Shocked, I leaned against the wall for support. "How'd you know her?"

"We danced together. Her, me, and her best friend, Colette."

Molly. I wanted to say that Louisa's best friend was Molly. Instead I asked, "What do you mean you danced? Like at concerts or something?"

Mary laughed a phlegmy laugh that sounded more like a cough. She placed her palm delicately on the top of a nearby chair and spun around it, landing in a seated position with her chin resting on the back. "No, like *dancing*, honey. We worked at a strip club together for a year until your mom got in a fight with the manager and she and Colette drove off to Oakland. Louisa never mentioned a kid, though. Colette had one. Nadia or Natasha or something. Little girl, way younger than you."

As soon as Mary and Jimmy left, I took two Valium so I could sleep without dwelling on the sickening image of Louisa twirling around a pole and thrusting her tits in guys' faces like some chick in a bad hair-metal video. But I left for Oakland the next morning.

Even though Louisa's life was a pathetic shell of what I'd always imagined, she did seem to be following the music.

She'd been in Boston right before the Pixies made their mark and hit the Bay Area when punk bands like Green Day and Rancid were starting out. And the Gilman, the place where those bands played, was still around. Within three months, I met a woman who'd been hanging around the punk scene since the late eighties. She vaguely remembered Louisa and Colette. She said all the two of them ever talked about was New Orleans. When they disappeared in 1989, that's where she assumed they'd gone. Given the time period, I would have expected my mother to go farther north and catch the beginnings of grunge in Seattle, but New Orleans was thick with musical history, so I could see the draw.

I arrived in New Orleans on a sweaty night in early July. I checked into the first hotel I found, right off I-10, a real dive in an area that was not meant for tourists, as I concluded by the sagging buildings with boarded-up windows and the gunshots I heard coming from somewhere nearby. The only things it had going for it were that it cost thirty dollars a night and that it was located above a twenty-four-hour bar.

I spent as little time in my room as possible. Its appearance was nauseating. The cigarette-burned carpet was the color of an old mustard stain. The furniture consisted of a bed with shit-brown blankets, a chair whose wooden arms had been used as an ashtray on several occasions, a scarred and drink-ringed dresser, and a matching (in the scars and drink rings, not the color of the wood) nightstand. No telephone or television, although I didn't want either. What I didn't like was that I had a sink and a mirror, but the toilet and shower were in the tiny bathroom that joined my room with my neighbor's—a greasy-haired man who winked at me every time we passed in the hall. Only two flimsy bolts separated me from him, one flimsy bolt if I was in the bathroom. Since my explosive breakup with Johnny, I'd taken to carrying a butterfly knife; I took it with me to the bathroom and kept it on the nightstand while I slept. It was convenient to have it there anyway, for cutting cocaine.

I'd been in New Orleans for a week when I celebrated my twentieth birthday. If you could call it a celebration. I'd been zigzagging across the country after Louisa for over a year. It was the second birthday without my dad and Regan, and I had to fight the urge to call them. I fought that urge every day, but the battles felt the worst on holidays.

Once upon a time when I ached like I did that day, I would have just played my favorite song. Now my music collection sat in the corner untouched as I scraped at the thin, white film that coated the scarred surface of my nightstand. There wasn't enough for one lousy line and I hadn't made any reliable connections in New Orleans yet. I took a big swig from the wine bottle I also kept on the nightstand and decided that since I'd been there a week, I might as well unpack. Maybe I'd get lucky and find more coke in the process.

I pulled a pair of jeans out of my bag and opened a dresser drawer to toss them inside. Something on the bottom of the drawer caught my attention. Painted in red nail polish in the back corner were the initials L.C.B., and a date, 4/81. My heart clenched and I dropped the jeans. I ignored the fact that there were probably a million people with the initials L.C.B.; I was convinced that those letters stood for Louisa Carson-Black. My mother had been in this room.

I yanked the drawer out of the dresser and slammed it on the nasty carpet. I traced the letters L.C.B., the date. I was sure it was her; the letters and numbers matched her handwriting on the back of photographs. I wanted to cut out that block of wood. Drive it all the way back to Carlisle. Show it to Molly and my father. Tell them, "Look, I found her. I finally found her!"

I was in no state to drive, though. I knew that. So I just sat with the drawer and drank my wine. Eventually, I retrieved my notebook to record my discovery. "St. Charles Hotel, New Orleans. Louisa's initials, April 1981."

Wait, 1981, I realized. I'd left Oakland looking for the place Louisa'd gone in the *nineties*. Louisa and Colette must have talked about New Orleans because they'd been there before, not because it was their destination. I'd driven halfway across the country only to end up farther from Louisa's trail than I'd ever been. I should have followed my instincts and gone to Seattle.

I ran my fingers over Louisa's inscription, hoping she'd left her mark in every place she went and that I could find those marks. Then I decided that I should try to get some sleep, so I could head west again as soon as possible. Before climbing into bed, I wrote "E.D.B. 7/96" next to "L.C.B. 4/81" and returned the drawer to the dresser. I washed down two sleeping pills with a mouthful of wine and turned out the light.

Taking sleeping pills after mixing coke and alcohol was dumb, and washing them down with wine, even dumber. I fell into a horrifying stupor.

The first light of dawn seeped in through the curtains.

Not only was it too bright to sleep, I convinced myself that I could see the veins in my eyelids, and they were moving like tiny red worms. I pulled the putrid brown blanket over my face to block it out. I relaxed briefly, but then I couldn't breathe. It felt like someone had shoved cotton up my nose and down my throat into my lungs, blocking all airways. Panicked, I ripped the covers off my face.

Things were fine for a moment. The room was dark. But I felt something weighing heavily on my chest, still preventing me from breathing properly. That's when I really started hallucinating.

I looked down and saw forty or fifty little people swarming me. They were about three inches tall, all wearing space suits. Little men and little women, distinguishable because the men wore full space suits, and the women wore black dresses with space helmets over their heads. They piled miniature chairs and tables on top of my chest.

"Stop it!" I yelled, trying to shake them and their stack of furniture off me. "I can't breathe! You're going to suffocate me. I don't want to die in some sleazy hotel room." One mini astronaut stopped his work and walked toward my face. He studied me quizzically and I knew he was asking why I deserved to live.

"I was something once," I told him. "I could have been this big rock star. Then I could have died in a sleazy hotel and it would have been glamorous." I sensed the little spaceman glowering at me. "Okay, you're right. It wouldn't have been glamorous, I was joking. I've got this bitchy, sarcastic sense of humor," I explained, even though part of me knew that I shouldn't be talking to him. He wasn't real. "All I'm saying is it wouldn't have been this pathetic. I really screwed up, and I'm going to die now, right? This is my life flashing before my eyes, and I'm supposed to regret wasting all the talents everyone told me I had, right? Well, I do."

Then he lifted his wee arm and pointed toward the dresser. I turned my head and saw my mother. She looked just like me except she had white-blond hair. She was skinny, dressed in a T-shirt and jeans, and wore smudged eyeliner around her green eyes, making them look bruised.

"Louisa?" I sat up quickly, and the woozy feeling I'd had while hallucinating teeny astronauts vanished. Suddenly, I thought my heart was going to pound right through my chest. I rubbed my hands up and down over my sweat-drenched face. I wondered if she was a ghost and seeing her meant that I was dead, too. What she said didn't help that confusion.

"Emily, I left so that you wouldn't follow me," she admonished. From old pictures of her, I'd expected her to have the too-many-cigarettes, cool-female-rock-star voice. Instead, it was soft, almost ethereal. That was it, I knew I was dead.

"I didn't mean to follow you. I didn't know you were dead. I didn't want to die," I babbled helplessly, tears slipping down my cheeks. "I don't know what happened."

"Yes, you do," she insisted, narrowing her eyes at me.

"No, I don't!" I cried, stumbling out of bed toward her, barely able to feel my own feet beneath me.

She stepped back, out of my reach. "Yes, you do, baby," she said, the harsh tone disappearing. "What went wrong?"

"I wasn't like this when I had my music!" I pouted, hurt that she avoided my touch.

"Exactly."

"When I was playing with my band, I had my shit together. Sort of. I mean, I got too obsessed, but I knew what I wanted."

"Exactly," she whispered again.

"I was pretty good, Mom. I wish you could have heard me play."

"Someday," she replied, her voice like a teardrop. Then she turned toward the dresser and disappeared into a drawer, dissolving right into it, like a ghost.

"Mom!" I shouted. "Come back!" I lunged at the dresser and opened the drawer. Of course, nothing was inside except our initials, but I slung it onto the bed. I didn't want to be alone. I didn't want to hallucinate again, and I didn't want to die. I drenched my head with cold water in the sink, trying to shock myself sober. Then I collapsed on the bed, unsure of what to do next.

I knew I had to sleep, but I was afraid I wouldn't wake up. I turned the drawer on its side, leaning it against the headboard of the bed, and placed my pillow on its back wall. That way, lying down, my mother's initials would be right above my head.

"I swear on everything that matters to me, if I make it through this night, I will go back to playing music," I promised my mother's nail polish and the empty room.

3.

I wanna be your Joey Ramone
Pictures of me on your bedroom door
Invite you back after the show
I'm the queen of rock and roll

—Sleater-Kinney
"I Wanna Be Your Joey Ramone"
Call the Doctor

ALL ROADS LEAD TO ROCK 'N' ROLL

Leaving New Orleans, I felt hopeful for the first time in thirteen long, lonely months. I sang along with my copy of She Laughs' demo, pleased to find that I still remembered every lyric and that even though my voice was rusty, I hadn't completely lost it. Anxious to get my hands on a guitar again, I didn't stop driving until the fuel light came on. My stomach growled at the sight of all the junk food in the gas station. It hadn't done that in a long time due to the appetite-suppressant side effects of the drugs I'd been using, but I'd flushed all my pills after that crazy hallucination back in New Orleans. Of course, legal versions of speed marketed toward truckers sat next to the cash register, so I bought cigarettes and a bunch of snacks to resist the urge. I also impulsively purchased a phone card, deciding I should call Regan to let her know that I was on my way to Chicago and that even though I'd arrive after midnight, I expected her and Tom to be ready to rock.

I opened a bag of chips and munched on them as I dialed the pay phone, but stopped eating when I heard a series of tones, followed by an automated voice telling me that the number I was trying to reach had been disconnected. I tried it three more times before determining that it had to be a problem with the phone card. I dialed the operator and told her I needed to be connected to Regan Parker in Chicago.

"We don't have any listings for that name."

A chill rippled through me before I said, "It's probably under her boyfriend's name. Tom Fawcett. F-A-W-C-E-T-T."

There was an agonizingly long pause before the operator spoke. "Nothing in Chicago, but I do have something in Forest Park."

The suburbs? I thought as I scrambled for a pen and scrawled the number on the back of my gas station receipt. She told me she would connect me, but I hung up before the call went through. *When had Regan and Tom moved to the suburbs? And why?*

I got back in the car, forgetting my food next to the pay phone. I was oblivious to hunger, to the music that came on when I started the engine, and to which direction I headed in when I got back on the highway. Suddenly, it dawned on me that I'd been gone over a year and time hadn't frozen when I left.

Tom and Regan could have settled down, gotten married, even had a kid. What if Regan had given up music to become a soccer mom? What if she and Tom had replaced me and formed a new band?

I mulled over a million different scenarios and then my thoughts turned to the woman I'd been focused on for so long. I still didn't know the truth behind why Louisa'd left, but now I had insight into why she hadn't returned. Maybe after she'd been out on the road for a year or two she'd wanted to, even drove in the direction of home. Then she thought about how I wouldn't be a helpless infant anymore; I'd be a little person who'd learned to walk and talk without her. She'd barely recognize me and I wouldn't know her at all. And my father, he could have moved on, gotten remarried for all she knew. She'd probably thought *They're happier without me,* exactly as I was thinking about Tom and Regan. So instead of facing the ways the people she loved had inevitably changed, Louisa went on to another city and hurled herself into an empty life.

I almost followed in her footsteps, but then I heard the click of the tape player as my demo tape stopped and flipped over again. The first song on side two, "Home," had a chorus that the kids at River's Edge used to really scream along to: *"Displaced in this place, the only home I know is sitting next to you, turning up the stereo."* They shared my sentiments about escaping small-town life with music, though I'm sure they thought the "you" referred to my best friend or boyfriend. But I was talking about my father. And no matter how much time had passed, I knew that home still existed for me.

I blinked back tears and checked the next highway sign to make sure I was still going north. I drove through Chicago, continuing on toward Wisconsin. But my uncertainty grew as I got closer to Carlisle. I wanted to see my dad, but I couldn't go back there. I remembered what a loser I'd felt like arriving home the last time, and things had only gotten worse. I'd thrown away my band for this insane quest to find Louisa. My failure was written all over me.

I stopped halfway between Carlisle and Chicago at a highway oasis suspended like a bridge over I-90. After using the bathroom, I studied myself in the mirror. The black tank top I wore revealed how much weight I'd lost and I could no longer use my hair to conceal my bony shoulders. My hair had hung to the middle of my back since I was three years old. I'd subconsciously mimicked the way my mother's bleached hair looked in all her photos. I realized this one night and cut my hair to chin length during a coke-fueled rage. Now I kept it in short, messy pigtails. I wore wide-rimmed sunglasses to disguise the circles under my eyes and nothing hid my ragged, chapped lips. I chewed on them all the time when I was high or fighting a craving. And speaking of cravings, my hands twitched uncontrollably.

I went out to my car and tried to sleep, but my mind spun, questioning what I should do next. At five A.M., I walked to the bank of pay phones inside the oasis and called my dad.

He answered on the first ring and his hello sounded wide-awake despite the early hour.

I took a deep breath and softly said, "Dad?"

"Emily? Where are you?" Urgency made his voice more high-pitched than usual.

"I'm at that oasis near Rockford. I wanted to come home, but I just can't face Carlisle. I can't . . ." I twisted around and stared at the highway below headed northwest to Wisconsin, and on the other side of the median, southeast to Chicago. I suddenly felt trapped. I didn't want to be in the Midwest at all.

My father seemed to sense this and asked desperately, "Honey, will you wait there for me? Please. I'll be there as fast as I can."

I glanced out at the road again. I didn't have the strength to keep running. "Yeah, I'll wait."

It took him an hour to get there. I waited on the eastbound side of the highway on top of a picnic table, smoking and watching the sun rise. He parked his truck and hurried over to me. The first thing I said when he got within earshot was, "I don't think you can smoke inside. This lady gave me a dirty look."

He pulled me into his arms. I didn't resist, hugging him back just as tightly. "Emily," he breathed. "Are you okay?"

"I am now," I mumbled into his T-shirt.

When we finally let go of each other, he held me at arm's length and looked me over with worried brown eyes. "How long has it been since you've eaten?" he demanded.

I shrugged, briefly removing my purple sunglasses to brush away tears. "Sometime yesterday."

He jerked his head in the direction of the McDonald's. "Let's go get something."

"Okay, as long as we can come outside to eat. I need to smoke."

"Those things will kill you, Emily," he chided.

"They'll kill you, too, Dad," I retorted with a half-smile, tapping the pack in the pocket of his T-shirt.

I put away two breakfast sandwiches while sitting across from him on the shady side of a picnic bench. It was quiet but comfortably at ease, the way our meals had always been. I wanted to forget the missing year and act like this was a normal thing to do, meeting for breakfast at six in the morning at a rest stop. But I couldn't ignore the way he kept sniffling. Tears clung to his long eyelashes and occasionally dribbled down into the creases around his eyes and mouth. His face hadn't been so lined when I left and his dark hair had grayed at the temples. My absence had aged both of us.

I said "Dad" at the same time he said "Em," and we both laughed weakly.

"Go ahead," he insisted, taking a long swallow of coffee.

I decided to answer the question I knew he was dying to ask. "I never found her."

"No?" If this news disappointed or upset him, he hid it well, keeping his tone even and his lips in a straight, emotionless line.

"Not really. I did have this weird drug-induced dream . . ."

His forehead wrinkled and distress blossomed in his voice. "What do you mean by that?"

I waved away his concern and lit a cigarette. "I need to start at the beginning. Did Molly tell you I called her?"

He nodded.

"And she told you that Louisa used to write her letters."

He nodded again, averting his eyes. He'd probably known about the letters for at least as long as I had, but I didn't have it in me to be angry at him for that or anything else anymore. Over the past year, I'd come to terms with it. He'd done whatever he'd done because he thought he was protecting me.

"The last address Molly had was in Boston. It took

months, but finally, I met a woman there who knew Louisa." To protect him, I eliminated the part about the woman being a coked-out stripper. "She said Louisa went to Oakland. So I drove across the country like she's done god knows how many times. In Oakland, it took a little less time to find someone who knew her, and they said they'd heard her talk about New Orleans." I sighed, taking a long drag to brace myself for the hardest part of the story.

I stared at the cars zooming by below, so I wouldn't have to see my father's disappointment. "I was pretty messed up. I didn't realize how much I needed to play music, how it keeps me focused and balanced. I've been doing a lot of pills and cocaine." I heard him inhale sharply through his nose and I rushed to say, "But I promise I'm not going to touch that stuff anymore. I'm done. Cold turkey." I pinched my cracked lips, tugging at a piece of dead skin. "And it's because of Louisa.

"I was staying in this crappy hotel in New Orleans on my birthday. I was rifling through all my things, looking for more coke, and I opened this drawer and found her initials. L.C.B. 4/81. I guess it could be a coincidence, but I—"

"Just knew," he finished.

I scratched at my bare arm. "Yeah. But then I got upset 'cause, 1981? I wasn't looking for that date, I was looking for 1990, 1991. So I decided I better just go to sleep. I took these pills to get down and reacted really badly. Felt like I couldn't breathe, had awful hallucinations. I thought I was going to die, but I saw her. Louisa. She spoke to me, made me realize I needed to stop destroying myself and get back to my music."

Relief washed across my dad's face. "So you decided to come home."

"Kind of." I gestured southeast with my cigarette. "I wanted to see Regan in Chicago, but I called and her number was disconnected, and when I found out she'd moved to the suburbs, I just assumed . . ."

He furrowed his brow. "What?"

I gazed through the dark glass doors of the oasis, watching the shadowy figures inside. I maintained a steady tone when I said, "She moved on," but my eyes grew damp beneath my sunglasses.

I felt Dad's hand on mine. "She and Tom moved because they wanted to live someplace cheaper, more low-key. But she wants the band back, she wants *you* back. She's never stopped waiting for you, Emily, and neither have I."

"Oh." I turned my head to face him.

Tears rolled shamelessly down his cheeks. "You know how impossible it is to give up on the person who left you."

I nodded. "And now I know how it is to be the person that leaves. You don't abandon everyone you love unless you're desperate. Drugs, punk rock, the excitement of seeing a new city—none of that fills the void left by the people you care about. Louisa might have gone off to follow the music, but she did it to try to heal something really ugly inside of herself."

"Yeah, you're right." He reached for his smokes, obviously preparing to answer the questions I'd asked over a year ago.

I panicked. Maybe I didn't need to hear this. Maybe I'd never found her because I wasn't supposed to know. As I watched him light his cigarette, I noticed something and found a way to change the subject. "Dad, what happened to your wedding ring?"

He rubbed his naked ring finger. "Took it off when you left." Exhaling smoke in a long stream, he explained, "When I got married, I got married for life. That's how I was brought up. I know even Prince Charles and Princess Di are getting divorced nowadays, but when I took that vow, I told myself I'd always be there for your mother. Even if it meant waiting twenty goddamn years for her to need me again." His voice cracked. He closed his eyes momentarily and regrouped. "But once you have a child, you always choose your child. *Above everything.* I *don't* love your mother more than I love you. You deserve to know whatever you need to know."

I wadded up my sandwich wrappers, passing the wad from fist to fist, packing it tightly like a snowball. It would have been easiest to tell him that I'd found out all I needed to know and just go back to my old life. But I'd learned too much about myself in the past year. I knew I could only play tough for so long. Maybe I'd manage to be strong for another twenty years. By that time I might have a kid of my own and when I inevitably freaked out about my mother and ran off again, I'd screw them up, too.

"Okay." I stared into my father's dark eyes. "Tell me everything."

He patted the spot on the bench next to him. "Come sit with me, then."

Sitting beside him, my head against his chest and his arm around my shoulders, reminded me of how he'd read to me on the couch when I was younger. When the story ended, I'd grin up at him and say, "Now tell me one about

Louisa." He was the best storyteller, describing every detail so I felt like I was there with them.

"What you heard from Regan was true," he said with a heavy sigh. "Eric Lisbon raped your mother." I shivered uncontrollably despite the humidity in the air around us. My dad pulled me closer and we both brought our cigarettes to our lips. "Eric was a violent guy. He beat her up badly just for talking to me once, but I didn't find out that he'd done worse until almost two years after he died. The day before Louisa's eighteenth birthday, I went to River's Edge to think. I was planning to propose to her and I wanted to come up with the perfect words."

My father stroked my hair and brought me into his memory. I could see him pushing the side door open, flooding River's Edge with violet-hued, evening light. He approached the stage from behind and saw Louisa sitting on the edge of it. Her pale hair illuminated her head like a halo and her shoulders curved so gently they appeared delicate, even beneath her heavy leather jacket.

Then, every muscle in his body seized when he noticed the gun in her hands. Her hands were in her lap, but the barrel aimed inward, angled toward her face. He started to say her name but froze, terrified of startling her into pulling the trigger.

Louisa heard his strangled whisper. She turned the gun away from herself and pointed it out into the cavernous room at some memory floating like a mirage in front of her. "This is the gun I killed Eric Lisbon with," she said robotically.

My father approached her slowly, shaking his head. She'd been beating herself up since Eric died, but my dad figured it was because people blamed her for breaking Eric's heart and making him suicidal. "Eric killed himself, Louisa. It's not your fault."

Louisa let her arm drop, lowering the gun. "It wasn't suicide, Michael. Molly and I just made it look that way. I shot him right in the head. I don't know how we got away with it. I should be in prison." She spoke without the slightest waver, staring at the gun. "After his funeral, I asked his mother for this, told her I'd get rid of it. I meant to use it on myself. But maybe I'll take it to the cops, turn myself in. I *deserve* to be in prison."

My dad sat down beside her. Louisa's tightly drawn mouth and glassy eyes made her look twice her age. He slowly lifted his hand and placed it against the middle of her back, burying his fingers in the ends of her platinum hair. He blurted without thinking, "Eric deserved what he got after the way he beat you up in the parking lot that night. I could have killed him myself for that. I should have."

"That's the night I killed him." Louisa proceeded to describe how she went to Eric's house to confront him about his abuse. He dragged her down into the basement and brutally raped her. He was drunk and eventually passed out on top of her, so she crawled out from under him and staggered over to his father's gun collection. She picked up a gun, contemplating killing herself with it, but unable to do so, she called Molly. Then Eric woke up and came after her again. She still had the gun in hand, so she fired.

"I can't tell you the details, Emily," my dad whispered. "I just can't."

"It's okay, Dad." I huddled against him. I knew some

of what Louisa felt firsthand. I remembered the stench of Johnny's alcohol-laden breath when he'd pinned me against the door of our apartment. But I'd ended up with a few cuts and bruises, nothing more. If Johnny had done what Eric did, if he had even tried, and I managed to wrestle that knife away from him, I would have stabbed him straight in the heart. "She knew it was self-defense, didn't she?" I asked.

I felt Dad shake his head no. "I tried to tell her that. Molly tried. I even thought about letting her turn herself in, so that a judge could rule self-defense, but in those days in a town like Carlisle, too many people would have said she was asking for it. Instead, I tried to help her forget. I suggested we leave Carlisle, go to Chicago. I'm the one who taught your mother that running away was the answer. I shouldn't have been shocked when she decided she had to keep running to escape the guilt."

His body quaked as he sobbed and I embraced him, soothing, "It's not your fault."

He shirked out of my arms and stared at me fiercely. "I let your mother leave you, Emily, and I promised her that I would never tell you the real reason why. You should hate me."

I ripped off my sunglasses. "Well, I can't and I can't hate her either. I need you and I still just want her to come home." I flung myself against his chest again and he wrapped strong arms around me.

"I do, too, baby," he murmured. "I still hope she'll come back for you."

I sniffled and scooted backward, lighting another Winston. "What about for you? Do you still love her?"

My dad borrowed my cigarette to light his own. "Yeah."

"You gonna put your ring back on now or do you have a new girlfriend?" I rubbed my dry lips anxiously, unprepared for that kind of a change.

He snorted. "In Carlisle? Are you kidding? Who wants to date the guy who wore his wedding ring for nineteen years after his wife left him? I'd have to move to the next county, probably the next state."

That succeeded in coaxing a laugh from me, but then my smile faltered. "I can't go back to Carlisle with you, Dad."

"I didn't think you would. I figured I'd be taking you to Regan's."

"You don't have to take me—"

"You don't have a choice," he chastised. "I haven't seen you in a year. You admitted you have a drug problem. And you're moving back to the city where that bastard—"

"Dad, I'm fine," I snapped, cutting him off before he could say Johnny's name.

"I'll believe it when I see it," he shot back.

We glared at each other until I bit my lip and said "Thank you"; at the same time he said, "Besides, you want your guitar back, don't you?"

"You have it?" I leapt up, heading for his truck. I crawled inside and retrieved the case, but hesitated to open it.

"I restrung it, had to play it myself a few times while I had it." He gently glossed over the condition it had been left in.

"Johnny did that." I faced my father and promised, "I won't make that mistake again."

He nodded and patted my back. "Let me drive you back to Regan's, then."

I looked across the bridge to where I'd parked on the westbound side of the highway. "What about my car?"

"Tom and I will come back for it," he assured me. "Give you and Regan some time to catch up."

Regan opened the door wearing a tank top and boxers, her hair—nearly as long as mine had been and just as black—piled on top of her head in a messy bun. She blinked sleepy hazel eyes at my dad. Then he stepped aside to reveal me, and both of her hands flew to her mouth. When she dropped them, she was smiling and crying at the same time. She said, "I don't know if I want to slap you or hug you," but she already had her arms around me.

She pulled me inside, shouting for Tom. He emerged from the bedroom, face stubbly and sleep-creased, and embraced me while Regan still clung to my hand.

Regan and Tom were renting an entire house in the 'burbs for what they paid for their apartment in the city. When Tom and my dad left to retrieve my car, Regan took me downstairs into their basement and we sat on the couch that had belonged to her parents. "Can you tell me what happened?" she asked.

Even though I was physically and emotionally exhausted, I knew I owed her that much. It took me an hour to tell her the whole story, including what my father had told me at the oasis. When I finished, I was curled up with my head on Regan's lap.

"God, Emily," she sighed, squeezing my shoulder. "You've been through so much, and Louisa . . ."

"She's strong, but not in the ways I imagined. And I just wish she was strong enough to come home."

"I'm glad you were that strong."

I laughed and sat up wearily. "I don't feel strong. Just tired."

"Want me to make up the couch for you?"

My gaze drifted to the right and fell on Regan's drum set. Her basement really was like a smaller version of her parents' and it felt so comforting. One of Tom's acoustic guitars leaned against a wood-paneled wall. The urgency I'd felt at the beginning of my drive from New Orleans stirred. "I want to play."

Regan and I ran through some of our old favorites as I loosened stiff fingers, but when my dad and Tom returned two hours later, Regan was following my lead, finding the rhythm for something new. My hands danced over simple chords and my voice scratched out the words: *"Where you going? Where you been? New Orleans, Boston, California. Where you headed now? Did you ever leave California? Don't know where you went, but I'm going home."*

I wasn't aware of my dad's presence until I heard him clapping. I looked up, face flushing. He offered me my favorite guitar, suggesting, "Try it electric."

I traded instruments with him. "Only if you sit in, lend me some acoustic texture."

"What are you calling this one?" Tom asked, approaching his bass.

"All Roads Lead to Rock 'n' Roll."

My dad stuck around for a week to make sure I got situated at Tom and Regan's. I knew it was hard for him to be in

Chicago; he saw Louisa's face sketched in the skyline and heard her voice in the traffic, the wind, the waves on the lake. We mostly stayed in Regan's tree-lined neighborhood and one day I commented, "I hate to admit it, but I think I like the suburbs. A twenty-minute train ride and I can be downtown in the thick of it, but it actually gets quiet here sometimes. I think I'll look for an apartment nearby."

"I think you should stay with Regan for a while," my dad cautioned.

He was adamant about me taking things slowly. He watched She Laughs rehearse day and night and played with us occasionally, but insisted, "Don't throw yourself back into it too fast."

Before I could object that I knew how to take care of myself, Regan piped up, "Don't worry, everything is going to happen on me and Tom's terms this time."

"We'll make decisions as a band," I agreed, recognizing that Regan and my dad were right. Part of the reason I picked up the guitar so often was to temper drug cravings. Whether I liked it or not, I needed someone looking out for me and She Laughs had to function collectively this time, so we didn't self-destruct.

We rehearsed for three months before picking up gigs around Chicago again. And even though everyone clamored for us to release something, it wasn't until a year after my return, in August of 1997, that we put out our self-titled debut album with Capone Records.

Regan had always wanted us to sign with them and maintained a friendship with Frank, the label owner, in my absence. After hearing "All Roads Lead to Rock 'n' Roll" and the other new songs that played like a diary of my year on the run, he said, "Please do one record with me before some major label comes and snatches you away." We eagerly shook his tattooed hand.

The record release party was held at Metro, the same place where we'd performed the radio station show two and a half years earlier, but this time Regan and I didn't argue. We rocked a six-song set that, short as it may have been, was undoubtedly the most successful show of our career. Reps from four major labels came to see it. Three of them had been hounding us for weeks. We'd gone to several fancy dinners, but always left without signing contracts because no one had been able to talk music with us like Frank did, even if they did have shaggy hair and a few tattoos to *seem* authentic.

"We don't have to sign with any of them," I assured Regan as we headed to Smart Bar, the bar below Metro, where our party would continue into the wee hours, execs trying to lure us to their tables as our album blared on the sound system.

Regan fingered her hair, cut short and spiky again and currently dyed blue. "Well, we're definitely turning down the guy who promised to take Tom to the Playboy Mansion."

Tom stuck out his lower lip in a mock pout, but added, "And I'm not so sure about the guy who brought Dom Perignon to us before the show either. He said something about courtside seats at the Lakers game if we come out to L.A. I don't think he has a clue."

We sat down at an inconspicuous table in the corner, sneaking past a third rep. I jerked my head in his direction.

"I wasn't pleased with that guy. He said he'd give us the biggest advance any female-fronted band had ever seen. If he can't see past female-fronted . . ."

"He doesn't get it," the three of us finished in unison.

Frank came over with his arm slung around the shoulders of a dainty, curly-haired girl with glasses. He flashed us his usual lazy grin and said, "If you're going to leave me for anyone, leave me for Lucy," introducing the mysterious fourth rep.

Regan spat her Coke back into her glass. "You signed my sister's band July Lies to No Wave Records in Minneapolis in 1992."

My jaw dropped as the girl pushed the cat-eye glasses up her nose. "You saw our first show at River's Edge."

"Yes and yes. You were pretty good back then, but this." She paused so we could listen to me snarl *New Orleans, Boston, California* over Regan's thunderous drumbeat. "This is the most honest song I've heard in three years."

"Thanks," I mumbled.

She tucked messy mahogany waves behind her ear. "Will you let me sit down and tell you why I left No Wave for Reprise?"

Tom glanced at Regan and me, then stood up, offering her his stool.

Ten minutes later, she slapped a business card down in front of each of us. "I'm not going to promise to take you to fancy Hollywood parties because I don't think *you're* interested. I'm not going to bust out a brick of cocaine to bribe you with because if you do that stuff, *I'm* not interested. I'm not going to cut you the biggest advance check in the world because you wouldn't outsell it and my bosses would drop you without giving you a real shot. Instead, we'll put the money into promotion and I'll get you a good contract so you'll have the same creative control you do right now. You pick the producer, the studio. But you'll have ten times the distribution. Think about it. Call me tomorrow."

When she left, the three of us sat speechless for a solid minute. I rarely drank since my return from New Orleans, but I announced, "I think I have to drink to that."

We wandered over to the front bar. I got a Midori Sour, Tom got a beer, and Regan got another Coke. We clinked our glasses together, toasting, "To Reprise."

Then Tom went off to talk to some friends while Regan and I daydreamed the way we had back in her parents' basement, where we'd diligently taught ourselves three power-chord punk songs and laughed at all the hair-metal guys on MTV. One day, we said, we'd turn the tables. Girls on top, where they belong. We'd play the boys' game better than they could play it themselves. Rocking harder. Having boy groupies. Dating movie stars and male models. Using rock gods as arm candy. Of course, Regan was in a committed relationship now, but she could still fantasize and I needed to, because my thoughts landed on Johnny more often than I wanted to admit.

Miraculously, I hadn't run into him at all during my first year back in Chicago. Initially I felt uneasy every time I entered one of his usual haunts, but he never turned up. I learned he was touring the album of songs he'd written while we were together. I'd hoped he was out of my life for good, but I should have known better.

"Here comes trouble." Regan's hazel eyes narrowed at the lanky guy with spiky, champagne-colored hair getting his ID checked at the entrance at the top of the stairs. From what I could see, Johnny looked almost exactly the same as he had when I left him, just another skinny boy in a faded T-shirt and jeans. But it was the way he moved—confident, eyes always scouting, the curl of his lip when he found what he wanted—that made him different.

"Jesus Christ!" I groaned. "He picks tonight to run into me? To-freakin'-night?"

Regan slunk off her stool, dragging me with her. I followed her through the door that divided the front of the bar from the dance floor, ducking, we hoped, out of his line of vision, but I couldn't help glancing back in his direction.

Two years after breaking up with Johnny, sometimes I didn't remember him in the way I knew I should. The end of our relationship, not the beginning, should have been playing on a loop in my mind. But Johnny shoved his way into my dreams again on summer nights when I lay twisted in my sweaty sheets and a hot breeze cascaded into my stuffy apartment, mimicking the air at River's Edge when we first met.

I dreamt about stage-diving. I let myself go limp, riding the current of the crowd like a dead body in a river. My head turns to the right and there, through the waving, pumping hands, is Johnny. I see him in slices that I won't put together until later: silver eyes, the curve of his jaw, the O of his lips cheering me on. And then, entwined in his fingers, I see the thing I won't notice I'm missing until I'm back onstage: my necklace, my mother's locket. He reaches out, trying to give it back, pushing past heads and hands, but my body rises up and away on the wave of grasping and releasing fingers. *Take me back.* His voice hangs in the air around me. *Take me back.*

I shook off the recollection as Regan and I found stools at the back bar. After about twenty minutes, Regan figured Johnny hadn't seen us, so she left me to use the bathroom. Of course, Johnny had probably been waiting for just such an opportunity.

"What are you doing here?" I asked without looking at him, feeling his shoulder brush mine as he sat down beside me. I stared straight down into the green of my drink, its sticky film coating the back of my throat and making it even harder for me to speak without my voice squeaking.

"Like I'd miss the most happening party in Chicago." His muscled arm rubbed against mine as he lifted his hand to signal the bartender. "Jack and Coke," he told her. She flicked her head in acknowledgment.

Instead of noting that he still drank whiskey despite its role in the incident that had broken us up, I scoffed, clearing my sickly sweet throat in the process. "The after-party for a record release show at Metro is hardly the *most happening* party in Chicago."

I refused to look at Johnny. My eyes followed the bartender, the drink she slid to him, the dark blue fingernails that pulled his crumpled dollar bills toward her. Next, she poured a beer for a red-haired girl down the bar. Beneath the straps of the redhead's shimmering gold tank top, she had wings tattooed on her back. As she walked away I watched the wings disappear to the other side of the dance floor. I wished I had wings to fly into the steamy August night. I wished Regan's tousled, indigo head would come through the door, Tom towering behind her. I combed the crowded room for someone familiar who could rescue me, one of the fans or industry people who'd swarmed me after the show, but they'd already gotten what they wanted from me.

"I've never seen so many A&R types. It's got to take something pretty interesting to get them out to see a local band on a Tuesday night." Johnny leaned even closer to me, so he didn't have to shout over the music.

"Oh, I get it." I finished my drink in one swallow and swung my bare legs around on my stool, finally facing him. "You, A&R types, flies, shit . . ." I flung my hand up to give my clichéd insult more impact. In the process, my stubby middle fingernail chipped against the bridge of his nose, marring his creamy skin with a little red line. My gaze hovered on the scratch, but avoided his silver bullet eyes. "I'm out of here," I said snottily, rocking off the bar stool and smoothing my shiny black skirt as I stood.

"Emily, you're not going to run out on your own release party, are you?" He lightly teased me like he used to, little competitive gibes.

My mouth twisted into a cruel smile. "Why not? Tomorrow morning, we're signing a major deal. I'll be back in the studio to record the next album within a year. I've got hundreds of songs in me, Johnny. What about you? I heard you're still playing the same set from two years ago. Writer's block? Lack of talent?" I wasn't normally one to brag. Hearing my voice, my guitar work on the CD blaring from the speakers that night had honestly made me uncomfortable until that moment. Then I let a choppy guitar riff punctuate my comment like laughter. "Hundreds of songs, Johnny," I repeated, meeting those gray orbs for the first time, dulled as scuffed marbles by the power of my words. "And you can't compete with a single riff."

I tried to storm off, my shoulder-length hair whipping around with me, but he grabbed my wrist and pulled me against him like he had that last time he touched me. I winced, my side expecting the tip of a blade. "Emily, please listen to me." A genuine plea, but I could only react to the whiskey stench it floated on.

"You can't hold me back now, just like you couldn't then. And this time you don't even have your knife." I planted the sharply pointed toe of my patent leather high heel into his shin.

His hand loosened around my wrist, but he let his body topple forward, leaning over me. "I'm sorry. Please, just come outside and talk to me."

His warm lips grazed my ear. The sensation made me shudder, and not out of fear like it should have, but I still resisted my twisted craving for his kiss. I flipped him off over my shoulder as I stalked away.

"It's not over between us, Emily," he called after me. I could picture the self-assured smirk on his face as he said it and knew that, unfortunately, it wasn't.

Other People's Daughters

September 1996

When Nadia entered middle school, Colette constantly said to Louisa, "I hardly recognize her." And she wasn't just talking about how the petite girl had suddenly gotten tall, changed the color of her hair monthly, and coated her eyes in glittery makeup. Nadia's personality had flip-flopped. She'd gone from a sweet, quiet introvert to a door-slamming, loud-music-blasting, boy-crazy social butterfly in a matter of months. "Is this normal?" Colette wondered.

Louisa shrugged in reply and turned away so Colette would have no idea how much the question stung. Emily had been completely lost to Louisa by the time she reached Nadia's age, and watching Nadia grow up made Louisa wish she'd kept in touch with Molly. Whenever Colette said, "The problem is that Nadia's turned in to me, but nowadays kids are so much crazier," Louisa craved reassurance that Emily had made it through adolescence in one piece and hadn't turned out like her. But all Louisa could do was hope for the best for Emily and play mediator between Colette and Nadia. Which was why she'd been the one to answer the phone on that awful night in September.

Colette's grand plans for Labor Day weekend—to go to a cabin in the mountains they could rent cheap from her co-worker's sister—had gone bust when thirteen-year-old Nadia pulled her usual attitude. "Who goes to the mountains?" she complained, crossing her arms and pouting bright pink lips. "Palm Springs or Vegas, or I'm not going."

Colette tossed her hands in the air. "Who taught you to act so spoiled, because it sure wasn't me!"

So, Saturday night, Nadia went out as usual, and Louisa and Colette sat around at home watching *Saturday Night Live*. Half an hour into the show, Louisa headed into the kitchen to make more margaritas and the phone rang.

"If that's Nadia, tell her I'm not extending her curfew," Colette shouted from the living room.

But Louisa was surprised to hear Brenda, Nadia's best friend, on the other end, and was even more shocked by the way she sounded.

"Colette?" Brenda's panicked voice came on the line. The haughty, self-assured, "back by midnight" snap of lips painted too thickly with red gloss was gone.

Louisa's skin went cold. "No, Brenda, it's Louisa. What's wrong?"

"Nadia . . ." Louisa immediately knew that Nadia was in trouble. She heard the tears in Brenda's voice, hard tears that ripped at the throat. "She . . ."

"What? Spit it out!" Louisa's words came out sharper than she intended.

"Just come to the motel where I live. Come to the p-p-pool," Brenda stuttered. And then she hung up the phone.

"Brenda, what happened?" Louisa screamed at the dial tone.

The drive to the motel would take less than five minutes, but it sounded like there was no time to spare. Louisa's bare feet slapped against the wooden floor as she ran down the short hallway to the living room.

Colette sat on the floor with the TV blaring, her long, snowy legs stretched out beneath the coffee table; she was cutting lines of cocaine on her mirror, clearly oblivious to the conversation that had gone on in the kitchen.

"Something's happened to Nadia!" Louisa yelled as she skidded into the room.

Colette scrambled up, knocking the coffee table on its side. The mirror, landing beneath it, cracked, and the white powder poofed up, forming a perfect cloud that hung in the air for a moment, then settled, covering the floor in a white film. Louisa's six years in L.A. had been coated in this same white dust.

When they reached the motel, the sight of Louisa and Colette, barefoot and disheveled, dashing around the side of the building for the gated-in pool caught the attention of the night manager. He stumbled up, shouting, "Hey, the pool is for guests only!" as he pursued them to the back of the building.

Propelling herself up and over the short chain-link fence—her heels hitting the cement hard, though she wouldn't feel them throb until much later—Louisa saw five kids squatted in a tight circle, shoulder to shoulder, heads bowed like they were performing a séance alongside the deeper end of the kidney-shaped pool. Louisa didn't see Nadia and realized that they were bending over her. She convinced herself that it was innocent, that the kids were chanting "Light as a feather, stiff as a board, light as a feather, stiff as a board" in a collective murmur and Nadia would soon rise.

Colette's ragged wail shattered Louisa's fantasy. "Nadia!"

The coven of teenagers took flight, scattering to the back fence. The chairs in which overbaked guests sunned themselves during the day clattered against the concrete as the kids knocked them aside in their hasty escape.

When the circle broke, Nadia was revealed, lying on her back, limbs flung out at her sides haphazardly as if she'd fallen from the sky when the clouds cracked open for a sudden downpour. Water puddled around her body, fanning outward and darkening the cement. Brenda staggered backward, away from Nadia, leaving wet footprints. Louisa clamped her hand around Brenda's wrist as Colette collapsed on her knees at Nadia's side, moaning, "No, no, no!"

Colette's ringed fingers prodded at Nadia's neck, digging for a pulse. The purple tone glistening through Nadia's translucent skin had to be the sign of blood trying to push through her veins. Colette's hands slid over the straps of Nadia's soaked, glittery black tank top and down her clammy arms. She rubbed her daughter's skin like Nadia was a tarnished treasure chest that had been submerged deep beneath the waters of the Bay Motel pool. If she massaged the waxy skin hard enough, perhaps words would be revealed, a magical spell that Colette could recite to unlock Nadia, cause her to sit straight up, spewing the water in her lungs freely like a fountain.

Colette quickly moved her hands from her daughter's arms to her chest, pounding on it. Her fingers pinched Nadia's nose as she forced her breath in through Nadia's wilted lips. Lifting her mouth from her daughter's and glancing into the night momentarily, Colette screeched, "Call someone! Help me!" The word "help" was breathless, Colette having given nearly all her air to Nadia.

The sallow-faced night manager had come to a halt at the gate, mouth hanging open, chin dangling like an undercooked dumpling. When Colette screamed, he sprang into action, his sausagelike legs propelling him back to his office.

Louisa wrenched Brenda out of the shadows toward where Nadia lay on the ground. Nadia's bright crimson hair, which Louisa had helped her dye just days ago, was plastered flat against the concrete beneath her, sticking out around her head like a flaming crown extinguished by the scummy pool water. Louisa got close enough to see Nadia's face. Her red lipstick smeared outward, giving her cheeks the illusion of pinkness. The black eyeliner and dark shadow Nadia had artfully smudged before going out that night spread down her face like mud.

At the sight of Nadia, Brenda faltered and stopped pulling away from Louisa.

"Did you call 911?" Louisa demanded as she stared into

Brenda's amber eyes, which were just as waterlogged as Nadia's.

Brenda's bony face shook like her voice. "Y-y-yes," she choked. Her answer was punctuated by the shriek of sirens drawing near. Louisa let Brenda lower herself to the ground. The girl wrapped her spindly arms around her legs. "I didn't mean for N-N-Nadia to get in trouble. We didn't want to get in trouble."

We didn't want to get in trouble, the empty eulogy for Louisa's time in California. Every time she'd tried to leave, Colette repeated, "You know we'll get into trouble without you."

Nadia, just last year, had mimicked her mother, blocking the door alongside her, arms crossed, hip cocked, blowing a strand of hair out of her face. "My mom is *always* in trouble without you," she sighed melodramatically before dissolving into giggles.

Louisa hurried over to Colette and knelt down beside her and Nadia. As if Colette couldn't hear the wail of the sirens, Louisa reassured her, "They're coming."

Colette's anguished scream matched the sirens' volume. "She won't wake up! Nadia, wake up!" Colette's hand lashed across Nadia's ashen cheek, leaving a red imprint that did nothing but upset Colette further. "Oh god, I'm sorry!" She pulled Nadia up into her lap, wrapping her arms around Nadia's body, wet and heavy as a pile of soaked towels. "Please wake up."

Though neither Colette nor Louisa heard him approach, an EMT put his hand on Colette's shoulder. "Let us take her."

"But *I'm* her mother. I have to be here!" Colette insisted.

"I know, ma'am, but if you could stand to the side so we can treat her." He squatted behind Colette. He had kind, brown eyes that reminded Louisa of Michael's, eyes she hadn't seen in twenty years. Like Michael, the EMT also had thick, tanned, hardworking arms. Arms that were stronger than Colette's and Louisa's combined. Arms that could revive Nadia.

"C'mon, Colette, he'll take care of Nadia. He'll wake her up," Louisa said soothingly.

She stood as Colette transferred Nadia into the EMT's arms carefully, as if she were a newborn baby. After Colette slowly backed away, his partner rushed forward, a woman with blond hair tied back in a tight ponytail. They surrounded Nadia the same way the kids had, shielding her with their white-uniformed backs. Their limbs moved in a blur as they worked to revive her

At first Colette stood right behind them, sobbing silently. After a minute of watching strange instruments pass back and forth, she started to whimper. Then her chest began to heave as she pulled at tufts of her black hair. "I can't see her," she implored. "I need to see her."

A police officer stepped up from somewhere, a lean, Hispanic man who raised both of his palms as he talked, addressing Louisa since Colette didn't seem to see him, her eyes still seeking Nadia. "They need some room. If you, the mother, and the other girl can please step back and tell us what happened."

Reminded of Brenda's presence, Colette whirled around like a tornado, arms outstretched and right index finger pointing accusatorily. "She knows what happened!"

Sobs wracked Brenda's skinny frame. "I . . . I . . . I . . ."

"How did Nadia end up in the pool?" Colette's red-rimmed eyes seemed ready to burst from her anger-stiffened face.

The policeman stepped between Brenda and Colette, putting one hand on each of their arms. He entreated Colette to stay calm, then swiveled to face Brenda. "Please tell us what happened as best you can. Don't leave anything out."

"N-Nadia went to the pool before any of us. When we got there she was already underwater," Brenda stammered. "We thought she was swimming . . . and then she didn't come up. We thought she was just messing around, but she was down there too long. We dove in and pulled her up. She's going to be okay, right?"

Brenda's face, wet with tears and pool water, glistened even though it was half shaded by the palm trees that cut into the hazy yellow lamplight surrounding the pool. Everyone always glistened in L.A. because it never got completely dark. Nowhere, Louisa had noticed over the years, got as dark as Carlisle. She'd run from that darkness, the way it cloaked nasty secrets that could destroy lives, but, she wondered, was it that much different in the light? What had Nadia and Brenda done out in the glaring California sun that she and Colette overlooked?

"Where were you beforehand?" the officer asked. "I need you to be honest with me. I need to know if there was drinking, drugs. Remember, this is Nadia's life at stake." He sounded rehearsed, but perhaps, Louisa thought, it was because she had seen this happen on TV so many times that it didn't seem real. The emergency workers and their frantic hands pumping on Nadia's chest; the cop with his notepad, his professional words working to both question and console; and the red-faced manager trying to keep curious motel guests from getting through the gate.

Brenda stared down at the cement, her wet hair swaying like seaweed. "We started at Nick's, and then we came here. I live here, me and my mom, in room 204." Her arm moved like it was pulled by a string, indicating the motel.

"What were you guys doing at Nick's?"

"And who the hell is Nick?" Collette snapped. "You didn't say anything about going anywhere with anyone named Nick!"

Brenda lifted her eyes, defiance returning to her face and her voice. "Nick's her boyfriend. Didn't you know that? Weren't you paying attention?"

"Don't you dare talk to me like that!" Colette would have lunged at Brenda had the policeman not been holding them apart. "*I* pay attention! *You two* keep secrets!"

The officer tried to redirect the conversation. "Let's just go back to Nick's. What were you doing at Nick's?"

"We were, uhh, drinking."

"How old is Nick?"

"Seventeen . . ."

"What the hell is he doing with my thirteen-year-old daughter, then?"

"Shh." Louisa trailed her fingers down Colette's back. There was so much they didn't know about Nadia, so much they hadn't known for at least a year. Or, rather, so much that they'd ignored. Just a few months earlier, on Nadia's birthday, Colette and Nadia had had their biggest blowout yet right on the front lawn. Colette had made a reservation at a much nicer restaurant than she could afford, and Nadia, dressed in a skirt Colette deemed way too short, had run off to a party with her friends instead. When Nadia stumbled in drunk that night, Colette didn't even pull her eyes away from the TV. She told Louisa through gritted teeth, "She's too much like me. I can't watch her make the same mistakes."

Louisa tried to map out the preceding years, six short years, and figure out when it had all fallen apart. Things had only been the way Colette had promised in Portland for six months, and then Brad's money had vanished. They moved from tiny apartment to tiny apartment, always staying in the good neighborhoods because Colette said, "My daughter is *not* going to a ghetto school. I'll move her back to my god-fearing father's house in North Carolina before she sets foot in one of those schools." Louisa wondered why they hadn't just gone to North Carolina then. Anywhere but L.A.

Dust coated the reasons, white dust Louisa had sworn she would never use again. Coke had transformed Los Angeles into a glittering, sun-streaked island, saying, *You live in the place born from the American Dream, why leave?* Numb, Louisa and Colette had listened, even let Nadia listen, and Nadia had grown up too fast because of it. The murmurs and secrets of L.A. were not intended for a child's ears. A little girl should not hear so many fairy tales that end in broken dreams.

Louisa squeezed her eyes shut, praying that Nadia was all right. Between each prayer was one for her own daughter. *Michael was smarter than me,* she reassured herself. *Please, as much as I hated it, please let him have stayed in Carlisle to raise her. Please don't let me find out Emily was like this at thirteen.*

Feeling guilty about the way she let thoughts of Emily overshadow those of Nadia at such a time, Louisa tuned back in to hear Brenda admitting, "He also had some pills. Ecstasy."

"Did Nadia take any pills?"

"Yeah, on the car ride over. She was just trying to have fun. That's all. And when we got to my room, she said it would be fun to swim, so she ran off . . ." Brenda broke down, crying inconsolably.

"Oh god," Colette moaned, shaking her head, white-faced, too terrified to be angry anymore.

Louisa caught the flurry of activity around Nadia out of the corner of her eye. The female paramedic stepped to the side as the man tried to start Nadia's heart with a defibrillator. Colette's gaze followed Louisa's, and at that point, no one could hold her back.

Colette arrived at her daughter's side just as Nadia started sputtering, coughing up the pool water, gasping for air. She rolled on her side, heaving, vomiting up more water. "Baby, baby, baby," Colette murmured, rubbing her daughter's icy shoulders, massaging her back as she shuddered. The paramedic who resembled Michael helped Nadia sit up and wrapped her in a blanket.

Nadia's eyes were cloudy, her head lolling on her neck

as she faced her mother. Dazed, she still managed to say "Sorry" between labored breaths.

"Shh," Colette sobbed. "I'm the one who's sorry. I've been letting you down for years."

Louisa watched the paramedics lift Nadia onto a stretcher. As the terror she felt for Nadia subsided, remorse rose to the surface. She stared at Nadia's delicate hands trembling in Colette's grip. Nadia's lips regained their natural pink hue beneath the lipstick stains, and her heavy lids slowly dipped over shocked, hazel eyes. Louisa had come to love this child, let Nadia nudge her way into the space in her heart reserved for the daughter Louisa had left behind. And the results had been disastrous. She'd infected Nadia the way she'd feared she would her own child. Just because Nadia wasn't flesh and blood didn't mean she wasn't susceptible to Louisa's bad luck.

Louisa's eyes drifted in the direction of the 101. It was time to go. She shouldn't have stayed so long. She shouldn't have come to L.A. with Colette and Nadia. She should have shut her door on Colette the very first time she'd shown up. *You were supposed to go it alone, so you wouldn't ruin any more lives,* Louisa reprimanded herself.

"Lou," Colette called over her shoulder, clinging to Nadia's hand as the stretcher wheeled forward. "Are you coming in the ambulance or following us to the hospital?"

Louisa shook her head. "I'm not going. It's not my place."

Colette's brow furrowed, but she was too focused on her daughter to question Louisa. "We'll see you back at the house?"

"Yeah," Louisa replied, but she honestly wasn't sure if she would still be there.

When she arrived at the apartment, Louisa carefully cleaned the living room. She picked up the coffee table, wiped the white dust off the floor, and stacked the magazines—the *Spin*s and *Rolling Stone*s that she and Colette bought and the *Vogue*s that Nadia pored over. God, Nadia was such an L.A. girl. Hopefully Colette would be able to get her out before it was too late. Then again, maybe L.A. would be safe for them once Louisa left, taking her bad vibes with her.

Louisa wandered into her bedroom and began to pack her things, but the panicked feeling she'd had before Nadia had been revived still seemed lodged in her chest. There was something she needed to do.

She went to the kitchen and picked up the phone.

"Hello," Molly answered sleepily.

"Molly?"

"Louisa?" Molly practically shouted. Then her tone dropped to a low whisper; Luke was probably beside her in bed. "Where are you?"

"I want to know about my daughter. I want to know about . . . Emily." Louisa's voice was scratched with tears.

"Okay." Louisa could hear Molly swallowing back shock. It had been nine years since Louisa had so much as sent a letter to her best friend, and Louisa had never mentioned Emily by name, even in writing. "What do you want to know?"

"Just tell me if she's okay," Louisa said.

"She's fine. She and Regan are living together outside of Chicago. They've got a band, and they're actually pretty good. If you want her address . . ."

"No, I just wanted to know that she was alive."

"She's fine, but she'd love to see you. She—" Louisa hung up. She imagined that Molly would sit in bed repeating "Louisa?" despite the sound of the dial tone. She tried not to think about the way Molly would cry when she finally had to hang up the phone and accept that Louisa was gone all over again. Louisa had a hard time not crying herself as she returned to her room and continued packing.

THE ART OF BAD ENDINGS

There are so many horror stories about touring. Someone in the audience throws a bottle at the bass player, resulting in a concussion. The drummer gets drunk one night and punches a wall, breaking three fingers. The singer/guitarist passes out on-stage and management blames it on "dehydration" or "nervous exhaustion," denying rumors of drug addiction. Sleep-deprived bandmates brawl backstage. Everyone quits at least once.

Yeah, the idea of touring freaked me out for a lot of reasons. Would it remind me of running after Louisa? Would that on top of a grueling schedule cause me to lose it and start using again? Would Regan and Tom's sharing a bus or hotel room with me strain their relationship and drive Regan to drink again?

Because of these concerns, we decided to take touring as slowly as we had everything else. We started the week after our first album came out, but only scheduled fifteen dates. Regan and Tom hadn't been outside of the Midwest, and when I'd traveled my focus had been on Louisa, so we took the time to do touristy things like visit the Lincoln Memorial in D.C. and the Space Needle in Seattle. We weren't a hard-partying band, so we got enough rest to truly enjoy playing legendary clubs like CBGBs and the Whisky. Touring didn't feel like work. Seeing kids all over the country who pushed to the front of the stage and sang along to every song was a dream come true.

We were asked to add more dates and didn't want to turn down the smaller cities because we identified with those audiences most. Then a phone call from our booking agent came: "They really want you in London. And how about Paris?" No way in hell we could say no. Ultimately, we ended up touring across the United States, Canada, and Europe for almost a year before heading to L.A. to record our new album.

It wasn't easy all the time. The bus stank and so did we more often than not. Regan got food poisoning in Texas. Tom twisted his ankle while carrying equipment in Denver. I sang with a sore throat for a week and got so sick in Toronto, I almost had my dad fly out to bring me home to Chicago.

I called my dad a lot because spending so much time with a couple made me lonely, but I didn't want to fall into a pathetic pattern of one-night stands. That's also why I couldn't help but take some pleasure from Johnny's little notes.

His band was on tour as well, opening for more famous labelmates. They played the same venues we headlined a couple of days before we got there, and Johnny started writing messages to me on the walls backstage. His first, at the Rave in Milwaukee, read simply, "All apologies, Emily Black." In San Francisco, he wrote, "Emily Black = Rock Goddess."

By Europe, things were more flirtatious. In Berlin, Regan came out of a doorless bathroom stall and found me writing on a cracked mirror so covered with stickers and handwritten logos that only a few inches in the center were clear for a last-minute check of hair and makeup. "What the hell is this?" she demanded.

I'd finished adding a swirl to the last *s* of She Laughs with my purple Sharpie, but she tapped the message a few inches above. "Johnny Threat Hearts Emily Black."

Horror-struck, she asked, "You aren't sleeping with him again, are you?"

I just laughed. "When, Regan? I've been with you guys every night. Have you seen me rush ahead to the next city to meet up with him?"

"No." She narrowed her hazel eyes suspiciously. "But this is creepy. Stalker creepy. We need to make it stop."

I brushed her off, playfully messing up her artfully disheveled plum hair. "Regan, it's harmless. It's not getting to me, so don't worry about it."

"This is going to end badly," she warned.

Of course, she was right. And I'd lied; Johnny's words were getting to me. They made me smirk, made me tingle, and—worst of all—sometimes I felt like my head was in the clouds. But, goddammit, I planned to keep control of the situation. I had my dignity, my self-respect, and power over my sexual desires. At least I did when Johnny was more than fifty miles away from me and notes were his only form of communication. I knew that if I ran into him in person, the chemistry would kick in. And not the kind of chemistry that brings about cures for diseases and solutions to the energy crisis, but the kind that explodes and leaves most everyone in the vicinity dead or deformed, and the survivors shaking their heads, going, "I wish I'd seen *that* coming."

I *should've* seen it coming, but I'm going to blame the hypnotic glitter of L.A., the excitement of recording in a real, professional studio, and large quantities of alcohol. Especially the latter.

We arrived in Los Angeles in July 1998 with more than an album's worth of songs written for our major-label debut. The first two days, we worked from noon until midnight, pounding out material with serious vigor. But on our third afternoon in the studio, I received a phone call that led to a series of horrible decisions.

Even though I hadn't actually spoken with Johnny since he'd crashed my record release party a year earlier, I immediately recognized his smug "Emily, I finally got ahold of you."

Keeping my eyes on the control room, where Regan was occupied, I hissed, "How did you get this number? Why the hell are you calling me?"

Johnny replied, smooth and cocky as ever, "You know how it is, when labels are interested in you, they'll do just about anything you ask. It wasn't hard to find out where you were recording."

Regan had hit the nail on the head. This was creepy. Stalker creepy. Johnny had to be dealt with.

My first bad decision was to try to do it on my own.

When Johnny invited me to his show at the Roxy that night, I accepted and snuck out of the studio before anyone could question me.

Bad decision number two: stopping a little ways down Sunset Strip for a few too many drinks to steel my nerves. I planned a speech that began, "Seriously, Johnny, things are over between us. I don't want to hear your apologies because nothing can make up for what you did to me." But by the time I got to the club, I was so sloshed that I could barely tell the door guy, "I'm on the lisssshhhht."

When I stumbled backstage, I found Johnny drunk as well. He was nervous about all the industry people in attendance, not to mention his harshest critic, me. Instead of berating him, I found myself sharing a bottle of Jack with him, giving the old pep talk we used to give to psych each other up back in the day. It was easier than telling him off, and wasted as I was, I preferred the easy route. Wasted as I was, Johnny seemed like the nice, normal guy from the beginning of our relationship.

While he performed, I stood at the side of the stage, swilling whiskey like it was water, and ogling his messy, dishwater-blond hair, the perfect cheekbones, the familiar muscled arms covered in inky spiderwebs, stars, and brightly colored hula girls. He performed the drunkest, sloppiest, most beautiful show I'd ever seen him play, and immediately afterward I pulled him and our bottle of Jack into a closet-size dressing room. Or maybe it was a bathroom. I couldn't really tell at that point, the lighting being rather dim and my vision rather blurry. Johnny stripped off my T-shirt and pushed me against a wall. I peeled off his shirt, a half-smile on my face as my eyes darted down to those seductive, washboard abs, where my name was inscribed in Old English–style letters.

Wait. I stared at the black lettering. *That hadn't been there before. When did Johnny get that tattoo?* My stomach lurched and I tasted vomit in the back of my throat. *He's stalker creepy, you idiot!* I scolded myself as my hands flew away from his belt buckle and grasped the walls for balance. Everything spun and I began to hyperventilate. *How did this happen? I'm not supposed to be one of those stupid, gullible, idiot girls who fall for the evil guy again and again.* I'd never hated myself more.

"Emily, what's wrong?" Johnny asked, slightly out of breath, his lips working their way down my neck, fingers fumbling at the clasp on my bra.

I shoved him off of me. "I can't do this. I won't do this. We're not getting back together, Johnny."

Shock replaced his eager expression. "Emily . . ."

I groped for the doorknob at the same time his bassist, Seth, started banging on the door. "Johnny, there's a label guy out here who wants to talk to us!"

I fell out of the claustrophobic room into half of Johnny's band. Mike, one of *my* label's A&R guys, stood behind them. "You didn't see me here. We're not together," I slurred. "I'm not part of any rock 'n' roll couple. The girl always gets screwed."

"Emily!" Mike called after me, confused. I waved him off, grabbing someone's hoodie from the couch and zipping it over my bra as I ran outside. I hoped the cabdriver that I hailed wouldn't notice my lack of shoes.

Upon my arrival at the swanky, corporate apartment

complex where Reprise had put up my band while we re-corded, I went directly for Regan and Tom's apartment in-stead of my own. When Tom answered the door in a T-shirt and pajama pants, I whimpered, "I know you guys are having a nice, quiet evening together, and I hate to interrupt, but I need Regan." I rubbed snot on the stolen-from-a-stranger hoodie.

Regan's violet-streaked head peeked up over the back of the couch. She quickly slid a remote and a bowl of popcorn onto the coffee table and rushed over to me. "Em, what's wrong?"

"Oh," I hiccupped, clinging to the door frame for sup-port. "You're watching a movie together. You guys are like a real couple. You're like . . . Oh shit!" I pushed past her, run-ning through the living room and just managing to slide the door to the balcony open before I retched.

When I finally finished and turned to apologize, Regan's lips were puckered in a combination of distress and disgust. Tom couldn't help snickering. "That was pretty punk rock, Em."

Regan smacked him in the arm. "Emily, why are you so drunk?" she asked with concern as I wiped my mouth on my sleeve. "And why are you wearing a hoodie for Johnny's band?"

"I am?" I glanced down at my chest to find My Gorgeous Letdown's logo scrawled across it. "Oh god, I am!" I promptly unzipped the thing and dropped it on the vomit puddle, mak-ing Tom laugh even harder.

He ducked out of Regan's reach. "I'm sorry, but that's so appropriate."

"Get her a T-shirt, Tom!" Regan snapped, on the verge of losing her patience. She growled at me, "Tell me you're not seeing Johnny. Tell me you're not that stupid."

I staggered forward, hugging her as I blubbered, "I am that stupid. I am! I thought I knew what I was doing. I thought I could take care of myself." As she led me inside, I blurted out the whole story. How I secretly felt complimented by the messages Johnny had been writing and part of me wanted to forgive him because they made me miss the good times we'd had. How that part of me must have taken over after I'd gotten the phone call from him and proceeded to get wasted before his show. How if it hadn't been for that tattoo freaking me out, I probably would have slept with him. "And then you would have hated me," I finished, putting on the T-shirt that Tom had brought me before excusing himself from the apartment.

Regan stroked my head affectionately. "I wouldn't have hated you. I just would have lost some respect for you."

"I've already lost respect for me." I sniffled. "And I need a cigarette."

We smoked silently for a moment before Regan smirked. "So, how big is the tattoo?"

"The letters are, like, an inch tall," I said soberly, trying not to laugh.

"Damn, he better get a record contract so he can afford the laser removal!"

"Well, I think Mike Nowell's going to take care of that."

Regan choked on her exhalation. "They're going to be on *our* label? Are you sure Johnny wasn't lying . . ."

"I saw Mike. Did I leave that part out?"

"Yes."

The memory of Mike seeing me with Johnny rekindled all of my concerns. "I told Mike not to tell anyone Johnny and I were together." But as I said that, I realized Mike wasn't the real problem. Things had gotten almost lighthearted with Regan joking about the tattoo, but it wasn't funny. Johnny's obsession was clear. I started crying again. "It doesn't matter what Mike says or thinks, though, because Johnny's not going away. When I ran out, I heard him say, 'We'll talk later, Emily.' *We'll talk later*," I mimicked. "Dammit!" I slapped my thighs. "He's not gonna leave me alone and he's gonna tell everyone we're together and he'll probably say he wrote all of my songs. I just want to make a good record. And for our music to be taken seriously. I don't want to be tabloid fodder!"

"Shh." Regan pulled me toward her. Her hands worked in small, comforting circles on my back. "It'll be okay. We'll use Mike to our advantage. Have him tell Johnny not to talk about you, that it could be damaging to his own career. That's what matters most to Johnny, after all. Maybe he can get that tattoo fixed to say 'Ego.'"

I didn't laugh. I didn't even try. I was on that drunken roller-coaster ride: I'd gone from horny to freaked to puking my guts out to tears, and now to full-on self-pity mode. "Maybe I should just be with Johnny. Maybe that's what I deserve. Maybe he's the best I can do. Girls like me, we don't get fairy-tale endings."

Regan wasn't about to let me wallow. "Emily, shut up! This isn't you. You broke a guy's nose for calling you a groupie, for Christ's sake. Don't lower yourself to taking back psychotic ex-boyfriends."

Her version of motivation didn't work; it just put me on the fast track to angry drunk. "Maybe I'm not lowering myself!" I spat. "Maybe I'm not the slut with the redemptive arc like you. Maybe I still wanna get drunk and screw wannabe rock gods. Maybe that's just me."

"Oh yeah, 'cause that's fun, right?" Regan rolled her eyes.

I looked hatefully at the evidence of her happiness. "More fun than eating popcorn and watching movies. This"—I pointed to the table—"was not why we wanted to be rock stars. Do you and Tom even have sex anymore?" I asked caustically. In my state, I didn't even know why I lashed out at Regan, but she did.

"Have you ever actually been in love, Emily?" She crossed her arms, wearing what I read as a self-satisfied, know-it-all expression.

I thought of the night Johnny held the knife to my side, when I knew what we had wasn't real love. "No, Regan. I haven't. I'm not capable." I rose and kicked the table, sending the popcorn flying. Of course, I still had bare feet, so as soon as the pain registered, I fell back onto the couch, bawling my eyes out. "Who cares? Love worked out really great for my parents, Regan!"

Her anger evaporated. "Jesus, Emily, I'm sorry I said that," she consoled, hugging me again. "Really sorry. Things are going to work out for you."

I sucked back tears and put my head down in her lap. "I just wish the Johnny thing was over. I wish it had never happened."

Regan untangled my hair with her fingers. "We'll get rid

of him and we'll find you a good guy. Seriously, Em, things are gonna get better. We're going to make an amazing record, and by this time next year, we'll be on the cover of *Rolling Stone*."

The album came out a couple weeks before Christmas and we had a low-key release party in Chicago at a dive bar down the block from Regan and Tom's, just friends, family, and some people from our label. We ceremoniously put the new CD in the jukebox and Lucy punched in the numbers for the first single, informing us, "It's getting a lot of play on KROQ in L.A." Ever the cautious businesswoman, she added, "They always try to break new punk bands. It doesn't mean the song will catch on nationwide. Your first record did extremely well for an indie, but don't get disappointed if you don't have instant success. Just keep touring like you have been and you'll sell through, if not with this album, with the next one."

So we toured. Phone calls came from the record company telling us which "markets" had the song "in rotation" and reporting numbers of albums sold that seemed extremely high. But the business talk was confusing. The real evidence of success came when our shows got moved to bigger venues or when second and third nights had to be added. Then, one night a fax from Lucy waited for us at our hotel in San Diego: the Billboard Hot 100 chart. She'd circled our album in the number two position and scrawled beside it: "Your gold records are waiting in L.A.!"

Regan screamed and dropped the sheet of paper. Embracing me as tears streamed down her flushed cheeks, she declared, "Maybe we can knock Britney Spears out of the top spot if we wear Catholic schoolgirl skirts in the next video."

Since Tom wasn't about to shave his legs, we never dethroned the princess of pop, but it didn't matter. The album had only been out for a few months when my dad came to our show in Milwaukee and I had a gold record to present him with for his birthday. It came in a rectangular frame matted against a red background. I wrapped it up and gave it to Dad while he relaxed on a couch backstage. He shook his head, confused, probably wondering if I'd purchased an overpriced piece of art and needed a lecture on the value of money. When he tore through the paper, his hand flew to his mouth and he just stared. Finally, he looked up at me, lip curling into a smirk, and said, "Didn't I tell you this would happen four years ago?"

But the biggest shock of all came a month later. We were in New York City and our manager insisted on going someplace nice for dinner. He gave no explanation, just asked, "Would you prefer Italian or sushi?"

I gagged into the phone. "Pasta, please."

Regan, Tom, and I beat him to the ritzy restaurant and were mildly irritated when he arrived guffawing away with a guy in designer vintage threads that were stereotypical of industry people trying to disguise themselves as hipsters.

Well, we were pissed until the guy was introduced as "from *Rolling Stone*," and immediately after he shook our hands, he said, "We want to do a story. A cover story."

Somehow we managed to order our food, but once the waiter left, I kicked Regan and Tom under the table. "Can you excuse us for a minute?" I said.

Tom was so dazed that he didn't even notice when we dragged him to the ladies' room. We all sank to the floor and lit up cigarettes. A woman in a silky dress that probably cost more than my dad made in a month walked in, wrinkled her nose at us, and stalked out, huffing, "Who do you think you are?"

"Rock stars," Tom mused with a kid-on-Christmas-morning grin.

"Yeah, look for us on the cover of *Rolling Stone!*" Regan shouted after her.

I collapsed against the marble tile, my black hair fanning out around me. "Holy shit, guys, *Rolling Stone.*"

So Regan's little prophecy came true, early in fact. If only she'd been right about being rid of Johnny. He never mentioned me in the press, seeming to understand that it would be best for both of our careers not to, but the creepy stalker thing continued. He lurked in the audience at a couple of our shows. He sent me flowers when the album went gold. I threw those, vase and all, off the balcony of my hotel room to Regan's and Tom's rowdy applause.

Then, a week before the *Rolling Stone* shoot, Tom got a voice mail from Johnny. At that time, I still didn't have a cell phone, an attempt to exercise control over who could reach me when, but Tom did. While checking it on the bus one day, he tossed it to me. "Crap, Emily, listen to this!"

When I put it to my ear, I heard Johnny's voice. "Hey, Tom, I don't have contact info for Emily, so if you could just pass this message on to her. I heard you guys are going to be in Wisconsin in a few days, doing yet another magazine cover—congrats, by the way, *Rolling Stone*'s the big one—and I'm actually going to be in the studio in Madison redoing a couple vocal tracks, so why don't you give me a call and we'll get together for some drinks."

I thrust the phone away as Johnny rattled off his number. "Delete!"

Tom shook his shaggy head. "I don't know, I think we should play this for Mike . . ."

"No." Even though it had been proven that handling Johnny on my own wasn't the best course of action, I still hated asking for help. "Mike's probably freaking out enough as it is. That album's supposed to be in the final mixing stages by now."

"Johnny Threat, punk-rock perfectionist," Regan quipped, but she was frowning. "I think Tom's right. We need to make sure Johnny doesn't show up or something." She deferred to me uncertainly. "Unless you want to see him . . ."

I glared at her, exasperated. "Regan, the only guy I'm hanging out with during the *Rolling Stone* thing is my dad."

To illustrate our roots, *Rolling Stone* had decided to do the cover shoot at River's Edge, which was as close to Carlisle as I was willing to go. I planned to drive up early and spend a little time with Dad while I got my picture taken and finished answering questions. I hadn't seen him since his birthday in Milwaukee. I didn't see him nearly enough because of my nonstop tour schedule. There was the added complication that I refused to go to Carlisle when I was off, and Chicago was tough for him to visit.

But at River's Edge we were both in our element. When I arrived and saw his motorcycle parked outside, I ran inside with my guitar in hand. We met in the middle of the warehouse and hugged. He kissed the top of my head and repeated what he said every time I called him: "I miss you, but I'm so proud of you."

I squeezed him tighter. "I miss you, too."

Then we finished the sappy stuff and turned to what we did best: playing music together. Sitting cross-legged on the stage, I strummed my guitar and mumbled lyrics. He nodded in rhythm with the song, the lines in his forehead puckering as he concentrated, still taking on the role of my coach.

Halfway through a song I'd been having trouble arranging, I slapped the stage in frustration, whining, "I don't like that bridge. It's been driving me nuts."

"Well, let me show you something . . ." My dad reached for the guitar. And then it happened: the camera flash that brought Ian Winters into my life.

I glared murderously at the lanky, dark-haired stranger. "What the hell do you think you're doing?" I snarled, hopping off the stage and standing protectively in front of my father, arms crossed.

"My job," he said, not fazed by my attitude.

"*You're* the *Rolling Stone* photographer?"

He had a baby face, round cheeks, and smooth olive skin that he probably had to shave about once a week. His messy brown curls would have dipped down below his shoulders if he freed them from his ponytail. He wore ragged jeans and a plain white T-shirt, both wrinkled, like he pulled them out of the hamper after deciding they were clean enough. In short, he appeared to be in his second year of art school.

"Yes." He didn't use any unnecessary words, and his expression was undecipherable. The look in his catlike green eyes and the slight curve to his lips could have been contentment or contempt. When I didn't reply to his one-word response, his dark eyebrows knitted together. "Is there a problem?"

"You're just . . . you're, like, nineteen or something," I stuttered, uncharacteristically.

He smirked, his amusement discernible for the first time. "Twenty-five, actually. Magazines like to do that sometimes—up-and-coming band, up-and-coming writer, up-and-coming photographer. Besides, you're a Chicago band, I'm a Chicago photographer."

"But we're not a Chicago band." I was inexplicably defensive about that. I mentioned it in every interview, but hated Carlisle so much I wouldn't even visit my own father there. "We're from here. That's why we're doing the shoot here. But you're early and I had no idea who you were . . ." God, why did he get me so flustered?

He extended his hand. "I'm Ian Winters."

"Emily Black."

"Hmmm." His lips snaked into a secret smile, but his eyes darted down to his paint-spattered sneakers, so I couldn't read him.

"What?" I snapped, put on guard by his aloofness.

"Obviously you're the singer," he murmured.

"What does that mean?"

He just blinked.

"I'm not trying to act like a diva, if that's what you're im-plying. My dad and I playing music together . . . that was a private moment, when you took a picture . . ."

"Sorry. I liked that moment. When everyone else gets here, you'll have to pose and put on more makeup, but that's not really the spirit of rock 'n' roll, is it? When you guys used to play here—"

"Whoa, you've seen us play here?"

The furtive grin once more, the forest-green eyes shoot-ing down to the shoes and back up again. "I'm not really from Chicago either. Freeport," he said. "And no offense or anything, but I've always liked your drummer's sister's band better than yours."

"None taken," I replied, impressed.

"Anyway, I can toss this film if you want. I just wanted to get some genuine shots before we go pose in the cornfields so people stop thinking you're a Chicago band and get tuned in to your roots or whatever."

"No," Dad spoke up. I turned, startled, having almost forgotten about his presence. He gave me a pleading look. "We don't have enough pictures of the two of us together. Her mom's gone, so there's no one to hold the camera," he told Ian, glancing down at the wedding ring he'd taken to wearing again.

The way he said "gone" was heartbreaking, so I quickly agreed. "Okay, take some pictures of us, but these are for my dad, not *Rolling Stone*."

"No problem. When everyone shows up, I'll change

rolls, set these aside, develop them myself, and we'll be in touch."

I climbed back onto the stage beside my dad and picked up the guitar again, but before I started playing, I added, "I'm not posing in a goddamn cornfield. When Regan and Tom get here, we're setting up our equipment and we're gonna rehearse. You can take pictures of that. My roots are not in those cornfields, they're in this dank, ugly warehouse, and if they want to airbrush some corn in . . ."

Ian laughed, and it wasn't short and razor-sharp like Johnny's sarcastic chuckle. It came from his belly and made his eyes dance. And I knew I wanted that laugh in my life.

We got the shot that would end up on the cover somewhere around one in the morning. Since it was a school night in May, there wasn't a show at River's Edge that evening. Around four in the afternoon, it had been determined that *Rolling Stone* owed us massive quantities of pizza and beer. My dad took that as his cue to leave. The writer, though amused by our antics and the fabulous stories Tom and I told about Carlisle once we were drunk—most of them exaggerated, like Regan and I beating up half the football team, Tom getting kicked out of his house the night he met us and living at River's Edge—decided to drive back to Madison because a hangover would only amplify the cold he already had.

Ian put his camera away and swapped tales with us about growing up in a small town and moving to the big city. I lay on my back at the foot of the stage, my hair hanging over the edge. The makeup artist long gone, I looked how I usually did after a show: my dark eye makeup streaky, but my red lipstick applied thick. Tom and Regan sat cross-legged on either side of me, facing each other, talking over me as I lazily strummed my unplugged electric guitar. Ian had been at my feet, involved in the conversation, but suddenly he slammed down his bottle and announced, "This is it. The shot."

After he took it, he said, "They'll airbrush the hell out of it, but we'll know what it stands for."

"The spirit of rock 'n' roll," I nodded drunkenly.

"Yep." Ian bent down and kissed me on the forehead.

It could have gone *much* further than that. Regan and Tom tried to convince me to go back to her parents' house with them, but the alcohol stirred a particularly acute belligerence toward Carlisle, so I refused. I ended up sleeping on the couch backstage at River's Edge and Ian slept with me. Literally just slept. I would have him in time, I told myself. A boy who laughed like he did deserved to be had under better circumstances.

But apparently "better circumstances" weren't in the cards for me.

I awoke to the sound of shattering glass. My eyes shot open, and I felt a stabbing pain in my arm as a shard lodged itself there.

Johnny stood by the stage door, a few yards away from me. When I registered his presence, he bellowed, "What the fuck is this?" He punctuated his words by launching another empty bottle.

I instinctively leaned in toward Ian, covering our heads,

but Johnny's aim went wide. Despite a pounding headache, I sprung up like a cat as soon as I heard the bottle clatter to the ground unbroken.

"What the fuck is *this*?" I gestured to the drops of red trickling down my arm. "Oh, I know what it is," I seethed. "The violent outburst that I knew would come eventually, just like last time. This is why we didn't get back together, Johnny. Get the hell out of here!"

Johnny tossed his hands up in the air and laughed so maniacally it contorted his face, making it look eerily skeletal. "No, Emily, I don't think so. This isn't *just like last time*. How the hell do you expect me to react, finding you in bed with someone else? With—who is this? The journalist?"

"I'm the photographer," Ian murmured, sitting up on the couch behind me and rubbing his temples, bewildered.

Johnny paced back and forth, three quick steps one way and then the other, whipping his head to the side each time he turned, so he could keep his crazed eyes on me. "You're so messed up, Emily. I don't get your logic. It would ruin your reputation as a musician to screw other musicians, but you can screw journalists? Is this why you don't want anyone to know about us? It would interfere with you sleeping your way to the top? How respected are you going to be when this gets out?"

I hurled a beer bottle at him, but it smashed against the wall by the door, slivers of glass glittering in the hot sun as they harmlessly spit outward toward Johnny's sneakers. "Shut up! First of all, there is no *us*. There hasn't been for four years and it's because *you're* crazy! Second, how dare you even imply . . . If anyone slept their way to the top, it's you. Whose label are you on? Gee, the same one I'm on." I covered my mouth in mock disbelief.

"What?" Johnny raged, his eyes dark as gathering clouds. "That's a coincidence. You had nothing to do with Mike coming to see us."

"Are you sure about that, Johnny?" The words popped like the safety catch on a gun. My lips spiked upward into a taunting sneer.

Blotches of red spread across his cheeks. "Yes! You were with me that night, drunk as hell. You didn't arrange that."

I cocked an eyebrow. "Are you sure that I didn't call Mike beforehand? And what about the media, how would they see it?" I lobbed his threat back at him.

"Well, let's ask the reporter you just screwed!" Johnny flicked his chin in Ian's direction.

Ian stood and cleared his throat. "I'm not a reporter. And Emily and I just passed out . . ."

But Johnny wasn't listening. "You're not special, you know that?" he said to Ian, stomping toward us. "Do you know how many guys she fucked here? I should know. I was one of them. She's a screwed-up little whore. Print that in *Rolling Stone!*"

Ian stepped up beside me. "Don't talk about her like that . . ." His voice was low and menacing, but with his rumpled clothes, bare feet, and hair half freed from his messy ponytail, he seemed powerless compared to Johnny.

The muscles of Johnny's tattooed arms went taut beneath the sleeves of his T-shirt, his fists clenched. I could tell that, unlike the last time Johnny and I fought, he was stone-sober. He swaggered forward until we stood toe-to-

toe. "You know why she's so messed up?" he asked, ostensibly talking to Ian, but glaring directly at me. "'Cause her mommy left her when she was a baby. She tells the cutest little story about it, makes Mommy out to be the holy spirit of punk rock. Has that been in an article yet? Do you want the real story? About how her mom just ran off one day and left her and her dad, who's hopelessly devoted to her? Is that sick or what? No wonder she's the love-'em-and-leave 'em type," he ridiculed, the corners of his mouth wet with spit like a rabid dog.

"Don't." I fought to keep my voice strong, my chin from quivering. I certainly hadn't shared anything about my mother with the press. And I regretted the moment of weakness after my grandfather's funeral when I told Johnny the full story—what I knew of it then—about her. "Just shut up. Louisa has nothing to do with anything."

Johnny's dark grin stretched wide. "Of course she does! Your mommy complex is everything. Admit it. You want to find her. And if you can't find her, you'll be her."

My agonizing year of running after Louisa flashed before my eyes. "You have no right to be talking about this, you goddamn psycho. What's your complex? What's the explanation for you stalking me for the past two years? Oh, I know"—I jabbed a finger in his face—"you're nothing but a leech, clinging to my talent because yours is nonexistent."

Johnny pinched my finger between his forefinger and thumb. Then he slid his whole hand around it. "Didn't anyone teach you not to point?" His eyes narrowed into snakelike slits. "I could end your career right now. I could rip this finger out of the socket, and you would never be the same. Who's in control now, Emily?"

Tears spilled down my face, but I kept my eyes locked on his and refused to bless him with a response.

"Tell me you're sorry. And admit it, your mother screwed you up and that's why we aren't together anymore. Admit—" But then Johnny sucked in air and lost his grip on my finger as Ian punched him in the gut. Johnny stumbled backward, and Ian, ignoring the broken glass beneath his feet, punched him once more in the stomach and then in the jaw.

Johnny head-butted Ian in the chest, knocked him to the floor, and fell on top of him. "Stop it!" I screamed, but they just pummeled each other harder.

It seemed to happen in slow motion, me jumping on top of both of them, one arm pinning Johnny's flailing arms, the other pressing against Ian's torso. As I held Ian back, Johnny scuttled out from under him, blood dripping from his lip, the left side of his face swelling. I couldn't hear anything except my heart pounding in my ears, but he seemed to be mouthing "Thank you."

"Thank you?" I roared. "Get the hell out of here before I . . ." I stomped on the palm of his left hand with my bare foot, certain not to break it but to make it throb like he had my finger.

He howled, pulling his hand away, clenching and un-clenching it to make sure it was okay before scrambling to his feet and running for the door.

"I'm sorry about all that," Ian said moments later, as the sound of Johnny's tires crunching over gravel filtered inside. He moved to embrace me.

"Don't!" I jerked away. "You should have just left. I can take care of myself. I don't need a goddamn prince on a white horse to save me."

And with that, I gathered my shoes and my guitar and ran out. I left Ian standing openmouthed among the beer bottles and the broken glass. I decided that as much as I liked him, I wouldn't be seeing him again because humiliation was not my cup of tea.

Blasting my car stereo as I sped out of Wisconsin, I told myself it didn't matter. *You don't need a boyfriend, it was never part of the plan.*

INDISCRETIONS

September 1996 through June 1998

Louisa left L.A. before Nadia got out of the hospital. When Colette came home in the morning to retrieve some of Nadia's things because the doctors wanted her to stay one more night for observation, she found Louisa slumped on the couch flanked by two suitcases. "I need you to take me to the bus station. You can keep my car. You guys need it here," Louisa stated numbly before Colette could even speak.

Colette blinked at her with wide, bloodshot eyes. "What?" finally scraped out of her throat. "You're leaving?"

Louisa nodded mechanically.

Colette's nostrils flared. "I almost lost my kid and now I'm gonna lose my best friend?"

"I told you that I couldn't stay in one place for very long or bad things would happen. Bad things happened."

"Louisa, it had nothing to do with you! It's my fault. I was irresponsible. I already talked to some people at the hospital about me and Nadia seeing a therapist together. I'm gonna be a better mom and I need you to help me do that."

Louisa couldn't help but laugh, a dark, drained cackle. "You want *me* to help you be a good mother. *Me?* I left *my* kid because I was no good for her. I can't help you be a mother. I can't be around your daughter anymore. I'm a bad person, Colette. A bad, broken person. Nadia doesn't need that. Besides, it's not fair to—" Louisa stopped herself before she said Emily's name and rose from the couch. "If you won't take me, I'll call a cab."

Colette trembled, but she pressed her lips together and nodded. "I understand, but won't you at least say good-bye to Nadia?"

"I can't." Louisa's head dropped into her hands. She bit her left palm before she looked up, tears glistening. "It's hard enough saying good-bye to you."

Colette wrapped her arms tightly around herself, head bobbing slowly. She still wore the same clothes she'd had on when they ran to the motel. They'd gotten soaked and dried wrinkled. Her hair stuck up in an unruly way, and all her makeup had washed away so that the deep circles under her eyes and worried creases in her forehead were painfully obvious. Louisa hadn't seen someone so hurt since the night she'd left Michael. She spoke to Colette in the same empty tone she'd used on him. "I've gotta go. I should've left a long time ago."

Still nodding involuntarily, Colette reached for Louisa's car keys. "I know," she whispered.

When they got to the Greyhound station, Colette hugged

Louisa. "Go see your daughter," she said, her breath warm in Louisa's long, golden hair. "Because you still can and you never know when that chance might slip away." She pulled back to meet Louisa's gaze. "I'll tell Nadia good-bye for you, tell her you went to see your own daughter. She'll feel good about that, 'cause it's gonna break her heart that you're leaving. You should write us, okay?"

Louisa didn't respond, so Colette urged, "Please go find Emily. Do it for me. Do it for no more regrets."

"No more regrets," Louisa echoed listlessly, staring out at the line of cold, metallic buses, one of which would bring her to her next life. She made no promises. Finding her daughter would only lead to remorse for everyone involved. But she'd let Colette think that was the plan if it would bring her and Nadia peace, not to mention keep them from following her again.

Louisa went inside the station and bought a bus ticket to Portland. It was the only thing she could think of, picking up where she'd left off before L.A. sidetracked her.

In Portland the routine began again. Late-night cocktail waitress. Dreary, lonely apartment. Louisa wondered if this was how it had always been when she wandered alone. On a night off, she ventured into a punk club. She'd stopped doing that in L.A., focused more on partying. *Follow the music,* she remembered. The music wouldn't be powerful enough to absolve her of her guilt as she'd once hoped—with Nadia's near death added to the rest, she had enough to run from for several lifetimes. But as she stood there, holding a watery beer, watching a girl who couldn't have been more than eighteen ferociously whale on the drums so that her chestnut curls flew in every direction, Louisa knew that the energy of the music could keep her going.

She spent every night off at some hole-in-the-wall listening to local bands. She craved more, like a junkie on a binge after years of sobriety. Ready to search out the next big wave, but no longer in tune with where it would hit, Louisa went to its last known location, Seattle—though, by the end of 1997, it was the center of the dot-com universe, not the rock 'n' roll galaxy.

The day after moving to her apartment on the outskirts of the Capitol Hill neighborhood, Louisa scouted for a job. At two thirty on a Thursday afternoon, she walked to the bar down the block. Since she was still without a car, working close to home would be ideal. There were only two customers inside, guys in their forties. Judging from their tired smiles and dusty boots, probably contractors, who started their workdays and nightly drinking before everyone else. They slouched at the bar, keeping the bartender company with their off-color stories. Louisa sat three stools down from them, and when the bartender, who was about the same age as his customers, loped over to ask her what she'd like to drink, she said, "Actually, I'm wondering if you're hiring servers. I just moved from Portland. I was a cocktail waitress there."

He smiled at her, took off his baseball cap, and smoothed the ginger hair beneath it. "Sorry, this place don't get enough business to pay for servers, just bartenders."

"You were looking for a bartender, though, weren't you, Ben? You tend bar, too?" one of the customers asked, swiveling on his stool to face Ben and Louisa. His skin crinkled around bright cobalt eyes when he smiled, and he wore his hair in a gray-streaked, dirty-blond ponytail.

"You tryin' to do my hiring for me, Finn?" Ben joked.

Finn shrugged. One shoulder seemed stiff, hardly able to go along with the movement. "She just seems nice."

"I've tended bar, too. Lots of different places, different cities," Louisa offered.

Ben scratched his pudgy cheek. "This is a shot-and-a-beer kind of place . . ."

She smiled. "My kind of place."

Ben glanced at Finn, who gave the thumbs-up. "Well, I guess if you got the Finn Leahy seal of approval, you're hired."

Louisa became fond of Finn because, like her, he had failed. Louisa had failed to escape Eric without resorting to the worst kind of violence, and because of that she failed at being a good wife and mother. She'd even failed at running away to seclude herself from everyone and everything but the music. Finn was a failed musician, so she liked him even more because their failures seemed connected. Finn was forty, just a year younger than Louisa. His first garage band had bombed in the late seventies—not quite punk enough. He'd had his last big chance in 1992 when his latest band—like many others from Seattle—garnered major-label attention. He was thirty-five, still young enough, he felt, to live the rock-star dream if destined.

"But it wasn't," he told her on her second shift. He was

the only one in the bar, a pattern that would begin most of her days. "'Cause unlike those other guys, kids really, who, sure, came from nothing, and worked a few shit jobs but gave 'em up to be struggling musicians, I'd struggled for too long, so I had a day job. Construction. And just days away from the gig that probably would have landed us the big deal . . . boom! Total freak accident. This stack of wood tumbled down behind me, a rain of boards and me caught beneath." He paused to rub his shoulder. "I got hit in the back, and now the weight of the guitar is too much. I can do a show every now and then when my back's feeling good, but when it's bad . . ." When it was bad, Louisa wouldn't see Finn for a few days. He didn't get out of bed, lying there in a haze of pain pills. "And it took years for me to be able to play that often. By the time I wasn't hurtin' too much or too drugged up to function, I had no band, and, well"—Finn smirked—"grunge was dead."

Finn kept going the way Louisa did. Not that Louisa felt their situations quite comparable, but she admired his outlook.

"It could've been worse," he said. "I could've been crushed. My dad was a logger. I went to work with him a few times as a kid and saw a guy crushed to death, smashed flat, no bones left in him, just a puddle of skin and blood. That's why I didn't end up a logger." Finn laughed, a smoky, deep laugh through which Louisa could almost hear his singing voice. "I've never gotten that image out of my head, and it's good. Whenever them pain pills drag me to the lowest of lows, instead of putting a gun in my mouth, I think, Finn, maybe you lost your dream of playing music, but somebody liked you enough to keep you around so you could still listen to it."

It had been years since Louisa had met a person with a passion for music that mirrored her own, so she found herself saying, "That's what I'm looking for, music. That's why I move so much, trying to pick up new sounds, new bands. Maybe you could tell me some places to check out here? If the music's still good."

"Of course the music's still good." Finn grinned. "That's what MTV and *Time* magazine didn't get. The music in Seattle has always been good and always will be. They just caught onto our secret for a little while. My back feels pretty good today, so how about when you get off, I take you to a place or two? You'll never want to move again because Seattle's got the best scene."

Louisa winced slightly. She knew she'd left the best music behind in Carlisle. "Well, okay. I was in L.A. for a few years, and everything seemed so fake and empty to me, I decided to keep going north till I found something. If the music here is that great, it'll stop me from going to Alaska."

"Alaska? They got something up there I don't know about?" Finn chuckled. He always laughed despite his pain, another reason Louisa came to like him so quickly.

"No, but I always told myself that's where I'd go if I felt like the music was completely gone."

"Hmm." Finn thought about that for a moment. She could tell by the look in his eyes that the idea of being surrounded by snow, being so cold he couldn't feel anything, appealed to the failed being within him. But he took a swig of beer and said, "If I were in L.A. for any length of time, I'd think music was dead, too. Nah, I'll revitalize your ears tonight."

Louisa soon found herself out with Finn at some club or bar every night that he wasn't in too much pain. She grew attached to him like she had to Colette. She thought about running, really going to Alaska, but she realized there was a part of her original plan she just couldn't force herself to follow anymore. She couldn't be alone. Thoughts of Colette and Nadia surfaced far too often for her liking, and she couldn't be with them any more than she could be with Michael and Emily. But being with Finn was a safe substitute. Being with Finn was okay because he was already damaged. And at first sleeping with Finn made her feel as guilty as any of the one-night stands she'd had through the years, but eventually she realized he was different. He'd been a friend before he became a lover. Still, Louisa knew she couldn't tell him any of her secrets, much as it hurt to keep them inside. They would poison everything she and Finn had.

After six months together, Louisa had all but officially moved in with Finn. They spent many a night both silently staring into the darkness, neither of them able to sleep because of the pain. Louisa gave Finn a reason to keep his head clear, but resisting taking the pain pills meant lying awake aching. Sometimes he would break down in the wee hours of the morning. Louisa would hear him turn over with a groan, then hear the pills rattle into his hand from the plastic bottle he kept beside the bed. He would sleep late into the following day. But Louisa couldn't take anything to ease the discomfort in her chest, where all her heartbreaking memories lived.

One night, Finn spoke her name into the black, knowing that she couldn't sleep either. "Louisa, nothing in this world scares me more than being alone."

"Yeah?" she whispered.

"I used to think that if I couldn't play music, it would kill me, but it hasn't. I thought nothing could be worse. But you know what's worse? Being stuck flat on your back in bed for two days, in too much pain to get up for food or water, and thinking that you could die there and no one would even miss you."

Louisa's face contorted, his despondent words sending a pang of worry through her. "I'd miss you."

"Yeah, but before I met you, I was goddamn lonely, you know? Of course you know, you were as lonely as I was. I saw it in your eyes that first day. That's why I made Ben hire you. I thought we might be able to help each other. And you really have helped me. Have I helped you, though?"

Louisa wanted to say that no one could help her, but even Finn would question that. And she appreciated the fact that he didn't usually ask questions, just accepted that she would tell him what she was able. She sighed. "Yeah. I'm not too good at being alone anymore, either."

That was enough for Finn. He fell silent momentarily. Then she heard him roll onto his side, but not in the usual way toward his nightstand; instead, he turned toward her.

He didn't groan in pain, just hissed a little bit of air through his teeth. "You know I'm lucid, right? I didn't take them pills."

"I know." Louisa's head lolled in his direction. She let her eyes drift over the shadowy outline of his nose, his chin.

"Let's get married, Louisa. So we don't have to worry about being alone."

Louisa wanted to tell him that her last marriage had resulted in her being more alone than ever. She parted her lips to say so, then closed them. It was time, she concluded, to bury her memories where she could never dig them up. Emily and Michael deserved to be set free, not locked up in her head next to the corpse of Eric and images of Colette and Nadia, her makeshift family. Her life with Michael had been a fantasy that kept her alive on the cold cement floor while Eric forced himself into her. She'd kept breathing like Finn had beneath the boards. Like him, she survived, but old dreams were unattainable. Mother, wife, it couldn't happen. It hadn't happened. She had crawled out of that basement blood-spattered and bruised, staggered barefoot down the driveway, through the fields, her torn clothing catching on the rough vegetation. She kept walking, shedding fabric, then stained and tainted skin. As she wandered all the way across the country to the tune in her head, her body regenerated. She wound up in Finn's arms as an entirely new person. There was no reason not to start over. "Yeah," she told Finn, "that sounds good."

Finn's hand found its way to Louisa's. He interwove his fingers with hers. She rocked onto her side to face him, pressing her body closer to his. Her lips found his neck, then his chin, and finally his lips. For the first time, she wasn't haunted by Michael while she kissed another man. It had been almost twenty-two years since she'd left him. Certainly he had given up on her, moved on, remarried. As he should have. As she was about to.

ROCK 'N' RUIN

Don't give your drummer a microphone even if she sings great harmonies. I learned that lesson at Reading Festival in England when Regan decided to embarrass me in front of fifty thousand people. To be fair, she warned me of her scheme; I just didn't think she'd go through with it.

I'd moped through our entire European summer tour over my fight with Johnny and, more so, because I couldn't be with Ian due to my wounded pride. Taking matters into her own hands, Regan confronted me in our dressing room, staring me down in the mirror as I applied eyeliner until I got irritated and shouted, "What?"

"You know who's here, don't you?" she teased.

But I misjudged her tone and responded nastily, "Yeah, I know Johnny's here. Do you think he'll try to fight me because we're second from the top of the bill and he's second from the bottom? Unfortunately, him having to stay fifty feet away from me doesn't apply in England, huh?"

Regan's face fell. "Oh. Yeah. Him."

"Yeah. *Him*. Who were you talking about?" I glanced over my shoulder at her.

She couldn't help but smile. "Your favorite *Rolling Stone* photographer."

"Great," I groaned. "Even worse."

"Emily, don't be so melodramatic." Regan unleashed that half-grin she wore back when we were fifteen when she thought she'd spotted some guy who would be perfect for me. "If you really like him, you should go for it."

She was so evil. "Regan . . ."

"Just try going about it differently. Hard as it may be, don't sleep with him right away. I'm not saying you have to hold out for a year like I did, but—"

"Regan!"

"I dare you." She smirked deviously.

"Nice try." I rolled my eyes, turning to face her with my hands on my hips. "That's not gonna work like it did when we were ten."

She ignored me. "Dedicate a song to him tonight. Just murmur, 'This is for Ian,' like after you take a drag off your cigarette or something. It'll be all sultry and mysterious." She pursed her lips, fluttered her eyelashes, and took a dramatic drag from an imaginary cigarette. Giggling, she fished in her pockets for a real smoke.

I shook my head and returned to my makeup. "No. I am definitely not doing that."

"Then *I* will. I'll be all Casey Kasem long-distance dedication about it. 'This one goes out to Ian of *Rolling Stone*, from Emily . . .'" She rubbed her palms together gleefully.

I whipped around, brandishing my eyeliner pencil like a sword. "If you do that, I will seriously break up the band onstage."

"I knew it!" she chortled. "You've got it soooo bad. Like me and Tom."

"Like my mom and my dad?" I huffed sarcastically. "And where did that get them?"

Regan's expression faltered, but then she met my gaze firmly. "You're not her, Emily. Look at yourself. Look at what you've attained. Just let yourself be happy."

Her words hit me hard. They followed me onstage that night and bounced around my head for days. Simple as they were, I needed them to counteract what Johnny had said back at River's Edge about me trying to be my mother. I needed them in order to let Ian in. Not that I did right away. Especially not after Regan's stunt.

She pulled it three songs into the set. I mumbled, "This one's called 'Home,'" and peeked back at her because she was supposed to click her drumsticks together and count it off, but instead I saw her pink, pigtailed head lean toward the mic. Her lip gloss gleamed in the stage lights as she did the bad Casey Kasem impression, dedicating the song to Ian from me. She'd called my bluff, knowing I wouldn't really break up the band. I could only shake my head and growl the lyrics, so it didn't sound like a love song. I did throw my guitar into her drum kit at the end of the set, but she dodged it, laughing. And as much as I wanted to watch the Red Hot Chili Peppers perform after us, I stalked back to the bus to avoid Ian.

But when I returned from England, Ian called me in the

middle of the night. His excuse? He wanted to show me those pictures of me and my dad, which he claimed to have just developed. He insisted on bringing them to me right then.

"It's one in the morning. I was asleep," I protested groggily.

"That's not very rock 'n' roll," he said with a laugh. Damn his adorable laugh.

"I'm still jet-lagged."

"Come on, where do you live?" he implored.

Since he was nice enough not to mention the dedication incident, I agreed to let him come over.

I answered the door in pajamas. While I blinked blearily in the searing light coming from the hallway behind him, his green eyes glowed bright, wide-awake. His washed-out Cheap Trick T-shirt and his jeans, which hung loosely enough to reveal the top of his boxers, appeared slept-in, but apparently he only owned wrinkled clothing. "You really were sleeping." He seemed shocked.

I tried to flatten my tangled hair. "Why would I lie about that?"

"Because you didn't want to see me. I mean, when you gave me this address, an apartment in the suburbs, I thought for sure that you were trying to get rid of me."

"Why? Should I live in a Gold Coast penthouse now? I don't like moving." I shrugged and held out my hand for the envelope tucked beneath his arm. "Pictures?"

"You're not even going to let me stay and look at them with you?" He frowned, nibbling on his lower lip.

"Okay." I shrugged again, too tired to resist. I led him

inside to my tiny living room and pushed aside the mound of dirty laundry on the couch so we could sit down.

Ian was good at what he did. He understood how to manipulate light and shutter speeds and all that stuff I didn't get, but he also recognized the emotional force of music. He caught rock 'n' roll in motion, and not just the notes being played, but the intensely personal reaction of the musicians. I studied the last picture. In it, my father's eyes were half closed, a curl untucked from behind his ear, his lips partially open as he hummed, his hands a blur on the strings. All you could see of me in the very corner of the picture was my hair, the curve of my nose and chin, and my hands in my lap.

"That's the best one," Ian said.

"How do you do it?" I asked, staring at the perfect image of my dad. "How'd you capture the essence of music without the sound?" I managed to rip my eyes away and meet Ian's.

Then we were kissing. It was familiar. It was easy. I slid my hand up his shirt, my nails down his back. He took my tank top off, tracing his thumb gently across my breast. I shivered slightly, sucked his warm breath into my lungs, and then drew back, wrapping my arms across my bare chest.

"I'm not going to do this. I know you heard all of those things Johnny said about me, but they weren't true. Well, they were. I am pretty slutty, but . . ."

Ian wore a placid expression. He was so hard to read. He picked up my shirt and pulled it down over my head. I clumsily lifted my arms, like I was a child letting him dress me. It seemed sort of sweet, but then he didn't say anything and I felt silly. I was about to get up and show him the door when he finally spoke. "If we just fell asleep together again, no one's gonna show up throwing things this time, right?"

"Right . . . ," I said uncertainly.

"Okay." He leaned back against the couch, opening his arms to me.

And so it began. Ian and I didn't use any sort of terms for our relationship, but we made out all the time, and stayed over to sleep—just sleep—in each other's beds. I pretended that my life was the way it had been a year earlier, before the record came out. I was a normal person, freezing on the 'L' platform, waiting for the train to his house, where we'd eat Chinese takeout and watch bad romantic comedies on cable.

Then, after three months of total bliss, I had to go on tour.

Nobody wanted to do that December tour, short as it was—a couple of second billings at holiday radio station concerts on both coasts with some extra dates thrown in to make it worth our while. Hey, kids, like the latest single? Ask for our album this Christmas. Definitely the record company's idea, not ours. Regan and Tom would have preferred to go back to Carlisle for a while. I had a feeling they were about to get engaged, because they were spending a lot of time with her family (his family was still nuts, Sarah Fawcett being one of those people who filled the basement with canned goods and bottled water in preparation for Y2K). And I wanted to spend every waking moment with Ian.

But admittedly, once I got out on the road, even though I still missed Ian insanely, I had a great time playing live. My newfound happiness restored my energy, and performing felt as incredible as it had back at River's Edge. The tour sped by, we got good reviews, album sales went up.

Seattle should have been an awesome show. Every show we'd ever played there had been great. And it was the second-to-last stop before home. After, we'd headline Q101's Twisted Christmas in Chicago and then be able to take a break until we went into the studio in the spring. But it didn't work out that way.

Afterward, I thought I shouldn't have toured. I should have stayed on Ian's couch watching movies. The very public airing of my private life still would have happened, but, holed up with Ian, I might not even have found out about it for a few days. Instead, I watched it unfold in real time, and then faced the world mere hours later.

Regan had control of the remote even though it was my hotel room—a really nice hotel room at the Four Seasons. We'd checked in at the crack of dawn and napped for a while. I slept the longest, so Regan and Tom came knocking on my door to force-feed me coffee before sound check. I was perusing the room-service menu when Regan squealed, "Holy crap, I can't believe they're doing this show! It's almost as bad as *TRL*. Remember they asked us to do this show and we said no?"

She'd flipped to MTV, which had *Live Punx!* on. It aired every Monday, with a different band in the studio introducing videos, answering audience questions, and performing their hit single. They did it live with the hope that crazy punk-rock antics would ensue: bleeped swear words, blurred-out nudity, and the occasional controversy.

When She Laughs rose to sudden success, the media called it a "punk-rock revival." They proclaimed Chicago the new Seattle and said that we'd come to save the rock world from "the postgrunge macho backlash." Groups fronted by girls or sensitive yet angry guys ruled the airwaves. Like all movements in music, it yielded mixed results. Great underground bands got their day in the sun, but shows like *Live Punx!* were born to make an edgy scene more palatable for the masses. As far as we were concerned, self-respecting punk bands didn't do *Live Punx!*

But Johnny never had much self-respect, and his was the band that Regan gaped at in my hotel room, laughing hysterically. My Gorgeous Letdown fell into the "sensitive yet angry male" category. They'd ridden our coattails to the top and now verged on real success.

I stuck my tongue out at the TV. "Change it."

"No, it's going to be funny," Regan insisted.

I doubted it. I knew they would ask him about me. Everyone had been asking me about him lately because they'd figured out that My Gorgeous Letdown's biggest single, "Blackout Girl," was about me. Every goddamn song on the album alluded to me, and since Johnny wasn't the most subtle lyricist, it wasn't too tough to decipher. But I always gave the same cold response when asked about it: "Johnny who? Never heard of him."

And Johnny, clearly frustrated by his failure to be enigmatic, kept spitting out "No comment" when questioned, his pretty lips contorting into a scowl. "No comment" was a stupid answer. It implied there was something to comment on.

I hadn't been too concerned about it anyway because I'd had Ian to distract me. But now my eyes were glued to the screen and I had a gut feeling that the whole Johnny-Emily thing was about to reach the boiling point.

They played the "Blackout Girl" video and then cut to the band in the studio. All four of them were crammed onto an obnoxious neon-blue couch, the spiky-haired, mall-punk-clothing-clad VJ seated next to them in a director's chair. He led in with the usual "Really rockin' song, guys," tossing that devil-horns hand signal at the camera so his viewers could concur, *Yes, indeed, that song does rock.* "But there are rumors flyin' about it. It was recorded right around the time She Laughs released their major-label debut last winter, and everyone wants to know, Johnny, is the song about Emily Black?"

Johnny rolled his gunmetal-gray eyes and sighed audibly, but as he yawned his usual "No comment," the VJ went from innocuous, trend-sniffing puppet to lecherous, hard-nosed reporter.

"Because, Johnny, you and your reps have denied any romantic link to Emily Black, but we did some detective work, and we've uncovered this lease in the names of Emily Black and John Thompson—your legal name—for an apartment in Chicago back in 1994, this restraining order filed against you by Ms. Black six months later, and another one filed just this summer. Unless this is a different Emily Black, it seems like the two of you have had a very rock—"

Johnny lunged for the papers in the VJ's hands, snatched them away, and started tearing them to pieces. Seth, the

bassist, leapt up, screaming, "End of interview!" as the cam-
eras cut to a quick, final shot of Johnny's fist connecting
with the VJ's jaw.

"Shit." I heard my voice but didn't feel myself talking.
Regan's hands flew to my shoulders, and Tom turned off
the TV. The phone sat beside me on the bed, the number
to room service in my lap. So I dialed. "Two bottles of Jack
Daniel's."

Regan and Tom tried to convince me to cancel the
show. Especially after I opened the first bottle of Jack. But
I thought drinking and playing would make me feel better.
I should have known by then that drinking and playing did
not mix.

Little things came back to me later in snapshots.

Halfway through the second song, I stopped, told Tom
and Regan, "Shut up! I have to ask these people something."
I tried not to slur. "Do you care about who I'm fucking, Seattle? Seriously, do you?"

There seemed to be a mixture of reactions. Some confusion, since half of my audience didn't watch MTV, but
somebody did and yelled out, "Johnny Threat!"

"Noooooooooo," I drawled into the microphone. Then
I took a long swig of whiskey. "And you don't actually care,
right? 'Cause you are a good rock city. You just want to rock.
So we'll start that song over again." And we did.

I played my way rather badly through a couple more
songs. A blur.

My next memory: plopping down on the edge of the stage
with my bottle, declaring, "I suck tonight. I need a second
guitarist so when I suck, they can take over."

The same guy yelled out, "Johnny Threat!"

"No, I need a *good* guitarist," I sniggered. "He's not very good." Some people jeered. "You *like* his band? If you do, you can leave now."

I struggled to my feet. "Listen to this. I can play his song better than he can even when I suck." My fingers flew over the power chords to "Blackout Girl," and I mockingly scream-sung, *"Ooooh, my blackout girl, you press my buttons, you conquer my world,"* making my voice crack like a pubescent boy.

Regan and Tom stood silently behind me, clearly disapproving of the joke. Whenever I whirled around to face them, they stared at me, terrified, like I was a suicidal person on top of a building and they feared that if they said "Don't jump!" I would wink and take a running leap.

I took off my guitar and shouted for a roadie. "I polluted the guitar. I need a new one now."

I was presented with another one, but before I strummed the first chord, I quipped, "I heard he's really bad in bed, too."

A few more songs. I forgot lyrics, entire verses. Regan and Tom played robotically behind me.

Another snapshot: I asked, "Do you really want to know who I'm sleeping with?"

People booed me. I'd never been booed before, not even at my first couple shows when I deserved it. I went on with my tirade anyway. "I don't fuck rock stars. They're boring. Ooooh." I covered my mouth and looked back at Regan, whose face was in her hands. Still speaking into the microphone, I added, "I'm sure it's not boring for you and Tom, since that all started before you were rock stars." She didn't lift her head. I turned back to the crowd and told them, "I'm doing this photographer. Actually, I haven't yet, but I'm going to. Will someone tell MTV to announce this for me?" I paused dramatically, staring into the bright white lights above me. Then I yelled into the mic, "Ian, when I get home, you are getting laid!" I giggled girlishly. "He'll be happy to know that. He was probably beginning to wonder."

"Emily!" Regan hissed.

"What?" I said into the mic, pivoting toward her. "Another song?" She shook her head no, but I said, "Okay, another song."

According to one of many devastating reviews of the show, I played a song we'd already played. I made it through two more and stopped again, contending, "Restraining order, pffft! You guys think I would need to take out a restraining order against some wussy-ass, wannabe rock god? I'm tough. I can take care of myself!" And to prove it, I jumped into the crowd. They scratched me. Tore out my hair. Ripped me apart. And I remember cackling, thinking it was good pain.

I returned to the stage in my underwear. I admonished the audience. "I have to go find some clothes now. My boyfriend would not appreciate this many people seeing so much of me." But I probably would have stood there half naked, sipping my whiskey and yapping about my love life, if Tom hadn't finally yanked me offstage.

In the dressing room, Regan muttered, "Emily. Jesus Christ, Emily."

And Tom told someone, "There is no way she's going back out there."

And I puked at Regan's feet, falling to my knees, clutching my gut and gagging.

The voice of the tour manager: ". . . spectacle . . ."

Regan to me: "It's okay, honey. Just let it out . . ."

Tom: ". . . should have canceled . . ."

Someone from the venue: ". . . going back out there?"

Manager: ". . . obviously . . ."

Tom: ". . . not . . ."

Me, suddenly sober, wiping my mouth: "Yes, I have to fix it."

Regan: "No."

Tom: "No."

But I splashed cold water on my face, put on a T-shirt and jeans, and made them follow me out for the usual encore. Dizzy as hell, I kept my eyes closed the entire time. I finished by saying "Sorry" instead of "Thank you, good night."

When I got offstage, I requested a 7UP and the cancellation of our show in Vancouver.

Regan combed her fingers through my hair. "Do you want to fly home tonight?"

"To what?" I snapped. There would be reporters and, after my outburst, no Ian.

"What do you want?" Regan persisted gently.

"I want to go back to the hotel, where you are going to bleach my hair."

She blinked back confusion. Though she'd been changing the color of her dark brown hair for years, I had never messed with my natural hair color. People killed their hair trying to get the black I was born with, so why screw with it?

And blond? As Regan knew, I never would have considered blond. In my mind, it was trademarked by Louisa.

But I'd started longing for her again when my band's popularity skyrocketed. I tried not to, but I couldn't help it. If Louisa had been following the music and now I *was* the music, maybe she would find her way home. I imagined her showing up at my father's door, the issue of *Rolling Stone* with me on the cover in her hands, too proud to stay away from us any longer. He'd bring her to a show in Milwaukee or Minneapolis or Chicago to meet me. I'd walk offstage, feeling unusually triumphant, like I'd just played the best damn gig of my life, driven by a strange presence—and it would turn out to be Louisa.

After every concert in the Midwest, I left the stage hopeful that my mother would be there, my parents holding hands. But that was a daydream. Louisa had probably never even heard of my band because she hadn't gone off to follow the music, but to run away from her demons. And now I had demons to escape, too.

I looked into Regan's bewildered eyes and explained, "Louisa's blond. And right now I want to disappear, just like she did."

THE LOST CHORD

When Louisa married Finn Leahy, he unknowingly gave her back her daughter. If it weren't for Finn, Louisa probably wouldn't have discovered Emily's music until she saw her own eyes staring out from the female version of Michael's face on the cover of *Rolling Stone*. But Finn had She Laughs' first album. He played it for her just a week after they got married, while they were on their way to see some other band. Sliding the CD into his car stereo and handing Louisa the case, he said, "This is a great little band from Chicago. Didn't you say you lived there for a while?"

"Yeah . . ."

Louisa didn't notice Emily on the cover of the CD. It was a live shot, so Emily's wild, ebony hair hid most of her face. But when Louisa turned the case over in her hands, the name stuck out immediately, red letters against black. "Emily Black = Guitar/ Vox." *No*, she thought at first, *it's a common name*, but just below it, "Regan Parker = Drums." That was too coincidental.

The first words Louisa heard her daughter speak rode a wave of distorted guitars and came in a ragged yowl. *"You're gone!"* Emily screamed the first line of the first song. *"And I don't miss you at all!"* It knocked the wind out of Louisa. Everything seemed fuzzy around the edges for a moment, but then Louisa stopped listening to the lyrics, focused on the music. She recognized the same sound she'd heard back in Carlisle when she was a teenager, "punk" before the word was used, a patchwork quilt of all the best music a kid from the middle of nowhere could cobble together.

"Good, huh?"

Fortunately, Finn didn't take his eyes off the traffic on I-5. If he had, he would have seen tears glittering on Louisa's face as she smiled. "Yeah, the best thing I've heard in a long time."

After that, Louisa followed She Laughs zealously, the way a teenager does when they discover their new favorite band. She blasted the radio whenever one of their songs came on. She bought all the magazines that featured them. At first, she had to dig for short, one-page articles, but soon She Laughs captured headlines and cover stories.

However, the first two times that they played live in Seattle, Louisa made excuses not to go with Finn. Emily was a picture in a magazine, a voice on the stereo, an image that sang and laughed and danced around behind the glass of Louisa's TV. That was all Louisa could handle. Being in the same room with her daughter would make her too real. Of course, since Louisa hadn't told Finn about Emily, she ran out of excuses the third time She Laughs came to town. Finn insisted that Louisa just *had* to see them live.

When Louisa saw Emily again, it was almost twenty-three years to the day since Louisa had left her. It would have been upsetting anyway, but the way Emily broke down onstage made it worse. Louisa hadn't heard about the interview a few hours earlier that exposed Emily and Johnny Threat's turbulent relationship, so she had no explanation for Emily's behavior until after the fact. Louisa watched for forty-five minutes as her daughter stumbled around onstage, clinging to her bottle of whiskey more than her guitar, ranting about who she was and wasn't sleeping with, and finally launching herself into the crowd, not getting fished out for what to Louisa felt like days. After Emily was set back onstage by two security guards, her clothes mostly torn away, Louisa released a long breath and grabbed Finn's arm. "I can't watch this anymore."

But Finn replied, "It's rock 'n' roll, baby!" And Louisa knew he was picturing himself, the way things could have been if it weren't for his accident, if he were a rock star getting wasted for wasted's sake, not just downing pills because his back ached.

Louisa shook her head and pushed her way out of the crowded venue. That night, she meant to leave Seattle, but her instincts faltered. She'd been off-kilter since Los Angeles, when she'd become attached to Colette and Nadia and stayed in one place for too long. Louisa no longer knew when it was time to go. Instead of packing her bags and getting out before Finn came home, she went to bed. Even when Finn left two days later to fill in for the guitarist in a friend's band in Portland, and the perfect opportunity for leaving presented itself, Louisa wouldn't have taken it if it wasn't for Johnny Threat.

She didn't recognize him at first, even though his picture had been in the paper next to one of Emily stopping midsong, clutching a bottle of Jack Daniel's. The headline over them read "She Melts Down," and the article theorized about rather than reviewed Emily's chaotic performance at the Paramount. Finn read it over Louisa's shoulder, shrugging. "I guess I should be glad I never made it. The media cares more about your dirty laundry than your music when it comes down to it."

And normally Louisa would have agreed, dismissing it as stupid celebrity gossip, but this was her daughter's life that had been splattered all over the newsstands. She followed the Emily-Johnny saga religiously and it broke her heart. She locked herself in the bathroom and sobbed after reading the police report that described how Johnny menaced Emily in Chicago years back. Louisa couldn't picture this girl who possessed her eyes and Michael's smirk pressed against a door with a knife pointed at her side. Tabloid stories flew around Louisa's head while she bartended. Her thoughts were so clouded that it wasn't until she served Johnny Threat his third drink that she recognized his sharp cheekbones and spiky tendrils of blond hair.

"Whoa!" Johnny barked. "Lose some of the ice!"

Louisa met his red-rimmed, aluminum eyes for the first time. The fury stirred in them during the *Live Punx!* interview had been glazed over by a night of heavy drinking. Perhaps he mistook Louisa's meeting his gaze for compassion, or perhaps he saw Emily in her eyes, but suddenly, he softened. "I'm sorry. It's been a rough week. Everyone's in my business. My career's in the toilet and instead of dealing with it, I came all the way out from the East Coast to apologize to my girlfriend . . . my ex . . . and she won't take my phone calls . . . I know her, though. If she's upset, she's out drinking. I've been all over Capitol Hill searching for her."

Extremely uncomfortable, Louisa glanced down the bar, hoping for the excuse of a customer to serve, but it neared midnight on a Wednesday, and except for a cluster of regulars whose drinks she'd just refreshed, there was no one besides Johnny.

He took a large gulp of whiskey, and rage crept into his melancholy again. "I can't believe she won't just listen to my side of the story. I mean, the things that happened, they were heat-of-the-moment things. Passion. Me and her, a lot of passion. She acts like I'm the one who's screwed up, but her life ain't perfect. Sure, she had this cool dad who taught her to play music, but I never met him. He didn't come to Chicago when we lived together because his no-good wife had left him there. Her mom. And she thought her life was normal. Her mom bailed when she was a baby. That's not normal. And her dad was still in love with this woman. No wonder she was afraid of any kind of relationship."

Louisa gripped her side of the bar to keep from collapsing under the weight of his words. Johnny didn't discern that her eyes were tearing up, just noticed their color. "You got eyes like hers. Green. Envy green. Emily green." He slurred "envy" and "Emily" so they almost sounded identical. He drained his glass. "How 'bout another refill?"

Louisa's lips moved without her willing them to. "Get out."

"What?"

"Get out, Johnny."

"Shit, you know who I am? You've known this whole time and just let me—"

"I said get the hell out of here," Louisa growled.

"Your eyes," he murmured again, screwing up his face as his alcohol-drenched brain slowly made connections. She probably could have gotten him out of there before the correct synapses fired if it weren't for the call from down the bar.

"Hey, Louisa, I need another one down here." A regular named Dan shook his bottle of Rainier and indicated a buddy of his with a few streaks of gray in his messy brown ponytail. They all looked like Finn, which saddened Louisa because she knew she wasn't going to see Finn again. As soon as Johnny started laughing, she knew she'd be fleeing Seattle and leaving Finn behind.

"*Louisa?*" Johnny said incredulously. His cackle, coated in whiskey and cigarettes, like Colette's laugh but darker, cut the air like a rusty razor blade. Johnny stood up, knocking his stool over. "Louisa." He repeated her name greedily, like a child who had just stolen his sibling's Halloween candy.

"Shut up and get out!" Blindly, she heaved the bottle of whiskey at him. She missed by a mile and Johnny continued to chuckle.

"Does she know? Does your daughter know you're here?"

"Shut up!" Louisa ran toward the other end of the bar, glancing back to scream at Johnny, "You stay away from her!"

"Lou?" Dan asked in confusion. He reached for her wrist.

She shook him off. "No, I gotta go."

Johnny's laughter followed her down the street.

Apparently, people don't just walk out of the Four Seasons hotel, Emily thought. The woman behind the reception desk repeated, "We were told to call a car for you. Won't you just let me call a car?" The whole thing still felt foreign to Emily: limos to the airport, the Four Freakin' Seasons hotel. "Ms., uhhh, Carson . . ." Checking into places using her mother's name. "It's been arranged for you by your people." Having "people."

"No, really, I can get there by myself," Emily assured the clerk, her eyes fixed on the woman's sleeve. She wore a neatly pressed tan suit. It was the most neutral thing in Emily's field of vision. The lobby made her nauseous. The walls looked coated in that liquefied gold they dip roses in to sell for Mother's Day. The salmon carpet's elaborate patterns spun, a crisscross of flowers, blocks of green framed by vines of gold. Suffering from lack of sleep and what felt like a hangover that had been lingering for days, Emily clung to the reception desk, gazing longingly at the escalators that would take her away.

The hotel clerk, her face woman-behind-the-makeup-counter-at-a-high-end-department-store flawless, stared at Emily squeamishly. Emily wondered if she looked as bad as she felt. She hadn't showered since before her band's disastrous show. She'd stayed up that night bleaching her hair, but just rinsed the chemicals off in the sink. The next two nights, she reapplied new makeup over old makeup before barhopping by herself all over Capitol Hill. Wednesday night, she hadn't even gone to sleep when she got back to the hotel at three A.M., knowing she'd have to be up in a few hours anyway.

Her "people" booked a nine o'clock flight back to Chicago on Thursday morning. The Vancouver show she'd canceled had been expendable, but she had to get it together and play Twisted Christmas in Chicago that weekend. She received many calls about this from the record company until she insisted that no one be put through to her room except for her father. But he alone had the courtesy not to call, seeming to know she needed to work things out by herself.

The clerk—probably prepped by Emily's "people" to make sure she didn't miss her flight—insisted, "Let the valet at least get you a cab."

He stood next to Emily, trying to take her suitcase out to the entranceway. She shifted her guitar case uncomfortably on her shoulder. "No, really, I just want to walk down to the waterfront, and then I'm going to take the bus."

"Well—"

Emily interrupted, too exhausted to continue the charade. "Listen, I'm from Middle-of-Nowhere, Wisconsin, okay? We didn't even have a bus. The bus is an exciting mode of transportation for me, all right?" she snapped, inwardly cringing at her rock-star outburst. Everything in her life had become a cliché. She should have trashed her room instead of politely straightening up for the maid. "Do I need to sign anything?"

"No, no, you're set," the woman stammered. "You didn't want any phone calls, but maybe you want the messages."

"Thanks," Emily murmured, taking them. "And I'm sorry, I just . . ." She couldn't complete the sentence. Her excuse would have taken hours. Then she glanced down at the messages. The top one was from Michael Black. "Hey, I said to put my dad's phone calls through!"

She flipped through the pink slips of paper. The first one said, "I'll be at the show in Vancouver. Flying out tonight." The next one said, "Didn't know Vancouver was canceled. Talked to Regan. Will be at Seattle Greyhound station Thursday morning 8 A.M. No money for another plane ticket."

"How do I get to the Greyhound station?" Emily asked desperately, trying not to fume at the hotel for not following instructions, at her "people" for not telling her own father what was going on, and mostly at herself for not calling him.

Louisa arrived at the Greyhound station at five on Thursday morning. She hadn't owned a car since Los Angeles. She didn't mind public transportation, but it limited her ability to leave when she pleased. For twenty years, she'd been able to decide in the middle of the night that it was time for a new town, throw all her stuff in the car, and head for the horizon. Instead, after the incident with Johnny, she had to catch a bus to Finn's (it never felt like hers), throw the essentials into two suitcases, and take a cab to the Greyhound terminal. She'd decided Canada was the place to go. The bus ticket to Vancouver was cheap, and she'd used up America—except for Alaska, and Finn would look for her there.

In the station, she dragged her suitcase over to the back row of plastic chairs and tossed her body listlessly onto one. She studied the ticket—her bus was to depart at 8:30 A.M.—and then squinted at the clock above the ticket counter. Since she had a couple hours to kill, Louisa pushed her limp hair out of her face and slid to one side, placing her balled-up hooded sweatshirt against the wall as a pillow.

Despite the noise of nearby arcade games, Louisa dozed, waking to a frantic male voice. "Miss . . . Miss! You can't smoke in here. There's no smoking in the station."

Louisa's lids flickered open, and since she'd been smoking in her dream, she mumbled an apology. Then, half conscious, she heard a female voice. "Oh . . . sorry."

The girl stopped in front of Louisa and stubbed a cigarette out under the toe of her black boot, her platinum hair swinging side to side as she did so. She started to walk off, but the station employee insisted, "Miss, you can't just leave it on the floor."

"Sorry." The girl's scratchy voice sounded tired but familiar. Louisa watched her bend down to pick up the cigarette butt. She glanced toward Louisa, searching for the garbage, and Louisa felt a shock ripple through her as she placed who the girl was. The green eyes, though circled by signs of sleeplessness and crusty eyeliner, gave her away despite her attempts to bleach out her identity by changing the color of her naturally black hair.

"Emily," Louisa whispered, as the combat boots clattered across the orange and brown tile toward a trash can. Louisa wondered if, after all these years, she should really speak to her daughter. She'd sworn to stay away, but if Emily found her . . . Louisa straightened up, smoothing the wrinkles from her clothing. "Emily!" she repeated loudly.

Emily halted in midstep, but seemed hesitant to turn. Her shoulders and neck visibly stiffened. Louisa realized how many people must call her daughter's name, must beg to be recognized. "Emily, it's me . . . ," she began, and then stopped herself, not knowing how to say the words she'd kept buried inside for so long. She just prayed that the girl would turn her head. After a long pause, she finally did. Tears sprang to Louisa's eyes and she had to hold on to the side of her chair to remain upright.

Everything about the woman in front of Emily looked faded, from the T-shirt and jeans she wore to her hair, so bleached it appeared whitewashed. Like an old photograph. Emily met eyes like scuffed, clouded emeralds that matched her own and staggered backward with her hand over her mouth. She lost sight of the bus station, suddenly able to see only the black-and-white picture that she'd kept on the speaker in her childhood bedroom, that she'd taped to the dashboard of her car as she'd run around the country, and that she had tucked into a notebook in her purse minutes earlier.

If she imagined that photo crumpled slightly, creating crinkly lines around the eyes and mouth, and if the bulge of the woman's pregnant belly was flattened, which of course it would be because Emily had been born over twenty-three years ago . . .

Emily blinked until her surroundings came into view again. When she removed her hand from her mouth, her words came out in a strangled sob. "No, it can't be . . ."

The woman seemed to be struggling to breathe as well. "I'm . . ."

"Louisa?" Emily gasped, her hands at her face again, fingers pressing against the bridge of her nose, the corners of her eyes, because goddammit, she wouldn't cry.

"Yes," Louisa confirmed with a nod, her chin quivering. She didn't know why she had expected this girl—this grown woman—to call her "Mom," but her heart sunk into her stomach when Emily didn't.

Anger and sorrow collided in Emily's chest. Of course, it hadn't happened the way she daydreamed, Louisa coming to her greatest-ever concert. Louisa was no longer moving, searching out the next band, the next wave. She remained where the last wave had crested five years before, and if she'd seen Emily play, she hadn't seen the best damn show but the worst. "Not like this," Emily stuttered.

Louisa didn't dare rub her own damp eyes because she didn't want to take them off of Emily for a second. With Emily's hair bleached to nearly the same color as her own, she felt as though she faced herself from over twenty years ago. Addressing that mirage more than Emily, she managed her first complete sentence. "I didn't imagine it happening this way either."

A million questions converged on Emily's tongue, but the one that spilled out was, "Where are you going?" As soon as she asked it, Emily knew the response she craved.

"Oh . . . I'm just moving on to the next place."

That was not what Emily wanted to hear. *Chicago. Wisconsin. Home.* She wanted Louisa to say that she'd heard Emily calling her home with her songs. Louisa hadn't named a specific destination, but Emily knew that home wasn't it.

Neither of them could figure out what to do or say next. Emily didn't sit down, and Louisa didn't stand up. Emily stared at the back of the pay television attached to Louisa's chair, and Louisa looked at the flashing arcade game behind Emily. Finally, Louisa asked, "What about you? You're kind of a big deal now, what are you doing at a Greyhound station?"

Feeling a surge of hopefulness, Emily clung to her mother's acknowledgment of her success. "You've heard of my band?"

"Who hasn't?" Louisa let pride spill into her smile. "You're good. Really good."

"Not that show a few nights ago," Emily tested, needing to know if Louisa had been there.

"It was hard to watch," Louisa murmured, without thinking that she shouldn't let on that she'd seen it.

"You were there?"

"That wasn't really you, though. I mean—"

Emily cut her off, demanding feverishly, "Have you seen any of my other shows?"

"No." Louisa saw disappointment flicker in Emily's eyes. Thinking that Emily was concerned about her seeing a bad performance, she quickly stammered, "I know that you're better than that. I mean, you had your reasons to be upset that night. What people do when they're upset—it's not really them."

"My reasons," Emily snorted. "You heard about that crap, too?"

Louisa thought about her encounter with Johnny just hours ago. How he would probably continue to pursue her daughter relentlessly. How Emily didn't need to be anywhere near that kind of bad love. "It doesn't matter. You can rise above it. You've got to," Louisa urged. "You're amazing. I've got both your albums. They're better than anything I've heard in years, probably since before you were born. And I'm not just saying that because you're my daughter."

Louisa's eyes landed on Emily and darted away. Both women went pale. The word "daughter" hung in the air between them. Louisa had almost choked on it, and it stung Emily, reminding her of how she felt after drunkenly flinging herself into the crowd at that last show. Was it a release from pain or was it something more painful?

She couldn't help it—she responded with a barbed remark. "I guess you would know, since you've followed rock 'n' roll all these years, right?"

Louisa blinked slowly at hearing her decades-old words to Michael thrown back at her. "Yeah," she mumbled, "that's what I do."

Emily wanted to scream at her, *So, why didn't my music bring you home?* But she couldn't even look at Louisa. She glanced at the clock near the ticketing area. Her father's bus would arrive soon. When she turned back to Louisa, she found herself answering Louisa's earlier question. "I'm here to meet my dad," Emily said carefully, training her eyes on her mother. "He heard about what happened the other night and couldn't reach me, so he went all the way to Vancouver, where I was supposed to play last night. Now he's on his way here. To take care of me."

Louisa flinched and swallowed hard, her voice small. "He's taken good care of you. I knew he would." Panic exploded in her stomach at the mention of Michael. She couldn't face him. She bent down to retrieve her suitcases, saying, "I gotta go." But when she stood, Emily blocked her way.

"No." Emily shook her head, tears welling up. Louisa had a glimpse of how she'd looked as a little girl, the childhood Louisa had missed. "You can't just go. It's not fair," Emily insisted, a whimper lurking behind her strong words. "You can just pick up a magazine and know all about me. You knew why I freaked out the other night, knew my reasons. I need to know your reasons, too!"

Louisa anxiously surveyed her surroundings. No one paid attention to her and Emily. A call for the bus to Spokane came over the loudspeaker, and people shuffled into a line next to one that had already been formed for the bus to Portland. A bedraggled young mother just a few feet behind Emily shushed her small daughter, who was clamoring for vending machine candy. "For the millionth time, no. I told you no!" The child's wail increased in volume.

Louisa bent back down, slid one suitcase onto its side, and unlatched it. Four black notebooks were stacked neatly in the left corner.

"I wrote you letters." Louisa kept her eyes on the notebooks instead of on Emily. "Letter after letter, trying to explain. And I think I finally did in the last letter, which I wrote on your sixteenth birthday. So, umm . . ." Louisa gathered the notebooks with trembling hands and rose. "You can read about me, too."

Emily stared at the stack of notebooks in her mother's outstretched arms. This was not enough. Louisa owed her a conversation. After all this time. After all she'd put Emily through. She gritted her teeth and said, "I spent a year of my life looking for you. Did you know that?"

Louisa fidgeted uncomfortably. "You did?"

Emily nodded. "When my relationship—which you clearly already know all about—ended, I asked Dad to tell me why you really left, but he couldn't. You mean so much to him. So I went hunting for the truth."

Louisa took a deep breath. "What did you find out?"

Sympathy melted Emily's cold, jade eyes and filed the razor's edge from her tone. "I know about Eric Lisbon."

The notebooks cascaded out of Louisa's arms. Two landed in the suitcase, one on the floor, and the other teetered in between, pages ruffled and bent.

"I've been there. Sort of," Emily said. "I've been trapped by someone I thought I loved, threatened. And I know it was worse for you. He raped you. You defended yourself. You felt guilty, but—"

"I guess you know why I had to leave, then," Louisa interrupted with a strained whisper. Her eyes returned to the notebooks. "The whole story is in—"

Emily snatched Louisa's hand before she could reach for them again. "No, Mom." Emily's voice shook on the last word. "I don't understand why you had to leave me. I understand why you did what you did, and I understand that you felt really guilty about it, but no, I don't understand how you or anyone could willingly walk away from her child."

Louisa stared at Emily's hand wrapped around her arm. Something about her touch differed from everyone else's. And then that word. Mom. Louisa felt faint. Emily's grip was the only thing holding her up. She dangled, a fish on the end of Emily's thin but sturdy line. "The whole story . . . ," she repeated. "The notebooks . . ."

"But is the real reason why you left me in those books? I don't want those books if they can't tell me that."

"You've already figured it out. The reason. Eric. Guilt."

"No." Emily shook her head adamantly. "That's not good enough. Dad loved you. I . . . I needed you. There's got to be more."

She studied her mother's face, the little lines around the corners of Louisa's eyes and mouth. Did they map out all the places she'd been? Emily lowered her gaze, trying to catch her mother's, but then she noticed something else. The ring on Louisa's finger. The tiny diamond set in white gold glistened. It was not the wedding ring that matched the simple gold band Michael had worn for years. Emily thrust Louisa's arm away from her like it was diseased.

The fingers on Louisa's right hand fluttered like the wings of an uneasy bird and landed protectively over her left hand as she realized what Emily had seen.

"Guilt?" Emily ranted. "If guilt kept you away from us, then why didn't it keep you from moving right on into a whole new life without us? If you wanted a family, you should have come back. Dad waited for you. He's *still* waiting for you! And I searched for you. Did I really give up? No, I disguised it as something more productive, touring with my band. And you married someone else? Do you have kids? Did you replace me, too?" Emily spat the questions rapid-fire, but felt her throat close around the last.

"Emily, no." Louisa shook her head so furiously it seemed like it could come undone from her neck, fly to the floor, and rattle around like one of the balls in the pinball machine behind Emily.

Emily's eyes flew to the suitcase. "I get it. You're still running. How many families have you started and left? Is that what you've really been doing? Find the music, start a family, feel guilty, leave them behind?"

"No! You are my only baby." But when she said it, Louisa immediately remembered Nadia, who'd been like another daughter. She'd followed the life of that child for thirteen years, first word, first step, every phase she'd missed with Emily. She was never a replacement for Emily, though, and Finn didn't replace Michael. "I still love your dad—"

"Then why are you married to someone else?" Emily shrieked. Her words were muffled by the announcement about the bus to Vancouver. Louisa thought, *If the bus going to Vancouver is ready to board, then the bus coming from—*

"Louisa?" Michael choked. Both Emily and Louisa whipped their heads around, as startled as Michael sounded.

Louisa met brown eyes gashed with pain. He'd clearly heard his daughter's question. Aside from the sorrow, his face was exactly the way Louisa had imagined it would be at forty-four. The same swooping cheekbones, little laugh lines pressed into his skin with all the smiles Emily had conjured, his curls flecked with gray, and the lips she once thought she would kiss every day of her life.

Emily's arms instinctively extended to her father, both protecting him and asking his protection from Louisa's betrayal.

"I couldn't be alone anymore," Louisa sputtered, tears coursing down her pale face.

"Then why didn't you just come home?" Michael asked, keeping his words soft and even somehow, forcing his mouth into a straight line to avoid crying, an outburst of rage, or both.

He and Emily stood entwined in front of Louisa. With no one to lean against, Louisa slumped into her chair. "I thought you understood, Michael. I know you understand. You can explain it to her, since she knows about . . . Eric . . . how afraid I was to hurt her, hurt both of you."

"No." Emily wept, rivulets of mascara streaking her cheeks. "There has to be more of a reason than that."

Michael smoothed his daughter's unruly hair. "Emily, there isn't. That's the reason."

Emily angrily wiped her nose with the back of her hand. "Eric Lisbon raped you. He would have killed you. You did what you had to do. You survived. You had a husband who loved you. A daughter who loved you." Each sentence came out staccato, no emotion behind the words, but then Emily's voice shot through with hysteria. "And you left us for *twenty-three years*? And it's not like you intended to run into me today. You would have left us forever because of your guilt. You should have fucking faced it! Feeling guilty is not a good enough reason to abandon your husband and child!"

Hearing Emily's version of her own life story in such simple terms made Louisa's whole body quake. "It has to be good enough," she pleaded softly.

Michael looked slowly from the gold band on his finger to the ring on Louisa's hand, then up to her desperate green eyes. "It's not. God, Louisa"—he sucked air through his teeth, containing his own tears momentarily—"it never has been." Michael turned to Emily. "I'm so sorry, baby."

"I gotta go," Emily murmured.

Louisa wanted to rise, to stop her daughter with the same imposing force Emily had used on her moments ago, but she didn't have the strength to move.

Michael gripped Emily's shoulder. "Don't you leave me," he whispered uneasily.

"I'm not. You can come with me, but I'm going. Right now."

Michael glanced back at Louisa and she forced herself to address him. "Michael, please wait. Just talk to me for a second."

He deferred to Emily, who ducked out of his grasp but squeezed his hand before walking away. He deserved his moment with Louisa, too. "I'll wait outside," she told him.

Louisa watched her daughter go, kept her eyes on Emily's blond head until she felt Michael's stare weighing heavily on her. He didn't speak. His chocolate eyes read plainly, *I didn't ask for this. Any of it.* She'd requested to talk to him and she'd have to do the talking. Finally, she managed to say, "She's perfect. You did such a good job with her."

Michael sniffed, cleared his throat. "I did the best I could. She needed you."

Louisa sobbed soundlessly, chest heaving. "Now she doesn't want anything to do with me. She'll never understand."

When Michael dropped his head and shoved his hands into his pockets, it caused Louisa to cry harder. She knew she didn't deserve comfort from him, but she missed his embrace so much. Gradually, she gained control over her breathing. She and Michael both stared at the ground, at the four notebooks of unsatisfactory explanations that lay between them. Louisa knelt to gather the books and wobbled to her feet, offering them to Michael. "Please give them to her when she's ready."

He nodded, slowly raising trembling hands.

Louisa cocked her head, trying to coax him into looking at her. "I don't know where I'm going, but I'd like to write you when I get there. So you and Emily can reach me if you want to."

Michael nodded again. His voice shook like his hands. "That's good. I have twenty-three years' worth of things to say to you. But my daughter needs me now."

Their eyes didn't meet, but their fingertips touched briefly as Michael took the notebooks. Louisa shivered, treasuring the contact and aching at the way he claimed Emily as his alone. But she couldn't change that, not for the moment anyway, so she simply said, "Thank you."

He exited through the same door Emily had and Louisa

dropped into her seat, where she remained until the last call for the bus to Vancouver came over the gravelly intercom. Then she numbly got in line to board.

"We're just about out of Iowa. We'll be flying over southwestern Wisconsin and will begin to make our descent right around Janesville," the pilot announced.

Emily lifted her eyes from the brown squares of land carved up by rivers and roads and asked her father, "Will we fly over Carlisle?" They were the first words she'd spoken since finagling a later flight and a ticket for him, and giving up the first-class seat that had been booked for her so they could sit together.

"Emily . . . ," he began, but she stopped him.

"I can't talk about it now. I just have to play my show this weekend. I have to do that and do it well because if I don't . . ."

"Emily, if your label is pressuring you . . ."

"No!" she bristled. "This isn't about business or Johnny or . . . her. It's about me. This is the thing I have to do right now, 'cause it's the *only* thing I know how to do."

"I know how that is." He leaned forward to look out the window with her. "Carlisle should be coming up."

Emily studied the patched-together land. "Will you know when we go over it? 'Cause it's all the same to me. It still looks like Iowa."

"No, I won't know any better than you."

She stared contemplatively for a couple minutes. "I think that's it. I sort of feel like down there's home."

"I thought Chicago was home," Michael said stiffly.

Emily turned to him, her green eyes glinting with tears. "I don't want to be like her, Dad. I'm not gonna be selfish and stay away from my family just because I have certain feelings that are tough to face. I don't want to hurt you like she did."

Michael bit his lip. "But *I* helped her hurt you."

"You didn't mean to, though."

"Neither did she."

Emily resumed gazing out the window. "I think I'll come home with you after the show this weekend. For Christmas. Maybe if Ian doesn't hate me, he'll come. He did call me a couple times in Seattle. Hopefully he'll forgive me for not calling back. You'll like those pictures he took of us. And I'll stay awhile if that's okay. I need a quiet place to work on the songs for the next record. Maybe we could renovate the basement, make it a home studio. I've got money . . ."

"Emily, did you hear what I just said?" Michael interjected. "Your mother did not mean to hurt you."

"Yes," Emily hissed begrudgingly. "I heard you, but it's going to take a long time before I can believe that."

After a few more minutes of focusing on the land below, she addressed Michael again but didn't look at him. "I saw that you took those notebooks."

Michael sighed. "She asked me to."

Emily accepted his answer with a curt nod. She fell silent momentarily, but curiosity beat out her stubborn desire not to care. "What else did she say to you?"

"She wanted to write to us, let us know where she goes. I said she could."

Hope rose inside of Emily for the first time since she'd stormed out of the bus station, but she couldn't allow it to pierce her tough exterior just yet. "Does she know that we're not searching or waiting for her anymore? That she has to come to us?"

"I think she knows that." Michael fumbled for his daughter's hand and she let him take it.

Emily finally faced her father, holding his gaze with her clear, emerald eyes. The tears that had almost spilled had completely dried. "Okay, then," she replied with a sense of release, the same feeling she got after belting out her favorite song.